.iviera

Evonne Wareham

Choc Lit

Where heroes are like chocolate – irresistible!

Published 2023 by Choc Lit Limited
Penrose House, Crawley Drive, Camberley, Surrey GU15 2AB, UK
www.choc-lit.com

EPUB: 978-1-78189-521-4
PRINT: 978-1-78189-533-7

PRINTED AND BOUND BY AMAZON

Riviera series:

Summer in San Remo
A Wedding on the Riviera
A Villa in Portofino
Masquerade on the Riviera

The events in this book take place in the summer of 2019, at the same time as the stories told in *A Wedding on the Riviera* and *A Villa in Portofino* – books two and three in the 'Riviera' series.

This one is for Phil – for all his enthusiastic support

Acknowledgements

As always, thanks must go first to the team at Choc Lit who get the show on the road, and to the Tasting Panel for their constructive input: Elisabeth Hall, Tracy Kean, Alan Roberton, Liana Vera Saez, Emily Smeby, Anne Eckersley, Lynda Adcock, Bee Master, Fran Stevens, Honor Gilbert, Jo Osborne and Gill Leivers.

Writers work better with friendship and support, in what can be a solitary occupation. I get mine from the Cariad Chapter of the RNA. Also laughter. And cake.

Thanks are due to local independent bookshop, Griffin Books, in Penarth, for sourcing and sending me the research and reference books that I needed to work on this story during lockdown. The efficiency and friendliness of the staff is much valued.

A special mention for the Egypt Centre at Swansea University, in particular the Museum Volunteer Manager, Syd Howells, for answering my questions about matters Egyptian. You can't get everything from books and help from professionals is invaluable. Any errors that I have still managed to make in turning information into a work of fiction are mine.

Chapter One

The gargoyles on the roof were watching him again.

Being the youngest member of the on-site security team for the University of Aquae Sulis – by several decades – Tyler was resigned to the fact that the last in-person round of the outlying admin buildings was his job. After 10 p.m., it was down to the alarms and the security lighting to protect this part of the campus. Although, to be fair, a gentle amble to double check the doors and make sure that there were no lights left on inside the buildings wasn't too bad – better now in late June than in the dark of November.

With the majority of the students on vacation, the place was quiet. The flower beds in front of the reception building were pretty and there were still a few birds twittering sleepily in the trees. It was all okay, really – except for those gargoyles on the front of the Graduate Library. Pentecost Court had been one of the former homes of the eccentric Pentecost family – renowned as notable collectors of art and historic artefacts. It was the only building still left standing from before the land had been sold and the University built, and had now been repurposed as a library. Tyler grimaced. Old Professor Mumford could rabbit on all he liked about "Gothic facades" – whatever *they* were (presumably the gargoyles) – the statues lurking on the roof didn't impress *him*. As far as Tyler was concerned, the Victorian architect who designed the things must have been three parts out of his tree, and Erasmus Pentecost, the old codger who paid for them, even worse. They were just … hideous. *And creepy*. Even on a sunny summer evening. The way they looked at you was bad enough, but when you walked away, knowing that they were behind you—

With a disgusted huff, Tyler hustled forward to try the wide double doors. He cursed under his breath when the round iron handle turned in his grip. Someone was still in the building – and there were no prizes for guessing who. *Old Mumbling Mumford, off in his own little world on the third floor, barricaded in with his books.* Tyler stepped back, looking up. Yes, he could just about make out that there was a light showing in the window at the right top corner of the building. With a sigh, he reached for the radio on his belt.

'Jeff? It's me. Yeah. Grad Library. Old Mumbling is still in there. I'm going up to chase him off now. The boss is going to have to have a go at the library staff *again.* They're supposed to make sure the building is clear. Yeah – three sugars, *and* a biscuit, if I have to climb all those stairs.'

Positioning the radio back in place, Tyler let himself into the library, crossed the black and white tiles of the slightly echoing hall, and started his climb up the majestic oak stairway. There was a lift at the back of the building, but it was strictly off-limits after hours, when the place was meant to be closed. Rules were rules – and, besides, Tyler had no desire to be caught in a skinny metal coffin for a couple of hours if the power just happened to fail.

He reached the top floor without getting out of breath, which was gratifying. All those sessions in the gym were paying off. He hesitated when he got to the doors leading onto the third level. While the lower floors had been remodelled since the University took over, up here had been Erasmus Pentecost's own library, and the fixtures and fittings had been left largely untouched. It still had the heavy old bookshelves, carved with all manner of weird creatures. *More faces, watching you.* Tyler straightened his shoulders and pushed through the doors. The place was shadowy. The sun, just going down outside, provided the only illumination, except for a small golden glow visible between the stacks – the light over Mumbling's carrel.

'Professor Mumford.' Tyler raised his voice, summoning the correct note of respect. 'Time to leave, sir.' *Yeah, well, actually that was about an hour ago*. 'The books will still be here in the morning,' he suggested jovially, expecting Mumford's face to appear over the wooden walls of the carrel, blinking like an owl behind the heavy frames of his glasses.

No reaction.

Sighing again, Tyler padded forward, knowing what he would find. And yes, there was the old boy, face down in his research. 'Asleep again,' he muttered. 'As if he hasn't got a home to go to.' It would take much longer to wake him and get him on his feet and out of the building than if he was simply engrossed in his work – and if Tyler wasn't back in time, all the chocolate biscuits would be snaffled.

'Come on, sir. Rise and shine.' He put a careful hand on the tweed-clad shoulder that was nearest to him and gave it a gentle shake. Really, the position Mumford was in, with his face all mashed up against the books, it couldn't be comfortable. Tyler sniffed suspiciously. No smell of booze, although there was a trace of something that might have been cigarette smoke, or maybe a vape – but it was a hanging offence to smoke in here with all the paper. Even the students respected that.

Tyler shook a little harder, gripping and pulling on the old man's shoulder to lift him up and away from the desk. *The old boy really is dead to the world.*

'Sir – Arghh!' Letting go, Tyler jumped back with a sharp and embarrassing squeal. Professor Mumford, instead of sitting up to stare blearily at him, toppled backwards. The old man's legs slid under the desk and his head and torso flopped against the leather chair.

Now Tyler could see his face.

Smothering a gasp, he reached blindly for the radio on his belt, thumbing the button. Jeff in the control room squawked an answer. 'Yeah, I'm still in the Library. Mumford is here ... He's ... he must have been taken ill.' The radio squawked again. Tyler swallowed hard. 'Yeah – you better call an ambulance, just in case … but I'm pretty sure he's dead.'

On the Devon coast, amongst the palms and ferns in the murky depths of a dark and silent Victorian conservatory, a mobile phone rang. It was swiftly answered.

'You're late.' The voice was brittle, laced with tension and impatience.

The caller simply laughed. 'But worth waiting for. We can cross Professor Mumford off the guest list.'

'We can?' Now there was doubt mixed with the annoyance.

'We can. He's dead.'

The grip on the mobile phone tightened. 'How do you know? Are you sure?'

'I'm sure.'

There was a long, heavy pause before the muffled response. 'Oh.' Another pause. 'The University will still send someone though?'

'Undoubtedly – but it will be a much bigger and better fish than Mumford.'

'Bigger than Mumford? Who?'

'Elliott Elwood'

'Elwood, that's—Are you sure?'

The caller made a *tsking* noise. 'You really must get over this unflattering tendency to doubt me. But really – who else *is* there?'

'You?'

‘Huh! – I don’t think so. Dr Elliott Elwood will be joining your little house party, you can bet on it. And he’s going to be a lot more use to us than Mumford.’

‘His reputation—’

‘Exactly.’

‘Do you have any scruples at all?’

‘Very few where money is concerned – and we’re talking about a great deal of money.’ There was another low laugh. ‘Honestly, did you really think I’d done away with the old boy?’

The uneasy silence spoke volumes.

Another laugh. ‘I told you – I have good contacts. I’ll ring you on Wednesday – same time.’

Chapter Two

'Will you speak at the memorial service for Professor Mumford?'

'I would like to.' Elliott Elwood settled into the visitor's chair in his old friend's office. The room in the Humanities Building in the centre of the Aquae Sulis campus was spacious, but the angular, ultra-modern chair had been chosen for looks rather than comfort – possibly designed to discourage undergraduates from lingering. The points it earned in that respect were quickly wiped out by the effect it was having on Elliott's overlong legs. 'Do you have a date?'

Benedict Bartram grimaced – an expression that was as close to a frown as was possible for him crossing his open, freckled face. Even with the grimace, Elliott was pleased to note that Ben was looking better than he had in a while – since his wife Sara had left, in fact. Now, two years on, Ben seemed to be relaxed and settled. Aquae Sulis suited him. He'd established himself as a popular lecturer in the English Department and found a niche. Elliott smiled. Ben deserved to have things going right for him for once.

'We can work around your commitments,' Ben answered Elliott's question. 'But there isn't even a date for the funeral yet. He died unexpectedly, so there has to be a post-mortem and an inquest.'

Elliott let his surprise show. 'Really? Even when he had a heart condition?'

It was Ben's turn to look surprised. 'You knew about that?' His pale hazel eyes widened. 'I understood that it wasn't widely known.'

Elliott nodded, but didn't elaborate. He had known because he'd unexpectedly run into Mumford in Harley Street when he was coming away from a second appointment with a cardiac consultant. Mumford had been shaken and needing to talk. 'He wanted to get his magnum opus completed, before being shuffled off into final retirement,' he said instead.

Ben looked slightly affronted. 'Being appointed an Emeritus Professor isn't exactly being shuffled off – and I'm not sure that he was ever going to finish his history of the Pentecost family. Talking of which—' Ben fumbled on his overcrowded desk, a contrast to the open and airy room, unearthing a thin folder '—Leyland wants you to go to this. I know it's terribly short notice, but Professor Mumford was meant to be attending.'

It was Elliott's turn to frown, not – he'd been reliably informed – that it made much of a difference to his face. In contrast to Ben's wide eyes and easy smile, the adjectives applied to him were always dark – brooding, saturnine, enigmatic. The last two were courtesy of a particularly irritating group of female students who called themselves "The Undergraduettes" and seemed to consider him as some sort of academic Mr Rochester, with an Instagram account apparently dedicated to pictures of him looking "saturnine and enigmatic". *But that's what you get for inheriting hair the colour of a crow and the Elwood nose.* Mobile phones with cameras were the work of the devil, he always thought.

He had to admit that the contrast between him and Ben had frequently worked to both their advantages in the dim and distant student days when they went clubbing together – before they got old and respectable. *And had reputations to maintain.* Now they were both here at Aquae Sulis, he looked forward to properly reviving that old friendship. Suppressing a sigh for nostalgic memories, he took the folder. He wasn't sure he wanted to do anything at the bidding of Dr Vaisey Leyland, Dean of the Humanities Faculty. He didn't officially move from being a visiting lecturer to joining the staff until the start of the Michaelmas term in October; Leyland had been one of the reasons for his hesitation in deciding that he *would* join, despite Ben's vocal encouragement. The man was a study in arrogance and ambition, confident of his intellectual superiority and with his sights firmly set on moving up from Dean of Humanities to the post of Vice Chancellor. Elliott had no interest in helping him get there – that included attending events with Faculty movers and shakers just to make Leyland look good. It also irritated Elliott that Ben was expected to undertake extra administrative tasks for the man, despite the fact it really wasn't part of his job. Sometimes Ben was too easy-going for his own good.

He opened the folder. It *wasn't* a Faculty event. He let out a low whistle, totally unsuited to a Distinguished Expert in Egyptology. 'The Pentecost Collections are finally on the market.'

'They are,' Ben confirmed. The glow of excitement in his eyes was unmistakable. 'But they're not going to an auction house.'

Elliott scanned the papers. 'You have to be joking. A house party!'

'Yep. Ignatius Pentecost died the year before last, but it's taken this long to sort out the formalities. His heirs – the last of the Pentecost blood line, although they don't bear the name – are the grandchildren of his three younger sisters: two great nephews and a great niece. According to the old boy's wishes, expressed in his will, the Collections are to be sold and the money goes to the three cousins, but *not* just by putting the whole thing in the hands of an auction house. There are four invited bidders for the whole lot, on the basis that the Collections are to be kept together and put on public display. Ignatius was a true Pentecost eccentric, but he did have a point – he didn't want his legacy broken up and disappearing piecemeal overseas, or into the vaults of private collectors.' Ben indicated the folder. 'As you know, it's really a group of individual collections gathered by the family and currently located at Pentecost Place in Devon. The Egyptian relics that Aristotle Pentecost brought back in the 1920s are the biggest and most notable part, but there are also secondary collections assembled by other members of the family who lived in the house over the years – they all had personal specialities. There are some valuable pictures, including a couple of Picassos, as well as sculpture, books, ephemera – it's all listed in there.'

'And the successful bidder gets everything?'

Ben nodded. 'The Collections go to a new owner and Pentecost Place is sold. Invitations to bid have gone to two small museums, a stately home with a distant connection to the family and us – the University of Aquae Sulis – because we have the Court. And probably also the deepest pockets,' he suggested.

Elliott nodded. He knew Professor Mumford's big dream had been to display everything at Pentecost Court – formerly a family property, now the Graduate Library on the University campus. Ben was looking at him with gleam in his eye that Elliott recognised. There was something going on here.

'Representatives of all four bidders are invited to spend the weekend at Pentecost Place, to view the Collections in situ and then submit sealed bids. Pentecost Place is in Torquay,' Ben casually added the reminder.

'Agatha Christie.' Elliott made the connection immediately. 'For crying out loud! What is it? Last person standing at the end of the weekend gets the prize?'

Ben gave a bark of laughter. 'Better make sure your revolver is in proper working order.'

'I think the lead pipe in the billiard room might be more my choice. Is the rest of the family as … eccentric ... as Ignatius?'

'Looks like it might be possible. At least one of the nephews, Barnabas, the eldest, has a bit of a reputation – he's the one coordinating the arrangements, apparently with great enthusiasm.' Ben's face sobered, laughter gone. 'It *was* Mumford's greatest wish that the Collections should end up here,' he emphasised, clearly sensing Elliott's hesitation.

Elliott felt a pang for the loss of an eminent colleague. 'So Leyland wants me to spend the weekend risking my neck by taking part in a murder mystery?'

'God, I hope not.' Ben shook his head. 'I know the Cleopatra Necklace is supposed to have a curse on it, but that's just superstition.'

Elliott looked up with a jerk of surprise. 'The Necklace *is* part of the Collections? It's been confirmed?'

'It's my understanding.' Ben gestured to the open folder resting on Elliott's knee. 'There's an inventory of the Egyptian items in there, at the back. Not that the Necklace has ever been authenticated – that's why Leyland wants you there, to evaluate the Necklace – and the other items, of course.' He grinned. 'He must have heard about the Elwood Magic Touch when it comes to Egyptian artefacts.' He laughed when Elliott waved away the teasing reference with a grimace. 'All right, I'll shut up. I know you don't like to talk about it. The whole Egyptian collection is supposed to be spectacular – Mumford always claimed it was, although he was no Egyptologist. But the Necklace – there's also the history attached to it. All that scandal and bloodshed – it's a collectors' piece on reputation alone. You know how *that* works.' He sat back, clasping his hands together over the edge of the desk. 'If it was only the Necklace being put on the market, there would be plenty of people vying for it, cursed or not. But the weekend is not just about the bids – all the candidates have to make their case for having the Collections and how they will use them for public display. The heirs will be considering that as well as the money. The brief for the University's pitch is in there, but you know already what Mumford intended. He *really* wanted it, El,' he repeated with earnest emphasis.

Elliott wondered if it was totally cynical to speculate on whether financial gain or public good would hold most weight with the heirs. Even divided three ways, there was a lot of money at stake – and with the Necklace ... Elliott sighed. *Do you really have a choice?* Having a conscience was a bloody inconvenience, but he didn't have any specific plans for the weekend and the Pentecost Collections *were* reputed to have some outstanding examples of Egyptian statues and sarcophagi. *You damn well know you can't possibly pass this up, even if it* is *at the behest of Vaisey Leyland.* He shut the folder. He was already sold. Rumours of murder, mystery and a cursed artefact. What else could a man want from a weekend?

Ben picked up on his expression, leaning forward anxiously. 'You'll do it?'

He smiled at Ben's worried stare. 'Yes, I'll do it.' His friend's relief was visible. 'I'll make the pitch, but can't guarantee to come first in the beauty contest.' He was pretty sure that the University could outbid the other candidates, with or without the Necklace, but would the lure of relocating the Collections to Pentecost Court be enough? The Court had been the Pentecost family's second residence. When the architect finished Pentecost Place, Erasmus had moved him on to create another Victorian Gothic marvel to amaze the inhabitants of Bath. It would be a fitting setting for the art and artefacts – and with the family connection ...

'Give it your best shot, El. I know you will, for the sake of poor old Mumford and the University,' Ben encouraged. 'Hell, you know I'm no expert—' Ben's engaging, self-deprecating grin lit up his face '—but even *I* know the Pentecost legacy is the most significant private collection to come on the market for decades. And Aquae Sulis is absolutely the best home for it.'

Taking his leave of Ben, Elliott walked slowly down the corridor, deep in thought, recalling all he knew about the Pentecost Collections. Reputedly as eccentric as the various collectors, they had been begun when Victoria was still on the throne and wended their way until almost the present day in the hands of a large, wealthy and decidedly odd family. Erasmus, the patriarch, entranced with the Victorian Gothic splendour that the Marquess of Bute was achieving at Cardiff Castle, had recruited a brilliant young architect of his own and set about creating Pentecost Place on the Devon coast and Pentecost Court, now on campus. The rest of the family were magpies – snappers up of trifles. Elliott couldn't remember who had used those words – probably Mumford. Different members, mostly men but a few women, had pursued their individual enthusiasms over more than a hundred years. With one, it was Pre-Raphaelite art – that collection was said to house a small gallery of "lost" masterpieces. Others had collected fine porcelain, items relating to clowns, first editions, music scores, books on alchemy, stamps ...

The element of the family hoard that most interested Elliott was the work of Aristotle Pentecost, a nephew and amateur archaeologist in the 1920s, who had allegedly brought back a collection of Egyptian artefacts fit to rival those discovered by Harold Carter at Tutankhamun's tomb – except that very few people outside the family had ever seen Aristotle's cache. Even so, the wonders it was reputed to contain had always been the subject of rumour and speculation. *And now you're holding an inventory in your hand.* Despite himself, he could feel his heart speeding up at the prospect that this weekend he might—

'Ah! Elwood. Glad I caught you.' Elliott jerked out of what was developing into a pleasant daydream to find the Dean, Vaisey Leyland, bearing down on him. With the academic gown that the man insisted on wearing billowing behind him, it was a bit like being swooped on by an ambitious hawk.

'Dr Leyland.' Elliott inclined his head and hoped he was looking suitably saturnine and enigmatic.

'Ah! Excellent.' Leyland's sharp eyes had spotted the blue folder. 'Bartram has briefed you, I see. A strange way of proceeding – this house party business.' The Dean gave a rather theatrical laugh. 'Been a development too, I understand,' Leyland ploughed on, nodding at the folder. 'A fifth bidder in the frame – some billionaire recluse.' Leyland frowned, before moving forward to pass Elliott, briefly patting his shoulder. 'Counting on you to do the thing for the University – unthinkable that the Collections should go anywhere but to their proper home. Know you'll make the strongest case.' He swooped importantly off, leaving Elliott standing in the corridor, feeling comprehensively patronised. With a grin that would have horrified The Undergraduettes, he strode off to find a quiet place to study the folder and think.

A little later, ensconced with a pot of oolong tea in a corner of the café in the basement of the Graduate Library – a space that would probably have been some sort of pantry when the Court was built – Elliott spread out the contents of the blue folder. There was a map with a picture of Pentecost Place in Torquay (red herringbone brick, more gargoyles and a turreted tower), a programme for the weekend, beginning with afternoon tea on Friday (that was tomorrow), the University's bid brief, and the inventory. Elliott scanned it, passing over pages of paintings, books and *objets d'art* until he got to the Egyptian section – sarcophagi, statues and funerary furniture; all items to quicken his interest.

Leyland, the supercilious sod, knew exactly what bait to dangle to catch Elliott's attention. *And it's succeeding*. Only a fraction of the pieces would be on display at the weekend, but the statuary alone would be worth the trip. He turned the page and there it was in the list: the mysterious star of the show. The Cleopatra Necklace. Baldly described as a gold neck piece, inlaid with lapis and semi-precious stones, it didn't sound like much. Elliott was sure that it would be beautiful. *And spectacular if it's genuine*. Its authenticity and provenance might be dicey for a purist, but its fascination was its reputation. At least three people who'd had the temerity to wear it had allegedly died shortly after. There were the usual tales of bankruptcy and ruin, suicide and sudden death, with whispers of madness and murder trailing in its wake. *Yet the thing has been in the possession of the Pentecost family for a few decades with no adverse effects.*

Elliott sat back, assessing what he knew of the legend. The term "necklace" was no doubt a misnomer. It was probably more like a torc or collar, possibly with ritual or ceremonial significance. That it was a genuine Egyptian artefact seemed possible. That it had ever graced the neck of Queen Cleopatra, exceedingly doubtful. How it had found its way into the Pentecost Collections was something of a mystery. Logic suggested that if the thing was a genuine artefact, it was most likely one of the finds that amateur archaeologist Aristotle had brought home, having acquired it in Egypt some time before his death in 1928 – but that origin story completely erased the spectacular mythology that had become attached to the relic. The flamboyant stories of multiple previous owners were in large part what gave the thing its allure.

Mumford's investigations suggested it had arrived at Pentecost Place sometime in the 1980s. Before that was a more shady and complex history, including once supposedly being in the possession of Catherine the Great of Russia. If the relic was finally emerging from the shadows, scholars would be queuing up to study it – and the exotic rumours that surrounded it would make it irresistible to a certain type of collector. Elliott wondered about the fifth bidder – the reclusive billionaire. But all of that was smoke and mirrors. If it *was* a genuine Egyptian artefact, the thing had never been officially authenticated.

Am I expected to do that?

Chapter Three

Maisie Webster walked slowly along the seafront, watching the waves and the gulls, and appreciating a few minutes to clear her head in the sunshine before she dived into her next assignment. Today, and for the rest of the weekend, she was Maisie Norris: trusted personal assistant to a wealthy eccentric.

Life as a working detective was certainly varied. If things had gone differently last month, she might have been well on her way to Nice right now, pretending to be the besotted fiancé of a con man who specialised in leaving his brides at the altar. That impersonation had not worked out, so here she was instead. Her mouth quirked into a smile – she'd swapped the French Riviera for the English version, but on a sunny afternoon in early July, Torquay wasn't at all bad. And this job – put together in haste by Jake McQuire, the owner of the detective agency where she worked – sounded as if it had the potential to be interesting. It was certainly different.

Her role this time was to attend a weekend house party to inspect and bid for a private collection of art, artefacts and jewellery, as the representative of a reclusive billionaire. It was one of Jake's special assignments – working directly for him, not for a client. Jake suspected that something shady might be going down in connection with the jewellery, of which the notorious Cleopatra Necklace was the most notable item. Was someone planning to steal it? He had managed to get the fictional Augustus Elladour – her supposed employer – onto the list of prospective bidders. Jake had some amazing contacts so she was confident her cover would hold, even though the details had been assembled in a hurry.

The whole setup was pretty weird – *a house party weekend to choose a buyer?*

Passing the pavilion and the entrance to the pier, she stopped for a moment to watch a seagull gliding on an air current. At some stage during the two-night stay, she would have to present a case for ownership of the Pentecost Collections to be awarded to the fictional Augustus, but all she had to do for the moment was keep her eyes and ears open and report back. This was very different from her last assignment, although that had also been unusual – Jake seemed to specialise in unusual cases – but, on the whole, that one had been fun. *Until the end, when it decidedly wasn't.*

She was sad about that, because Sir Gerald had been an absolute sweetie. The agency had been called in originally at the instigation of Sir Gerald's finance director and long-standing business partner, who had some nagging worries about his old friend's safety. Sir Gerald had refused point-blank to have a bodyguard from the agency's protection team, denying that there could be any threat. It was Jake's wife, Cassie, who came up with the idea that Maisie, who had all the training and qualifications to provide personal protection if necessary, should pose as Sir Gerald's new midlife-crisis trophy girlfriend. Sir Gerald had been sufficiently amused and flattered by the idea to go along with it, although still doubting it was needed.

She'd had a lot of fun for a few weeks, posing as Maisie Flynn, the ditsy gold-digger who'd managed to snare a rich businessman who was old enough to be her father. Sir Gerald had proved to be a perfect gentleman, a fiendish chess player and an excellent co-conspirator, playing the bemused and besotted sugar daddy to perfection. The ending had been a bad one, though, with the threat proving all too real – a long-planned kidnapping which Sir Gerald had not been intended to survive. The businessman's eldest son had been looking forward to both a cash payment and to stepping into his father's shoes to take over the family empire. Maisie had the satisfaction of knowing that she'd protected the client, but the fallout was emotionally devastating for a man she had come to like and respect. All in all, she was ready for a weekend by the sea, even if it was for work.

She'd spent the previous night at a small, discreet hotel at the opposite end of town to Pentecost Place, giving her a chance to scope out the location – and really the building was something else; not quite Dracula's Castle, but definitely leaning that way. The gargoyles on the roof wouldn't have looked out of place on Notre Dame …

Overhead, a gull squawked and a nearby clock chimed. Brought back to the present, Maisie turned to retrace her steps to collect her car and her luggage. It wouldn't do to miss the weekend's first event – a formal afternoon tea.

Half an hour later, she parked her car in a designated area behind Pentecost Place as instructed, unloaded her suitcase and rolled it round to the massively imposing front door. She yanked the bell pull, hearing the echo inside the building, and stood back for a second, admiring the facade of red herringbone bricks and the rest of the Victorian Gothic embellishments. The gargoyles on the roof crouched to peer over a parapet at her, and roses scrambled up a turreted grey stone tower tacked onto the side of the building.

The front door opened. Maisie was mildly disappointed that it didn't creak. A man stood in the doorway holding out his hand. 'Ms Norris? Welcome. Do come in.'

Maisie shook hands and was ushered over the threshold as she mentally reviewed the briefing note that was now safely locked away in a box in the boot of her car. This was Barnabas, eldest of Ignatius Pentecost's heirs. Forty-five but looked older, mainly because of the old-fashioned glasses and not-quite-but-almost period dress – checked shirt, tweed tie, corduroy trousers and an olive-green cardigan. *The squire in casual clothes or an off-duty vicar?* She was glad of the wardrobe that Cassie had picked out for her – modern nostalgia with a sprinkling of Cassie's favourite vintage pieces. Jake's understanding that the weekend was themed to match the heyday of the house – the 1930s, when the then Pentecost owner had entertained lavishly – appeared to be correct. Her wardrobe would be a subtle way of fitting in and scoring points.

A woman with almost white-blonde hair and a flower-patterned afternoon dress that was a more droopy version of Maisie's stood behind Barnabas. 'My cousin.' Barnabas waved a hand. 'Dorothea. Oh. Thank you, Jefferies.' A dark-suited man had come forward out of the shadows of the hall to take Maisie's suitcase. 'Ms Norris is in the Blue Room.' Dorothea was in her early thirties, but like her cousin, she looked older, probably because of her badly styled hair – a wispy attempt at an up-do that was escaping from its pins – and her ill-fitting, dowdy clothes. Armand, the third of the cousins was of a similar age. He didn't seem to be in evidence as one of the welcoming party.

Maisie looked around from shaking Dorothea's hand – limp like her dress – to take in the huge tiled and panelled entrance hall. Doors led off to other parts of the house. A staircase in the centre of the hall, opposite the front door, was a wide wooden affair, heavily carpeted in dark red with some sort of motif in the weave. Two passageways disappeared into the murky depths of the building on either side of its looming bulk. Barnabas was expressing his pleasure at her arrival again, urging her towards the drawing room where tea was about to be served.

'Just in time. Just in time,' he muttered happily. 'Jeffries will attend to your case.'

Maisie made suitable noises of appreciation, which was all that seemed to be required, and allowed herself to be drawn forward. She was slightly stunned, although she hoped she was not letting it show. *Honestly, is all this for real?*

Dorothea had disappeared into the bowels of the house, apparently leading the way. Maisie was about to follow when a noise from the staircase made her look up. A man was coming down, presumably also bound for tea. Youngish, tall, dark, expensive but unassuming tailoring – *one of the museum staff or the academic?*

He paused, one hand on the banister, looking towards them.

Maisie's heart turned over as recognition poured over her like a shower of ice.

Dr Elliott Elwood, distinguished academic, eminent Egyptologist with his own TV show, was looking down his supercilious nose at her.

Again.

Chapter Four

If anyone sitting at the low tables in the chintzy drawing room had ever seen a better furnished afternoon tea, Elliott would have been surprised. He knew he hadn't. There were four versions of the beverage itself – in an array of china teapots, all with distinct flower patterns to differentiate the contents – with both milk and lemon, a bowl of sugar lumps with silver tongs, and a discreet pot of coffee with hot milk and cream for non-believers. The central table was covered in tiered stands of sweet and savoury offerings. The choice was impressive there too – sandwiches with assorted fillings, small savoury pies and tartlets, three different types of scone with a choice of jams and clotted cream, plates of bread and butter, both white and brown, celery in a tall pressed glass jar, and a large bowl of watercress, as well as small sponge cakes, macaroons, éclairs, slices of Battenberg and miniature trifles. A magnificent chocolate cake and an iced fruit cake stood sentinel, one each end of the table.

Dorothea was presiding in a listless fashion beside a beaming Barnabas, who was attempting to fill people's plates and getting in the way. The museum contingents – they had both sent delegations, one of four and one of five people – were eating enthusiastically. Lady Something hyphen Something from the stately home – Elliott hadn't caught her mumbled introduction – was worrying the single piece of bread and butter on her plate with restless fingers and an expression that conveyed deep distaste for her companions and surroundings. Which left Ms Norris, who had served herself a pair of smoked salmon sandwiches and a handful of watercress.

The very interesting Ms Norris.

Elliott helped himself to a roast beef sandwich and a slice of quiche. On meeting his host and hostess – there was no sign yet of Armand, the third heir – he'd felt that something was off key, although he wasn't quite sure what. Possibly it was the effect of the pseudo period dress. With Ms Norris, he *knew* that there was something wrong.

He studied her over the teacups. All curls and curves. What his reprobate Great-Uncle Angus would have called a nice little armful. The non-PC part of him, that Elliott did his best to stifle, had to agree. *Very nice indeed*. And the last time he'd seen her, that was exactly what she had been – a delectable vision, hanging on the arm of one of the city's leading entrepreneurs and falling out of a low-cut pink dress that clashed horribly with her hair. She'd been egging on an entranced Sir Gerald, her "companion", to bid high on a diamond bracelet in a charity auction evening. And her last name *hadn't* been Norris.

Elliott narrowed his eyes. She looked quite different now; the auburn curls tamed, short pale pink nails rather than multi-patterned talons, make-up understated and expertly applied. The tea dress still gave an idea of the curves and Elliott felt a disturbing flicker of attraction. With a jolt, he brought himself back to the current situation. He had no doubt that it was the same woman. She'd stuck rather vividly in his mind. *You've always been a sucker for that particular shade of dark auburn.*

With another jolt, he forced himself back to the problem at hand. *Given that she isn't who and what she purports to be, then who is she and why is she here?* The obvious answer, given past form, was the jewellery – presumably the Necklace. She'd shown no recognition or discomfort when introduced by Barnabas as the representative of the unexpected billionaire bidder. Either she didn't remember him or she was very good at pretence. Elliott suspected the latter. What about the billionaire? Was he real? Was she involved in some plan to steal the Necklace? After the distressing scandal involving his son, Sir Gerald had retreated to his family home in Scotland. Presumably the trophy girlfriend had been ditched with everything else? Had she been part of the plot? Elliott studied her, under cover of putting cream on a scone. She'd made a remarkable recovery if she'd avoided detection and already started a new scam. He needed to know. Contacting Sir Gerald to ask about the clever and alluring Ms Maisie Norris would be difficult. *But not impossible.*

And Elliott knew someone who would be able to do it.

Maisie slid quickly out of the gates of Pentecost Place and paced along the seafront until she came to a bench that afforded a view of the gates and the sea, and flopped onto it. She was far enough away to be able to see in good time if anyone approached from the house. If anyone did, she would claim a landlubber's fascination with watching the waves. She needed to make a phone call where she would not be observed or overheard, but she also needed a few moments alone to process the meeting at the bottom of the stairs. Dr Elliott bloody Elwood! Of all the damn luck.

He'd shown no sign of recognising her, but she couldn't be sure. She certainly remembered *him* and the snooty way he'd looked her over at that charity bash. Okay, so he was a friend of Sir Gerald – they sat on some museum committee together – and he was obviously concerned that she was taking an older man for a ride. She'd sort of respected him for that – but that snooty look still rankled. He'd got a good eyeful of her in that pink dress while he was at it.

In a reflex action, Maisie settled her skirt more comfortably over her knees. Had the change of persona been enough? *There weren't many men that evening who were looking at your face.* All she could do was carry on regardless. It would have been nice to have known she would be meeting with Elwood – although that probably would have meant being pulled off the job. She would be stuck in the office as the handler and Michelle would have been here, out in the field. Her friend and colleague was much more of a geek than she was. Michelle *enjoyed* being back at base with the computers.

Maisie frowned. Elwood wasn't supposed to be here – with the sudden death of the university representative, Professor Mumford, Jake had expected the replacement to be a man called Leyland. That's who had been profiled in the hastily assembled notes that Michelle had put together in the short time available – which meant that Elwood was a problem on more than one level. She needed to call in.

With a sigh, she fished out her phone and selected Michelle's number. Conscious that she'd already sat there too long and that she needed to get back to Pentecost Place as soon as possible, she launched into her report, with only the barest greeting, as soon as the phone was picked up.

'Hi – I'm here and I'm in, but we have a problem – the university rep isn't Leyland. It's Elliott Elwood. I ran into him when I was undercover with Sir Gerald, so there's a chance he might remember. I need background on him ASAP.' *Other than that, he's a snooty, supercilious—*

There was a strange noise coming out of the phone. It sounded as if Michelle was … laughing?

Maisie glared at the phone but it made no difference. It was definitely laughter. 'Look, I don't know what the hell is so funny. I really need that briefing—'

The spluttering at the other end dialled down a notch.

'Sorry, hon – but you're not the only one.' Michelle began to giggle again. 'Dr Elwood just rang Jake to ask about *you.*'

Chapter Five

It took a few minutes to sort out that Dr Elwood hadn't known that she worked for Jake when he rang – but that he did now. He'd made the call to have *her* investigated. *Pompous, patronising ...*

The spike of indignation wasn't helped by the knowledge that it was actually a logical and practical thing to do.

'What did he think? That I was planning to steal the damn Collections?' *Of course he did. Why else would you be here?*

The question seemed to have set Michelle giggling again. Maisie enquired acidly what was funny *now*.

'I just had this image, hon – of you making off with a couple of sarcophagi on the roof rack of the car.'

'My car doesn't have a roof rack,' Maisie informed her with dignity. 'What does Jake want me to do?'

'Work with Elwood,' Michelle responded immediately. 'I'll send you a briefing, but Jake confirms he's one of the good guys – they're on some committee together.' *Another one!* 'Thing is,' Michelle continued, serious now, 'he *is* a leading Egyptology expert – if he authenticates that part of the Collection and especially the Cleopatra Necklace, it can only enhance its value.'

'Particularly to someone who *is* planning to steal it.' Maisie could see where this was going. 'Which also makes Dr Elwood a valuable commodity.'

'Valuable, and maybe vulnerable.'

Maisie considered this. Somehow, she couldn't see the possessor of that supercilious nose being browbeaten into anything – but if he was threatened in some way? 'Of course, we don't know that there is anything *at all* going on with the Necklace, or any other part of the Collections,' she said after a moment. 'Some of the paintings are worth a fortune – even the ones with clowns.' She resisted a small shudder.

'Yeah, but maybe not so easy to transport? Which is not to say that it can't be done.'

'Jake's tip-off was only about the jewellery though.'

'Yeah. Something connected to an insurance case he's working on. Hush-hush – you know how it is? – maybe something, maybe nothing,' Michelle said. 'In the meantime, you need to play nice with Dr Elwood.'

'Huh!' Maisie huffed. 'I'll talk to him.'

'Sounds like a good place to start,' Michelle agreed cheerfully. 'Jake's given him your phone number. And your real name.'

Maisie huffed again, then reminded Michelle about the briefing and rang off.

Getting up from the bench, she was almost at the gates of Pentecost Place when her phone pinged with a text message. *Meet in the Conservatory in 15? E.*

"E" for Elliott or for Elwood? Whatever, he'd wasted no time. With a sigh, she flipped back the answer – *yes*.

There was no point in sulking because … well just because … *Just because, in other circumstances, he'd tick all your boxes for an attractive man?* She gritted her teeth. She was here to do a job, as was he. Never mind if he'd thought she was a tart and/or a thief. *Be professional.* She straightened her shoulders and headed into the building.

Elliott prowled the humid depths of the conservatory, looking amongst the ferns and palms for a suitable place for an "impromptu" meeting with Maisie. It had been a disconcerting surprise to find that she was working for Jake. *Although it does explain a few things.* She was the operative who'd thwarted the kidnap attempt on Sir Gerald. Elliott wasn't quite sure where that left the disturbing and inappropriate attraction he'd felt when she was playing the part of gold-digger. *Uncle Angus's disreputable genes coming out? Maybe you inherited more from him than his flat and his beloved car?* Hmm – he wasn't unpicking that right now. There were more important things to worry about. *Which does not stop her being gorgeous*. He pushed the thought firmly away. She was a competent professional who was *working* here. If Jake's ambiguous but disquieting concerns were true, he might need that competence.

He found a stone bench in a small clearing beside a tiny indoor fountain. He sat down, listening to the water tinkling softly into a shell-shaped basin. He'd read somewhere – probably some spy novel – that the sound of water masked conversation. He wasn't certain that there would be anyone around to overhear, but it couldn't be ruled out, so it was best to be … circumspect.

Barnabas had reminded the participants of the programme for the weekend as they'd finished tea. There was a three-hour gap before drinks and dinner – time allocated for the guests to settle into their rooms, for those who needed to set up for their presentations tomorrow to have time to do so, and for a brief guided tour of the Collections, overseen by Barnabas. The group had been divided into two – the largest museum contingent and Lady Something were viewing the house and its treasures now. The other museum group were busy with equipment in the room allocated for them to make their pitch in the morning, which took care of everyone but himself and the undercover Ms Norris, whose real name was Maisie Webster. Dorothea, their limp hostess, was apparently supervising the arrangements for dinner, which would be followed by a talk from a local expert on Agatha Christie.

In amongst the presentations tomorrow, there were various Christie-themed events on offer, as a diversion from the exigency of the bidding process, and the day would culminate in drinks and dinner at a hotel with links to the author's books. On Sunday there would be free access to the Collections before sealed bids and departure after lunch. A real house party weekend, presided over by the beaming Barnabas. The whole setup was totally eccentric, but also totally in line with what he expected from the Pentecost family.

The participants invited to the bidding war were a varied bunch. The museums had sent experts covering all aspects of the Collections. According to Ben's folder, Lady Whatsit from the stately home, despite her obvious uneasiness at the situation – and Elliott couldn't entirely blame her – had a stellar reputation, vast experience as a curator, and had written books on the display and presentation of exhibits. *Which leaves Maisie Norris/Webster ... and me*. Jake had explained that Maisie's role was as trusted agent for Augustus Elladour, the reclusive billionaire that Jake's team had invented for the assignment. She was here at short notice to view the Collections on behalf of her fictitious employer and present his proposals, rather than as any sort of art expert.

Elliott shifted uneasily on the hard stone bench, wishing that it had a back to lean against. His own experience was limited to one aspect of the Collections. True, it was the largest, the most notable and possibly the most valuable, but even with all that, one particular item in it stood out – the Cleopatra Necklace. Professor Mumford would have attended alone, but he had been the acknowledged expert on the Pentecost family.

Leyland could have assembled a team from the University to match those from the museums, even at short notice and in the vacation. The Art History Department would have fallen over themselves to get to the paintings. *Instead, there's just me.* That was undoubtedly down to Leyland's arrogant assumption that Aquae Sulis was the natural home for the Collections – that there was no real competition. It would not have occurred to the Dean that more than one person would be needed to make the University's winning bid – and Elliott was the one who was expected to deliver.

But information that Jake had stumbled on raised a question ...

Is someone else expecting you to authenticate the Necklace while you're here?

But how ...?

A rustle amongst the palms jerked Elliott out of his distracted thoughts. Maisie stepped into the clearing and stopped, as if surprised. She inclined her head. 'Dr Elwood.'

'Ms Norris,' he returned the greeting. 'I was hoping for the chance to speak to you. Would you join me?' He indicated the space beside him on the bench. 'I'm afraid I can't recommend its comfort.' He tried a smile. She didn't exactly smile back, but there was a slight softening in her expression. And she did sit down.

The muggy warmth of the conservatory was enhancing her perfume; something warm and spicy that overlaid the ambient scent of soil and vegetation. Her hair was frizzing slightly, tiny curls forming around her face. Elliott grasped the edge of the bench to stop himself reaching to touch one. *For heaven's sake!*

He took a deep breath. He knew what he had to do. He'd realised it as soon as he'd ended the call with Jake. 'When we last met,' he said quietly, 'I formed an erroneous impression of you. I'd like to apologise for that.'

He studied her face – perfect skin with just a tiny hint of freckles over the nose and very dark grey eyes. She hadn't expected an apology, he decided. Her mouth, wide and full, had crimped a bit at "erroneous". *So shoot me – I'm an academic.* 'You were working,' he continued, dropping his voice so it was even softer. 'Jake confirmed that you're a bodyguard, when necessary. Um ...' He tightened his hold on the bench. 'Jake didn't exactly spell it out, and I'm not entirely sure how it could be possible – but if I'm reading things right, he seems to be suggesting that this weekend ... *I* might be the body that needs guarding.'

Chapter Six

Well! Maisie knew her eyes had widened. She hadn't expected the man to put two and two together quite so fast. *But I suppose they don't hand out doctorates on a whim*. She certainly hadn't expected the apology. The cynical part of her suggested that one might be connected to the other, but even so, the words had been said.

He was looking at her now with a hopeful expression, and she really couldn't do anything else but respond to the olive branch.

'You disapproved of the role I was playing,' she said stiffly, shifting quickly away from the admission and on to the conclusions he'd drawn. 'Jake made it clear that, in this case, we don't actually *know* anything.'

Know – no. Suspect – maybe. Jake had a *lot* of contacts, and recently there'd been a small buzz about something unusual and of major historical significance that was about to come on the market. Something that would attract a certain kind of buyer, with certain expectations. Something that could also attract a thief?

The Necklace fitted the description perfectly.

The thing that was giving Jake cause for concern over Elwood's safety was another rumour, of a different kind. In the art world, provenance – the documented history of an object and its owners – was very important to prove that an item was genuine, but the opinion of an acknowledged expert could also be significant in cases of doubt. Six months ago, an eminent art historian had unexpectedly expressed decisive support for the authenticity of a painting with a slightly questionable provenance. When this became known, the value of the piece had rocketed. A bidding war had taken place between two wealthy prospective buyers. The painting had subsequently disappeared, stolen en route to a major exhibition in London. Nothing had been said, or even hinted at in public, but in the underground circles, from which Jake occasionally obtained information, a dark rumour whispered that the expert's wife and teenage daughter had been threatened, possibly abducted for a short time. The man had subsequently resigned his post and relocated to his wife's family home in Switzerland.

Had the expert and his family been threatened to influence his opinion, establish the painting and raise its value?

Perhaps.

And now a mysterious Necklace and a prominent Egyptologist were here under the same roof, along with a rumour of a historic piece of jewellery that might be worth stealing. And might be even more worth stealing with an expert endorsement?

If it had worked once…

As the sole representative of the University, without a team surrounding him, Elwood was potentially more vulnerable if there was someone out there.

Which is where you come in.

You're his team.

If there is *anyone out there.*

'It's all speculation,' Maisie continued. 'We don't really *know* anything,' she repeated.

Elliott's dark eyebrows were drawn together in a frown. 'I can't really see how something could have been planned. I didn't know myself that I was going to be here until yesterday.'

'True.' Maisie remembered that her own briefing pack had profiled Vaisey Leyland. 'But now you *are* here – if there are professional thieves interested in the Necklace, they'll have excellent intelligence networks – Jake doesn't like to take chances if he can avoid it.' She shrugged. 'In all probability nothing will happen, except that everyone goes home knowing more about Agatha Christie than they did when they arrived. And possibly having gained a few pounds in weight.'

She tilted her head to look sideways at Elwood. The frown had faded. When he wasn't being stuck up and supercilious, he really was … She headed off that thought once again. *Concentrate, Webster.* 'And, of course, someone will have secured the Pentecost Collections for their employers,' she added. 'I fully intend it should be Augustus Elladour,' she tacked on provocatively, playing up to her cover story.

'Of course.' He nodded, but she didn't miss the competitive gleam in his eye. 'Might I ask what your employer intends to do with it?'

'Put it on public display,' she responded glibly. 'There will be a new building to house it – with an architectural contest for the design. And obviously the building will be named after him.' She could see from Elwood's eyes that he was assessing her pitch. She could also see when he reached the conclusion that, if Elladour and the bid had been real, it might have stood an excellent chance of winning.

'This weekend is going to be interesting.' Elwood smiled suddenly. Maisie felt several things inside her react. Her breathing was one of them. The smile faded regrettably quickly. *Luckily* not *regrettably*. 'In the meantime, we wait and observe?'

'That's about it.' Maisie looked at her watch. 'I think we'd better find our way to the entrance hall to begin the grand tour.'

Elliott couldn't remember the last time he'd had an experience like this. The Pentecost Collections were sublime and unconventional, sometimes both at the same time – particularly the items in Bourdene Pentecost's so-called Clown Room; although "clown" was really only convenient shorthand. The exhibits owed more to the theatre and the *commedia dell'arte* than the sawdust ring of the circus. Sketches and paintings of harlequins and *pierrots* by Picasso and Jean Cocteau rubbed shoulders with soft focus Rococo canvasses of rural landscapes with costumed figures. There were sculptures in metal and glass, vintage posters, props and costume sketches, an antique toy theatre with figures from the Commedia, and a score of the opera *Pagliacci* signed by Caruso. Life-size models of Harlequin and Columbine stood together in an alcove, their costumes of pastel patchwork glittering with stage jewels. A note on a side table indicated that they had possibly been created for principal dancers from the Ballet Russes, but if so had never been worn in performance.

The room was strange and beautiful and parts of it were slightly creepy. Maisie was standing before one of the small canvasses hung in a corner of the room, looking at it with an incredulous expression. He sidled up to her. 'What?' he asked quietly.

No one else was looking their way. The museum people were clustered in front of a display of four Picasso sketches. 'I could be mistaken, but it *looks* like a Watteau – one of his *fêtes galantes* paintings – a sort of open-air masquerade concert.' She gestured. 'You can just see Harlequin, there beside the tree, behind the man with the lute. If it *is* a Watteau, it's a lost painting. I've never seen it before.'

Elliott studied the picture, taking in the shimmering quality of the paint and the dreamy subject matter – groups of beautifully dressed friends and lovers, dogs, musicians and children, disporting themselves in a Sylvan landscape. Its quality was obvious. Maisie's suspicions could easily be correct. That was how the Pentecosts were – rich, eccentric and eclectic connoisseurs of the rare and exquisite. *And Ms Webster seems to know about these things. Interesting.* 'It's beautiful.'

‘And very valuable,’ Maisie breathed. ‘Collectors would go nuts.’ She shook her head. ‘This place is crazy.’

Elliott touched her arm. ‘Looks like we’re moving on. You should get a look at the provenance tomorrow.’

The next room housed Victorian paintings. Elliott stood at the back of the group, watching and listening as Barnabas showed off a succession of treasures. This was obviously one of his personal enthusiasms. Many of the paintings were by the Pre-Raphaelites, assembled when the Place was under construction. At least three – a Rossetti and two by Waterhouse – were known only as names on lists and two others, supposedly by the “lost” Pre-Raphaelite, John Bateman, would keep his History of Art colleagues debating for years. The house really was a treasure box of the lost and the extraordinary.

He tuned out Barnabas’s commentary, simply looking at the art. Almost all the paintings featured beautiful women. *And Maisie Webster could pose for at least half of them.* He watched her studying one of the supposed Batemans, standing in front of another canvas depicting a woman with tumbling Titian curls. The painting was lovely, but the living, breathing woman standing below it … Elliott felt a strange constriction in his chest, and only part of it was down to the knowledge that the next room housed the Egyptian collection.

The group shifted forward, across the corridor, and here it was. Elliott swallowed hard. Two magnificent painted sarcophagi guarded the doorway, with another towering against the wall at the end of the long room. Large statues depicting the cat goddess Bast, and the lioness-headed Sekhmet patrolled the perimeter. Their eyes were inset with crystals that glittered under the old-fashioned florescent lights. Two seated representations of Horus and Anubis, slightly larger than life-size, stared out over a museum-style glass case that ran the length of the room and contained small objects – grave goods, jars, statuettes, the glint of metal and the flash of paint and gems. It was an impressive display and this was only part of it. Larger and more fragile items were off-site in climate-controlled storage. And in a case by itself, sectioned off in the centre of the exhibit, was the Cleopatra Necklace, displayed on a stand. Gold and jewels stood out against black velvet. Undoubtedly, it was an impressive piece of craftsmanship, but none of the inset gems – crystals, turquoise and lapis lazuli – were especially remarkable. It was the history of the collar that could make it very valuable indeed.

Abruptly, Elliott understood the stories and the fascination. His fingers itched to take hold of the thing, run it through his hands, to fasten it around the neck of a beautiful woman – a living, breathing woman.

One particular woman.

And to crown that gesture with a kiss—

With a quick indrawn breath, he jerked his head up slightly and met Barnabas's eyes across the glass case, watchful and aware in his round amiable face. Elliott shook his head to clear it. For a strange, breathless moment he'd been drawn into the legend. Displayed as it was, the thing was lovely, no question. *But it doesn't mean it's a genuine artefact.* It *looked* right, but he wouldn't have expected anything else. It would have to be examined, along with its documentation. *But that's not really the point – the point is the legend – the cachet of owning a piece with its supposed history ...*

Barnabas was still watching him with a strange expression, then one of the museum staff asked a question and they moved on to where Dorothea stood waiting in the hall, ready to show them into the library – the province of Lucinda Pentecost – filled with grimoires, antique alchemical texts and signed first editions of Agatha Christie.

Examining herself critically in the bedroom mirror, Maisie settled the bodice of her dress so that it fitted properly across the shoulders. She smoothed the vintage copper silk – Cassie's choice – down over her hips and hoped she wouldn't have to do any running in the narrow skirt. *No reason that you should. Drinks, dinner and a lecture – what can go wrong?* She'd change into something more practical later for her exploration of the house.

Jake had sent copies of blueprints and architect's drawings for Pentecost Place to her by courier under the guise of proposals for the Elladour Museum, which she actually already had. The papers included original drawings and details for the current security system – heaven knew where Jake had got hold of them. They'd hashed out a plan of sorts, but it was still more or less a watch-and-wait operation. Michelle had done an initial background check on all the guests and the staff that had been hired for the weekend and there had been no obvious alarm bells, but there probably wouldn't be until she'd had time to dig a lot deeper. If anything was going on at all, it was more likely that the weekend would be used to check out the house for a raid later.

Even so, Maisie had that little prickle along her spine that told her something wasn't right. She slid a pair of heavy gold studs into her ears. The prickle was for the setup – nothing to do with Elliott Elwood. *Nothing at all.*

He'd had his own reaction to the Cleopatra Necklace, she was sure of it – for two maybe three seconds, surrounded by those massive statues, he'd tuned out. *Does that mean that the thing is genuine?* Barnabas had picked up on it too. She'd spent more time covertly watching her fellow guests than the exhibits, but she hadn't missed the fact that the whole building was stashed with stuff that would tempt a thief. It was the *reputation* of the Necklace that was the attraction. According to Jake's latest intelligence, there was a ring of four or five wealthy collectors who came together to bid against each other for particular items that were stolen to order – and the bidding process was of just as much importance as possession of the object itself. *A very expensive pissing contest.*

Somewhere in the depths of the house an old-fashioned dinner gong sounded, summoning the guests for pre-dinner drinks. Maisie reached for her evening bag and looked around for her shoes.

Most of the rest of the party was already in the drawing room when Elliott slipped quietly in. He'd felt self-conscious packing his dinner jacket, but a quick scan showed that everyone else had dressed up too. From the look of the fit, some of the museum staff had rented their evening clothes, as it appeared had Barnabas. Their host was energetically flourishing a glass cocktail shaker, his overlong jacket cuffs flapping around his hands.

Elliott spotted a tray of ready-filled sherry glasses on a side table and took one with a sigh of relief. The venomous green potion that Barnabas was pouring out looked as if it ought to be smoking as it hit the glass. It was almost the exact colour of the dress Dorothea was wearing; another droopy affair of sad looking satin. Sipping the sherry – an acceptable Fino – Elliott drifted over to where Maisie was standing before the fireplace, also sipping sherry and looking up at a large portrait of Erasmus Pentecost. Her close-fitting dress rippled with a coppery sheen – the wide neck setting off delicate collarbones and a glimpse of creamy shoulders. She'd gathered her hair up into a pleat, revealing the line of her neck. For a second, Elliott remembered the Cleopatra Necklace and the sensation of fastening it—

‘Hi!’ A large bearded man, part of one of the museum contingents, stuck out his hand in greeting. ‘Bill Chisholm. We didn’t get to speak earlier. I read your piece in the last edition of *Historical Excerpts*.’ He nodded to another man who was hovering. ‘Chris and I were wondering …’

With a carefully muffled sigh, Elliott gave himself up to talking shop. At least here no one was asking for autographs. Being accosted by strangers for his signature had been an unexpected consequence of fronting a series of television programmes on Egyptian archaeology. He continued to keep an eye on the rest of the room. *Or at least on one particular part of it.* Maisie had been joined in front of the fireplace by Dorothea, who had a slim, sun-tanned man in tow; slicked-back dark hair and what appeared to be a vintage evening jacket gave him the look of a 1920’s lounge lizard.

‘Don’t you agree, Elwood?’

Elliott pulled his attention away from Maisie’s smile of welcome for the man and back to the conversation he was meant to be having. ‘Oh, yes ... that is ... can you just run that by me again?’

Barnabas had embarked on a second round of green cocktails by the time Elliott was able to move over to where Maisie was standing. Lounge lizard was introduced and proved to be Armand, the third of the cousins.

‘Professional gambler,’ Maisie said softly as Dorothea shepherded him off to make more introductions. ‘Not too welcome these days in most of the casinos and clubs in London and the South of France. Concentrates now on private poker games.’

Elliott frowned. ‘He cheats?’

Maisie shrugged. ‘He wins – often. Could just be that he’s really good – and lucky.’

Elliott watched Armand bowing over the hand of one of the female museum staff, who was giggling. ‘Might he be in need of money and have dubious friends?’

‘Possibly – but his share of the inheritance should fund him for quite a while.’ Maisie sipped her sherry. ‘What did you make of the Necklace?’

‘It’s … beautiful.’ He shifted uncomfortably. He couldn’t explain the strange feeling that had come over him when he looked at the thing and he certainly wasn’t admitting to it. *Not to the woman around whose neck I wanted to fasten it.* He diverted himself quickly away from *that* thought. 'If it's genuine, then it's worth a lot more than the sum of its parts.'

'It's not the only thing of value in the house. The whole place is pretty overwhelming.' Maisie looked up at the portrait of Erasmus Pentecost. 'They were all trying to outdo each other. All the members of the family,' she said softly. '*He* began it with the two houses and the paintings, then the children and grandchildren and great-grandchildren carried on with their own collections.'

Elliott was startled, then he nodded. 'I never thought of it that way, but you're right – it was one-upmanship – each one with their own area of interest. And maybe it wasn't just within their family. Agatha Christie's family were notable collectors. Dame Agatha had a lovely set of Commedia figures that she'd inherited. They're on display at Greenway, her summer home. It makes sense that a family like the Pentecosts might be tempted to emulate – or even try to outdo them.'

'Well, imitation is the sincerest form of flattery,' Maisie observed. 'And I do get the feeling that the Pentecosts were generally a competitive lot. Apart from the Necklace, what's the Egyptian collection like?' she asked abruptly.

'Hard to tell. There's nothing particularly unusual about the items on display here, although they're all impressive and valuable. The bulk of that collection is stored elsewhere – a private hoard – but on the basis of what I've seen so far, I think the University should be very pleased to acquire it.' He looked around. 'Everyone will be bidding largely sight unseen. That was an accepted condition.'

'But there's plenty here to make it worthwhile.' She finished her sherry and put the glass down on the mantelpiece, grinning suddenly. 'If it were me, I'd case the place this weekend and arrive back with a fleet of vans on Sunday night when everyone has gone home, and clear the whole lot out.'

He shared the grin. 'Good thing you're not on the wrong side of the fence then.'

'Isn't it just? Oh!' She nodded towards the door behind him. People were moving through it. 'Looks like dinner is served.'

Mercifully, dinner was a much lighter meal than the afternoon tea – a shallow bowl of clear soup, chicken served with asparagus in a delicate sauce, followed by platters of fruit and cheese and small cups of sorbet. Elliott, seated between Bill and Chris, the two museum staff he'd chatted to earlier, had just helped himself to a pear when he felt a soft touch on his ankle. *Accident? Or is someone playing footsie under the table?* He got his answer when a set of stocking clad toes began making their way determinedly up his shin. For a moment something in his chest tensed, then he realised that Maisie was sitting three seats away from him and at an angle. With a discreet cough, he drew back his foot. The girl sitting across the table, the giggler he realised, jumped a little in her seat, giving him a wide-eyed look before a rosy blush began to climb from the neck of her blue dress. *Not meant for me then.* He treated the woman to a bland smile and picked up a knife to cut the fruit on his plate.

Something had awakened him.

A door opening somewhere?

Elliott rolled over and looked at the clock on the bedside table. Half-past one. The lecture on Agatha Christie had been interesting and had provoked discussion until the party broke up just after midnight – but from the sound of stealthy footsteps in the corridor outside, not everyone had retired to their rooms to sleep. Curious, he rose quietly, crossed to the door and slid it open a crack. At the far end of the passage, light spilled out for a second as a door opened and closed over muffled laughter. A familiar sound. The giggler had found the correct recipient for her advances this time. At least he hoped it was the correct recipient.

On the other side of the passage another door opened. Maisie's head appeared. 'Musical beds,' he whispered. Maisie nodded. In the faint sliver of light through the crack of her door, he could see she was fully dressed in a dark sweater and jeans. He shut his own door quickly and was already reaching for his trousers and shoes when he heard it – a soft scraping noise followed by a thump …

From overhead.

That was what had awakened him, not the sounds from the corridor. He scrambled into his clothes and let himself out into the passageway. Maisie was a dark blur on the way to the stairs. He caught up with her in a few strides. 'You heard it?'

'Heard what?' She blinked up at him, but he didn't buy the innocence for a second.

'Either the gargoyles are throwing a party, or there's someone on the roof.'

Chapter Seven

He'd expected her to try to shoo him back to his room. Instead, she just led the way forward. *Probably knows you wouldn't go back.* There was a cool draught of air coming from somewhere. When they reached the stairs, Maisie gestured to a shadowed recess just beyond them. The door to a short set of steps giving access to the roof was open, propped with a fire extinguisher. Maisie indicated they should stop. They both stood still, listening. Elliott found that he was counting silently. *Thirty-four, thirty-five* ... He'd reached one hundred and forty-four with no further noise from the roof, when Maisie moved cautiously forward and up the steps.

There was a nearly full moon, drifting in and out between clouds. 'I'm so glad you reminded me about the gargoyles,' Maisie said softly.

Apart from the hunched and winged figures crouching on the parapet, the roof was empty. One of the statues appeared to be wearing a belt.

'Fashion statement?' Elliott suggested.

'Not quite.' They both looked over the parapet to see the end of the rope, stretching away to the ground. Maisie stood back and considered the surroundings. 'I don't think anyone climbed up that to get in here. It's an insurance policy.'

'An emergency exit,' Elliott confirmed.

'Which means that whoever put it there is already inside.' She started to make her way back to the steps. Elliott followed. Once they were through, she moved the extinguisher and shut the door. 'Just in case.'

They made their way down through the dark and silent house. Elliott wondered about alarms, but Maisie seemed to know what she was doing, and if there *was* someone else here, they hadn't set anything off. His eyes had adjusted to the dark; there were occasional patches of moonlight coming in through un-curtained windows, but by night the building was … disturbing. Furniture and large ornaments that he didn't remember seeing by daylight loomed from odd corners. There was an intense and uncomfortable sense of being watched by the family portraits hanging on the walls beside them. Snatches of light glinted off a display of swords. A figure standing still and silent near the top of the stairs had his heart surging to beat in his ears until it resolved into a suit of armour. Maisie padded easily beside him. He thought he could pick up a trace of her spicy scent. She stopped at the top of the stairs, looking down. There was a faint light coming from one of the rooms below, through the open door to the hall.

'That's the Clown Room,' Elliott whispered.

Maisie nodded to confirm. She started forward cautiously for the first stair when there was a small clatter and a muffled curse. A woman's voice. Maisie shot back to the landing as the light inside the room wavered, as if a figure had moved in front of it. Then the light went out and the door closed softly.

Abruptly, from somewhere else in the house, there was a muted rattle of crockery. Another door opened, a switch clicked, and the lower hall was flooded with light. Half dazzled by the unexpected brightness, Elliott instinctively reached for Maisie's hand, pulling her into the relative shelter of the armour as Barnabas strode across the hall, carrying a tray full of plates to the dining room. He was singing. Elliott recognised the chorus of the Beatles' 'Yellow Submarine'. Elliott dropped to his knees, but pulled himself up on the banister so that he could see over the top, aware that Maisie had done the same. *Like kids watching the grown-ups down below.*

From outside, there was a sound of a car pulling up on the gravel. Then there was a movement at the entrance to the Clown Room. Barnabas's head came up with a start, almost endangering his burden. The plates rattled. 'Oh hey – I didn't realise—' He didn't get any more words out. A figure rushed towards him, clearly intent on getting to the front door.

The subsequent encounter had an awful inevitability. With some sort of instinctive reaction, Barnabas thrust the tray at the woman barrelling towards him. China flew up and crashed down and so did the figure, slipping on something on the hall floor. Amongst the chaos of breaking plates and the idling car, there was a scream and an ominous thump.

Elliott realised he was still holding Maisie's hand when her fingers crunched hard around his. He took a chance and stood up, dragging Maisie against his shoulder. She was soft and warm and craning to see. Barnabas was still on his feet, making ineffectual sounds of distress. The woman's body lay on the hall floor. Her grey wig had slipped, revealing short, spiky blonde hair beneath. The bag she'd been carrying had bounced away from her, scattering picture frames across the floor.

Paintings and sketches of harlequins, *pierrots* and clowns spilled splashes of colour across the black and white chequer-board tiles.

Hours later, in the depths of the conservatory, lit by the first faint light of pre-dawn, slightly shaky fingers keyed in the number. The phone rang for a long time, until at last—

'What?' It was a groggy growl. 'Do you know what time it is?'

'Yes, but I had to ring.' The story of the attempted robbery tumbled out.

'It was only the clown pictures?' The growl was no longer groggy. 'She didn't go near the Necklace?'

'No. Not even close. The police have been and gone. We can still go ahead – the Necklace is fine.'

'And Elwood definitely reacted when he saw it?'

'Definitely. I was watching – I made sure.'

'That's good.' The interruption was impatient. 'That's what we want. We don't need to change the plan. Act normal,' the voice ordered. 'Go to bed. I'll ring you when I've had a chance to think.'

Maisie considered the cup of coffee in front of her. The foam on the top had been sculpted into a perfectly shaped heart. It almost seemed a shame to disturb it, but she was craving the caffeine. She'd only managed to grab an orange juice at breakfast before escaping to a café near the marina.

Not unexpectedly, the weekend programme had been knocked somewhat out of shape by the events of the early hours. Amongst the hubbub of police, an ambulance for the dazed thief, guests emerging from their rooms in various states of undress and a quantity of broken china, no one had paid any attention to her and Elliott. By unspoken agreement, they'd stayed in the shadows on the landing until they could mingle unnoticed with the crowd.

Without the grey wig, "Lady Whatsit" had proved to be a member of the stately home's staff who'd been taken on temporarily for the summer season. The real Lady Whatsit had been given a message that arrangements had been rescheduled to the following weekend. Apparently, she was now on her way to Torquay. The police had apprehended the failed thief's boyfriend, who was still sitting outside in the getaway car with his ear-buds in when they'd arrived. He was at the police station, helping with enquiries; she was in the local hospital with concussion. The art had been retrieved with no more than a slightly chipped frame on a Cocteau drawing. Some of this information had come from an early morning phone call with Jake, the rest in snippets from a distracted but excited Barnabas over a running buffet breakfast. There was a noticeable shortage of plates. Disturbed and jumpy, the guests milled around, noisily rehashing what had happened. Maisie had been glad to forego breakfast to get away.

Now she was enjoying coffee and a croissant, waiting for Elliott to join her. *And since when has it been* Elliott*?* They had things to discuss, but before that she had issues to sort out in her own mind – and that was one of them. Holding his hand, leaning against him in the darkness had felt … good. Too good. It was one thing to have him close so that she could keep an eye on him, quite another that she should enjoy it.

She pursed her lips. She needed to have her mind on the job. She'd called Jake as soon as she could. He'd already heard about the raid through his contacts and was of the opinion that last night's disturbance was simply a coincidence. They did happen. The would-be thief had concentrated entirely on the Clown Room – there'd been no attempt to go anywhere near the Necklace. Another piece of information that Jake had picked up from his police contact – she could never work out who was whose confidential informant in that setup – was more disturbing. She'd put that on one side until Elliott – *Dr Elwood* – turned up.

She shifted restlessly in her seat, looking at her watch. With the rumpus kicked up by the attempted robbery, she hadn't been able to have an uninterrupted look around and, in particular, to study the security arrangements for the Necklace. The case containing it was supposed to be alarmed, but she wasn't entirely convinced about that, and she couldn't shake a nebulous feeling of unease whenever she thought about it. She had a mounting suspicion that her vague disquiet was going to compel her to stake out the room for the coming night, which left her with the problem of Elliott. Did she watch him or the Necklace*? Both?*

Her brain flipped to an image of getting cosy with Dr Elwood under a glass display case – she drew the line at sharing a sarcophagus with him. With an effort, she ushered her thoughts back to where they belonged – assessing what she knew about the layout of the building and the security. She couldn't do any more for the moment, and Elwood was late.

Elliott let himself out of the front door of Pentecost Place and set off briskly in the direction of the pier and the marina. Too little sleep was making his mind woolly. The sea air would do him good. *As would seeing Maisie Webster*. Shortage of sleep had only been partly due to the nocturnal disturbances. His thoughts kept going back to the softness of Maisie's curves pressed against his chest. He really needed to get his mind out of *that* groove before he saw her.

He cut through a quiet side street. Ahead of him, a stocky man and a woman wearing a brightly coloured headscarf and tightly belted black trench coat were standing on either side of a parked car, talking across it. As Elliott approached, the woman peeled abruptly away from the car and crossed the road, walking off down the street and disappearing around the corner. As the man turned towards him, Elliott started with surprise. 'Ben!'

'Oh!' His friend stopped, blinking with confusion. 'El … I was coming to look for you, but that woman—' he gestured '—she wanted directions.' He took a quick look round, clearly off-balance. 'I had some disturbing news.'

'The attempted robbery? It wasn't the Necklace.'

'Robbery?' Ben asked carefully.

'Oh – not the robbery. Of course not.' Elliott shook his head. *Just because it's uppermost in* your *mind ...* The story would hardly have got out yet. 'Look, I think we'd better compare notes.'

He guided his friend towards the sea front and a convenient bench, and succinctly described the events of the night. Succinct because it could only be what a guest roused from sleep to find a dazed thief on the floor and the police on their way would have known.

'That's awful.' Ben put his hand to his head. 'And with what I came to tell you …' He gave a sudden shudder.

'What *did* you come all this way for?' With a rush of concern, Elliott realised his friend looked pale in the morning sunshine. Pale and worried. Ben waved his hand in an uncoordinated way. A curious seagull, checking whether they had any food, twitched its wings and scuttled off with an indignant squawk.

'I've got a great-aunt in Brixham,' Ben said, as if it was an answer. 'With what happened yesterday, I felt I had to see you. I couldn't tell you something like that over the phone. The police came to the campus just after lunch.' Ben's eyes were wide now and pained. 'They've started an investigation. They said ... they said that Professor Mumford was *murdered*.'

Chapter Eight

Elliott got to the café at last. Maisie was sitting at a corner table. She glanced at the clock and pushed a pot of oolong tea towards him as he sat down. *How does she know ...?*

He remembered the teapots yesterday. *Observation.* It looked as if she was on her second cup of coffee and there was a plate with crumbs and a few flakes of almond on it.

'I'm sorry I'm late,' he apologised, once he'd got his breath back. 'I was diverted. Benedict Bartram – an old friend from the University – came to see me. I met him on the way. He said ...' Elliott swallowed. He'd been too intent on getting rid of Ben, who'd shown signs of wanting to linger – which had made him impatient and guilty – for the news to properly sink in. 'He said Professor Mumford was murdered.' He swallowed again. Unperturbed, Maisie poured a cup from the pot and passed it over to him. 'You knew,' he realised.

'Jake heard it from one of his police friends last night. The toxicology results showed up something that shouldn't have been there.' She gave a small shrug. 'As he had a heart condition, it might have slipped through as natural causes – except his consultant wasn't happy about it and asked questions.'

'Not many people at the University knew about his heart.' Elliott explained that he had been one of them, after the Harley Street meeting. 'He didn't want any fuss that might stop his research.'

Maisie frowned, considering. 'I'll get Jake to pass that on to the police – it might narrow the field.' She gave him a level look, which he returned. He knew what was in both their minds.

He shivered, hoping it didn't make him look too pathetic. 'It's difficult to know of anyone who would want to murder William Mumford,' he said. 'He's got no close family. He lived for his work.'

'And that work was to bring the Pentecost Collections to Pentecost Court. But his expertise was on the family, not on any particular artefact.'

'Maybe they'll find a former colleague with a grudge, or a vengeful old flame.' Elliott thought about it, then thought about Mumford. It didn't seem likely, but the alternative ... Elliott drew a line on the table with one finger, then looked up. 'It seems ... outrageous to think that he was murdered so that I could take his place.'

'Which is why no one will be suggesting that idea to the police.'

'I should hope not.' He gestured restlessly, aware of how still and composed she was. This was clearly the real Maisie, as opposed to the ditzy gold-digger of their first encounter. 'It can't be true. There must be another reason, something in his private life that we don't know about. And, anyway, Leyland might have decided to come himself – that would have been far more likely than sending me.'

'True,' she agreed, although he wasn't sure how much she believed it.

You're the man with the reputation as an Egyptologist – the talking head off the telly.

The unspoken words hovered, making him shift uncomfortably in his seat. Even normally easy-going Ben had been rattled, asking Elliott if he couldn't just give a written authentication for the Necklace and leave, then laughing awkwardly about fear of the curse. He'd mentioned it again as they'd said goodbye, with a clumsy joke about Elliott returning to Bath with him, leaving a note to say the Necklace had been validated remotely using the Elwood Magic Touch.

'The police are interviewing everyone at the University now.' Maisie broke into Elliott's thoughts, giving him an assessing glance. 'They'll want to talk to you, but if you weren't on campus you're probably in the clear.'

'As a murderer, yes. I was in London when Bill Mumford died.' Elliott found his hand tensed rather hard on the delicate teacup. 'But as a murderee?'

Maisie shook head. 'I think you're probably worth much more alive than dead.' She smiled suddenly and Elliott felt warmed all the way down to his toes. 'It's my job to keep it that way.' She leaned over to briefly touch his free hand.

Elliott took a large gulp of oolong. 'Good to know,' he managed to acknowledge. What with the potential threat and the smile and the feel of her skin … He took another gulp of tea and pulled his mind away from scary speculation and back to practical matters. 'Well – now – as everyone had a disturbed night, the cousins have decided to rearrange the programme – unlimited access to the Collections today and presentations and bids tomorrow morning. Barnabas announced it just before I came out. The extra-curricular activities are still happening, if anyone wants them.'

‘What are you going to do?’ She seemed to have accepted that they were moving on.

‘Spend some time with the archives,’ he said promptly. ‘I can’t actually handle the Necklace today – something about the security locks on the case – so I want to look at the provenance of the Egyptian collection. Then maybe take a nap and do the Agatha Christie walk around the town before dinner.’

‘Sounds like a plan.’ She looked thoughtful. ‘I’ve got some research I want to do in the library.’

Maisie pulled a thick volume off the library shelf and carried it to her seat overlooking the garden. At the other end of the library, one of the museum staff – last night’s giggler – was engrossed in an alchemy text. She was making notes, her head bent so that her heavy plait of dark hair brushed the edge of the pages. They’d nodded to each other, then steered clear. Maisie didn’t want anyone paying too much attention to what she was doing. She’d found what she wanted in an alcove of the library. Erasmus Pentecost had been a keen amateur magician. He’d built up a collection of books on the topic and some of his old equipment was in one of the attics.

After half an hour, Maisie left the books for a while to investigate the upper floors, taking the time to step out onto the roof to say hello to the gargoyles. They simply sat, silent and brooding, but they still told her something that might or might not be important. The rope remained in place. The police hadn’t found it, or had not felt the need to remove it. She looked at it thoughtfully, then let herself back into the building and into the attics.

Erasmus had some interesting props; he’d been particularly fond of cabinets and devices involving carpentry. She prowled around a trunk adapted to have swords thrust through it, and another, the purpose of which she couldn’t quite make out, but she suspected would involve the magician disappearing before his mystified audience. There was another life-size construction, shaped disturbingly like a coffin, which had a false back.

Having seen everything there was to see, she went back to the library to find Erasmus’s personal notebooks.

She was just returning the last book to the shelves when Barnabas and Dorothea entered the room. For a moment they both stared at her, poised next to the cache in the alcove with the slim leather-bound volume in her hand. She was struck, in a brief flash, at the resemblance between the cousins. *They have the same eyes.* Flat, dark eyes, surveying her now with something that looked like suspicion. Then Barnabas smiled his wide, toothy smile and began to burble, enquiring solicitously whether she had found all the information she needed. Dorothea turned away to pick up a mug that the giggler had left on the table, tutting a little under her breath, and the strange moment passed.

'Secret passages?'

'I'm sure of it.' Maisie smiled at Elliott's surprise. They were dawdling at the back of the group from Pentecost Place who were getting some sea air before dinner by taking a guided tour of Torquay's literary landmarks. The bulk of the group was gathered around their guide, admiring a bust of Dame Agatha.

'Isn't that a bit – I don't know – Scooby Doo … or Enid Blyton?'

'Erasmus was interested in conjuring. He had a lot of devices made for him.' She'd found the specifications in Pentecost's notebooks for several of the illusions she'd discovered in the attic. 'When I looked at the plans of the house, there are a couple of places where the dimensions don't seem quite right. Erasmus used to give magic performances for guests and the family where he mysteriously disappeared and reappeared in different parts of the building. I think that was how he did it.'

'You're not planning to go around tapping the walls?' Elliott still looked sceptical. Maisie felt a twinge of the old annoyance. *Superior Dr Elwood.* Then he grinned and her insides did something very strange. 'Actually, secret passages sound a very Pentecost thing – and Erasmus *was* the first of the family eccentrics.'

'He made big money from industry and shipping. He could afford to indulge.'

Elliott nodded. 'So what *are* you going to do?' The group was moving forward. They kept in position at the back.

'I'm not intending to go exploring, just keep in mind the possibilities. It might be that the current family members don't know. As far as I'm aware, none of them have ever lived in the house. Passages could have been blocked up.

'Or not.'

'Or not,' she agreed. 'How was your afternoon?'

'Productive. If the stuff that's in storage matches the various documents, and I have no reason to believe that it won't, it's a significant collection.' There was an excited gleam in his eyes. The stab of something that felt almost like jealousy was very weird. *He's excited about a load of old mummies. So what?*

'What about the Necklace?'

'Nothing.'

'Nothing at all? Could the relevant paperwork be stored somewhere else?'

'Maybe. Or perhaps there isn't any …' His mouth twisted in disapproval as he paused. 'Or it could mean that it's been removed,' he added quietly. Something in his tone made her look up at him. 'There are no *obvious* gaps.'

'But you've got an instinct that something isn't right – exactly like I got with those house plans.'

He nodded. 'I'll ask Barnabas about it, if I can find an opportunity to do it discreetly.' He watched the other members of the group snaking out in front of them, trailing after the guide. 'The Necklace is an aberration. The rest of the Collections – all the different parts – are well worth the University making a bid. That's what enthused Mumford – all the pieces assembled by the family, not some legendary Necklace.'

'Even if he died for it?' Maisie said softly. When she looked up this time, there was a hard edge to Elliott's expression – something formidable and angry, and for a second she was glad she wasn't the target of his feelings. Then her self-confidence reasserted itself. She was quite capable of going toe-to-toe with Dr Elliott Elwood. *And wouldn't that be fun?* She ignored the provoking voice in her head. She was here to do a job. As it happened, he was part of it. *That's all.* 'Hey, we'd better move.' She gestured to the rest of the group. 'They're getting away.'

It was ten-thirty. After the previous disturbed night, the other guests had gone yawning to their beds – or someone else's bed. The early July night had turned surprisingly chilly and there was a fire lit in the drawing room. Elliott sat watching the flames. Maisie sat opposite him. It felt very peaceful but he knew that it wasn't. There was a tension in her that had been growing as the evening progressed. He had an inkling of what that might be. *May as well find out.* 'What are you going to do?' he asked softly.

She took a deep breath as if still deciding whether to tell him. 'I'm going to watch the Necklace.'

The buzz of satisfaction that she'd confided in him was sort of a surprise, and yet also not. 'You'll spend the night in the room?'

'Yep.'

'Want company?'

She hesitated. He saw her turning the request over in her mind, wondering why he'd asked. *About three different answers to that one – all of them valid to varying degrees.* He wanted to protect the Necklace; her body guard skills would be welcome if there really was someone with their sights on him, although that seemed pretty far-fetched – *yeah, like someone murdering a man like Bill Mumford?* Maybe not so far-fetched? The simplest answer was that he wanted to spend time with her, even if that involved sitting up all night in the dark with a cursed Necklace. He could think of more pleasurable things to do in the dark, but he'd take what opportunity he could get. *That* thought was a bit of a shock.

She hadn't answered, but she was clearly still thinking.

'Why does it have such a dark reputation?' she asked abruptly.

'Why does any Egyptian artefact? It's nonsense really – certainly no harm came to the last Pentecost owner. Ignatius died peacefully in his bed at the age of ninety-four.'

'He had no family though.'

'I think that was by choice. And the three cousins seem to be doing okay.' He sat back, gathering his thoughts. 'The Egyptian civilisation is very old, thousands of years in the past – much of it is still a mystery to us – yet they valued sculpture and painting, used colour and constructed monumental edifices in a way that still speaks to us. It's probably not surprising that stories and legends grow up. Some pieces acquire them like barnacles.'

'Like the Necklace?'

'Like the Necklace,' he agreed. 'There are all sorts of outlandish stories surrounding it. It has its own alternative history. It's supposed to have migrated first from Egypt to Italy – from Cleopatra to Lucrezia Borgia. Raphael is alleged to have painted Lucrezia wearing it just before she died, although the painting has never been found. Then there was Catherine the Great, who reputedly wore it in bed with her lovers. It then came down to the Romanovs, dooming them on the way, with a side trip into the hands of the Nazis during the Second World War, and then to a 1940's Hollywood starlet – who is supposed to have died mysteriously in a villa in St Tropez – before it finally fetched up here, acquired by Ignatius Pentecost after the fall of the Berlin Wall. The last part is the only bit that is in any way likely. The rest is all hearsay, rumour and conjecture – lost portraits and obscure references in letters and so on. Some of the dates of the supposed owners simply don't add up. And the curse is similar. Curses are very popular myths. If you actually read up on Tutankhamun's treasure, for example, far more people have survived coming in contact with it than those who died strange or grisly deaths.'

Maisie frowned. 'You wouldn't think that anyone who believed in the curse would want to own it.'

'If there is a collector, or collectors, who are looking to acquire it, they don't believe, but they like the cachet of its reputation – like the Koh-i-Noor or the Hope Diamond. For them, a curse would be a bonus. And the collector who goes after that kind of artefact has ego and obsession enough to believe nothing will happen to them.' He smiled. 'And on the law of averages, it probably won't. Also anything that has the name of a celebrity or royalty attached to it commands a higher price too. It's all about the drama and the romance.'

She nodded, as if it made sense now. 'And you think it *is* a genuine Egyptian artefact?'

'Without the benefit of properly examining it, it's hard to tell. Even then, you'd want paperwork to back it up. If it is authentic, I think it's most likely that it was uncovered clandestinely in Egypt between the wars at the height of the archaeology boom, and then lurked in a private collection somewhere in Europe until Ignatius Pentecost acquired it, which was possibly in Berlin, but equally possibly not. That was where Mumford's thoughts were leading – with the jury still out on Berlin. But it could be that Aristotle Pentecost brought it home with his other finds and it's lurked in the Pentecost Collections all that time.'

'So where did the legend come from?'

'That, if the University does acquire it, will be a question to unravel. Best guess – it's a compilation of stories and a selection of necklaces, many of which have nothing to do with each other, or with Egypt. The idea of a long and romantic history would cover up that it was most likely looted from an Egyptian tomb somewhere, early in the twentieth century. And, of course, a mysterious artefact *must* involve a curse.' His mouth quirked again in that wry grin. 'But then I don't have a romantic soul.'

'Hmm.' He couldn't tell from her expression whether he'd disappointed her. *Do you have a romantic soul, Ms Webster?* 'Well.' She exhaled. She'd come to a decision. He held his breath. Would he be joining her in her vigil? 'I ... I would like company.'

Yes! He kept the jubilation out of his expression. 'In that case, I'll be happy to join you,' he said gravely.

She gave him a slightly baffled look. 'You realise that there might not even be a threat to the Necklace, and that sitting up all night to watch it is absurd and could prove deeply embarrassing if anyone finds us there?'

'Yes – but we're going to do it anyway.'

Suddenly, she grinned, and Elliott knew exactly why he was planning to spend an uncomfortable night on what he hoped devoutly was going to be the wild goose chase Maisie had just outlined.

'I'm not actually sure what we would be able to do if someone does try to pinch it,' she admitted.

'We'll think of something,' he assured her confidently.

'I hope so.' They both looked up as a small carriage clock on the mantle struck eleven. 'I suggest we give it until midnight, for the house to settle, and then I'll meet you in the Egyptian Room.'

Chapter Nine

Maisie buttoned up her plain navy shirt. That and the black jeans would help her blend into the darkness in the Egyptian Room, but might look a little suspicious if she and Elliott were surprised there by one of the family, the staff or the other guests. If that happened, it was going to be embarrassing to say the least. There was a distinct possibility that *they* would look like the ones trying to lift the Necklace.

She frowned at her reflection in the mirror on the wardrobe door. Logically, she knew that sitting up all night to watch the Necklace was – well – not logical. That knowledge didn't help with the feeling of unease that was driving her. It had been building all evening, leading her to the conclusion that she *had* to watch the damn thing. She couldn't explain it, but the idea of going to bed and trying to sleep, with the Necklace alone and unprotected on the ground floor ... she just couldn't do it. Elliott had picked up on her unease. She wasn't going to poke around at the implications of *that* for the moment. *Think about it in the morning, after your wasted sleepless night.* It *had* to be wasted. She didn't even know what they might do if there was an attempted theft, except raise the alarm, but she still had to *be* there.

She and Elliott had hashed out an excuse of sorts to explain their presence on their way upstairs. It was thin, but they hadn't been able to hit on anything better than a mutual bout of insomnia. She didn't want to break her cover and reveal the real reason for being present this weekend. *Not opening that can of worms.* They had decided that both being unable to sleep and drawn by the lure of the Necklace, they had met by accident in the room, stopped to chat and admire the artefact, and managed to fall asleep while doing so. It was just stupid enough to be plausible. What else was there? No one was going to imagine a secret tryst in a sarcophagus. For a second, her mind hovered over that idea, thinking of the giggler, only to discard it. Who would swallow that, when both of them had perfectly good beds available? Sex in a sarcophagus seemed a complete kink and, anyway, she did *not* want to go to bed with Elliott Elwood. All right, he *was* a good-looking man, with a much more appealing personality than she'd suspected.

Oh please ... The man is gorgeous, intelligent, funny ...

Maisie pursed her lips, frowning hard. The only reason she'd invited him to spend what was undoubtedly going to be an uncomfortable night with her, surrounded by a collection of creepy Egyptian relics, was the need to keep an eye on him, along with the Necklace, just in case any of this crazy stuff *was* real. That sounded a lot better. *Well, if you want to tell yourself that.* She huffed. She did. She *definitely* did. *Get through tonight and wave goodbye to Dr Elwood after lunch tomorrow.*

She was proud to be part of a small group from the agency, along with Michelle and Mickey, who Jake trusted with particularly confidential assignments – the ones that flew outside the box and a little under the radar. This time she sincerely hoped that Jake's hunch was wrong. He would have to decide if there was any need to provide Elliott with continued security once the Necklace was back in storage.

She looked at her watch. *11.30*. Time to go. She'd told Elliott to meet her at midnight, but before then, she needed to check out the ground floor to make sure that everyone else was in bed, and then examine the Egyptian Room itself. She'd been just a bit economical with the truth when she'd said she wasn't going to explore.

Explore, no – but she was going to tap a few walls in one particular place ...

She hadn't shared it with Dr Elwood, but one of the anomalies she'd found in the plans of the building was alongside that room.

She was sitting on the floor, back to the wall in the darkest part of the space, when a shadow appeared in the doorway. She raised her hand to indicate her position. After a tiny pause, she saw Elliott register her presence. He moved towards her, sliding down to the floor to join her. He settled next to her, warm and ... big. He was tall *and* built – he might be an academic but the man had *shoulders* – and he moved easily and silently. She was glad he was with her. The surroundings were disturbing, even though the ground floor of the house wasn't totally dark.

There was a shaded lamp burning in the hall at the bottom of the staircase, spilling dim light through the open door. Someone, probably Barnabas, had placed a small battery-powered night-light in the case with the Necklace. In the flickering flame, the jewelled and enamelled gold collar seemed to float, glittering and disembodied, against the black suede of the display stand. Around them the tall statues loomed. Two of the cats had crystal eyes that gleamed even in the diffuse light. The huge sarcophagi, one each side of the door, made strange shapes – a darker mass against the darkness. The room was long and narrow, with an old-fashioned museum-style display case of wood and glass running down the middle, the tall compartment with the Necklace rising up in the centre of it. If it wasn't for those cases, she could imagine the room as the antechamber of an old tomb, lit by burning torches in sconces on the walls, flames leaping and twisting with every draught. The place smelled of ancient dust, old wood and parched stone.

'Atmospheric, isn't it?' Elliott's words were barely more than a breath in the dimness.

'Yes,' she breathed back. *Actually, I'd have said creepy.* 'You're used to all this.'

'Yes and no.' There was a hint of amusement in the whisper. 'I have been in dark places with statues, although not for a while ...' He paused. She sensed that he was thinking about that. 'My job is much more desk bound these days. I don't get out much.' She caught a glimpse of white that suggested a brief smile. 'Very boring. This is more excitement than I've had in months.' He looked around with interest at the looming artefacts. 'I've never spent the night in what is effectively a museum. D'you think they come alive at night?'

Maisie swallowed hard. 'Nah,' she managed, glad she could only whisper back. 'It's gone midnight – it would have happened by now. Definitely alone in here.'

She wasn't sure why that assurance should feel disturbing. Nothing was going to happen, and they *were* alone. She'd checked the ground floor and the panelled walls of the room before Elliott joined her. The place was deserted and she hadn't found anything significant in the walls. The passage that the plan seemed to indicate, if it really existed, was at the end of the room. She'd tapped and prodded, but found no evidence of an entrance *into* the room.

She stifled a sigh – it was going to be a long, boring, uncomfortable night. *Good – that's good. Exactly what we want.* Somehow, in the gloom, she was very conscious of Elliott sitting beside her. She could feel his warmth, although they weren't touching. The faint scent of his aftershave overlaid the dry dustiness of the place. She knew they really shouldn't be talking, but she also knew that she had to stay alert. Conversation would stop her from dozing and there was a question that had been flitting into her mind all day that she hadn't got round to asking. 'It's the vacation – how come you're not somewhere digging things up?'

She'd wondered first when she'd noticed his hands, long-fingered and elegant, but with old scars and calluses – workmen's hands.

'I don't get to play in the dirt so much these days – as I said, I'm driving a desk instead.' There was whisper of resignation and maybe regret in the low voice. 'I might be able to fly to Cairo before Christmas with a group of students, to get a look at a promising site near Luxor. Perhaps do some digging.' He gave a soft laugh. 'Anything we did uncover would *not* be piled into crates to be shipped home for my private collection.'

'If I wanted to see it then I'd have to come to Egypt?'

'You'd be most welcome.' The warmth in his voice made something inside her flutter. For a moment, her mind wandered – hot sunshine, exciting sights and smells, a different world. She hauled her attention back to a dark night in Torquay. Just before she'd let herself out of her room, she'd heard the sound of rain drumming against the windows.

July on the Riviera. The English *Riviera.*

They continued to talk in a desultory way and finally fell silent. Maisie wondered if Elliott was asleep. After the disturbance of the previous night, she could feel her own eyes getting heavy. She adjusted her position, forcing herself to sit more upright. She guessed, from the numbness that was creeping into her limbs, that it was probably about 2 a.m. In four hours, maybe less, it would be getting light and their vigil would be over.

She stared into the dark. The small night-light flickering in front of the Necklace illuminated only a limited area within the case, and the lamp in the hall was heavily shaded, but now her eyes were fully adjusted, it was enough to pick up the silhouettes of the objects ranged around the room, creating shadows. Solid unfamiliar shapes made inky black outlines against dark walls.

For a second, she thought she saw a movement close to the door leading to the hall. She peered that way, skin prickling, concentrating hard. If someone was coming, that was the only entrance. The room was totally panelled, with no windows, depending on artificial light even in the daytime. She kept staring.

Nothing there.

Imagination.

She shivered. The room seemed to be getting colder. She should have worn a sweater. Beside her, she could hear Elliott's soft, even breathing. *Asleep.*

She had to force herself not to shift a little closer to absorb some of his body heat. Ideally, she should get up and move around ... but if there *was* anyone watching…

As carefully as she could, she flexed her limbs, one by one.

Have to stay awake. Only a few hours to go.

Chapter Ten

Maisie started violently, abruptly aware that her head had been nodding towards the warmth of Elliott's shoulder.

How long had her attention lapsed?

She'd been dreaming; a muddled scene from an old tomb, as she'd imagined before, with flaring torches, smoke and the smell of incense. She shook herself, looking around. The room was still dark and still empty, the light still burning in the display case, the Necklace and the jewelled eyes of the cats still glittering. She let out a long breath of relief. Nothing wrong … except …

Her nose twitched. There was a heavy, sweet scent coming from somewhere, drifting across the room, and a draught of air drifting with it; damp, rain-washed air – coming from outside? As she sat forward, holding her breath now to listen, her fingers groping for the torch she'd stuffed in her pocket, there was a small scuffling noise.

'Something's happening.' Elliott's voice was a whisper close to her ear. If he had been asleep, he wasn't now and she couldn't prevent the tiny spurt of gratitude that she wasn't alone.

'Mmm,' she murmured in acknowledgement, preparing cautiously to get to her feet, when a loud and distinct creaking noise broke the stillness. Instinctively, her head turned towards the sarcophagi beside the door, expecting to see one of them gaping open, dimly aware that Elliott was doing the same, but the carved cases were still closed and the light still glowed in the hall.

She was breathing another sigh of relief when the light in the hall went out.

She had a sudden blurred impression of something moving in the doorway and at the same time a cold blast of air hit her, coming from the other direction.

'Someone is here.' Forgetting caution, she hauled herself upright, heart thumping, fingers closing on the torch.

Beside her, Elliott was also on his feet. She heard him mutter, 'Lights,' as he melted away towards the door. She wanted to pull him back but he was already out of reach. She had to concentrate on the Necklace. Something dark seemed to be hovering beside the display case, but she also had a confused sense of movement at the other end of the room – where the cold air was coming from. Cold air that smelled now of leaf mould and wet soil.

She flicked on the torch at the same moment as Elliott pressed the light switch with an audibly hollow click. No power, no light. Taking a deep breath and hoping that Elliott would stay where he was, or slip into the hall to raise the alarm, she ranged the small torch around the room. The light skittered off statues, lighting up jewelled eyes. There was a gasp that she was sure wasn't Elliott and a distinct shuffle of feet. *Definitely not Elliott.*

'Who's there?' she demanded. Adrenaline was surging, making her heart beat fast, but her voice was steady.

For a long second, everything went still. The whole room seemed to be holding its breath. Maisie shifted the torch, playing it around the case holding the Necklace.

Her heart slammed hard in her chest as the narrow beam caught and held an object floating in the darkness beside the case. Shock raced through her. She heard Elliott give a soft *oof* of surprise and disbelief. It was a face, hovering close to the glass.

The unmistakable golden mask of the boy king, Tutankhamun.

'Stop!' Despite the abrupt dryness of her mouth, the command croaked out. The narrow beam of light skidded off the drifting face with its blank, dark eye-sockets as the mask moved. Attempting to focus the torch again, she was aware, a split second too late, of a presence beside her.

'Elliott?' She spun, knowing even as she turned that it couldn't be him, that the position was wrong. 'Who …?' The demand died as a hand grasped and jerked her arm, knocking away the torch. It was gone before she could strike out in defence. The light hit the floor and rolled, illuminating the legs of the cabinet and a pair of booted feet that were already stepping back.

From the middle of the room there was a clunk and a whir and a strange rasping noise.

The light in the Necklace cabinet lurched and went out.

Movement swirled around her. Figures in the darkness. More than one.

Something – someone – pushed violently against her and she cannoned into the cabinet, making it shudder. Her heart was thumping almost out of her chest. Behind her in the doorway there was the noise of a struggle, the sound of a body falling, and then running footsteps that were half muffled by another loud creaking noise. Cold air brushed her face again.

'Elliott?' Alarm raced through her, making her voice rasp. 'Elliott?' Oh God, if she'd let him get hurt…

'I'm fine,' he spoke breathlessly out of the dark. Relief flooded through her. 'What the hell just happened?'

'I don't know. I—'

Abruptly, with a sudden blaze, all the lights in the room came on. Wincing, Maisie put her hands up to shield her eyes, aware that Elliott had thrown his arm across his face for the same purpose. She could hear his laboured breathing over the sound of her own.

This was a mess. She knew with gut-wrenching certainty that she had blown it, big time. Cautiously, she dropped her hands, blinking in the pitiless light of the overhead fluorescent tubes. The glass display case housing the Necklace was intact, apparently untouched – and empty.

She moaned softly, aware that Elliott was staring at the empty cabinet in the same way that she was.

'I swear …' He paused, still getting his breathing under control. 'There was no way anyone got that thing open in those few seconds – and the guy that pushed past me, his hands were empty. He shoved me in the chest,' he finished, still staring at the empty case and rubbing the front of his sweater.

'But the Necklace is gone.' Willing her heart to settle, remembering the blast of cold air and the creaking noises, Maisie turned towards the far end of the room. The smaller sarcophagus was now sagging away from the wall. She moved quickly towards it to find that it wasn't sagging – merely open, like a door.

Dank, earth-scented air blew in from a dark, narrow space, chilling her face. She looked down at the thing wedged between the two halves of the casket, preventing it from closing – the black suede display stand that had supported the Necklace. But now the neck of the model was bare.

The Necklace was *definitely* gone.

Hours later, in Pentecost Place, the phone was snatched up at the first ring.

'At last! Where have you been? Is the thing safe?' the caller demanded.

‘It’s safe. I couldn’t get to the phone. The police are all over the house—’

‘What the *hell* just happened there?’ The furious question cut across the attempted explanation.

‘I don’t *know*. Elwood and the Norris woman were in the room when I came down. I almost walked in on them.’

‘Huh!’ The exasperated huff came clearly down the connection. ‘It was meant to be fast and simple – in and out through the passage, all done, an outside job. It was bad enough that you insisted on being there—’

‘You know why that was. We agreed.’ Another irritated grunt was audible. *You’re not getting away with that.* ‘If I hadn’t, you’d have been caught.’

‘Maybe.’ The concession came grudgingly, but now the rage and blame were fading. ‘Jesus, when you loomed out of the dark in that bloody mask, I thought *I* was going to have a heart attack.’

‘I *told* you I needed to be there.’ Difficult not to sound smug.

‘You did. And it worked. We did it!’ Now there was the laugh of triumph. ‘We did it, babe. The Cleopatra Necklace is ours. And now you need to go, before anyone misses you. You know how to handle the cops. All we have to do is sit tight and wait.’

Chapter Eleven

'I hear you were mugged by Tutankhamun?' Maisie glowered at Mickey James across the side table in the conference room where they were both fixing themselves coffee, waiting for Jake and Michelle to arrive. This Monday morning debrief was going to be humiliating enough without *him* sticking his nose in. Why did he have to be here *today*, on one of his infrequent trips back to the office from whatever top-secret undercover work he was doing on the Riviera for Jake?

She knew that she had to make a report about the debacle in the early hours of Sunday morning, but she didn't need an audience who hadn't even been involved. The hours spent with the police had been both uncomfortable and embarrassing. They'd stuck to the insomnia story, which Dorothea and Barnabas had accepted with exclamations of sympathy for their unexpected ordeal, and gratitude that they had raised the alarm so promptly. Armand had proved to be off the premises at an all-night poker game. The detective sergeant investigating had not been impressed with tales of Egyptian masks and secret passages, although the passage, a tunnel leading out into the grounds, had proved to be real. He had clearly wavered between suspicion that Maisie and Elliott had either taken the Necklace themselves, which he would establish with forensic evidence, or that they had been indulging in kinky sex in a sarcophagus, falling asleep afterwards to wake in confusion when surprised by the thieves. The latter was marginally better than being arrested for theft, but not much.

Maisie braced herself for mockery, but Mickey surprised her, meeting her eyes.

'Don't take it to heart, Maze.' He pushed a mug of coffee towards her. 'Jobs go pear-shaped. It happens.'

'Even to the famous Mickey James?' Flustered, she blurted out the question, still not sure if she should be defending herself.

'Yep, him too.' Mickey grinned. 'Especially when it's one of the boss's off-the-books jobs.' Softening and slightly reassured, Maisie picked up the mug. 'Speak of the devil.' Mickey indicated the door behind her. Jake had arrived.

Once Michelle had joined them and they all had coffee and were seated at the table, Jake gestured to Mickey. 'As he was unexpectedly available,' he nodded to Maisie, 'I asked Mickey to join us to help unravel what we have here.'

'A hot mess.' Maisie tried to keep the bitterness out of her voice. On the whole, she thought she had succeeded until Jake snagged her with a gently reproving ice-blue gaze.

'This assignment was *not* a failure.' He glanced around the room at Mickey and Michelle to confirm that. To her surprise, they were nodding in agreement. 'You went in there at short notice, with a watching brief that was based on rumour and hunch. No client was let down. If we'd been doing official security for the Necklace, there would have been a lot more protection and a lot more people. You maintained your cover. The Pentecost heirs accepted your story and I've spoken to the investigating officer – he understands now what you were doing there. I really didn't expect you and Elwood to sit up all night with the thing. That was above and beyond the call of duty.' He gave a sudden grin and Maisie understood why Cassie Travers-McQuire so often wore a very satisfied expression.

'The Necklace still got stolen,' she said sadly.

'It would have been stolen if you hadn't been there, or if you'd been blamelessly asleep in bed, like the other guests. As it is, we have first-hand information about the theft. Now we figure out what it tells us and what we can do with it. So …' He sat back in his chair. 'Go over everything you remember about the whole weekend.'

Maisie did as she was asked, finding it was easier to speak when she got going. Michelle made notes and drew a rough sketch plan, marking the doorway, the passage and the items of statuary. All three asked occasional questions.

When it came to the hours spent in the Egyptian Room after midnight, Maisie hesitated. Seeing only encouragement around the table, she plunged on with everything – the strange sweet scent, the noises and the cold draught, the extinguishing of the light in the hall and cabinet, the mask.

'You're *sure* they were a team?' Jake asked at one point. 'That they definitely worked together against you and Elwood?'

She drew in a startled breath, pulled up short by the suggestion. 'I don't ... Yes,' she said, after a second of thought. 'The person who came from the house was the person in the mask. I think they were the one who turned out the lights too.' She shook her head. 'The alternative ... another innocent bystander or two thieves arriving independently at the same time? There would have been a confrontation – maybe the Necklace wouldn't have been stolen. They were together,' she affirmed. 'It all sounds weird and I know the detective was sceptical – he thinks we imagined the person in the mask – but that *is* how it happened. And the Necklace disappeared in a matter of seconds. It's difficult to know how that was done, but it *was* done, and the display stand was dumped at the entrance to the passage.'

Nods of understanding encouraged her to carry on until the end of the story. It didn't take long to finish.

'Right,' Jake said, when Maisie finally ran out of steam and he'd checked that there was nothing more. 'Observations? Questions?'

Michelle waved a hand over the plan. 'Two thieves, working together – but the theft could have been done by just one of them from inside the house *or* through the secret passage. Why both?' She looked around the room, grinning. 'Wow – secret passage – I really got to say that *in real life*!'

Mickey and Jake both laughed. Maisie felt the cold lump she'd had in her stomach since the early hours of Sunday warming up a little.

Mickey frowned, clearly thinking. '*We* know that one of the thieves came from inside the house. Bringing in the secret passage—' He shot Michelle a swift grin '—that puts the focus *outside* the house. It waves a flag at the police that this was the work of an intruder and shifts suspicion away from the occupants.'

'Wouldn't the family be expected to know about the passage?' Michelle objected. 'They'd still be suspects.'

Mickey nodded. 'But it inevitably widens the field – previous guests, past and present staff, casual visitors, workmen. It could be a long list, going back years.'

Jake looked thoughtful. 'An outsider working with a member of the family?'

'One contributes information on the Necklace, the other organises the mechanics and the sale of the goods, keeping suspicion away from the insider,' Michelle said. 'Sounds feasible – but why did the insider risk involving themselves in the actual theft when they could have stayed innocently in bed?'

'Confirming that the coast was clear in the house?' Mickey offered.

'Something had to be done that only the insider could do?' Maisie suggested. 'The locks on the cabinet, maybe?' She still couldn't figure out how the case had been unlocked in a few seconds. 'Or ... partners who didn't quite trust each other?' she speculated hesitantly. 'Keeping an eye on each other?'

'No honour amongst thieves.' Jake tapped idly on the table. 'If it's a member of the family working with an outsider, any of those might fit. But which one has the Necklace?'

'The outsider – has to be,' Mickey said. 'They went out through the passage, taking the Necklace away from the inevitable search.'

'So the insider trusts them that much.' Jake scowled, obviously frustrated at not having answers. 'None of it makes sense,' he declared. 'But we have two impeccable witnesses who say that's how it happened.'

The cold lump in Maisie's stomach melted a little more.

'Whatever the answer to the puzzle – and we will find it—' Jake declared, '—they worked together when the plan began to go pear-shaped – when you and Elwood turned up.' He nodded to Maisie. 'They might have expected someone to be awake in the house, but actually in the room? They probably didn't understand why you were there, but once you were, they improvised – making the story for the police even more outlandish.'

'Someone who can act fast,' Mickey pondered. 'And who is currently congratulating themselves on how clever they've been? Would that make them careless, going forward? We can hope.' He looked at Maisie. 'No one seems to have questioned your cover.' He looked over at Jake. 'We need to do whatever is necessary to make sure it continues to hold up.'

Jake's quick nod indicated that was already in hand. Maisie let go of some further tension she hadn't been aware of holding.

Mickey was looking at her, smiling. 'I know you think your excuse for being in the room was thin, but look at it from the other perspective. Why would two rival bidders be standing guard over the Necklace in the middle of the night? The idea that you both crept down to have a private view is plausible. In general, people see what they expect to see, even thieves. I think you did the best you could in the circumstances, and it worked.'

'I do too,' Michelle agreed. She looked at her notes. 'The rope on the roof – did the second lot of police find it?'

'Yes – eventually,' Maisie replied. She hadn't told the police about it. Things had looked bad enough as it was, without admitting that she and Elliott had found that *too*. Now she was feeling a lot more cheerful. 'They didn't know if it was part of the first robbery.'

'I don't believe it had anything to do with the robbery on Friday,' Jake chipped in. 'I think it was meant to be found after the Necklace went missing. It wasn't necessary for the theft, but it was a useful distraction to muddy the water. Did the thieves come and go through the passage? Over the roof? Was it a gang?' He looked at the plan. 'There's a strange vibe coming off all this. It doesn't feel like the crew that we originally suspected might be involved.' He shot a glance over at Mickey. 'That's not to say that they aren't mixed up in it somewhere along the line, but this ... The whole thing seems a bit over-clever but also clumsy – an amateur effort?' He shrugged. 'It got the thing done.' He leaned his elbows on the table. 'We need to dig deeper into the background of everyone who was in the house that night. The cousins are the obvious suspects.' Jake nodded to Maisie and Michelle. 'Start there. Does one of them want a bigger payday than a third share?'

'We're going to keep working on it?' Maisie was trying to get her head around the idea of bumbling, well-meaning Barnabas, limp Dorothea or lounge lizard Armand as one or more of the players on Sunday morning. She couldn't do it. *Which doesn't mean that it isn't possible.*

'Certainly,' Jake confirmed. He smiled. It was not a pleasant smile. 'Now we know that there's *definitely* something to work on.'

Michelle was studying her notes again. 'I'm wondering about those noises you heard before the light in the cabinet went out. I'd love to be able to have a poke around.' She looked up. 'And what are we going to do about Dr Elwood?'

Chapter Twelve

Maisie's heart gave an involuntary jerk of surprise and, disconcertingly, alarm. A whisper of memory, the warmth of Elliott's shoulder as he sat beside her in the dark and the sharp, woody scent of his aftershave drifted through her mind. Inexplicably, her heart rate speeded up. 'Why do we need to do anything?' she objected. 'His part is over surely? They have the Necklace. What more could they want?'

Mickey grimaced. 'It depends on whether the rumour about that art specialist and his family is true. Now the thieves have the Necklace, why wouldn't they want it authenticated by an expert?'

Maisie's mood, which had risen with the sense that the assignment had not been a complete failure, slid steeply downwards again. In the chaos of the robbery, she'd lost sight of the threat to Elliott. *We have no real idea who these people are. Who they might be connected with.* If the rumour was true, two innocent women had been kidnapped to get an expert's signature on a disputed painting. And with the Necklace's mysterious history ...

Now her heart sank. The threat to Elliott hadn't disappeared along with the jewels.

They all turned to look at Jake.

He exhaled heavily. 'That art expert is keeping his own counsel, but I think it's safer to assume that *something* happened.'

Safer. The word echoed ominously in Maisie's head. Elliott *had* to be safe.

'If the Cleopatra Necklace was stolen either to order, or for some sort of bidding war between possible collectors, Elwood's imprimatur would boost the price,' Mickey observed coolly. 'An expert authenticates the thing as a genuine Egyptian artefact and all the rest of the legend is icing on the cake.'

'I agree,' Jake put in quietly. 'Elwood's authentication would be valuable, even if done in private with no one but the buyer knowing.'

'How do you even do that, with jewellery that old?' Michelle queried. 'It's not as if it has a hallmark or anything. I know paintings can be analysed, but even that's not always conclusive.'

'Which is why, in the end, it sometimes comes down to the opinion of an expert,' Jake countered. 'Like all art, the paper trail is important, but with a piece like this, with a colourful history?' He shrugged.

'And if our thieves decide that they want an expert, Dr Elwood is currently the one with the highest profile, after the television programmes and the exhibition at the British Museum.' Michelle was looking thoughtful.

Maisie didn't like the gleam of calculation in her colleague's eyes. Knowing the way Michelle's mind worked, she had an idea what she might be thinking. She rushed to speak before Michelle could voice it. 'We have to do something to protect him ... and his family.' As she added the words, she realised she didn't even know if Elliott *had* a family. She knew he wasn't married, but that didn't mean there weren't significant people in his life. If necessary, they needed to be protected too. *You'd expect to do that for anyone who was threatened. It's not just because it's Elliott.*

They'd all turned to look at her. An embarrassing flush stirred at the base of her throat, but she wasn't giving up the point. 'If we're assuming that the thieves might still attempt to get his authentication, then we have to offer protection,' she repeated.

To her great relief, Jake was nodding. 'I think we do. I spoke to Dr Elwood early this morning. He's fully aware of the situation. He's confirmed that there is no close family who might be used as levers. No children or spouse, current or ex. His parents are deceased, and while he does have an older sister, she lives off the grid in New Zealand. Elwood speaks to her twice a year when she travels to town for supplies – and a phone and internet connection.'

No close family. Even as she registered relief that there were no innocent parties to be drawn into the equation, Maisie felt a pang – a tiny tinge of envy immediately overwhelmed by sadness. Her relationship with her own family was ... difficult – but not to have anyone ...

'If this is the gang that we suspected at the start, New Zealand is not impossible. But you don't think so …?' Mickey was reading his boss's expression.

'No, I don't. Although I take your point. Arrangements will be made to contact the sister, but for the moment we work on the premise that if the thieves are looking for authentication, they will focus on Dr Elwood himself. Of course, if they decide to recruit a completely different expert we won't know, but given Dr Elwood's reputation and that he's already involved in the case, I think it's a fair bet that he'd be their first choice.'

'So what do we do?' Maisie was relieved that her voice didn't betray the turmoil of nerves she was feeling. *It will be all right. These people want something from Elliott – they aren't going to hurt him.*

'I don't think there's any immediate danger of Dr Elwood being snatched off the street. He's been warned and Liam will take a crew to his home and office later to check the security and improve it as necessary. The University has on-site security who'll be discreetly advised that threats, unspecified, have been made, so that they're on the alert. If Elwood takes care, I have no worries for the moment. If anything disturbs him, he'll let us know.' Jake sat back in his chair. 'Going forward, we concentrate on the robbery and, in particular, how the Necklace might be disposed of.'

He looked at Mickey, who nodded, understanding that was his brief. 'If we can find the Necklace then the threat to Elwood disappears.'

'Exactly.'

Jake quickly allocated tasks to follow up on the house party guests and the meeting wound up within a few moments. Maisie made her way back to her desk in a cloud of unease. Okay, she had a job to do on this, alongside her regular assignments. *And it isn't protecting Elliott Elwood. Not any more.* Liam was good, very good. He'd make sure security was tight. *But no one will be watching.*

She sat down and leaned over to wake up her computer. Jake seemed to have some ideas about the robbery, but he wasn't disclosing any details. *What does he know that he's not sharing? Is it just another hunch?* An even more uncomfortable thought made her scowl at her computer screen. She'd guessed what Michelle had been thinking. Did Jake have the same idea? Was that why he'd already spoken to Elliott, even before the meeting?

Is there a plan, and does that plan involve using Elliott as bait?

Elliott took the last items out of his suitcase and returned them to their proper places. There were a couple of specialist workmen fitting a security camera to his front door and another doing something to the windows. He wandered through to the kitchen to make coffee to offer them. Jake McQuire's phone call this morning had been … disconcerting.

He was okay with the extra security but he really wasn't sure about the reason. Now that he was back in Bath, the idea of some gang forcing him to authenticate the Cleopatra Necklace just seemed … a bit too

Hollywood? Pressing buttons on the coffeemaker he kept mostly for guests, Elliott grinned. Maybe Dan Howe would get cast for his role? He knew that protecting him had been on Maisie's mind over the weekend and he respected her judgement, so maybe he *did* need to be careful. He fished the teabag out of his own mug and dumped it. He'd gone along with her concerns for his safety because ... because it had seemed a lot more plausible then, when the whole weekend had been completely outlandish. *And because you were not adverse to a beautiful woman watching your back – or any other part she might be interested in?*

He distributed coffee and took himself back to the small bedroom that he used as a library-cum-office. The situation was all a bit off-the-wall, doubly so because if anyone actually put the Cleopatra Necklace in his hands, he'd be quite prepared to give them his opinion on it. But it would only be his opinion – and would it be the opinion that they wanted? There was no certainty on that. The thought did give him a tiny frisson of concern. He made an instant decision to continue to co-operate with McQuire and keep his wits about him.

No harm in that.

He picked up a pen from his desk and put it down again, glancing discontentedly around the office. There was work he could be getting on with – lectures to prepare, a conference paper to research and a book of academic essays that he was editing, not to mention assignments that had been handed in from postgraduate students. Besides that, Ben and Vaisey Leyland would be expecting an update on the reaction to the University's presentation and the lodging of the bid for the Collections. He really did need to get that done before lunch. His report would *not* be what they were expecting. With Pentecost Place invaded by police, the programme for the remainder of the weekend had been rapidly abandoned. Instead of making a presentation the previous day, guests had submitted written proposals and bids and departed after questioning, leaving their contact details.

Elliott shuffled a few piles of papers, staring unenthusiastically at a book on the pyramids – another one – that he was meant to be reviewing. A chart on the wall set out his various deadlines for the month. Nothing was on fire yet and this morning none of the listed tasks appealed. He really should telephone Ben before any stories leaked to the press.

He lifted the phone and put it down again. *Need to get your thoughts in order*. If he wasn't careful, he was going to sound as if he'd come unglued. The house party idea and the whole bidding thing had been eccentric, but then to have two robberies in the space of twenty-four hours …?

Elliott cupped his hands around his mug of tea and sipped thoughtfully. The weekend had certainly been … different. And now he was restless. *Come on, you might as well admit it – the whole thing was exciting.* He'd felt alive. Alive in a way he hadn't for quite a while. And a good part of that aliveness – *was that a word?* – emanated from a close association with Maisie Webster.

He put down the mug and contemplated it. Maisie had challenged him in ways of which she was probably completely unaware. *Let's face it, you've got staid ... and boring.* Too much of his work these days involved administrative jobs, and his social life revolved around academic and campus events, interspersed with dinners and drinks parties mixing with the right sort of people – where he was guaranteed to meet the "right" sort of women. He grinned. Maisie was definitely *not* the right sort of woman. She was a lot more than that. Maisie was ... stimulating.

He shifted in his seat as some of the excitement came back to him. She was dedicated, competent, intelligent – and completely different from any woman he'd ever dated. Well, any woman he'd dated recently. A brief flicker of the recollection he'd experienced in Ben's office – their undergraduate days – came back to him. He and Ben had met on a pub crawl in freshers' week. They'd hit it off and been friends ever since. In their second and third years, they'd shared a flat. They'd supported each other. He'd dutifully cheered Ben on in Intervarsity swimming contests – muggy hours poolside, breathing chlorine-scented air – until his friend had been unfairly dropped from the team because of some jealous rivalry from another competitor. They'd switched their allegiance to supporting the rugby sevens, where they could cheer on their side together. Those had been good times. Ben had eaten Elliott's first experiments in cooking without complaint – well, only a few – and he *had* got better. They'd studied, partied, picked up and broken up with girls, endured hangovers and exam jitters together ...

When did you lose all that?

He sighed over a wash of nostalgia. In the last term before graduation, Ben had been dating Sara, while he'd paired up with her friend. He couldn't even remember the girl's name now – neither of them had been serious about a relationship. Then the next thing he knew,

Ben was marrying Sara and settling into a steady job and domesticity, while *he'd* gone on to his doctorate, focused on academic advancement and his career. As he'd climbed the ladder, expectations and responsibilities had gradually accrued like anchors round his feet. He drummed the desk with restless fingers. Okay, so this past weekend had been a crazy one-off, which didn't mean that he couldn't try to hold on to some of that sense of being alive. He knew where he wanted to start. *Take action, then you can write the damn report.*

Leaving the remains of the tea cooling on his desk, he grabbed a jacket, skirted the workmen at the door and headed for the small parade of shops around the corner. He could arrange what he wanted there. After that, it was all down to hope and a little luck.

Elliott had never realised how irritating Ben's laugh could be. He was certainly noticing it now. His friend seemed to find the events of Saturday night in Torquay hilarious. Elliott didn't really see the joke.

'Sorry.' Ben hiccupped to a stop. He was actually mopping his eyes. 'I know it isn't really …' He giggled again. 'It's just … It sounds like something out of the *Keystone Cops* or a French farce or something. But, of course, it wasn't … I wasn't thinking …' He'd finally cottoned on to the fact that Elliott was sitting stonily in his visitor's chair and definitely not laughing. He patted his hands on the surface of his desk, clearly composing himself. 'Of course, it was serious. Getting involved with something like that, you could have been hurt – or Ms Norris,' he added, his face sober now. 'Do the police have any ideas, about the thieves?'

'If they have, they haven't shared them,' Elliott said. The stressful weekend was catching up with him. There was the suggestion of a headache forming behind his eyes. Maybe that's why his sense of humour seemed to have deserted him. *And you're just a little tense, wondering if your phone is going to ring. If—*

Elliott jerked back to awareness of his surroundings. Ben was still talking. 'Quite a coincidence that both you and Ms Norris had the idea of looking at the Necklace in the early hours.'

Elliott shrugged. 'Coincidences do happen.' He'd gone with the much-used insomnia story, for want of anything better, realising too late that with a little finesse he might have avoided mentioning Maisie at all. *Definitely not firing on all cylinders – and she's definitely on your mind.*

'You think that maybe she was in on it?' Ben gave him a considering look. 'That the thieves are working for this mysterious employer and she was there to like … supervise?'

'No.' Elliott was pleased that his tone hadn't come out as sharp as it might have. To someone who wasn't in the know, it might have been a reasonable question. Maisie and her mysterious employer *had* been shoehorned into the house party at very short notice. 'I'm confident that Ms Norris had nothing to do with the robbery. She was as shocked as I was,' he added stiffly.

'Good. That's good,' Ben said, nodding vaguely. His thoughts had clearly moved on. 'I don't know what Leyland is going to say when he finds out about the Necklace. I expect *I'll* have to tell him.' He gave a long-suffering sigh. 'I suppose it will all end up being my fault, as usual.'

'How can he hold you responsible for a robbery?' Elliott protested, slightly impatiently. 'You overthink things – you can't be blamed for this! And you don't have to worry about telling him, because I e-mailed him my report at lunch time. If he's read it, he knows. I'm not sure—'

Almost as if on cue, the door of the office opened and Leyland strode in. *Entrance of the demon king?* His face lit up when he saw Elliott.

'Ah! – Elwood, you're here. Excellent. Excellent. Just read your report. Good work. I've written to express the University's thanks for the hospitality and re-confirmed the bid in writing, as you recommended.'

Elliott saw that Ben's eyes had widened in shock. 'But, Dean – surely without the Necklace …?' He cast a worried and vaguely accusing glance at Elliott. 'The Necklace was *stolen.*'

'Hah!' Leyland made a sweeping gesture of dismissal. 'A bauble, merely. The rest of the Collections fully warrant the Aquae Sulis bid – the library and the art. Three Watteaus.' He was actually rubbing his hands.

'I'm not an expert on those and the University's bid does *have* to be accepted. There are other contenders,' Elliott cautioned.

'Hah!' Leyland exclaimed again, with another sweeping gesture. 'Mere hoi polloi. Aquae Sulis is the natural home of the Pentecost Collections, and I'm sure that the family members will take that fully into account. Now,' he addressed Elliott again, 'we must schedule some time to discuss the disposition of the pieces when we receive them. My secretary will be in touch.' His eyes gleamed in anticipation. Elliott never recalled seeing him so animated. 'We can afford to be generous also to the unsuccessful applicants – perhaps an offer of a short loan of some of the choicer pieces? And, in due course, a touring exhibition. America, naturally – the universities, and of course our colleagues in Egypt for that collection.' He shifted slightly to look directly at Ben. 'Bartram, write up a proposal in consultation with Dr Elwood. The end of the week will suffice.' He nodded decisively and strode back out.

There was a short, freighted silence. 'Well,' Elliott said on an out breath. 'He's certainly confident.'

'Yes.' Ben's voice had a distinct edge to it, and for a second Elliott caught the flash of what might have been anger in his eyes. *And with some justification – sometimes Leyland treats him like a lackey, and it's not even really part of his job.* Ben seemed to have rapidly shaken off the emotion though. His face creased in his normal open, easy-going smile. 'Looks like I know what's top of my to-do list. Will you ask Jenni to fix us up a meeting?'

Elliott nodded. 'Whatever you need.'

Hmm. Now Leyland was disposing of his time, as well as Ben's!

'I hope it won't be wasted work. So many of the things he demands are. Keeps me out of mischief though.' Ben smiled again, then narrowed his eyes. 'He's probably right about the University having the edge on the museums and the stately home, but what about the billionaire bidder – is he going to be interested now the Necklace is gone?'

Elliott shook his head. 'Having talked to Ms Norris, I think I can safely say that the Necklace is the thing that caught his attention.'

'Good. Good,' Ben murmured absently, seeming to be distracted again for a few seconds, before his focus came back to Elliott. 'You know, we really must get together one evening next week for a drink. Find a good local pub – just like old times.'

'Sounds like an excellent idea. How about Tuesday? As long as you're not planning to get us involved in any cider drinking contests.' Elliott laughed. 'Worst hangover I ever had.'

Ben grinned. 'I remember that. I didn't know human skin could actually turn that shade of green. Tuesday is fine.' He picked up a paper from this desk. 'Before you go, this is the rough draft for the order of service for Mumford's memorial. See what you think.'

Elliott let himself out of Ben's office and walked down the corridor, checking his phone. Nothing from Maisie. No text, no missed calls. *Come on – she's at work.* As you should be. *Yeah – but how long does it take to tap out a text?* He frowned; something he'd noticed in Ben's office when Leyland had interrupted them was niggling at him. A faint echo of something from Saturday night? *Something that might be important?* He couldn't put his finger on it. With a frustrated sigh, he paced down the corridor. If it was significant, it would probably come back to him.

He'd reached the lift that would take him back to the foyer. Then where? Pentecost Court, he decided. If Leyland wanted plans of where to display the Collections, it was going to be a major undertaking. Probably need an inter-disciplinary working party. Leyland had seemed very confident that Aquae Sulis would be selected.

Does he know something? Or someone?

The lift swooshed up and the doors opened. Elliott stepped inside, still pondering. Leyland had no connection to any of the Pentecost family that he knew of, but a scrap of campus gossip surfaced – the rumour that in his down-time, the Dean was a skilled and heavyweight poker player. Elliott had never been sure whether the scuttlebutt was someone's idea of humour. If it was correct, might his poker playing connections include Armand?

The delivery boy propped the old-fashioned bicycle, decorated with flowers and streamers, outside the offices of Kings Detective Agency, entered the foyer and advanced towards the receptionist. 'Delivery for Ms Maisie Webster?'

'Flowers for Maisie.' Michelle, passing the reception desk, held out her hand. 'I'll take them.'

'Is that okay?' The delivery boy looked at the receptionist, who nodded. 'Oh. Right. Here you go then.' He handed them over. 'Can you apologise to Ms Webster? They were ordered this morning, should have been delivered then, but I had a bit of a problem with the bike.' He jerked his head to indicate the flowery confection gracing the front of the offices.

'I'll be certain to tell her,' Michelle assured him solemnly. The boy, relieved of his burden, retreated to reclaim his conveyance. Michelle bore her prize up to the office and put it carefully down on Maisie's desk. 'Late delivery, for Ms Webster, with apologies from the florist. It's not your birthday, is it?'

'No.' Maisie looked at the flowers, bemused. 'You sure they're for me?'

'That's what it says on the envelope.' Michelle indicated the flamboyant black print. 'You've got a secret admirer, hon.'

'Not so secret if there's a note.' Maisie detached it from the wrappings. The last time she'd had flowers in the office they'd been an ostentatious mix of roses and hothouse lilies. A "Dear Jane" bouquet from a con artist. This was a jaunty bundle of sunflowers and blue delphiniums, with some sort of daisies and sweet-smelling foliage.

'Oh.' She got the envelope open. The message on the card was short. But enough to get her heart beating faster. 'It's from Dr Elwood. He wants me to have dinner with him.'

Michelle laughed as Maisie stared at the flowers and the card. 'Don't look so surprised. People do that, you know? Go to dinner. It's called dating.'

'Yes, but …' Maisie stared some more at the card, as if it might speak. Okay, she'd fantasised a bit, but she'd never really expected to hear from him again. 'It was work … I didn't think …' She tailed off. She didn't know what to think, except that her heart was going a mile a minute. *Excitement or apprehension?*

'He's not a paying client, and he's interested,' Michelle said patiently. 'It's just dinner.'

'Mmm.' Maisie's brain had begun to work again, dealing firmly with the parts of her anatomy that had perked up at the idea of another encounter with Dr Elwood. *An off-the-clock encounter.* 'He probably just wants to know about the investigation.'

Michelle gave her a pitying look. 'He can get that by ringing Jake. D.A.T.E,' she spelled it out. 'Text the man. Say yes,' she ordered.

'I'll think about it,' Maisie replied, with dignity. She reached for the flowers. They *were* lovely. 'I need something to put these in.'

In Torquay, the phone was ringing again in Pentecost Place. It was answered with a reluctant stab of the thumb.

'Where are you?'

'Where do you think? The police are *still* here, poking about and asking questions.'

There was a muffled laugh. 'They're not going to find anything, are they?' There was just an edge of threat under the scorn. Or was that imagination? '*Are* they?' The voice sharpened. 'Do you have it yet?'

'No. I'm not chancing it. It's safe enough where it is. No one is going to find it.'

'They'd better not. We've risked too much. When you've retrieved it, we have to meet. You bring it to me, understand? As we agreed.'

'Yee-esss, we did.'

'You don't back out now.' The threat was more overt this time. 'We stick to the plan. No more theatrical stuff like Saturday night.'

'That was necessary – and it worked.'

'So you say. Just get the fucking thing and bring it to me.'

'Why? Why do you have to have it?'

'Because I need it to show potential buyers? We agreed – we set up an auction. I can do that. You need me, remember? I'm the one with the contacts. You know you won't be able to sell the thing on your own.' There was heavy pause. 'Come on.' Abruptly, the voice softened. 'We've got this far. All we have to do now is get the merchandise into the right hands. I'm the one to do that. The hard part is over and you were *great,* even with the theatrics.' The laughter now was soft, triumphant. 'We did it. We pulled it off. Now it's money, all the way. The police can't hang around forever. Once they've gone, you bring it to me, just like we said. It'll be great. You know it.'

The line disconnected.

Sceptical eyes regarded the quiescent phone screen.

'Yeah. *We've* risked too much. And of course it's going to be *great.*'

Chapter Thirteen

Maisie sat on a high stool at the breakfast bar that divided the kitchen area from the main living space of her shoebox-sized flat. It might be a shoebox, but it was *her* shoebox. Well, hers and the bank's.

She'd eaten a chicken sandwich and was sipping from a careful half a cup of coffee – because she was on surveillance later. She had nearly an hour before Eddie picked her up for their nightshift. Spending the evening watching a guy who may or may not be cheating on his wife was in no way the most rewarding part of her job, but the bread-and-butter work was what paid the mortgage, so she really wasn't complaining. *Much.* The chance of getting involved in Jake's special projects made up for it, but she wasn't going to think about that now. She had something much more pressing to ponder.

She stared at the flowers, which she'd arranged in a vase on the breakfast bar in front of her, and then at the card that had come with them, then at the telephone which lay beside her empty plate. She picked up the card and tapped the edge on the counter surface. She had time to ring the number before Eddie arrived. Plenty of time …

She jumped as the phone rang. Her heart skittered. It couldn't possibly be *him*. He didn't have her number.

Did he?

Of course he does, Jake gave it to him.

Letting the card go, she hurriedly scooped the phone up without looking at the screen. 'Maisie Webster,' she answered automatically.

'Mariette?' Her skittering heart plummeted. She really needed to fix the phone so she got a distinct ring tone and a few seconds' warning when she was about to talk to her mother.

Or you could just check the number.

She breathed in. 'Hello, Mum.'

'Darling.' Her mother's voice, smooth and restrained, like everything about her, drifted softly into her ear. 'Is it convenient to talk? You're not getting ready for a date or anything?' Maisie heard the note of hope. No – not unless a couple of hours in the car with Eddie, happily married, three kids and a fondness for custard creams, counted. She wasn't about to share *that* though.

'No – no date,' she confirmed. 'Not on a work night.' Instinctively, her eyes strayed to the flowers and the card. *Not sharing that either.*

‘Oh, well.’ Stella Webster gave an unconvincing laugh. ‘That’s very dedicated of you, darling.’ Maisie sat up a little straighter, picking up immediately on the forced gaiety. *What now?*

‘That’s actually why I’m calling. Your work, that is … at least ...’ Mrs Webster stopped. Maisie knew instinctively where this was going. Yet another attempt to get her into a job where she would meet what her mother considered to be the right kind of man. Good husband material. Unlike the type she might meet staffing the reception desk of a detective agency. She stifled a sigh. Why she’d never divulged to her family that she’d left her temporary student job on the agency’s reception desk years ago and was now a fully-fledged and trained member of the detective team, about to enrol part-time for her Masters’ degree in criminology, she didn’t really know. *Yes, you do* – she could imagine the horror. It wasn’t the sort of thing that happened in the Webster family.

What would the neighbours think?

Whatever would your grandmother have said?

She pushed away the suggestion of a shiver that was trying to crawl down her back. “My family doesn’t understand me” was fine for a teenager. At twenty-seven, it sounded like a whine, even if it was true. As far as Mum, Dad, Françoise and Henry were aware, she was still a receptionist. And her mother was talking about that now. ‘You must remember him, darling ... he was up at Oxford at the same time as your brother. He’s setting up his own legal practice and he’ll need someone reliable on reception. It would be perfect for you, darling.’ *Too many darlings*, the detective in Maisie registered. But her mother couldn’t possibly be nervous. ‘Lovely new offices in Bristol, very smart. And perhaps you could even think about retraining. Maybe as a paralegal?’ Not a lawyer. That role in the family was firmly occupied by big brother, but Maisie recognised that gambit too – “my daughter the paralegal” sounded a step up from “my daughter the receptionist”.

‘I’m not looking to make a change, Mum. I’m happy where I am,’ Maisie pointed out firmly.

‘Yes, so you say.’ Her mother’s huff of frustration sounded clearly over the phone. ‘But, darling, you really need to think about the *future*. It would be so good to see you *settled*.’ For a moment, a shade of petulance layered the smooth tones. Stella Webster didn’t like things that didn’t fit her perfectly ordered view of the world. Her younger daughter definitely didn’t fit. *Yeah, square peg, that’s me. My daughter – the detective? No way!*

Her mother was still speaking, 'You know your grandmother would be *so* disappointed,' she pronounced, as if it was a clinching argument. Maisie ignored it. Stella might want to remember her own mother's attitude to her younger daughter as disappointment – all Maisie could remember was the chilling stare of disapproval. 'At least promise me that you'll *think* about it. I'll give Kevin your number. You can have lunch with him. Talk about what he has in mind for the office. I'm sure he can convince you.'

Maisie prodded her memory. Which of her brother's friends was Kevin? She couldn't be sure but she suspected that he was the one with the loud voice and the sweaty hands. The sweaty *wandering* hands. *That would be a "hell no" to the lunch then.*

'I wouldn't want to waste his time, Mum. Like I said, I'm happy where I am.' She pretended not to hear her mother's low-pitched hum of annoyance. 'How is Dad? Did Françoise bring the girls over at the weekend?' Diverting her mother onto the subject of her twin grandchildren usually worked. Maisie settled down with genuine interest to hear about the latest achievements of her two nieces.

When her mother finally rang off, with another instruction that she really must lunch with Kevin – "such a marvellous opportunity, darling" – Maisie returned to studying the flowers and the card, picking it up to read the invitation again.

As if you don't recall exactly what it says.

Will you please have dinner with me? followed by his name – *Elliott Elwood* – and a reminder of his phone number.

She might have known that the spiky black script was his, even without the signature. He'd written it himself, not left it to the florist. *What does that tell you?* She wasn't quite sure how she felt about what she *thought* it was telling her. Why? *Why does he want to have dinner with you?*

Michelle had been convinced that she should accept and repeated her opinion several times before they left the office. 'Live dangerously. Give it a go.' She'd fixed Maisie with a provocative grin. 'After all, you did spend the night together.'

'Yeah, and we nearly ended up sharing a jail cell.' The suspicion of the detective investigating the robbery was still quite vivid in her mind.

'There you are then – a match made in heaven,' Michelle retorted. 'It's just dinner, Maze. You might even enjoy it.' She gestured to the flowers 'He's serious, or he wouldn't have sent you those.' For a second,

Maisie had registered complex emotions flitting across her colleague's eyes; a touch of envy, longing, pain, gone as fast as they had come. There was someone in Michelle's past that she still thought about, or maybe not in her past? Maisie sometimes wondered—

She snapped herself out of her speculation. She didn't *know* anything and Michelle would never tell. She was sure of that. She tipped her head back to stare at the ceiling. Her friend said to go for it. Her mother, Maisie knew, would be *ecstatic* at the idea of her difficult second daughter having dinner with *Doctor* Elliott Elwood.

What about you? How do you *feel?* She took a deep breath, listening to the inner voice. *Really – there's no reason to turn him down just because your mother would approve.* She let out a heartfelt sigh. She knew that being the underachiever in a family of massive overachievers had shaped her life more than it should – it made her sensitive to anything that looked like failure. *Like letting the Cleopatra Necklace get stolen from right under your nose*? Did she want to go on a date with Elliott Elwood and be reminded of that?

The feeling of a warm body sitting beside her in the darkness flitted through her mind again. Oh yes. She could certainly fancy Dr Elwood, and it seemed that he could fancy her. *Yeah, well, he did get a good eyeful of the merchandise the first time you met. Does he think if he buys you dinner you'll fall straight into his bed?*

Not going to happen.

He'd be having dinner with the real *Mariette* Webster. Would he find her a disappointment?

She'd got used to being one of *those*. As the afterthought of the family, twelve years younger than her accountant sister and ten years than her lawyer brother, she hadn't followed her siblings to Oxford. Her degree was History of Art at a redbrick university. No kudos there. The "Oh so funny" jokes about Sherlock Holmes and Colombo around the Sunday lunch table when she got the vacation job as a temporary receptionist at the agency had stopped her talking about it. It had also stopped her going regularly to lunch. She'd eased herself out gradually, with just an occasional appearance here and there when her conscience pricked or her mother's complaints got too much; the family embarrassment, not much missed.

With the new generation of overachievers coming along nicely in the twins, there was plenty for them to talk about at the Sunday get-togethers without her being there. To be fair, her brother Hal got a bit of the "settling down" flack too, but it was apparently different for a guy to be focused on his career.

Their father had long ago accepted the reason that Hal never showed anything but polite interest in the succession of eligible young women their mother pushed in his direction. Mum had never quite got it. *Or didn't want to*. Stella Webster was nothing if not persistent. *Well, good luck with that.*

And none of this has anything to do with whether you have dinner with Elliott. For heaven's sake, as Michelle said, it's just a date. You do remember those. You want to do it, so do it.

And it would give her the chance to make sure that he was taking proper care, just in case there was a real threat from the thieves. She looked at the clock. She still had just enough time before Eddie got here. She reached for the card and the phone.

'Maisie, have you got a moment?'

Maisie turned with a smile – when it was the boss asking if she had a moment, then of course she did, even though Jake wasn't that kind of boss. He'd never expect his employees to dance attendance on him. She had a pretty good idea what this might be about from Jake's slightly furtive expression. He'd caught her in the corridor that housed the agency's interview rooms. It would be easy to duck inside one of them. Her grin widened and she felt the glow of being the one in on a secret. Jake – fed up with a running joke that he wasn't a real detective, that he only owned the agency – had enrolled in the training courses that would give him the same certificate to hang on the wall as his staff had. No one else knew, not even his wife, Cassie. Maisie guessed the big reveal would come at some fancy office celebration. Jake was good with celebrations and bringing the staff together, making everyone feel that they belonged. He was pretty good all round – a qualification would just add gloss to his abilities – although she could understand why he felt the need.

An ex-Wolf of Wall Street, a billionaire through inheritance from his father and his own efforts, he'd grown up around the agency when his divorced mother was still running it and before his father carried him off to New York to play the son and heir. Jake *was* pretty good at what he did, which was organising and delegation. But Maisie knew about the compelling attraction of a bit of paper – the need for validation. As the member of staff who had most recently completed the formal training, if he had any questions about what he was studying he came to her. She liked that. As long as Cassie didn't think they were having an affair. *As if.* A reformed rake, Jake was completely devoted to his flamboyant wife, and now that Cass was expecting their child—

'Ah – the two people I need.' Startled, Maisie looked beyond Jake. Michelle was steaming towards them carrying a thick file and a small electronic tablet. Jake's frustrated huff told her that her reading of the situation was the correct one. He had questions. 'Later,' she mouthed, getting a tiny salute in response as Michelle swept them into the first empty interview room.

'Pentecost, I presume?' Jake asked after they closed the door.

'Yep.' Michelle was depositing her burdens on the table. 'Been digging into the family. Barnabas—' She pointed to the top sheets of computer printout '—he's an administrator at a homeless charity, which we knew. Long-term divorced, which we also knew. Apparently amicably. Ex-wife is now living with a younger lover at his vineyard in Tuscany. Some suggestion that the vineyard and the relationship are not doing so well and a few cracks on social media from "friends"—' Michelle made the quotation marks '—that Barnabas might now be worth coming back to. No indication that's anything other than a slightly malicious joke ... Barnabas has a discreet friends-with-benefits arrangement with a female colleague. No sign that the lady has ambition to change that, but money has a loud voice.'

'Mmm.' Jake nodded. *Well, he would know.*

Michelle indicated some press cuttings. 'He's on record as saying that he and his cousin Dorothea intend to use their shares of the proceeds from the sale of the collections to buy back Pentecost Place and turn it into a shelter for homeless teenagers.'

Jake raised his eyebrows. 'A worthy cause.'

Michelle nodded. 'Very.' She looked thoughtfully at her pile of paperwork. 'Nothing from Dorothea to show she's on board with that though.'

'But nothing to say that she's not?' Maisie frowned, conjuring up the image of Dorothea. It was difficult to imagine that limp and colourless woman being enthusiastic about anything. 'A reason for one of them looking for an extra pay-day on the side?' she speculated.

'It's a thought,' Jake agreed. 'What about Dorothea's background?'

'Not a lot.' Michelle's grimace indicated frustration. 'No recent social media.' *Which is practically a crime in investigative circles,*

Maisie thought. 'She had a quite successful career in arts administration but gave it all up two years ago to care for her aged great-aunt, living in Cheltenham. The aunt finally died at Christmas. Dorothea inherited, but there doesn't seem to have been much money. I'm still digging into that. Not much social life since she's been caring for the aunt – but, apparently, she has a modest reputation as a poet. She's appeared at fringe events at a few literary festivals – Cheltenham and Hay-on-Wye – and done some volunteer admin work for a couple of small local ones.'

Jake nodded. 'And Armand?'

Michelle restacked the papers and pulled the tablet towards her. 'Now he is *very* interesting.' She looked up with a grin. 'Apparently, he's a married man.' A picture of a sultry brunette in a form-fitting red dress appeared on the screen. 'Sabine St Clair, also a professional gambler – quite successful.' She flicked through a gallery of photographs showing Armand and Sabine together, including a shot posed on what looked like the steps of a register office. She was wearing a low-cut white jumpsuit and carrying a tight cluster of white rosebuds. 'A quiet ceremony, in London, almost eighteen months ago. No indication that his cousins know anything about it.'

'Eighteen months ago,' Jake mused. 'Just about the time that the terms of Ignatius's will became known?'

'Around that time,' Michelle confirmed. 'I'm attempting to tie down dates, but that's not all.' She looked over at Maisie. 'You had the impression that Armand hadn't been in the house before his late arrival at the weekend?'

'That was certainly how it appeared.' Maisie frowned. Had she been told that or had it simply been implied? Dammit, she couldn't be sure.

'Well, apparently, he was in Torquay the week before and he was actually the one who collected the keys and opened the place up for the cleaners and the maintenance staff before Dorothea took over. He stayed in the house overnight, then left again.'

'Hmm. So each of the cousins potentially had time to do a little snooping around?' Jake speculated. 'Armand's finances?'

'I'm still digging into that too, but so far I'd say erratic, although he seems to have had a bit of a winning streak since the wedding.'

'The couple who play together stay together?' Maisie suggested.

'Maybe.' Michelle clicked the tablet back to the screensaver; a shot of an oil painting of a rural scene that Maisie thought might be a Corot. 'He was out playing poker when the robbery occurred. He could have set that up as an alibi of sorts. He certainly looks like the front runner for involvement from the family.'

Maisie, thinking of blustering Barnabas and pallid Dorothea, had to agree.

'Yes, he does,' Jake concurred. 'But the police have more or less nixed the idea that there was inside involvement.' He shot Maisie an apologetic look. 'Apparently, there was a power cut in that part of Torquay for about ten minutes in the early hours of Sunday, which would account for the lights failing. The rest is just being written off as confusion in the dark.'

Maisie clenched her hands into fists. The mask and the movement in the room and the strange noises were in no way confusion. It rankled, although she knew she didn't have to defend herself to Jake, who was still speaking. 'They're treating it as an outside job. Currently sifting through all the staff and workmen who've been in the Place over the last twenty years.'

'I wish them joy on *that*,' Michelle commented. She was grinning. 'And it leaves the house and the family to us.' She turned towards Jake. 'Have you got anywhere on permission for us to look inside?'

'Working on it,' Jake confirmed. 'Once the police have finally finished. All the valuables have been returned to secure storage, so it's only the mechanics of the passage that are keeping them. I'll let you know.'

Chapter Fourteen

Elliott looked down at the fancy embossed invitation sitting in the centre of his desk. He knew that Jenni, the PA he shared with two other staff members, would have put it there deliberately, so that he couldn't pretend he hadn't seen it. *She knows you too well.*

When he'd agreed to give a couple of guest lectures for the Academic Society in London, he hadn't realised they would be linked to an exhibition sponsored by a firm of jewellers, who were launching a new Egyptian-themed collection. The invitation was to the gala that would open the exhibition at the Society's headquarters – which he was clearly expected to attend. *The price of fame*. He knew that the sponsorship was important to the Society, enabling it to refurbish its building and to add to its grants and bursaries programme. He was happy to help, but he was going to have to re-think the lectures. Something told him his plans to speak on funerary statues – *shabti* – was not what the sponsors would be looking for. *Can't seem to get away from Egyptian jewellery.* He was aware there was possibly something else going on at the Society too. Twice when visiting its building in London, he'd entered a room to have the sensation of conversations abruptly stopped and then restarted. *Or maybe you're just being paranoid?*

He looked at the invitation thoughtfully. It didn't mention a plus one, but he could get Jenni to ask. He reached for a sticky note, scribbled a message and stuck it to the invitation, tossing it into the out tray. Proof that he'd not only looked at it, but taken some action. *Won't Jenni be pleased?*

Glancing at his watch, he reached for his suit jacket. He was due at a meeting with the University facilities manager in less than five minutes to talk about possible building alterations to accommodate the Pentecost Collections. Knowing the facilities manager, that would see off the rest of his afternoon. At least he had one good thing to look forward to: Maisie had agreed to have dinner with him next week. That *was* good – even if she had stipulated next Friday because of work commitments in the evenings. He understood and could live with that. After a tense wait when he'd almost decided she was going to ghost him, the call came. He grinned. It was enough to make even the facilities manager tolerable.

Elliott had suggested a small Italian restaurant, just outside the city centre, that was one of Maisie's favourites. It made things a lot easier; she knew the layout, the menu and the dress code – she only needed to upgrade her work-wear trousers and jacket with a silk blouse and some upmarket jewellery. She'd been careful too to check out the security situation before they met. The team keeping Elliott under observation was satisfied that there was no one else doing the same and had already scaled down their operation. It could be scaled up again if there was any definite news on the Necklace. Everything had gone quiet. Jake was speculating that the thing had been stolen to order and had already disappeared into some collector's vault.

As far as Maisie herself was concerned, all Jake's operatives automatically kept a low profile around the office, frequently coming and going through a small courtyard at the back that gave onto four other premises, as well as regularly swapping cars out of the firm's pool. When working undercover, or tailing someone, it was common sense to avoid being spotted entering the headquarters of a local detective firm. Michelle had put together some "business commitments" that would account for Maisie's presence in Bath in her undercover persona as the billionaire's assistant, should it be needed. Having by fortunate coincidence found herself in the same city as Elliott, and having hit it off during their fraught weekend in Torquay, it was really only natural that they should get together. She was as confident as she could be that seeing Elliott would not draw undue attention and spark questions.

Tonight, they had arranged to meet at the restaurant. Anyone watching Elliott would have to be shadowing him pretty closely to follow him there, and Liam had seen no signs of that. Which meant that she could relax and enjoy the evening. *Relax – oh yeah!*

Even so, she made certain to arrive ten minutes early, although she knew the place, in order to check out the surroundings, confirm the exit routes and observe the other diners. To her chagrin, Elliott was already seated at a table when she arrived. She noted that he'd chosen a discreet corner location and left her the gunslinger's seat – the chair with her back to the wall, facing the room. Was that in acknowledgement of her detective status or old-fashioned courtesy? She'd read somewhere that the woman was meant to face outwards, to see and be seen, but the guy was supposed to look only at his companion. *Adoringly, no doubt.*

With a small sniff, she gave herself a mental shake. She was here to meet an interesting man. She knew she was prickly, defensive and overvigilant, not all of which was down to her job. *And once you've done your job, you really need to leave all that at the door.* She cast a careful professional look round. Everything normal, nothing out of place, familiar staff, familiar surroundings. The professional part of her stepped down, which just left the rest of the bag of nerves. *It's dinner. Just dinner.*

Polite greetings, sampling the wine that Elliott had ordered – similar to one she'd drunk in Torquay, he'd clearly noticed – and choosing from the menu took up the first few minutes. With nothing more left to divert her, Maisie braced herself for a proper look at Dr Elwood. He looked ... good. In the two weeks since Torquay, he hadn't aged, or gone bald – or sprouted horns? *Come on girl – he's still gorgeous. And you still would. Well – might.*

Swallowing down that disturbing thought, Maisie took a deep breath and a slug of the wine. This was *it*. She had to get it out *now* before they went any further. 'Why are we here?'

She winced internally as she heard herself. *That could have been way smoother, Webster.* She'd blurted out the words that were uppermost in her mind, unadorned.

Elliott was looking at her quizzically. There was a gleam in his eyes. 'Well – speaking personally, I'm hoping to have dinner.' There was just a suggestion of a smile at the edge of his mouth. He had a very nice mouth. She'd been aware of it in Torquay.

He was watching her carefully, waiting. Whatever he saw – rabbit in the headlights, probably – it made him give a soft laugh. But he wasn't laughing *at* her. He was inviting her to laugh too – and suddenly they were both laughing and it was going to be fine. Elliott took a sip of his own wine. It occurred to Maisie, now that some of her brain had begun to function again, that he might also have been a little uncertain of how things would go.

'When we met before, both times, you were working … Playing a part?' He stopped to check with her. He looked as if he might like to take her hand. He didn't – but Maisie realised that she wouldn't have minded. 'I've already apologised for the way I misjudged you the first time,' he went on, shrugging. 'Maybe I was playing a part too – the distinguished academic – I'm not keen on these charity things, but some of the proceeds were going to finance displays for schools in small museums around the country.'

'And the organisers were parading their lions?'

He grinned. It was definitely a grin. 'Exactly. For my sins, I seem to have become a lion.' He sipped his wine again. 'That's what appearing on television does for you.' Now his mouth twisted self-deprecatingly. That and the grin seemed to be unwinding the wary ball of apprehension that Maisie had been nursing. 'The second time we met, you were working again – this time the consummate professional.' He saluted her with his glass.

'Huh!' She rolled her eyes. 'I didn't manage to keep hold of the Necklace.'

He gave her a narrow look. 'But that wasn't why you were there, was it? You were on a watching brief. And I'm sure that Jake McQuire hasn't given up on the case.'

'Well – no, he hasn't,' Maisie admitted.

Elliott waved his hand, dismissing the Necklace. Maisie could imagine him using that gesture in a lecture theatre about a theory that didn't hold water. *You'd like to watch him doing it, even if you probably wouldn't understand one word in ten.* It was an ... interesting thought. He looked her full in the eyes, serious now. 'Tonight, we're just two people having dinner. I'd like to get to know you better and I hope you would like to get to know me.'

Abruptly, the tight ball of nerves dissolved completely. Somehow, he *got* it – the mixed feelings that she barely understood herself.

'I'd like that too.'

After that, everything was easy. The food was good and the conversation better. There was no further mention of the Necklace. They talked about books, films, music, theatre – the sort of thing people talked about on a date. Maisie found that she had relaxed, more than she had in weeks. The gentle light of the restaurant and the candlelit tables set blue-black glints in Elliott's hair. His dark eyes were frequently warmed with humour. She admired the set of his shoulders in a slouchy linen jacket. She remembered the warmth of those shoulders, sitting beside her on the floor of the Egyptian Room in Pentecost Place, and suddenly felt herself blushing a little. Elliott was good company and the perfect gentleman. No accidental-on-purpose brushing of hands or attempts at footsie under the table. When the evening ended, he escorted her to her car and saw her into it without even a kiss on the cheek. She started the engine and set the car in gear as he walked away and found herself wishing that there *had* been a kiss on the cheek – and maybe more than that …

With a mental and physical shake, she switched herself away from the personal into her professional mode, watching in her rear-view mirror. Elliott was signalling to the taxi that he'd called from the restaurant, which had just pulled up. He'd mentioned that he didn't always use his car for short trips in the city. She quietly guided her own car around the corner, stopped in an empty residents-only parking bay and waited. When the taxi went by, she fell in behind it. Ten minutes later, when they reached Elliott's address, an apartment conversion at the top of one of Bath's Georgian buildings, she knew that no one had been following him. *No one but me.*

She double parked at the top of the road while he paid off the cab. When he went inside, she cruised slowly down the street, as if searching for a parking space, until she saw the light go on on the top floor. The cars lining the road were dark and quiet. None had occupants. She breathed a long sigh of relief. Dr Elwood was home and safe for the night, locks and alarms engaged, and in telephone contact with the special response team at the agency if the need arose. She was pretty sure that it wouldn't.

She changed gear and speeded up to drive home.

Now she was free to think about the evening, and she had plenty to think about. Elliott Elwood attracted her in a way that no man had in quite a while, but she still wasn't sure where this might go – or if she wanted it to go anywhere. She'd enjoyed herself tonight – Elliott had been an entertaining companion – but she couldn't quite forget the circumstances of their first encounter. Did he look at her and still see *that* woman – the one who was cheap and available? He, on the other hand, was damn near perfect – in her mother's terms. Even her grandmother might have been just a *little* impressed that the family failure could attract a man like Dr Elwood.

Maisie suppressed a habitual involuntary shudder at the memory of her grandmother, whose shadow loomed large, even nearly ten years after her death. Her grandmother – never nana or granny – probably wouldn't have believed it. *And would she have been right?* Did it really matter? Maisie wasn't about to fall headlong into a casual affair with Elliott, however much she was tempted, but neither of them were looking for anything more. She was sure of that.

But she *had* agreed to have dinner with him again next Wednesday,

Before that, she and Michelle would be in Torquay, exploring Pentecost Place. Jake would get the keys on Monday.

Chapter Fifteen

Michelle turned the key, waiting for the soft click of the lock disconnecting, then pushed open the door. Maisie darted through to take care of the alarm. For a heart-stopping few seconds, the thing flashed and twittered before falling silent, showing a green light.

'Phew!' Michelle ostentatiously wiped her brow. Maisie frowned. She wasn't too happy about being back in Pentecost Place, the scene of her recent disaster.

'Jake doesn't make mistakes about things like security codes.' The disaster had been because they were working on rumour and hunch; she kept reminding herself of that. Although in that case, the rumour and hunch had, in fact, proved correct. The Necklace had indeed been targeted. *But not by the people we anticipated?*

'Always a first time,' Michelle said cheerfully, pulling her back to the job in hand. 'Let's go and look at the Egyptian Room. I want to see the secret passage.'

Maisie led the way through the back premises – a large kitchen and a warren of small rooms, which she had only inspected in a cursory way when she'd been studying the house – until they fetched up in the main hall. 'This way.' Maisie directed Michelle into the long gallery where the Egyptian exhibits had been displayed. Everything had been returned to storage. The cabinets were empty and the statues that had ranged the walls were gone; even the two huge sarcophagi guarding the door, which had looked as if they were part of the building. Only the smaller one remained – the one concealing the passage. Maisie wasn't sure if it was an imitation, good enough to convince Elliott, or whether it was real and had been sacrificed to form the entrance.

Michelle stood back, giving it a considering look, then leaned forward to tap the surface. It didn't sound particularly hollow, but Maisie knew that it opened like a door. Behind was a slim space, not much bigger than a cupboard, which dipped abruptly into a set of roughly cut steps. A narrow tunnel led to an old icehouse in a wooded and shady part of the garden. They had checked the icehouse on their way in. The exit was sealed now with police tape. The passage was off-limits.

The carving stood tall and impassive and firmly closed. Jake's police contact had confirmed that the entrance lever could only be operated from inside, not from within the house. The space behind the carving had showed signs of occupation, presumably on the night of the robbery.

'You were here and someone else was inside that.' Michelle voiced Maisie's thoughts. 'Creepy.' They both looked up at the painted face that stared out blankly over their heads. Michelle was clearly disappointed that the thing was closed and she wasn't able to poke about inside. Maisie found she was faintly relieved. 'What about this display case then?' Michelle asked.

Maisie gestured behind them. 'The Necklace was there, in that raised bit in the middle.' They both turned to study it. Two old-fashioned glass museum cases stretched out like wings from a central wooden plinth. On the top of the plinth, there was a lantern-like structure – oblong pieces of glass held in place by narrow fillets of polished wood, topped by a "roof" of more wood and glass. The roof hinged off like a lid, secured on either side with two small locks bedded into the wooden frame. Maisie made a mental note to confirm who had held the keys, even though she was sure the case had not been opened. There simply had not been time.

The cabinet was more a piece of craftsmanship than secure storage for a valuable piece of jewellery. A thief with a heavy bat or a blade could have made short work of it, but that kind of assault had not been attempted. The Necklace was still gone. The glass box was intact. And empty.

The Necklace had simply disappeared.

Maisie stared morosely at the scene of the crime. Michelle was prowling around the cabinet. 'How was the Necklace displayed?'

'On one of those black velvet stands – not the whole head, just the neck and the suggestion of shoulders. There was a battery-powered tea light in the case. They flicker a bit like real candles, so with the rest of the lights out you couldn't see it clearly. It was just a shape glittering in the dark, but it was *definitely* there.' She was sure of that.

The theft had succeeded, right before their eyes. In her head, Maisie was back in the room, in the early hours of that Sunday morning – the sudden blackout, the indefinable scent of ancient artefacts and a strange elusive sweetness overlaying the tang of Elliott's aftershave, the moving shadows, a swirling shift in the gloom. The tiny light flickering in the case and then the uneven gleam of her torch. The eerie face that simply floated – golden, disorientating, black-eyed … It had been a King Tutankhamun cardboard mask with whoever was wearing it dressed in dark clothes. It was obvious *now* – but then, unexpectedly in the darkness …

With an effort, Maisie shook off the memory – and the guilt. She focused back on the room in full light and on Michelle still prowling.

'What are you looking for?'

'Not sure.' Michelle leaned over, peering at the wood and glass lantern. 'You said there was a noise?' Now she was bending down with much of her upper body *under* the glass case.

'Ye-ees. Kind of a whir and a click? And then there was a cold draught, which of course came from the passage – and movement.' Maisie looked around. 'I don't care what the police say, there was more than one person here, and one of them came from inside the house. What exactly *are* you doing?'

'I believe you. And I think …' Michelle ducked right under the cabinet, letting out a satisfied grunt. She swung back out again, feeling underneath with one hand, before standing back. 'There you go.'

Maisie watched, fascinated and disbelieving, as the wooden floor of the case jerked, dropped an inch, split and started to slide back, accompanied by a soft whirring noise. Her breath hissed as a black velvet neck and shoulders mannequin rose up slowly, wobbled and then stabilised, settling into place with a click. The stand was empty, but faint indentations in the velvet suggested where a jewelled collar may have rested.

'Hell.' Maisie breathed out now, finally understanding what had happened. 'That's how it was done.'

Michelle was grinning. 'I'm guessing that the Pentecost who made the passage designed that too – the one who liked conjuring tricks. Look.' She indicated under the case. Stooping, Maisie looked. The part of the wooden frame below the case was as deep as the glass lantern above. 'There's a lever, right up underneath. It's almost flush with the wood. You can feel it rather than see it. Looks just like a piece of fancy moulding. But who puts fancy moulding *under* a cabinet?' Michelle leaned over, fumbled for a moment and set the process in motion again, in reverse. The velvet stand sank back into its hiding place.

'Yes,' Maisie confirmed. 'That's the noise I heard. That's how it was done,' she repeated. 'The nightlight didn't go out, it dropped into the cavity when it opened. Then the whole thing, Necklace and stand, lowered into the box underneath and the floor closed back over them. The display case appeared empty —it *was* empty.'

‘And the Necklace stayed hidden under the cabinet, still on its stand. The one that was abandoned at the sarcophagus door, that was holding it open, was simply a decoy. That, and the exit and entrance through the passage, cemented the idea that it was an outside job – that the jewellery had been removed and taken away. Clever,’ Michelle said admiringly. ‘The workmanship of the cabinet is exquisite. You really can’t see that the floor divides and moves back into the sides of the pedestal.’ She leaned close to the glass, peering in. ‘The join doesn’t show. There was a risk that it might be spotted or the mechanism would be tripped during a search, but it was pretty small. The Necklace was safe, where no one would think to look. Someone knew a lot about Erasmus and his toys,’ she added thoughtfully.

‘The Necklace never left the room – not until someone removed it after the police had left.’ They had reconvened in the office conference room late on Tuesday morning, for Michelle and Maisie to report what they had found to Jake, Mickey and Liam – who had been drafted in as backup. Mickey would be returning to the South of France on an afternoon flight to continue to do whatever it was he was doing there. It had never been properly disclosed what that was, but he was already sliding back into his undercover persona. Maisie caught the glint of a small diamond stud under his long hair, and his clothes and his body language were subtly different.

‘Right.’ Jake put his hands flat on the table. ‘What does this tell us?’

‘Definitely an inside job,’ Michelle responded.

‘Someone who knew the house,’ Mickey chimed in. ‘Which strongly suggests the family.’ He looked over at Michelle. ‘You established that the cabinet was made and installed when the house was built, but Aristotle took it over for his Egyptian artefacts when he shipped them home. I guess that lets off the installers themselves – unless we have a *very* old thief.’

‘The knowledge might have been passed on,’ Maisie pointed out. ‘Or there might be family papers with drawings that we don’t know about.’ She had a sudden flash of recall – Barnabas and Dorothea coming into the library when she was returning one of Erasmus’s notebooks to the shelf. Had there been a reaction from one or both of them? There might have been *something* – but she couldn’t be sure. And Armand had had the house to himself overnight – time to investigate, if there had been a family rumour about the glass case.

Everyone around the table was nodding at their conclusions. There was a distinct air of frustration.

'Whoever it is, they're okay with an element of risk,' Liam suggested. 'The Necklace might have been found before they had the chance to remove it and they *did* have to remove it. Someone might have been sweating a bit before the police left.'

'Yes.' Maisie tried to think if anyone had given the impression of strain, but it had all been pretty chaotic. She still had a gut feeling though. 'My money's on the family. Someone had to have knowledge and access to the house.'

'I agree,' Michelle said. 'On current form, Armand is the front-runner, aided and abetted by the new wife. I did a bit more digging on her. When she's not jetting around playing high-stakes poker, she helps out in the family business – an upmarket antiques gallery in New York. She would potentially have the contacts to arrange a sale, know the collectors who would be interested – maybe just one collector?'

'I think we concentrate our efforts there,' Jake decided. 'Maisie, you check with Dr Elwood about collectors – shady ones, if he knows any.' He looked over quickly at Mickey but Mickey didn't speak. Maisie could feel the beginnings of a blush at Jake's casual acceptance that she was still in touch with Elliott, but no one else seemed to have picked up on it. He was now looking rueful. 'I'm going to have to share this with the authorities.' Michelle gave a muffled groan. 'I know.' Jake looked at her. 'But we really can't keep it to ourselves. And there is one good thing. I spoke to the insurers. They're not prepared to actively engage us, but there *is* a reward for recovery. So we have a justified interest in poking our collective noses in. The police will be all over this, of course, but we're still in with a chance.'

The meeting broke up once Jake allocated some follow-up tasks. He stood back as his employees left the room, talking softly amongst themselves. Mickey lounged near the door.

'What do you know?' Jake asked quietly.

Mickey put up a hand to fiddle with the diamond stud. 'I think if the thieves have the contacts, the most likely way to dispose of a piece like this is an auction for specialist collectors. That's the way to maximise the price – assuming it's not simply been stolen to order for one client. I'm ninety-five per cent certain that none of the people we're interested in are involved. Vibe seems to be that it was amateur hour. I might find out more when I'm back in Cannes. The Collections and the Necklace *did* come up on the radar, but the general opinion seems to have been that neither was worth it at this stage. Too short a time for the organisation that would be involved. There was no rush. The Necklace and the key pieces from other collections could be picked up once they were with the buyer.' He gave a crooked grin. 'Might want to have a word with whoever that is.'

Jake nodded. 'Probably the University. We can talk to Elwood or Dr Leyland, the Dean. Any chance that there would be indignation in professional circles that an amateur has waltzed in?'

Mickey shrugged. 'Maybe, but the Necklace isn't intrinsically valuable. It's a specialist piece. The art is of far more interest.' He took a deep breath, looking through the open door at the empty corridor. Jake waited until he'd gathered himself, abruptly disturbed about where this might be going.

'Even if no one we know has lifted the Necklace,' Mickey said evenly, 'it doesn't mean the Countess isn't involved.'

'Ah.' Jake understood. Mickey was undercover, working for a pseudo-Countess who was part of a gang of international art and jewel thieves – dangerous and violent people. The woman was as dangerous as any of her associates. One of her roles was to "place" stolen items with interested buyers.

'She does have a few private clients. When I get back to Cannes, I'll dig,' Mickey confirmed.

'Carefully,' Jake warned.

'I'm always careful.'

Chapter Sixteen

'We need a plaque, something to commemorate Professor Mumford. Here in the entrance. We can unveil it on the day of the memorial service.' Vaisey Leyland looked around and pointed. 'Over there.'

Elliott followed him across the hall of the Pentecost building to consider a wall that was currently exhibiting a mournful and moth-eaten stag's head. The chance to remove the sad thing would be welcome. The Dean's unexpected arrival on the scene this morning had been a surprise. Elliott wasn't quite sure what the motive was. He didn't think it was the plaque. Or not just that. *No doubt you'll find out soon enough.* 'It's a good location,' he agreed. 'Will you let me have a wording?'

Leyland nodded and they moved on to look at the room selected for the clown exhibit. It hadn't been publicly confirmed that the University was the successful bidder for the Collections, but Leyland was pressing ahead, so Elliott assumed he had been told unofficially. Knowing the Dean, it made sense that he would keep the news under wraps until the start of term, when he could announce it with a suitable fanfare.

Now the subject of Professor Mumford had come up, Elliott took the chance to ask a question that he'd been wondering about. He knew the answer from Jake, but he was curious about what had been shared with the University. 'Has there been any progress in the investigation into Mumford's death?'

Leyland exhaled. Suddenly, he looked tired. 'Not much. The police *seem* to be focusing on a feud with a neighbour about some overgrown trees, but I really don't know ... It's just difficult to imagine anyone wanting to murder old Mumford. And certainly not over a few trees. Maybe they will decide after all that it was an accident with his medication,' he added hopefully, visibly perking up at the prospect. He looked at his watch. 'Must get on. Good to speak to you this morning and I'll let you have that wording.' He was already at the door when he turned back. 'Oh – there was one other thing – almost forgot. You are intending to go to that reception at the Academic Society?'

'Yes.' Elliott hoped his face wasn't showing his confusion. Since when had Leyland paid any attention to his off-duty diary?

'Good, good. Hoping to be there myself. Should be an interesting evening.'

He flapped off, leaving Elliott standing in the middle of the hall, wondering what that Detective Colombo moment had been about and why Leyland would be attending an Egyptologists' event. And why did he have a ridiculous feeling *that* had been the real point of Leyland's visit this morning? He shrugged and turned to take the lift to the top floor. At least it had reminded him to ask Maisie if she was free.

When he got back to the office half an hour later, Jenni was frowning at her computer. 'Problem?'

'The Library can't find one of those monographs you wanted. There have been quite a few things going missing recently, some of them quite valuable.' The frown deepened. 'They had a couple of interns working there a few months ago and a lot of volumes seem to have been mis-shelved. They still haven't tracked down a first edition of *Lorna Doone* that Dr Brown asked for *last month*,' she grumbled, clearly irritated. 'Shall I see if I can persuade them to request the monograph through inter-library loan?'

'If you can,' Elliott agreed. 'It will save me a trip to the British Library. And say yes to that invitation, please.' He didn't need to tell Jenni which one. She'd already waved it under his nose when she'd confirmed that he could take a guest. He'd waited to see how things worked out with Maisie. The answer was that, so far, things were going well. Well enough to invite her.

'Oh yes.' Jenni nodded. 'The Dean was asking about that this morning.'

'Mmm. I just saw him.' *Curiouser and curiouser.* 'Tell them yes, and I hope to be bringing a guest.'

Leaving Jenni to speculate on who that might be, he returned to his office. Closing the door, he put the puzzle of the Dean's behaviour out of his mind in order to concentrate on an e-mail received that morning from a colleague in Munich, advancing an intriguing theory on a hieroglyph they had both been studying.

The gold collar glinted in its nest of black velvet. Gold, crystal and lapis that had circled the necks of some of the most famous women in the world – the Cleopatra Necklace.

He wanted it hidden away, in a safe deposit box.

But it's not going anywhere. It's staying right *here.*

Where I can keep my eyes on it.

Told him I was superstitious – don't want to risk activating the curse.

He *isn't happy about it, but that's too bad.*

Can I trust him?

'I love you.' That was what he'd said, and 'I have the contacts.'

But it was over four weeks now and nothing.

Just silence.

And somehow the police had found out about the trick with the cabinet. *Not much they can do though, when met with a blank stare and an outright denial.* An outsider who knew about the passage could easily have known about the cabinet. *Didn't give anything away.* A sharp, restless movement snapped the lid of the jewel case shut.

Time to break the silence.

The phone lay on the table, beside the case.

This time I'll *be the one making the call.*

'What?' The answering voice was a sharp, irritated demand.

No more than expected really. 'You haven't rung.'

'Nothing to report.' There was noise in the background, but it wasn't clear what. Traffic, voices, a radio playing? 'I told you, I'll ring when I have it set up.'

'It's been over four weeks.'

'So?' It was voiced like another demand, but it sounded distracted. *Where are you?* 'These things take time to arrange. You don't just take out an advert in the newspapers.' Now it was hard not to laugh. *Actually, lover, that's almost what we did do* – the theft had been reported locally and nationally. Luckily, two juicy scandals, involving a politician and a spy and a famous footballer and a Hollywood star, had filled column inches in the summer "silly" season. The theft of an obscure Egyptian relic from a private collection merited only a short paragraph. No enterprising reporter had dug deep enough to run with a cursed necklace story. 'As I *told* you, I'll be in touch when everything is in place.' There was an edgy note under the terse replies – a tension. Simple annoyance and frustration, or something else? *Time to change tack.*

'I miss you.'

'I miss you too, darling, but we knew all along it had to be like this. There will be news soon, I promise, and it will be big.'

The hand not holding the phone reached to drop the jewel case into the open drawer of the desk, pushing it shut with a decisive click. 'We're going to make it?'

There was a noise like a door closing and the voice dropped, quiet, confiding. 'We will make it. An auction. Three bidders. Just like we said. You just need to give me time.'

'Okay.' As intended, the breathy response sounded like acceptance.

Straining ears caught the tiny sigh of relief at the other end, before the call terminated.

Fobbed off. Placated. Humoured. You have the Necklace. How much longer should you wait? The police are investigating. Can you afford *to wait?*

A long, shaky inhalation.

Time to look for another way?

Tonight, she was going to kiss Dr Elliott Elwood. It was time. Maisie took a last look in the mirror, checking her make-up, and was pleased with the result – subtle but effective. They'd been seeing each other for three weeks now – four if you counted Torquay. She could admit cautiously that it was going well.

On all their dates Elliott had continued to be the perfect gentleman. The occasional touch of her arm, the offer of his hand on a staircase, the brush of fingers over a menu. *Actually, if his plan is seduction by not touching, he might just be acing it.* She grinned at her reflection, adding a final slick of lip gloss. She didn't think that was it. She was pretty sure that the no touching thing was all about their first encounter. *Not making any assumptions.* She liked that. It had allayed her lingering suspicion that he saw her as an easy conquest. She continued to enjoy his company, so it was a good time to move things along. *Just keep it light. It's a few dates, not a marriage proposal.*

Tonight, she was going to get that goodnight kiss.

They'd come close to it a few days ago, by accident. She could smile about it now, but at the time it had been ... disturbing. *Actually, downright scary.* They'd had dinner at a new restaurant. The bill paid, they'd been on the point of leaving when a woman stepped straight in front of Elliott, waving a knife. Maisie reacted instinctively, shoving Elliott to the wall to confront the attacker – only to find that the weapon she was wielding was actually a pen. It had taken a few embarrassing moments to unscramble the situation, make fulsome excuses, mendaciously claim a twisted ankle, and give the confused fan the autograph she was seeking. *The perils of dating a TV celebrity*. While

Elliott posed for selfies with the woman and her daughter, Maisie stood at the door, waiting for the burst of adrenaline to subside.

And, actually, the adrenaline hadn't all been the sudden alarm. She knew that a small part of it was down to the pressure of Elliott's body against hers, the closeness of his mouth. If she'd simply lifted her head ...

Of course, she hadn't and the whole thing had ended in laughter. She'd learned to look out for potential fans and her involuntary reaction had confirmed where dating Elliott was leading.

But she was going to stop overthinking it, and let whatever was going to happen ... happen.

The trill of her phone broke into her thoughts. She glanced down as she answered. Not a familiar number. *Not Elliott.* 'Yes?'

'Maze? Is that you, sis?'

'Hello, Hal.' The words "What do you want?" were on the tip of her tongue. Heroically, she held them back. 'How are things?'

They chatted for a few moments, Maisie with one eye on the clock. At last, she heard it – the slight indrawn breath on the other end of the line. *Ah! Now we get to it – what this call is* really *about.*

'Er ...' Her brother sounded uncharacteristically nervous. *Why?* 'Will you be coming over on Sunday, for lunch?'

'To Mum and Dad?' Even as she said it, she realised it was a silly question. Where else? Had her brother suddenly noticed that she'd been MIA for months? 'Well ... I don't know,' she stalled.

'I'd like you to be there, please.' The note of entreaty took her by surprise even as her door buzzer sounded. *Elliott, bang on time*. She scooped up her bag and took the call with her as she secured the door and started down the stairs. 'It's ... it's important, Maze,' her brother insisted quietly. 'I really would like you to be there.'

'Well ... yes ... okay. What about Françoise and Paul and the twins?'

'I don't know.' There was a muttered undertone that sounded a lot like "other fish to fry". 'As long as you're there.'

'I can do that.' She let herself out of the front door. Elliott was leaning against his racing green Morgan. The classic car had been a surprise and yet not a surprise when he first picked her up in it. He'd inherited it from his great-uncle. *And it suits him.* He was wearing a light linen suit, his hair ruffled from the breeze in the open car.

Mmm, yes ... very kissable. Could she? Should she? Now?

No, she decided. Not yet. Hal was still speaking in her ear.

'I'll be there,' she confirmed. 'Now I have to go.' She said her goodbyes and clicked off the call.

'Hi.' Elliott grinned at her. *Extremely kissable.* 'Work?' He nodded at the phone.

She shook her head. 'My brother. Wanted to make sure I'm coming to the ritual feast on Sunday.'

'Ritual ... ah ... family lunch?'

'Yep.' Maisie couldn't help the grimace. 'For my sins.'

'You don't get on?' He looked concerned. *Which is sort of nice, I think?*

'I don't really fit.' She shrugged. 'Not really on the same wavelength,' she said lightly. She wasn't going there. Not now, with this *kissable* man in front of her. She dismissed her brother and her family from her mind as she turned the phone to silent and dropped it into her bag. 'I hope the food at this place lives up to its reputation. I'm ravenous. I didn't have time for lunch.'

"This place" was a gastro pub in a picture-perfect setting a few miles out of the city – a mellow old church, a ring of cottages around a village green and a traditional duck pond. The food was very good indeed. Maisie enjoyed her meal and listened with interest to Elliott's report on the latest developments in the re-modelling of Pentecost Court and the Dean's strange fascination with the reception invitation.

'He's probably cooking up some grand plan to do with the Egyptian collection – a joint exhibition, I expect, with a big announcement at the Society's reception. He'll want someone else from the University to be there to witness his triumph. I don't know why it needs to be a secret, except that the University doesn't actually officially *own* the Collections yet.' Elliott made a wry face. 'The man is an excellent administrator but does like to make a show, so I will be there, ready to be suitably awed and amazed by his brilliance.' He smiled. 'Having offered that as an enticement – the invitation includes a guest. Would you like to come with me?'

Maisie felt a sudden surge of pleasure at being asked. And maybe another kind of pleasure at the hopeful expression in Elliott's eyes. A small warning bell was also ringing in the back of her mind. *If this guy Leyland is behaving strangely, maybe you* should *be there.*

'I too can do awed and amazed,' she disclosed. 'I'd love to come. Thank you.'

Elliott's smile widened. 'In that case, it's a date.'

When the meal was over, they walked back across the green to where the Morgan was parked. The ducks were settling for the night at the edge of the pond, with sleepy snuffles and quacks. Twilight was closing softly into darkness. Impulsively, she reached out to Elliott. His fingers closed warmly over hers and they completed the short stroll to the car hand in hand. They'd passed a milestone tonight. The reception in London that was now firmly in her diary would probably require an overnight stay ... but that was for the future.

For tonight ...

The kiss could be now, in the romantic fading light ...

No, not yet.

She let go of Elliott's hand as they reached the car. He must guess what she was working up to, but he was waiting for her to make the first move.

The journey home didn't take long, on quiet roads.

Her stomach fluttered with anticipation.

As always, he walked her from the car to her door. This time, instead of reaching for her keys, she reached for him, hands on his chest – and how good did that feel? – slightly raised on her toes, lips slightly parted …

For a moment, they just looked at each other, and, for another swooping half second, she thought she'd got it horribly wrong, that Elliott was not expecting … didn't want … Then she realised, on the edge of freefall, that he was *looking* at her, drinking her in, his eyes warm and dark and intent. And in the next half second, she understood. This man *knew* her, who she was, what she was. No disguises. The thought was as heady and breath-stealing as the prospect of the kiss. And then Elliott bent his head and everything coherent in her mind evaporated.

She would swear there were fireworks going off somewhere, lighting up her skin. Every nerve ending in her body was focused on her mouth and the feel of Elliott exploring her, invading her, kissing her. *Sensation. Just sensation.* She leaned in, desperate to get closer, deeper. *More.* His mouth, his tongue, the faintest rasp of stubble, warmth, scent. She was enfolded and she was *melting.*

When he finally eased back to let them both have air, she couldn't help herself. She had to follow him and then he was pressing tiny nibbling kisses around the edge of her mouth and his hands were caught in her hair and she *still* couldn't get close enough. A car passed on the road and then another. Headlights raked across them, and at last they had to move apart. Her breathing was ragged, heart racing. Under her hand, still resting on Elliott's chest, she could feel the thumping rhythm, feel him pulling in deep breaths.

'That was …' He leaned down, resting his forehead against hers. 'Um … epic?' She couldn't do anything but nod. 'Thank you,' he whispered in her ear.

'No!' She moved back, startled. 'It's not … I wanted …'

'I know.' His smile started the melting all over again. She was a wreck. 'And it's still thank you.'

Across the street a taxi was disgorging its occupants, voices were raised, doors opened and light spilled. Elliott touched her mouth briefly with one finger and then he was gone, loping back to the Morgan parked at the curb.

Maisie managed the door and the stairs in a blur. She shut her own front door and leaned against it, taking a long, very shaky breath. She'd expected the kiss to be pleasant, that Elliott would be a thorough and accomplished kisser. She hadn't expected an explosion. She'd never felt like that before. Chemical combustion. Pure lust. If there'd been a bed, she'd have dragged Elliott into it. If it hadn't been for the taxi, she might have dragged him up *here.* She touched her face, feeling the blush. *Maybe you wouldn't have needed to* drag *him?*

What the hell, they'd just taken the relationship to a whole new level. One that she'd never experienced before. She ran unsteady hands down her body. What the hell was it about a snooty academic that could make her feel like *this*? Like her whole being was on fire?

She walked unsteadily over to the kitchen, flipping cupboard doors until she found her bottle of emergency whisky. She poured a glass, taking it to the window and sipping it slowly. The moon had risen and it was almost full, hanging low over chimney pots and tiles and shiny aerials. *Moon madness.* She splayed her fingers on the glass, as if she could catch it in her hand. What had she gotten herself into? Right at this moment she didn't know, but she wanted more.

Elliott guided the car around the corner and pulled into a parking space. If he didn't … compose himself, he'd be driving into a tree. Kissing Maisie … he'd never expected …

He leaned his head back against the seat to look up at the sky, steady his breathing and wait for his body to calm down. The top was down on the car, the moon was hovering over him and the night air had a slight chill. Not quite enough to shiver, but verging on it. *Or maybe that was something else?*

He'd known Maisie was different. He'd had affairs – civilised, sophisticated arrangements with friends of friends or colleagues distant enough not to make waves, but this … Hell, he'd gone back to college days; the heat, the excitement, the sheer overpowering sensation. *And now you're thirty-six years old and not being fuelled by adolescent hormones and cheap alcohol.* After another moment, he leaned over and started the car. He had no idea where this thing with Maisie might go, but he was more than ready to find out.

How much longer are you going to wait?

Lying in its box on the table, the gold of the Necklace was cold to the touch. The jewels glittered fragile fire, keeping their secrets.

You can do this. Sell it yourself. You don't need him. *All you need is a way to a buyer. Just one.*

The whispered words were so strong they seemed like a real voice. A siren song.

But how to find that way ... the way to Augustus Elladour?

A frustrated huff. Too risky to ask the lawyers, even if they could be persuaded to tell.

So how?

A swift glance towards the laptop open on the side table spiked another burst of frustration. The internet was very little help on the possible identity of the reclusive billionaire. Elladour's presence was there in the bigger galleries and auction houses, but it was shadowy. The most that was known about him was through the things he bought and bid for – historical jewellery and paintings. Things with a certain reputation. *Things like the Cleopatra Necklace.* The declaration almost screamed out of the screen.

He *would* want the Necklace. Of course he would.

But how to locate him – this shadow man? Best guess at his identity? There were plenty of those. He was a Russian oligarch, a

Japanese tycoon, a lottery winner, a retired Texas oil man, even a female cryptocurrency speculator from New York. It didn't really matter, if Elladour *wanted* the Necklace …

How to find out?

There *was* one way to trace him.

Can you remember?

Concentration.

A label on a suitcase. An apartment block in London. Yes!

A thrill. Excitement and fear.

You can do it, but carefully, carefully.

You have to go to London.

Maisie stood on the doorstep of her parents' house, gathering herself together. She'd dressed carefully – not in a skirt, she wasn't going that far – and brought flowers. When she'd had time to think, she'd formed an inkling of what this might be about, and could understand why Hal wanted moral support. And if it *was* what she thought, she would be *glad* to be there. However far apart they'd drifted, he was still her brother. But if, instead, it was some sort of plan to set her up …

She wouldn't be letting the door hit her on her way out.

With a deep breath, she pushed the bell. The door opened so fast, she was sure her mother must have been standing behind it. 'Mariette, darling.' Stella took the flowers when Maisie offered them. 'Oh, how pretty.' The quick glance her mother gave over her shoulder, checking that she hadn't brought anyone with her – anyone, i.e. a man – before enfolding her in a scented embrace – probably Penhaligon's Bluebell – suggested that it wasn't a setup. She extracted herself with more relief than she'd expected in order to turn and receive a brisk hug from her father.

A teasing imp inside her head wondered what would have happened if she'd brought Elliott along. *No!* She pulled herself up short. It was unthinkable even as a tease. Some of the residual tension inside her softened a little though, with the thought of him. They'd gone to the theatre yesterday evening. The goodnight kiss in the quiet darkness of the car, instead of on her doorstep, had been just as devastating as before. Afterwards, when he'd gently hooked a stray lock of hair behind her ear, he'd looked serious and intent. 'I wondered ... when we go to London …'

She hadn't let him get any further. 'Yes. I'd like that.' They'd already agreed that they would stay over and a shiver of excitement fizzed through her at the thought. She squashed it ruthlessly.

Not here, and definitely not now!

Lunch went as well as could be expected. The food was good. Her mother fussed and fretted but Maisie was used to letting it wash over her. There was no sign of Fran and her family, but the wine in Hal's glass went down slightly faster than usual. Nothing was said about her own intermittent absences from the table, although she caught her father looking speculatively from her to Hal. Conversation was mostly polite, only teetering a little when her mother made a clumsily laughing comment about her children always being welcome to bring guests. Maisie just smiled blandly. She thought her brother winced a little.

At last the meal was over, and Mum was stacking dishes to take to the kitchen and twittering about bringing coffee through to the lounge. Hal took a determined swig of the last of his wine and sat up straight in his chair. Maisie felt her heart speeding up in anticipation. 'Mum, Dad, Maisie …' Hal looked round at all of them. 'I'm … I'm getting married.' He shut his eyes briefly as his mother surged to her feet, arms outstretched.

'Darling! But who – Belinda? It must be. Such a lovely girl. I knew you'd get on. I—' Both Hal and her father made almost identical restraining gestures. Maisie put out a hand to gently pull her mother back into her chair. Stella subsided with a cluck of disapproval, wriggling to free herself, but Maisie left her hand resting lightly on her mother's arm. Hal needed the space to say this. His eyes were strained but his chin was level.

'Stephen and I went to Paris last weekend. He proposed. I said yes,' he announced to the sudden silence. Then her father was on his feet, clapping his hand on his son's shoulder and jerking his head towards her. 'I think this calls for champagne. Come with me, Maisie, and find the glasses?'

Looking back as they left the room, Maisie caught a glimpse of her mother. She was staring at Hal in bewilderment. As the door closed behind them, Hal moved to sit beside Stella, taking her hand.

Maisie couldn't decide whether their escape to the kitchen, leaving her brother to cope, was cowardice or strategy. Then she saw her father's face and understood – it was strategy. Hal could always be relied on to talk Mum round. Leaving them alone together was the best way. But there was something else going on too. 'You knew about this,' she accused as she opened cupboards, looking for the champagne flutes.

Her father pulled out a bottle that was conveniently chilling in the fridge. 'Suspected,' he agreed.

'You've met him – Stephen?' she asked curiously.

Father nodded. 'He's a nice guy. I think they'll be very happy together. He loves Hal, I'm sure of that. Your brother is nearly forty years old. I think he knows his own mind by now. He's never made a secret of the fact that he's gay.'

'Except Mum …' Her mother had always done the genteel equivalent of sticking her fingers in her ears and humming loudly whenever the subject came up. Maisie thought for a moment – her mother *had* recently stopped talking vaguely about "going through a phase" and pushing the daughters and nieces of friends Hal's way, so maybe—

'She'll come round. Best thing to leave them together,' her father confirmed as he extracted the cork with a satisfying pop and wrapped the bottle in a tea towel.

'Will she?'

'It's a wedding,' he said simply with a sideways tilt of his head.

Maisie let out a breath, then laughed. 'You know, you're right.'

'Should be. I've known her for fifty years.' *And loved her all that time,* Maisie acknowledged silently. Her mother's hidebound views and attitudes, inherited from her own mother, might drive Maisie mad, but she could never fault the solid nature of her parents' marriage. It wouldn't suit her but it suited them.

'You know, poppet …' The note in her father's voice and the use of her childhood nickname made her raise her head from the glasses. 'Anyone you want to bring home – anyone at all – they *will* be welcome.'

'I know, Dad.' She did know, but she just couldn't contemplate it. The thought of introducing Elliott—she shut down on the thought. The consternation in her mind, skirting the edge of panic, cut too deep. Understanding that this reaction was illogical was no help.

Content that he'd made his point, her father hefted the champagne, gesturing to the glasses. 'What'll you bet me that when we get back in there your mother will be talking about wedding venues? And Hal will be more than ready for a glass of this?'

Maisie was glad she hadn't taken the bet when they opened the dining room door.

'—and there's that hotel outside Cheltenham with the really lovely ballroom ...'

They both began to laugh. 'Come on.' Her father nudged her forward. 'Let's toast your brother's happiness.'

Chapter Seventeen

Despite enjoying her work, Michelle had never been keen on Monday mornings. This one had brought something that perturbed her. She padded down the corridor to Jake's top floor office and knocked. The sound of scuffling and a soft feminine laugh stopped her from opening the door straight away. Instead, she waited for Jake's call to enter.

Jake was sitting at his desk and his wife Cassie was leaning casually against it. Behind her the interconnecting door to her own office in the next building was ajar. It *might* have been a work consultation, except for the disorder of Cassie's hair and Jake's tie. 'Hi.' Jake had automatically risen to go to his fancy coffee machine in the corner of the office to fetch her cup. 'What's the trouble?'

He'd seen it in her face. After a wave of greeting, Cassie slid off the desk, preparing to leave.

'No.' Michelle put out a hand. 'Don't go, unless you need to.' She knew the value of Cassie's quick mind when there was a problem. Jake handed her the coffee and gestured for them all to take their places in his seating area. Cassie settled with her now visible baby bump in one of the low chairs and gave her husband a warning glance. 'You may have to help me out of this.' Jake acknowledged the statement with a grin.

He turned to Michelle. 'Not Thackeray?' Michelle shook her head. Everything on the wedding scam was going to plan. 'It's the Necklace.' She knew that Jake would have shared the information on that with his wife.

Cassie leaned forward, interested. 'Something happened?'

'Yes.' Michelle shifted uncomfortably, not happy with what she had to report. 'It's Maisie. Someone is sniffing around the identity we created for her for Torquay.' She could see from Jake's expression that he hadn't expected that. Hell, she hadn't either, even though they had kept the cover story in place – an excess of caution that was now apparently justified.

'What and when?' Jake asked, serious now.

'Just in the last couple of days, as far as I can tell,' Michelle replied. 'Nothing big – just some mail to the flat in London that I used as an address for her. Whoever it is, they're on a fishing expedition, because they don't have the full information. It has to be someone Maisie met in Torquay.'

Jake was nodding. He'd understood the implications straight away. 'Someone looking for Elladour. All the arrangements for the weekend were handled by the solicitors dealing with the estate. And everything to do with Augustus Elladour was meant to be kept strictly confidential. This isn't coming by any official route.'

'I don't think so,' Michelle confirmed. 'I wouldn't expect the solicitors to have disclosed anything and it doesn't look as if they have, or the snooper would have tried the business address we used for Elladour – although I will check to see if anyone has been asking questions.' She glanced over at Cassie, who was looking at her enquiringly. 'The heirs didn't get personal details about those attending – only about the organisations they represented and their names. There was no need for anything more,' she explained. 'Because we didn't know what was out there, I still did a full cover identity for Maisie – or the best that could be done in the time.' She grimaced. 'I deliberately left a couple of small gaps though – things that wouldn't look particularly unusual. Anyone taking undue interest would have to do a little bit of work, which would hopefully set off alarm bells that someone was looking. And it has.' Michelle was aware of a sense of relief that instinct had prompted her to build in those small safeguards and they had done their job. 'This morning someone tried to deliver a parcel. Like the mail, it only had Maisie's name and the name of the block. The concierge took it as agreed, without comment, but it looks like an attempt to find a flat number. Maisie is the only channel available if someone is trying to contact Elladour, but they don't have a full address.'

Cassie's head was tilted in her thinking position. 'Someone who had access to Maisie's cover ID from things she had with her at Pentecost Place – things you seeded – or from talking to her? And someone who wants to keep on the down-low? They wouldn't be asking the solicitors, even if the solicitors were likely to part with the information,' she decided.

'I think that too,' Michelle agreed. 'It can only be someone that Maisie met in Torquay.'

'Hmm. It certainly looks as if that's the case.' Jake steepled his fingers in a characteristic gesture. 'Which apartment in London did you use?'

'The service flat in Chelsea.'

Jake nodded. 'Good choice. Big lobby and plenty of front-of-house people and security. The staff there will do whatever we need.' He flashed a grin at Cassie who made a face at him. Michelle knew they had history with that service flat but she'd never found out what it was. 'Maisie should remember if she talked to anyone about where she was living,' he added.

'I hope so, but haven't spoken to her yet – she's out doing interviews for an insurance claim. I wanted to run it by you first.'

Jake nodded. 'So – someone is trying to contact Augustus,' he said reflectively. 'Our reclusive billionaire.'

Cassie's glance was sharp. 'Someone with something to sell? Like a Necklace that a reclusive billionaire *collector* might want to own?'

'It has to be,' Michelle breathed, focusing on the positives, not the alarm she'd felt when she'd got the message from the apartment block's Head of Security. Against all expectations, they suddenly had a lead. Her chest tightened – an approach from someone who might actually *have* the Necklace? 'What do we do?' She looked at Jake.

'Looks like it's time for Maisie to step back onto the stage.'

Maisie was startled but not worried when the receptionist intercepted her on the way back into the building with a message to go straight up to Jake's office. The worries started in the lift. What was wrong? Was it something to do with Elliott? Surely he would have rung her himself? What if he couldn't …?

Her heart was thumping as if she had actually raced up the stairs by the time the lift reached the top floor. Jake's office door was open. He waved her in and gestured to the welcoming cup of coffee on the table, inviting her to sit. She looked at him, then at Cassie, then at Michelle. They looked engaged, not concerned – well, maybe a bit concerned. Her shoulders relaxed a fraction as she sat down.

'What's going on?'

'Someone is trying to get hold of you at the London address.'

'Oh!' Maisie clutched the coffee mug, knowing her eyes had widened. 'The Necklace?

'It looks like a distinct possibility.' Michelle quickly filled her in on the attention that her Torquay persona was suddenly generating.

Maisie sipped her coffee. 'Whoever has the Necklace is having trouble finding a buyer and decided to go after Elladour?' she said after a moment. 'It makes sense,' she acknowledged. 'But who is it?'

'Can you remember if anyone at the house party was particularly interested in where you were living?'

Maisie frowned. 'Lady Whatsit – the fake one. We were talking about property in London and she said her sister had a place in Bywater Street and, of course, that's just round the corner. We were having drinks and there were a number of people who could have overheard. There was a label on my case with the name of the apartment block. And if anyone went through my handbag, there was an old envelope with a shopping list on the back, as part of my cover.'

Michelle was nodding. 'It was torn, so there was no flat number. But why would someone have been searching your handbag?' They both looked over at Jake.

'Maisie was a late addition to the party. Someone could have been checking up – which is why the envelope was there in the first place. We thought then we might be dealing with a professional gang,' he reminded them. 'According to Mickey, if the Necklace wasn't stolen to order for one collector then the most lucrative way of going forward would be to set up an auction. Whoever the thieves are, they'd need time to assemble a field of potential bidders. Maybe someone on their target list wasn't interested – or they have everyone on the list but thought it was worth a punt to add Elladour to the bag?' Jake suggested. 'They know that he was looking to acquire the Collections so he might be prepared to bid for the Necklace.'

'So – we may be looking at an auction.' Maisie's heart was beating very fast indeed. She knew she should be cool and professional over this but she was unable to damp down her excitement that a potential lead had suddenly fallen into their laps. She put her mug down with a thump. 'I need to go back undercover – be there, wait for them to get in touch.'

'I think so,' Jake agreed. 'But we're going to have to be very careful.'

'It's risky.' Maisie could see that Michelle wasn't happy.

'I know. If I put a foot wrong, we could lose them.' Maisie could feel a flush seeping up from her neck. Her last two special assignments had not worked out the way they had hoped. *This time you have to do better.*

'I don't think Michelle is talking about your acting ability.' Cassie glanced between the two of them. 'She's worried about *you.*'

'Oh.' Maisie was taken aback until Michelle gave her an unhappy nod. 'You'll be exposed – a stalking horse – and on your own.'

'It was the same in Torquay,' she pointed out gently, touched by her colleague's concern.

'Yeah – but we were only working on a hunch then.'

Cassie was looking at her husband for a lead.

'We do this,' he confirmed. 'Maisie goes in with her eyes open but we take *all* precautions. Minimum risk. This guy, whoever, is looking for an introduction. As soon as possible, we shift them over to the real target – the billionaire collector.' His grin had gone wolfish. 'And that would be me.'

Maisie felt an unexpected swell of relief – that she was going to be able to do the job, but also that she would be able to pass it on to Jake. A win-win.

'I *want* to do it. And I'll be careful.'

'I'll leave you to your planning.' Cassie extended an imperious hand and Jake leapt up to help her out of the low chair. Maisie and Michelle both pretended not to see the quick kiss they shared. It made Maisie think of Elliott. She shifted uncomfortably. What was his attitude going to be to her taking this job? *Well, it* is *my job.*

Jake came back from seeing Cassie to the door. 'Right,' he said briskly. 'Most likely candidates for our snooper, as always, are the family. Do we know where they are at the moment?'

'Barnabas is on a walking tour in Scotland,' Michelle informed him.

'Which could cover a multitude of sins.' Jake had a reminiscent smile on his face. 'See if you can get hold of that PI in Edinburgh who worked for us before, ask him to check it out. What about the others?'

'Dorothea is back at her aunt's house, doing the final clearing before new owners move in. She was overheard talking to a neighbour about taking a holiday. A train trip around Switzerland was mentioned.'

'Very nice,' Jake approved. 'And Armand?'

'Dropped off the radar.' Michelle's irritation was clear. 'Not unusual. He's been known to disappear before – underground poker tournaments. Secure locations and high-stakes – that sort of thing is his jam. Missus isn't with him. She's back in New York with her family.'

'Setting up the sale?' Maisie jumped in before Jake could say it.

'Seems plausible,' he agreed. 'She could have recruited help in London to find Elladour – or that could be Armand if he's in London somewhere. Those two seem like front runners.'

Maisie sipped coffee. It *did* make sense that someone from the family was involved. The thought that one of them had been watching and taking note of her that weekend gave her a little frisson of distaste though. *But that's the job.* Moving to London would make problems for seeing Elliott … and that raised a question. 'Er …' she began awkwardly. *Oh, get it over with.* 'I've been seeing Dr Elwood – socially, I mean … That is …' She glared at Michelle who was ostentatiously mouthing the word "dating".

Jake didn't seem surprised. *He already knew?*

'Don't see that's a problem. You met in Torquay, you hit it off.' He narrowed his eyes. 'It might even be an enticement. You're access to a billionaire *and* an expert.'

Maisie's heart, which had settled down a bit, began to thump for a different reason. 'Could be risky – inviting attention to him?'

'He's already on the radar. You might be able to find out if they do have any intentions in his direction,' Jake countered. Maisie breathed a bit easier. 'I don't think you should relocate too soon. Give it a few days. We don't want to look like we're responding to attempts to trace you.' He glanced over at Michelle. 'Can you stir the cover story a bit? Give our mystery watcher something to watch.'

'On it,' Michelle agreed.

'Good …' Jake looked at his watch. 'We'll reconvene on Wednesday, same time, to assess and fine-tune.'

Michelle and Maisie rose, taking their cue. When they had gone, Jake strode over to the connecting door, tapped on it and let himself into his wife's office. She looked up from her computer.

'Planning done?'

'It is.'

'But?' Cassie tipped her head to one side. 'You wouldn't be here if there wasn't a "but". You're worried about Maisie? She *can* do this, you know?'

Jake wasn't ducking that implication. 'I know she can, but she's had a couple of setbacks in recent jobs – although neither of them was her fault.'

'You're afraid that it's made her too eager to take this one on?'

'A little … but no,' he decided. 'She's more than capable. I'm just uneasy about putting her on the line. We're going to have to make sure that she has plenty of support.' He frowned, shaking his head. 'It may be totally unconnected, but all this began when Professor Mumford died. And there's no doubt that the man was murdered.'

Chapter Eighteen

Elliott was worried. He hadn't said anything, but Maisie could see it in his eyes and the small frown between the classically arched eyebrows.

Not wanting to explain the situation in a phone call, Maisie had suggested a quick meeting at a coffee house in town, knowing the place would be relatively quiet mid-afternoon. During the day, it was a venue for coffee and cakes, catering mostly to tourists. The place really got busy in the evening when it turned over to cocktails and live music. The thought flickered across Maisie's mind that it would be good to come here one evening. The decor was meant to match the building – authentic Georgian – spindly chaise longue, heavy drapes and ornately framed mirrors, with fans and gloves, swords and riding crops displayed on the walls. To Maisie it suggested a Georgian brothel rather than a coffee house. *Maybe it's all the red velvet and the riding crops?*

They carried their drinks – Americano for Maisie and a Four Seasons Oolong for Elliott – up to the top floor. By day, very few people ventured up the narrow stairs to what was once the servant quarters. Dividing walls had been removed to open up the space, but the skeleton of the original rooms remained as nooks and alcoves. After a quick look around, Maisie had chosen to sit near the window, well away from the only other occupants: a couple hunched together at a table at the back. The closeness of the blonde and dark heads suggested that they would have no interest in anyone else's conversation, but Maisie kept her voice low as she explained.

And now Elliott was worried.

About me.

She didn't know how she felt about that. It was strange, having someone *to* worry. Her colleagues knew a certain amount of risk was part of the job, and her family didn't know enough about what she did to worry. But now there was Elliott, with concern in his eyes. It sent a strange shiver through the pit of her stomach. She knew he wouldn't try to dissuade her – not that kind of man – but she found she didn't like putting that frown on his face.

'It's not really that big a risk.' She answered the question he wasn't asking. 'Whatever this is, if it is really anything at all, they want something from me. They're not going to mess that up. And I'm only the go-between – once they make contact, I'll be handing the whole thing off to Jake.'

'Yes. I see.' He nodded, understanding, and she was glad that some of the worry seemed to have lifted. He took a sip of his Oolong and gave her a sideways grin that was becoming very familiar. 'And if something came up that I had to research – something that required an urgent visit to the British Museum perhaps …?'

'Then perhaps we could have dinner. Or something,' she suggested. That "or something" vibrated in the air, sending another shiver through her.

'Good.' He didn't say anything more. Didn't need to – she could see that he was already planning that research trip. She dug in her bag for one of her cards, writing the address and the phone number of the apartment on the back and handing it over.

Elliott put it carefully into his wallet, which gave her a chance to admire his hands. Long fingers, square tips, elegantly shaped, but still working hands. Capable … She could imagine—

With an effort, she dragged her mind away from where it was going, looking at her watch. 'I need to get back to work. I'll phone you later.'

Elliott finished the last of his tea and they both stood up. In the back of the room the other couple were also on their feet. The man reached out to grip the woman's arm. 'Frankie, please—' He got no further. The woman shrugged out of his hold and headed for the stairs. Maisie put out her hand to halt their own exit, pausing in the shelter of a full-size model of a sedan chair that guarded the way down. She held her breath, very aware of Elliott still and silent beside her. The woman had her face averted, but Maisie caught a brief glimpse of her profile as she swept onto the stairs and clattered down. The man followed her with a muffled curse.

The room echoed with the movement. Maisie waited, counting to one hundred, until the sound of footsteps on the stairs faded.

At last Elliott shifted, turning to look at her. 'Someone you need to avoid? Work?'

Maisie shook her head, her stomach churning. 'Not work. That was my sister.'

But the man who was sitting so close wasn't my brother-in-law.

When Elliott returned to the University to check that nothing urgent had arrived in his in-tray before the end of the day, he found that Jenni had left a post-it note in her favourite place at the centre of his desk, reminding him that the deadline for an article in a popular women's magazine was approaching. His publisher's PR machine was keeping his latest book in the lower reaches of the bestseller list and the article was something that they'd arranged. There was no problem; it was done, just needing a last check before he sent it. He picked up the note and dropped into his office chair, making it creak as it took the strain. Normally the P.S. Jenni had added to the bottom of the note would have had him rolling his eyes, but not today.

They want a photograph of you, with a mummy! Suggested something at the British Museum?

He grinned at the note. *Yes!* On this occasion, Dr Elwood would be very happy to pose beside any number of the British Museum's mummies. He leaned back in the chair, carefully replacing the note on the desk.

Now he had a legitimate reason to go to London.

Excellent.

He wasn't so happy about Maisie's assignment, but this was her work. He had to trust McQuire wouldn't place her in a position of risk. His heart had begun to beat uncomfortably fast when she told him about the job. It had tripped again when they'd nearly run into her sister, Françoise, in the coffee house. He'd assumed that too was work related – someone she needed to avoid – until Maisie explained who the woman was. She'd been vague about the male companion and the reason for avoiding a meeting, and Elliott hadn't asked questions. She had implied previously that there was some sort of family estrangement. He didn't need to know more.

But if this thing is going where you think it's going, then you will eventually have to meet them ...

Whoa! Hold on a minute! Meeting the family?

He scoffed at the notion, pushing it out of his mind. Obstinately, it showed signs of hanging around. He pushed harder and it retreated a little. It wasn't gone entirely. He realised with a jolt that it *wouldn't* be leaving any time soon. What was happening between him and Maisie was unlike anything—

He was thrown out of his thoughts by a familiar thump on his door, followed by Ben's head appearing around the doorjamb. 'Fancy a quick drink?'

Elliott looked at his watch. It was a little early for him, but the bar in the Senior Common Room would be open.

Once there and settled over pints of the current guest beer, they chatted for a bit about campus gossip before Ben brought up the subject of the Necklace. 'Leyland was asking this morning if you'd heard anything. He seemed to think it was my responsibility to know.' He gave an exaggerated sigh. 'He always does.'

'Nothing to report,' Elliott said easily. He certainly wasn't sharing that McQuire's agency might have a lead.

'Gone for good then?'

'Looks that way. Into someone's private collection, I guess.'

Ben gave him a half smile. Elliott could see calculation in his eyes. *He's fishing for something*. It wasn't long in coming. 'Talking about private collections – someone said you'd been seeing the young woman who works for the billionaire. You met in Torquay?'

Elliott took a sip of his drink. He had his story. 'Ms Norris has business in this area – we've had dinner a couple of times,' he confirmed casually.

'Good. That's good.' Ben nodded enthusiastically. 'About time you started to circulate again – it's been what? Nearly a year since Annabel?'

'Araminta,' Elliott corrected. He would have left it there, having no wish to discuss either Maisie or his previous affair with a fellow academic he'd met at a conference. That liaison had faded from lack of attention, on both sides. From Ben's eager expression, he was waiting for more. His friend *loved* campus gossip. 'Ms Norris is based in London, so I'm not sure that anything will come of it.'

'Even so, it's good that you're seeing someone. All work and no play ...' Ben remonstrated. 'Will she be going to that fancy bash in London with you?'

'I have asked,' Elliott admitted.

Ben's face lit up in his characteristic beam. 'That's *great*.' He nudged Elliott with his elbow. 'Don't be slow off the mark, old son. If you're interested and the lady is interested, go for it. Make it happen.' His face clouded a little and the smile dropped. 'Might be better to avoid introducing her to Leyland though.'

'Why?' Elliott asked in surprise.

‘Oh well …’ Ben looked uncomfortable. ‘Just … well, he was speculating this morning, in the office, that the mystery billionaire was the one who had the Necklace. That he might have commissioned the theft. Stupid thing to say. You put me right on that, when *I* was being stupid about it. I wouldn’t want him to make that kind of remark to Ms Norris.’

‘I don’t think it would worry her if he did,’ Elliott responded. ‘I don’t know where the Necklace is, but I’m pretty certain her employer doesn’t have it.’ Actually, he was completely certain. ‘She’d probably tell Leyland so.’

‘Good for her,’ Ben approved, with a wide smile. ‘I really don’t know what the man is thinking about. He’s made a few weird remarks lately – and his mysterious trips to London.’ Ben shrugged. ‘Got some scheme on the boil. He’ll tell me in the end – when he wants some work done. Probably at an hour’s notice!’ He made a comic grimace that still had some chagrin behind it, putting down his empty glass. ‘You ready for another?’

The next morning, the plot thickened again when Leyland waylaid Elliott, walking beside him on the way back to his office from the library and pumping him – there was no other word for it – for details of collectors who might be interested in the Necklace. Elliott knew McQuire had three names. He only knew one of them and he wasn’t parting with that.

Leyland’s movements were jerky, his shoulders hunched, brow knitted in a frown, staring intently at Elliott, as if trying to read something in his face. Elliott stared back, confused. Then, abruptly, Leyland straightened up and started to talk about weekend plans. Mind whirling, Elliott made up a noncommittal response about seeing a friend.

‘Good, good.’ Now Leyland seemed lost in his own thoughts. Elliott suspected that if he’d claimed to be spending the weekend lion-taming, the response would have been the same.

‘And yourself?’ he asked, wondering if he would get any reaction.

‘Oh.’ With a jolt, Leyland came out of his distraction, focusing slightly bloodshot blue eyes on Elliott. ‘Playing this weekend.’ His voice dropped and his expression could almost be said to be conspiratorial. ‘High-stakes you know, but I have hopes.’ He gave a bark of laughter. ‘Glad to have this talk. Very glad indeed. Completely sound – knew that nonsense couldn't be right – totally unreliable.' Muttering the last sentence to himself, he turned on his heel and strode off.

Blinking, Elliott continued on down the corridor, passing Jenni's desk on the way to his own room. She looked up. 'The Dean was looking for you.'

'Yes, he found me.' Elliott cast a look back over his shoulder, still confused over what the exchange had been about. Was Leyland losing it? Overworked, with too many plots hatching? Or did he have something weighing on his mind? *Or his conscience?* 'He was talking about the weekend. Playing for high-stakes.'

'Oh.' Jenni was sorting paperwork into bundles and clipping them together. 'That would be his poker school.'

Elliott let himself into his office and settled down to work, although the conversation with Leyland lurked on the edge of his mind. Hadn't Maisie said something about the lounge lizard cousin, Armand, being a high-stakes poker player? He filed the thought away to pass on.

It was nearly an hour later before it occurred to him that the Dean might have been clumsily attempting to discover if *he* had the contacts to dispose of the Necklace. He leaned back in his creaky chair, remembering those last muttered and cryptic words. *Was that it?* If so, it seemed that he had passed the interrogation, which was good to know – but what might have put that idea in Leyland's head in the first place? And why?

Chapter Nineteen

Maisie let herself into the apartment and dropped her suitcase by the door – the kind of small case that would be used for a business trip. She had packed some necessities from her own place but everything else she needed would already be here. She looked around. It was an upmarket service flat with comfortable but non-descript furnishings. She knew that Cassie had been drafted in to add the throws, cushions and artwork, as well as books and potted plants, which lifted the place into something that looked like someone's home. There would be toiletries in the bathroom and groceries in the kitchen with bottles and packets opened to indicate use. There were even clothes in the wardrobe, although they weren't actually hers. Towels and bed linen were supplied as part of the service arrangement for the block.

She prowled over to the window. The flat was on the fifth floor. Cars and taxis flowed by in the street below, but there was only a very faint sound of traffic. Jake thought it unlikely that anyone would try to break in to snoop, but they weren't taking any chances. Maisie crossed to the smaller bag she had put down next to her suitcase, taking out the photo frames, ornaments and holiday mementos she had gathered up before leaving Bath. She wandered around the sitting room and bedroom arranging them. Hector, the stuffed hippo that she'd had since she was five, sat on the small dressing table. When she'd unpacked her cosmetics, hair brush and straighteners, it didn't look much different from the bedroom in her own flat.

She drifted back to the main room and over to the desk in the corner. Carl, the recently promoted Head of Security, had brought up the accumulated post for Ms Norris and left it in a neat pile, along with the parcel that had been taken in by the concierge. There was also a handful of bills and letters under a glass paperweight, faked to support her identity. Maisie shuffled through them, curious. It appeared, from the two credit card bills, that the Maisie Norris who lived here had a taste for expensive underwear, liked the theatre and frequented the Italian restaurant at the end of the street. *Hard to fault any of that*. She was pretty sure that she'd find the underwear in one of the drawers in the bedroom. She detected both Michelle and Cassie's hands in this, and if that was the case all the details would be perfect.

She was as set up as she could be. She frowned. Elliott had passed on the information that Vaisey Leyland had been quizzing him on his knowledge of collectors and was a poker player. She'd relayed the details to Jake. Irrelevant, or a piece of the puzzle they needed to make fit? She didn't know, but at the moment she wasn't going to worry over it. She felt safe enough. Carl was a first line of backup in an emergency. There was history there with Jake, but she didn't know what it was. Maybe she'd ask Cassie.

She went to the kitchen to make herself a cup of coffee and brought it back, sitting down to go through the unopened envelopes that Carl had brought – the fishing expeditions from her unknown correspondent. She inspected the outsides first – not much point in wondering about fingerprints, not without something to compare them with – and the postage details were uninformative. Five assorted envelopes, some of them brightly coloured, all posted in the Greater London area within twenty-four hours of each other. It suggested to Maisie that someone had taken a trip around the city on the Tube, stopping at post boxes along the way.

The contents didn't tell her much – advertising material and charity appeals, the sort of thing that dropped through thousands of letterboxes every day. Easy to get hold of and recycle into fresh envelopes. Maisie looked them over carefully, but cute puppies and exotic holidays didn't suggest anything that could be remotely considered as a clue. There was no note or message of any kind. Whoever had sent them was being super careful. What had they hoped to achieve? Confirmation that she did actually live here? The possibility of overhearing some remark about them from a member of staff? She considered two oversized envelopes in lurid pink. Something easy to identify if the snooper could get a look at residents' mail being delivered?

Making up her mind to think further about that one, she turned her attention to the parcel. A box of books – a mix of brand-new bestsellers, travel books, thrillers and romances. At least she'd have something to read. She lifted them out, one at a time, but again the shiny covers and pristine pages didn't tell her anything.

Until the last book in the box.

She recognised that one. The glossy coffee table book that accompanied a recent TV series on Egyptian archaeology written by one Dr Elliott Elwood. Coincidence? A message? A joke? Maisie examined the book carefully, page by page, but yet again it didn't tell her anything.

It was brand-new and untouched, like all the others. She rested her hand on it, looking down at the small author photograph on the back. Elliott stared moodily up at her, serious and snooty, every inch the eminent academic.

Something in her chest twisted. She'd thought that was what he was like, but she'd been wrong. She picked up the book with the others to place on a half empty shelf. Its presence could have been random, an accident, but somehow she didn't think so. It felt like a marker. "I'm watching you." "I know something." "I *want* something"?

Disturbed at her own thoughts, she went back to the box, rummaging in the bottom, but there was no paperwork, no invoice. It had been arranged to look like a delivery made in error, but with no originating address. After a moment, she gathered up the books again and returned them to the box. *Do what any honest citizen would do – hand them back to the concierge.*

Why the books? A hope – an anticipation – that they would be brought straight up to the apartment? It was a valid idea and might have worked if the staff had not had specific instructions on how to deal with post and deliveries. The sender would have needed to wait and watch in the lobby for the courier. Maisie experienced a mixed swirl of emotions – a slight visceral unease at the idea of a watcher, but a much stronger surge of frustration that the thief could have been so close and she had missed them.

There would be another approach, she was sure of that. Her instructions from Jake were to act naturally. She had to remember that and resist the impulse to make too much of a display – no hanging around in the foyer, no ostentatious conversations with the doorman, the concierge or the reception staff. Whoever this was, she sensed nervousness and caution. There would be no confrontation in a public place. The message to be delivered, the transaction to be arranged, was a private matter, not one for an audience. It would happen. No point in trying to force it.

Put it out of your head. Think about something else. Think about Elliott.

Actually, maybe thinking about Elliott wasn't such a good idea. Wondering where he was ... What he was doing ...

She picked up her cooling coffee and crossed the room to sit on the sofa, resting against the well stuffed cushions. She was tired and on edge, understandable in the circumstances. The quiet and the untouched feeling of the place was oppressive. Impulsively, she rose again and, pushing aside the protective glazing, opened the window, letting in late afternoon sun and the scents and noises of the street; she immediately felt better. It was stupid to be missing Elliott. She'd only known him a matter of weeks. The book had clearly unsettled her.

She ground her teeth a little as she thought back to their meeting in the coffee house. He was *worried* about her. She hadn't entirely unpicked the implications of that yet and wasn't sure that she wanted to. He hadn't said a word to dissuade her, recognising this was her job, which did tell her a lot. He hadn't said anything about them almost running into Fran either. *And that's a whole new can of worms.* What the hell was her perfect sister doing huddled with a stranger, when she should have been playing the yummy mummy, picking her daughters up from school? Who *was* that guy?

Do you care?

The thought made her frown.

Do you?

Maisie found on a sigh that she did. Fran had looked unhappy, bolting to get free from the man. Was her sister in some sort of trouble? Despite trying to cut her ties with her family as far as she could, it *did* matter. *Something else to be unpicked.* Elliott hadn't quizzed her, but he had to be curious about her relationship with her family. Should things develop …

A picture of her mother's delighted and astonished face rose in her mind. The family misfit managing to snare a man – and not just any man!

With a shudder, Maisie shut down on the very idea. She couldn't do that to Elliott. Couldn't do it to *herself.* She swallowed the remains of the nearly cold coffee and put down the mug. If she stayed here, looking at four walls, her brain would keep leading her down alleys she had no desire to explore. She had to *focus.* She was here to do a job. At the moment, that job was to look like the personal assistant to a reclusive billionaire who had just arrived home for the weekend from a business trip. What would that woman do?

She got up, dithered about closing the window, then decided to leave it open. *Sign of occupation.* Hunting in the cupboard under the sink, she found a supermarket bag. She would do what any woman might do, coming back from a trip. Go to the supermarket for milk and bread.

She was wandering down the King's Road, enjoying the sunshine and the shops when her phone vibrated. *Elliott.*

'Hi.' The warmth in his voice seemed to push the heat of the sun up a few notches. 'Are you there yet?' She heard him laugh softly. 'The classic question.'

'I am. Right now, I'm walking down the King's Road.' She dodged past a woman with a double buggy, smiling at the older child who was waving a one-eared rabbit and laughing.

'Sounds good. I was wondering – I know you're working, but could you use some company? Only I have this photo shoot at the British Museum …'

Maisie knew that her smile was very wide indeed as she ended the call and dropped the phone back into her bag. Elliott would be arriving tomorrow evening from Bath, to stay at a hotel off Sloane Square. They would have the remainder of the weekend together, before he had his picture taken with a mummy on Monday morning. She breezed into the supermarket, not even wincing when a blast of air-conditioned cold hit her as she passed through the doors. The brief for this job was to act natural. What could be more natural than to spend the weekend with your … friend? There was no way she could call Elliott her *boy*friend and he wasn't her lover. *Not yet*, a provocative voice whispered in her head.

Hmm. She looked at the crowded aisles of Friday night shoppers. The weather forecast was good. Maybe on Sunday they could go out for the day? Kew Gardens, perhaps? Picking up a basket, she headed for the deli counter and the ingredients for a picnic.

Chapter Twenty

They'd rattled down to Kew on the Tube, entering the gardens by the Victoria Gate. Elliott lifted his face to the sun, squinting over a shining body of water, before they crossed to go into the Palm House. His train from Bath had not arrived until nearly midnight, after some problem with signal failure. When he'd finally checked into his hotel and phoned her, Maisie's suggestion that they spend the day here together had quelled a lot of his frustration at not being able to meet her for dinner. He'd thought she might want to remain visible, close to the apartment, but she'd vetoed that. Her instructions from Jake were to act naturally. Not to look as if she was waiting to be approached. He could get on board with that, so now they had the whole day.

And maybe more …

He banked that thought to concentrate on the moment, inhaling the humid air of the huge conservatory, heavy with the scent of damp vegetation.

'It's amazing. This place was built in 1844.' Maisie had her head tipped back, looking at the bowed metal frame that supported the expanse of glass. 'Some of the plants are older than that.'

Elliott wasn't looking at the structure or the plants. He was looking at Maisie. Her hair was loose, curling widely around her face in the damp air. The strappy blue and green sundress and the expanse of tanned bare leg on show were far more interesting than a potted plant, however venerable. She laughed, fanning herself. 'It's also very hot. Let's get out of here, before I melt.'

He wasn't going to argue. The floppy brimmed hat he'd chosen to wear felt too small in the humid heat, but that and the dark glasses contributed to a disguise of sorts. He wasn't recognised too often as "that man off of the telly", but it did happen and he didn't want anything interrupting their day and putting Maisie into her professional mode 'Shall we look for somewhere to eat this feast you've packed?' The backpack wasn't heavy, but he'd rather eat the contents than carry it.

Maisie took Elliott's hand, letting her fingers linger on the intriguing calluses, and navigated them to the nearest door, gasping a little as they emerged into the fresh air. 'This way, I think.'

They found a spot in the Mediterranean garden, close to the King William IV Temple, shaded by some cypress trees. When Elliott nodded his approval, Maisie unfolded the blanket she'd been carrying and collapsed inelegantly on it. Elliott followed her down, drawing up his long legs and removing the ridiculous hat and the glasses, running his hand through his hair and looking around, inspecting their surroundings. She'd laughed when they'd met at Sloane Square station and she'd seen the hat, but then she understood. There had been a couple more occasions, since the one in the restaurant, when they'd been together and people had asked for an autograph or selfie. She'd had to steel herself to be on her guard, but not overzealous. Sometimes people simply stared, nudging each other and whispering. It was disconcerting and she couldn't imagine being watched like that. *But isn't that what you're doing, letting yourself be seen by some watcher?*

That was the reason she'd wanted to escape here for the day. She inhaled deeply, picking up the scent of rosemary and lavender, and looked at Elliott. Today, in cotton chinos and a dark T-shirt that fitted over some interesting muscles, he was a million miles away from the stuffy academic she'd thought he was. The academic was still in there somewhere, but today she had the man, relaxed and laughing. As if feeling her scrutiny, he turned. Her breath caught as she met his eyes. She leaned forward, heart thumping suddenly, reaching for his shoulder. His mouth was soft and warm, pressing against hers, but not starting anything that couldn't be finished in a public place, she realised as he finally pulled away. There was a promise there though; one she fully intended to collect on.

'Shall we eat?' She dived into the pack Elliott had shed along with the hat and glasses, drawing out baguettes, roast chicken and a container of salad from the cool bag.

Once they'd finished the meal with grapes and tiny pots of rich chocolate mousse, she lay back on the rug, watching the sun playing on the pale leaves of a clump of olive trees. They might almost have been in the South of France. 'I could have been in Nice right now, getting ready for my wedding,' she said idly, without thinking.

'What!' Elliott had been collecting debris from their meal and slipping it back into the bag. 'You were going to get married?'

'Um, well, not really.' Maisie bit her lip, knowing she'd been indiscreet. She was relaxed in Elliott's company and had let her tongue run away with her. *And a couple of glasses of rosé wine might have helped a little.*

Elliott was leaning over her, looking confused and maybe a little angry.

And hot. Very hot. Like ... smoking.

'It was a job.' She explained briefly about the scam to catch the scammer. 'He didn't take the bait, not with me.'

'Then I can only say that he had very poor taste.'

The anger and confusion were gone, but not the hotness. Maisie wasn't sure that was a word but she really didn't care as he was running a finger gently along the line of her jaw with an air of discovery.

'Your job. It's a masquerade isn't it, always being someone else?'

'Not always,' she said softly. 'And never with you.' She raised her hand, pulling him down, sealing the pledge with a kiss.

I saw her. This morning. Coming down the steps of the apartment block.

Maisie Norris.

No mistaking that red hair.

None of the ploys so far have worked. I knew they would need luck.

But today I *saw* her.

I was too far away to follow. By the time I'd crossed the road, she was out of sight.

It doesn't matter now. Now all I have to do is watch and wait.

And finally be bold.

Worth the risk.

What is it they say – "seize the day"?

I know now what I'm going to do.

This *will* work.

Chapter Twenty-One

Maisie and Elliott emerged gratefully from the fug of the late summer Tube into the evening sunlight of Sloane Square. Elliott looked around at the numerous restaurants, with tables spilling onto the pavement. It was early, but they were already filling up. 'Um. I can walk with you to your flat. Or we could have dinner – pick one of these places.' He gestured to the selection. 'Or there's the restaurant at the hotel. I think they have a terrace.'

When Maisie shook her head, his heart sank a little. They'd had a brilliant day and now—

'Does your hotel have room service for food?'

'Er, yes, it does.' Now his heart had shot up so hard it was almost lodged in his throat.

She looked up at him, clear-eyed. 'Then that's what I would like. I'd like to go to your hotel room and then maybe later we can order dinner.' He heard her breath hitch just a little. 'If that's what you would like too.'

'Oh yes,' he said fervently. 'I would like that very, very much.'

Elliott's sinfully abused heart was beating double time. *Like an overexcited teenager on a first date.* He waved the key card in front of the lock on his room and stood aside to let Maisie in. He couldn't remember when being with a woman had felt like this, had been so … important. *Maybe not since you* were *a teenager?*

'This is nice.' Maisie moved to stand in a patch of sunlight, turning slowly to take in her surroundings. It *was* nice. Arriving late on Saturday, he'd got an unexpected upgrade and there was a palatial bathroom and a seating area, as well as a king-size bed.

But the room faded into insignificance when he looked at Maisie. Her hair was curling wildly, a golden red halo around her head and spilling onto her shoulders which had caught a little of the sun, just slightly flushed to a rosy warmth. She dropped the blanket and her handbag on the floor. Abruptly he realised, with just a hint of shock, that he needed to lose the hat, sunglasses and backpack. By the time he'd unceremoniously dumped them, she had crossed the room again, putting a hand on his chest, laughing as she felt the tell-tale race of his heart. She lifted his hand and placed it just over her breast. Her heart was beating just as fast.

'What … what do you want … need?' He had to get the words out while he still could.

'I want you to take me to bed, Dr Elwood.' She looked up at him with a wicked smile. 'Show me how an Egyptologist makes love.'

'Uh. I think that would be the same as anyone else does.' His words *were* making sense but his mind was scrambling around "make love".

'There's really only one way to find out then.' She lifted a finger to tap his chin.

He knew then, with perfect certainty, that this would not be like anything he'd experienced before. It would be much, much better.

The first kiss was soft, just a gentle meeting of mouths. Sensation vibrated through him. Maisie's hands crept under his T-shirt, exploring the planes of his abdomen and running her fingers around to his back, pulling him towards her. He cupped her breast through the cotton of her dress and deepened the kiss, excitement flaring as she rose on her toes to meet and match him, holding herself close against him.

'Skin.' She did no more than whisper the word, but it felt like she'd lit a fire. It took seconds to haul the shirt over his head and let it drop, who cared where, so that she could have what she wanted. Her hands played over him, tracing pectorals and ribs as he reached to unbutton the straps of the sundress, so that the bodice fell away. What was underneath was a vision of turquoise silk and lace, but it was the creamy skin and deep valley of her breasts that stuttered his breath. He reached around her back – the skin there smooth and warm – to unfasten the clasp and then he had it all in his hands as the silk and lace drifted to the floor.

Holding his breath, holding his control, he traced a line of kisses along her jaw and down her neck as she tipped her head to give him access. *Not yet, not yet.* Her breasts lay in his hands and he stroked them with his thumbs, softly, teasing, hearing her whimper and feeling the pulse thunder in her throat. *Perfect. She's perfect.* He worked downwards with butterfly kisses, inhaling her scent until at last his lips closed on the tight, rosy-brown nipple and her body spasmed against him. He caressed and nuzzled, licked and kissed, her hands buried now in his hair, pulling at his scalp in a way that sent shockwaves through him. The chemistry that had exploded when they first kissed was flaring now – adrenaline, endorphins, *something* – pulsing so strongly he could barely keep on his feet. Maisie was clinging to him, body rocking against him. 'Have to make it to the bed,' he half gasped.

If they didn't, they'd be a tangled heap on the floor.

'Yes.' With an effort he could feel, Maisie pulled away from him, taking a faltering step back, wobbling in his grasp. Without even thinking he pulled her up into his arms, carrying her over and letting her fall back onto white linen sheets.

Maisie looked up, eyes dazed with lust. *Not lust. Elliott.* She hadn't imagined it could be like this. His scent, his smooth skin, the sleek muscles under her hands, the feel of the hard outline trapped in the cotton of the chinos. She lifted herself up on her elbow to watch as he shed the remainder of his clothes and she got to see – everything.

Then he was back, helping her out of her dress, still tangled at her waist, and then the remaining scrap of turquoise silk. She giggled as his fingers unintentionally tickled and he kissed her shoulder in apology, laughing too. His mouth found places on her skin that were so sensitive it almost hurt, she wanted him so much. Her head was swimming but she focused when he paused, searching her face and she saw the small packet in his hands.

'Yes.' Her attention suddenly sharp, she reached to take it from him. She would do this. The feel of him as she smoothed and stroked, the way his breath hummed, stirred the heat of her core to fever pitch. And then he was *there*, with a smooth powerful glide, and they were together in the most elemental way as her muscles tightened around him. He stopped moving, holding himself above her for a long breathless moment, looking into her eyes, trapping her gaze in a dark, steady stare and holding it as the rhythm began and built between them.

Then he was urging her up, until the world shattered and they both came undone.

Elliott put down his knife and fork and leaned back. Maisie was sitting cross-legged on the end of the bed, wrapped in an oversize hotel bathrobe, munching on a fully loaded hamburger and dipping fries into a glass pot of very upmarket tomato sauce that had come with the room service meal. He watched as she licked salt off her fingers, trying to imagine Araminta, or Rochelle or Eliza doing the same. He couldn't imagine it. Maisie was nothing like the cool-eyed and cool-blooded women he usually dated. She wasn't like any woman he had ever known.

She'd powered her way through that template – shattered it – the moment he saw her at that charity bash, falling out of the screaming pink dress. *You just didn't realise it.* Those sophisticated, civilised relationships, the meeting of sophisticated civilised minds ... There had been sex – very good sex on occasion – but the earth never really moved. *And you never wanted it to.*

Maisie hadn't just moved the earth, she'd completely reorganised the world.

The whole day – the picnic, the sunshine, the laughter, making love, eating hamburgers. It should have been hundreds of miles out of his comfort zone, too strange to be even contemplated. It wasn't. It just felt … right.

She looked up and saw him staring. 'What? Have I got ketchup on my chin?'

'No. I was just … Can you … will you stay?' Just for a second, he thought her eyes clouded. Then she nodded and he could breathe again.

Chapter Twenty-Two

Jake McQuire lounged against the headboard of the bed and watched his wife dress. Not quite as good as watching her *undress,* but good enough. She was fastening her earrings and looking around as if searching for something.

'Over by the door,' he suggested.

'Ah! I knew I got them out.' Cassie padded over to where her shoes stood beside her handbag and slid her feet into them. 'Are you planning to stay there all day?'

'I'm not the one who organised an 8 a.m. site meeting with a client,' he reminded her loftily. 'And I am working. I'm thinking.'

Instead of the mocking response he expected, Cassie crossed the room to sit on the edge of the bed. He moved his feet to give her space. 'Maisie – and the Necklace,' she said softly.

'Yes.' Jake put his hands behind his head. Cassie knew him so well. 'Mickey came through late last night, after you and junior had gone to sleep.'

'And you were here mulling it over all night? You could have woken me.'

'Nah – It wasn't all night and you both need your rest.' The idea that by next year he would be a father curled around his heart with joy and trepidation.

'What did Mickey say?' Cassie pulled him back to the concerns of the night.

'He's now one hundred per cent sure that none of the players we've been watching were involved in the theft. He thinks the Countess may have an approach from one of her private clients a few weeks ago about acquiring the piece, but it didn't go any further.'

'So, whoever the thieves are, they're not professionals – or not one of the bigger sort,' Cassie corrected herself. 'That fits with the idea that one of the family is involved. But that's not what's bothering you, is it?'

Jake grunted. His wife always knew when and where to dig.

'If this isn't a professional thing,' she continued, 'then the likelihood of Dr Elwood being forcibly pressured into a valuation is a lot less … But if one of their prospective buyers is Mr Elladour, Maisie is right in the frame.' Cassie tilted her head enquiringly. 'And it continues to bother you.'

Jake nodded. 'The trip to Torquay was meant to be a watching brief. It was never intended to expose her like this.'

'But it has, and she will do her job, like the professional she is,' Cassie pointed out.

'I know. I just don't like it.'

'Softy.' His wife found one of his feet under the mound of the duvet and squeezed. 'She's not in danger. She's a valuable commodity, the conduit to the mysterious billionaire. Once the contact is made, her part is over.'

'And I step up to the plate.'

'Mmm …' Apparently forgetting her appointment, Cassie settled herself more comfortably on the bed. 'How are you going to play that, given that Mr Elladour has about six possible identities?'

'That's what I was wondering about while you were snoring.' Jake hastily drew up his feet, out of Cassie's reach. If she started to tickle him … *Discretion is the better part of valour*. 'I take it back, you don't snore. Much,' he added softly under his breath.

Cassie gave him a suspicious stare, but let it go. 'Do you have an identity ready for Mr Elladour?'

'Michelle is organising something.' Gingerly, he extended his legs again, ready to move if there was an ambush. 'As long as the money is in place, which it will be, I don't think anyone will be too worried about where it's coming from.'

'Probably not,' Cassie agreed with a pout, before pointing a finger. 'You be careful too.'

Jake leaned forward to pull her into his arms. 'Always.'

Maisie fastened the straps of her sundress and smoothed out a few creases. Elliott was fixing cufflinks into an expensive-looking shirt, getting ready for his photo shoot at the Museum. Without thinking, she crossed the room to offer a hand. He looked up with a smile. 'Thanks. Are you sure you don't want breakfast?'

She shook her head. 'Coffee is fine.' Her cup was cooling on the dresser. In a few moments, she would leave to walk back to the flat – she absolutely refused to think of it as a walk of shame. What had happened between her and Elliott last night, and again early this morning, was nothing to be ashamed of. It had been glorious, but even so …

The link fastened, Elliott turned his hand to capture her fingers, looking down at her, his eyes dark and intent. Was there a question there?

Ignoring whatever it was, if it was anything at all, she pulled away gently, scooping up the cup to gulp down her coffee before picking up the backpack and the blanket. 'Good luck with the photos. I'll call you.'

She wasn't sure whether she heard a sharp intake of breath. He hadn't moved but she knew his eyes were still on her as she walked to the door with a deliberate tread.

'Maisie …'

Hand on the doorknob, she turned and took one last look, fighting the thrill of sensation that ran through her. In tailored trousers and that shirt, he looked …

She swallowed down the emotions that were trying to brim up through her chest. She knew the words. She had to say them. 'This …' Instinctively, her eyes flicked to the spectacularly unmade bed. 'This doesn't change anything.'

This doesn't change anything.

The words she'd uttered fizzed around Maisie's brain as she left the hotel and started towards Sloane Square. No commitment. That was the golden rule, the mantra for her relationships. Choose carefully. Stay in control. Keep it light. Over when it's over – no looking back, no hard feelings.

Sleeping with Elliott really *didn't* change anything. *Yeah – and who are you kidding? It doesn't change anything – except that it does. That it has.*

Who would have guessed that her snooty academic would be the perfect lover?

This – thing – with Elliott was unexpected. *But it feels right.* She brushed the idea away. Elliott was dangerous, to her poise, to her self-control – to her heart? With a burst of something like panic, she shoved that crazy thought ruthlessly out of her head.

Friends, now lovers. That's *all.*

Over when it's over.

Maisie dodged around a couple of shop workers who were dawdling along the pavement, sipping coffee from take-out cups and nibbling doughnuts. The scent of the coffee and sugar made Maisie's stomach growl. She needed to get home – well, back to the flat – and put herself back together. She had things to do.

So that she could continue to work while maintaining her cover, Jake had set her up with a delicate investigation into a financial adviser with a taste for modern art who had disappeared, alongside a large chunk of clients' money. The guy's parents were insisting that their son was a missing person, not a thief, and had commissioned the agency to investigate. The places those inquiries would take her would fit with those that the PA to a billionaire might visit in the course of her work. All it had to do was look right from the outside, and if the guy really was missing, she owed him and his parents her best shot.

She had to think of that and not how good it felt waking up this morning in Elliott's bed. She was independent, self-contained, *not* needy and clinging. It was a fling, an affair, nothing more. She *couldn't* want more. *If they were to become an item*—that thought was too conflicted to contemplate.

She'd come to the corner of Sloane Square, joining the clump of people waiting at the crossing for a string of nose-to-tail double-decker buses to pass. Even at this time in the morning, the area was busy with early commuters. The buses finally passed and the crowd surged forward. Maisie went with them, her mind still on Elliott. Yesterday at Kew … She should never have suggested it. She could see that now …

She had almost reached the far curb when she felt it – a thump in the small of her back – and suddenly she was falling, jerked out of her thoughts with the road coming up to meet her.

'Hey! Careful!' A hand grabbed her, holding her back from contact with the ground and half shoving, half scooping her onto the safety of the opposite pavement as a taxi skidded by, horn blaring. Maisie found herself looking up into the concerned face of a tall black woman in a London Underground uniform. 'You okay?'

Maisie shook her head to clear it. 'Yes, thanks. I thought I was going down.'

'So did I.' The woman grinned, then her face sobered. 'I think the guy behind elbowed you. In a hurry to get to the Tube, I suppose.' She shrugged in a what-can-you-do gesture.

Maisie looked around. Whoever the guy was, he was long gone. Her heart rate was coming back to normal and the tide of pedestrians was swirling around them like a break in the flow of a river. 'I'm fine now, thank you.'

Her rescuer gave her another smile and a small salute, and melted back into the crowd. Maisie walked slowly down the quieter side streets that would take her back to the flat. Had someone pushed her? She'd felt *something* but it couldn't have been intentional. She took a breath and walked on, only getting a few steps before her phone began to vibrate in her bag. *Elliott?*

Her heart started to thump again as she extracted the phone. 'Hello?'

'Maisie? It's me.' She wasn't sure if she was happy or crestfallen when she identified her brother's voice. *Happy. You're happy.*

'Hal. You're an early bird.' She squinted at her watch. It wasn't eight o'clock yet.

'I wanted to catch you before you went to work. Is it a good time? Are you already on your way? I can hear traffic.'

'Er ... yes.' Maisie diverted under the awning and up the steps of an Italian restaurant that would not be open for a few hours yet. It was a fraction quieter. 'What do you need?'

She heard Hal give a bark of laughter. 'Could it be that I just thought I'd like to talk to my sister?'

Well, no, but she wasn't going to say that. 'Is Mum giving you grief over the wedding and you want a shoulder to cry on?' she suggested.

'If I want a shoulder, Stephen's are wider, but no, she's fine. Apparently, someone from her book group organised a wedding for her gay son six months ago.'

Maisie didn't need to know any more. 'Yours will be bigger. And better.'

'Of course.' Hal laughed again; this time it was soft and easy. *He's happy and he's in love.* 'As long as Steve and I manage to get hitched somewhere in all the fuss, I don't really care.'

'Well, if it gets too much and you want help to elope, just say the word.'

'I'll bear your offer in mind.'

If grandmother was still alive, that's what you'd have to do. Maisie could almost see the soul-shrinking glare of the coal-black eyes, the perpetually disapproving downturned mouth. The idea that instead of a carefully selected *suitable* bride, her grandson would walk down the aisle with another *man* ... Well, at least Stella Webster was doing her best to shed some of her own mother's rigid opinions and expectations – although not all of them. Some of them were just too deeply ingrained. Maisie straightened her shoulders. She refused to acknowledge that her grandmother's lingering presence had any influence on *her*. She'd built a life, she was in control. She didn't need anyone's approval.

Hal's voice drew her back to the phone call, away from her drifting thoughts 'I'm not thinking of eloping just yet – but it is about the wedding that I was calling.' Hal paused.

'Yes?' Maisie felt a small flicker of alarm run down her spine.

'I want you to be my best man … woman … person,' Hal said in a rush. 'Steve's sister is standing up with him, and I'd like it if you'd do the same for me.'

'You want me?' Maisie only just kept the squeak out of her response. 'But what about Fran …?'

'I want *you*.' For a second, Maisie could hear the steely lawyer in her brother's voice. 'Please.'

'I …' She dragged in a breath. It was the *please* that got her, of course. 'All right, yes. I'll do it. If you really want me.'

'I do. Um …' The steel was gone now and Hal sounded almost nervous again. 'Can you come to the family dinner next Sunday, meet Steve, and we can talk about it?'

Maisie found herself agreeing that she could do that. Next weekend, she'd be back in Bath, her job here done. *And Elliott will be back in Bath too.* She shut her mind down on that, said goodbye to Hal, and stuffed the phone back in her bag. Life seemed to be getting damn complicated. What the hell did a *best person* have to do? Cassie would know.

She gathered her scattered thoughts again and walked briskly along to the mansion block, smiling at the uniformed doorman as he let her in before looking carefully but surreptitiously around the foyer with its large plants and shaded lights. There were people about, sitting on the pink velvet sofas or queuing to speak to a receptionist. A woman in a hijab was playing peak-a-boo with a toddler beside the door, possibly waiting for a taxi. A family with a large amount of luggage seemed to be checking in for a short stay. A dark-haired woman sat alone, head down, intent on an e-reader. As Maisie walked across the expanse of burgundy carpet to the lift bank, another young woman stepped out, waving to a man who was waiting for her by the desk. *All low-key and normal*? Any of them might be there to get a sight of her, or none of them. She caught the lift before the doors closed and pushed the button for the fifth floor.

Once inside the flat, Maisie disposed of the folded blanket on a footstool and shrugged the backpack off her shoulders, lowering it to the floor to take a quick look round. A brief inspection showed there was no sign of anything being disturbed. She hadn't really expected it, but knew that her deep exhale was a signal of relief as she returned to the backpack.

She was reaching forward to undo the zip, so that she could empty it, when a flash of white took her eye. An envelope, tucked into one of the deep panniers on the side of the pack. Holding it carefully by the edges, she drew it out.

It was an ordinary, plain white office envelope. It had her name typed on it – *Ms Maisie Norris*. Her heart rate escalated. She breathed in to steady it. This was what had nearly made her fall on the crossing. Not a man elbowing her out of his way, but sliding the envelope into the pannier. *A hand under the pack, steadying it for the manoeuvre perhaps?* It must have shaken him when she'd pitched forward. Whatever, there was no way to trace him now. She'd barely seen the back of his head as he brushed past, never mind his face.

Her heart settled into a heavy thumping yet again as she carried the letter over to the desk, armed herself with gloves and a paper knife, and carefully slit the envelope, pulling out the single sheet of paper by its edges and smoothing it flat.

The message was short and clear.

Should your employer wish to participate in an auction for the purchase of the Cleopatra Necklace, further instructions may be obtained from the number below.

The number meant nothing to Maisie. It was undoubtedly a burner – a virtually untraceable single-use mobile phone. Her fingers itched to dial it, but she knew that would be wrong. This had to be handled from the office. She pulled out her own phone to call Jake.

Chapter Twenty-Three

Elliott posed beside a statue of Sekhmet, the lioness-headed goddess, in what he hoped was an elegantly studious fashion, while the photographer snapped what seemed like enough shots to fill a hundred years' worth of magazines. Backed up by the museum official who was escorting them, he'd managed to persuade the photographer, and the editorial assistant who had accompanied him "to get some off-the-cuff quotes", that tasteful pictures next to statues would be better than poses involving a mummy. The young woman, whose name was Sophie, chatted enthusiastically about how thrilled the magazine was to be running a feature on him at this exciting time.

When she repeated that for the third time, Elliott tuned her out and thought about Maisie instead – specifically about that last remark, "This doesn't change anything". She'd lied, he knew that, and it wasn't wishful thinking on his part. But there had been a trace of something else in her eyes. He couldn't completely identify it, except that it almost looked like panic.

He was called back to his surroundings when the photographer asked him to move to stand in front of a plaque – a stele – showing the gods Anubis and Osiris. The escort was looking at his watch – the Museum would be opening to the public soon. Sophie was still bubbling on – something about honour and recognition. For a second, he thought he heard Leyland's name in the flow of words before the girl shut up abruptly, blushing a bright pink. But Leyland wasn't involved in the arrangements for this photo shoot. With his mind wandering, he must have misheard. Sophie, poor girl, had obviously noticed that he wasn't listening to her and been embarrassed. Feeling a heavy twinge of guilt, he sent her a smile of reassurance and apology. The guilt receded a bit when she tentatively smiled back. *The poor kid is only trying to do her job.*

At the request of the photographer, Elliott crossed to stand on the other side of the stele for a couple of dozen more shots.

'Are we done?' He turned to the photographer, who had at last let his camera drop. When the man nodded, he held out his hand. 'Thank you. It was an interesting experience.'

The museum official looked relieved as Sophie and the photographer turned to leave, muttering to Elliott that there was coffee waiting in the offices – and colleagues eager to hear the details of the Egyptian items from the Pentecost Collections. Elliott stifled a sigh. He was happy to talk shop with an interested and informed audience, but now it would be a while before he was able to concentrate on texting Maisie.

Maisie couldn't decide if it was a feeling of disappointment or relief that was uppermost in her mind. The contact was made. Her part was over. She'd gone through everything with Jake and Michelle over the phone and sent pictures of the note. They would put things in place to take up the invitation to the auction. It had been agreed that Maisie would stay in London to investigate the missing financial adviser and maintain her billionaire PA persona for the rest of the week, before quietly fading away. The original note was being sent back to Bath by special courier. Carl from Security had arranged it. It was unlikely to have fingerprints or anything else useful, but it would be checked, just in case.

Showered, dressed from a wardrobe distinctly more upmarket than her usual work-wear and replete with a breakfast of eggs and toast, Maisie took the lift down to the basement car park. The first stop in her investigation was Uxbridge, so she had decided to drive there rather than take the Tube. The lift doors opened out onto the gloom of the underground space. Her car, another upgrade on her regular wheels, was parked in the furthest corner.

She'd almost reached it, about to flip the controls to unlock the doors, when she sensed a movement behind her.

'Don't turn around.' The voice was robotic but clear. *A voice distorter.*

'What do you want?' Maisie kept her hands slightly away from her body in what she hoped was a non-threatening pose, breathing deeply to quell the spurt of alarm. *What is this? An attempted mugging?*

'I want you to take a message. To your boss, Mr Elladour.'

Relief, surprise and a thrill that she couldn't deny was excitement jostled through Maisie.

What is *this?*

'I can do that,' Maisie agreed, keeping her voice level. 'What do I have to say?'

'He wants the Necklace. He can have it. Just him. Five million. Tell him that. You'll be contacted within twenty-four hours. *Tell him that.*'

It was difficult to be sure, but Maisie thought she detected a trace of nervousness in the staccato delivery. Or maybe that too was excitement?

'I will.' She repeated the message word for word, to confirm that she understood.

'Good.' There was a distinct huff. Also relief? 'Now – don't turn around. Wait five minutes. If you don't, no Necklace.'

Maisie let her breath out through her teeth in a frustrated hiss. If she had something to act as a mirror, if there was a reflective surface here in the dim corner of the garage that would give her a clear view behind her – but it was no use wishing. There wasn't. There *was* CCTV installed, but would her unexpected visitor have known enough to avoid the cameras?

'I understand. I won't turn around,' she confirmed.

'Five minutes.' The voice was already retreating. Maisie strained her ears and thought she could hear footsteps. A light, fast tread.

That – and the voice? It hadn't sounded deep, even with the distorter.

A woman?

She waited the full five minutes. In that time, the lift doors opened and closed twice, three vehicles started up and left the garage and a single car came in.

Once the five minutes had passed and she was sure she was alone, Maisie retraced her steps, back to the apartment.

You did it! You did it! You did it!

The scheming, the waiting, the watching. It had all come good.

Maisie Norris would deliver the message.

Within twenty-four hours, Augustus Elladour would agree to buy the Necklace.

Doubt shivered in the air for a moment.

He *would* want it. He must.

You're on your own now. Pull it off and then disappear ...

Hands clutching the steering wheel were gripping too tightly in an effort to stop the shaking. *Excitement. It's just excitement.* And driving in unfamiliar streets, in London …

Can't afford an accident. Not now, not when it's almost done. Five million, free and clear. And no need to share it.

You can do this.

Maisie followed her escort along the corridor on the top floor of the City office block. The shaded glass of the long windows dimmed the brightness of the strong afternoon sun and the thick carpet muffled footsteps – the slightly eerie quiet of power and money. Jake had borrowed an office for the afternoon, or maybe he owned the building. Who knew? When she'd rung with the news of the second approach, there'd been an abrupt change of tack. He and Michelle had flown up – plane, helicopter – again, who knew? – so that they could work on a plan together. The second thief had pulled her back into the mix. It was scary and exciting.

She wondered, fleetingly, what Elliott might say, but her work really wasn't anything to do with him. He'd texted her to let her know that the photography was done and he would shortly be heading back to Bath. She'd had to swallow a lump in her throat when she read the sweet "morning-after" message. *And you can stop thinking you don't deserve that.* She'd acknowledge the text with a promise to ring.

Right now, she needed to focus on her job. They'd arrived at the correct door. The young man with the sharp suit and the even sharper haircut, who'd brought her up from reception, knocked, ushered her in and then withdrew.

The office was big, with a breathtaking view. Maisie identified the familiar shape of St Paul's as she greeted Jake and Michelle. Jake gestured her to a seat at the long table. Michelle had a speakerphone set up at the end of it.

'You haven't rung the auction number yet?' Maisie realised as she slid into her seat.

Jake treated her to one of his wolfish grins. 'It seemed like a good idea to wait for you, in view of the new development. Will you take us through both encounters?' he invited Maisie.

She recounted the incident on the crossing again, in as much detail as she could remember.

'No way that the note could have been put in your bag before you crossed the road?' Michelle queried.

'Not unless Elliott put it there.' Maisie met her colleague's questioning stare. She'd explained, briefly, how she'd come to be crossing Sloane Square at that time in the morning with a bag full of picnic debris, and she wasn't going to be embarrassed about it. Michelle had been the one urging her to go for it. 'It wasn't there when I picked the bag up. Whoever planted it – it had to be the man on the crossing – he knew where I was. He was waiting for me.' She could see from Jake's face that he'd already reached the same conclusion. Even though the object of the exercise was for her to be seen, she wasn't very happy with the thought of being followed.

'This thing is embedded in that weekend in Torquay. The thieves know about you – but they're only interested in you as a conduit to Elladour,' Jake reassured her. 'What about the encounter in the garage?'

Maisie took them through that one too. 'Carl, the security guy, ran some of the CCTV, but that part of the garage doesn't have a camera at the right angle. I suspect that was more luck than judgement on the thief's part. There's normally a security officer on the barrier, but he was dealing with a resident who had found some damage to the rear light of his BMW and was making a fuss about it. The rest of the CCTV footage is being checked, but it will be difficult to distinguish an intruder from a legitimate visitor. There *are* security patrols but they can't be everywhere.'

Carl had not been at all happy with the situation. He'd already begun a complete review of the security arrangements for the garage.

'Impressions?' Jake asked when she'd finished.

'Two players,' Maisie said decisively. 'I *think* the one in the car park was a woman, and I'm *sure* that the one who shoved me on the crossing was a man. And two personalities – the person in the garage seemed a bit hesitant, nervous. The intercept at the crossing wasn't – it was risky, flamboyant.'

'Hmm.' Michelle tapped a pencil on the table top, 'A man and a woman ties in with your impression of the thieves at Pentecost Place,' she acknowledged. 'If it was a woman, it wasn't Armand's wife – she's definitely in New York.' She dropped the pencil with an annoyed clatter. 'But why the two separate contacts? The note and the garage? Are they *trying* to confuse us?' Michelle huffed in frustration. 'I have to tell you that it's working.'

Maisie looked over at Jake. 'What do you think?'

'Your encounter in the garage could be some kind of con from the thieves. A double dip at extracting money for the Necklace.'

'But?' Maisie prompted.

'The devil is in the detail.' The wolfish grin was back. 'We suspect we have two players. We *know* we have two approaches – both want to get to Elladour, but they're not the same. The first is an invitation to participate in an auction, the second a direct offer, naming an explicit sum, to a man who has already shown an interest in acquiring the

Necklace. If it's not an attempt to con Elladour, I think what we might have here is a good old-fashioned double cross.'

It took a moment to consider it, then Maisie nodded, enthusiastically joined by Michelle.

'It's simple and it fits,' Michelle affirmed. 'Thieves falling out.'

Maisie frowned, casting her mind back to the weekend. The man could be anyone, but the woman? After two mystery encounters, she was more or less sure it *was* a woman. *Dorothea*? Maisie still couldn't cast that limp, colourless woman in the role of jewel thief and potential double crosser. They'd focused on the family, but abruptly another face rose in her mind – the giggler from the museum staff. She'd certainly been out and about in the house at night, which might be an alibi of sorts, should one be needed. Would a lover be perfectly sure at what time she'd left his bed? Or even be aware that she had? The theft had only taken a matter of minutes. The woman would have researched the house and the Collections for her job, she could easily have eavesdropped or snooped to learn Maisie's address, *and* she'd been in the library on Saturday afternoon. *Was she watching me?*

'What have you thought of?' Michelle had seen her expression.

'Not what, who. One of the museum staff.' Maisie shared her ideas. 'She could be working with Armand and his wife,' she suggested. 'They could have supplied details that she didn't know.'

Nodding, Michelle added the woman to her list of ongoing investigations. 'Sounds plausible,' she agreed. 'Maybe she always intended to cut them out? Although why has it taken so long to do it? Why would the partnership suddenly go sour now?'

'Maybe she just got tired of waiting?' Maisie suggested. 'Maybe *she* thinks she's being double crossed?'

Michelle sighed. 'We really don't have enough information to go further with this at the moment.' She glanced from Maisie to Jake. 'How is Elladour going to play this? Two people offering him the same goods?' she asked.

'What I would do if I was still a businessman instead of a detective …' There was a quirk of a smile that Maisie appreciated and Michelle didn't pick up on. 'Continue to negotiate with both until the situation becomes clearer. Only one of them can actually produce the Necklace. Where is it? Do both of them have access to it? Has Player B offered it to anyone else besides Elladour?' He shrugged. 'We can't answer any of those questions. We can only work with what we have – and a bit of intelligent speculation.'

'I hope it *is* intelligent,' Michelle retorted. 'If we have got thieves falling out ... This is getting a lot more edgy, isn't it?'

'It is,' Jake agreed levelly. 'But that's on them, not us. Things have been okay so far. We stay careful and alert and keep it that way. These people, both of them, want to sell to Elladour. He's the potential golden goose. No one will be looking to damage the source of the golden egg.'

Unless they find out that the golden goose isn't real? Maisie pushed the thought out of her mind. That was not going to happen.

'So where do we go from here?' she asked instead.

'Elladour listens to what both have to say, and follows instructions. It will be interesting if Player B produces the Necklace in twenty-four hours.' Jake grinned.

I'd say it would be a bit more than interesting.

From her expression, Maisie could see Michelle was thinking the same. Neither said anything.

Jake grimaced slightly. 'Just so you know, I have shared both approaches with the authorities – they're prepared to let us run with it. I get the feeling that they think we're being conned.'

'Are we?' Michelle raised an eyebrow.

'Only one way to find out. We've got a lot of unknowns, so we need to be careful, *very* careful – but we have leads and I think we have to follow them.' He made a sweeping gesture. 'If all else fails, I'll buy the bloody Necklace. It'll save me hunting for an anniversary present for Cassie.' He turned to look at the phone setup Michelle had arranged. 'Shall we dial the magic number?'

Maisie found she was holding her breath as the ring tone sounded and the phone was answered. 'Elladour?'

Maisie kept as still as she could as Jake crisply confirmed his false identity, knowing Michelle was staying equally still. The voice on the line was male – a flat monotone, undisguised but undistinguished. 'If you wish to bid for the Cleopatra Necklace, be prepared to travel at short notice.'

'Where?' Jake barked out the demand. 'And how do I know you have the Necklace?'

There was a pause. 'Further instructions and … proof of life ... will follow in due course. Thank you for your interest.' The call ended with a click.

'Call back?' Michelle asked.

Jake shook his head. 'We wouldn't get a reply, and the phone will be at the bottom of the Thames, or some other convenient body of water, within the hour.' He sat back in his chair. 'So what more do we now know – other than the fact that I need to keep a bag packed? I hope it's not Australia,' he added.

Maisie smiled, then started to count off on her fingers. 'Male, nothing in the voice sounded familiar, although it's not easy to tell with so few words, confident to a degree – no attempt to disguise – but he *was* keeping it short. We might get more from the recording you made—' she nodded to Michelle '—but I doubt it.' She turned to Jake. 'I think he was ready to end the call at the point where you challenged him. The bit about proof of life – there was a hesitation there.'

'He doesn't have the Necklace to hand?' Michelle suggested. 'He has to retrieve it from somewhere?'

Jake was nodding slowly. 'I wonder? Does Player B have it? Or is there now going to be a race to retrieve it? A tussle over possession?' He leaned back, speculating, '*Did* the request wrong-foot him – and if it did, is that bad preparation? I really can't see other buyers taking the goods on trust, but maybe that's how it's done in these circles – you accept the invitation but you don't inspect the goods until the actual auction? And there was no indication that he knew about any other approach—' he paused '—but we mustn't get ahead of ourselves. Both parties promised further contact. Now, we wait.'

Chapter Twenty-Four

Elliott was surprised to find the Dean in Jenni's office when he stepped in to let her know that he was back from London.

'Dr Leyland? Did you want me for something?'

'No, no, Elwood. No problem.' Leyland waved his hand in a dismissing gesture. 'Just doing some diary coordination.' He bustled off.

Jenni looked after him with a thoughtful expression. 'He's up to something.'

'Agreed.' Elliott nodded. 'Any idea what?'

'No, but that's a third time he's checked what appointments you have coming up.'

'Do I have any interesting ones?'

'Apart from that reception, there's nothing that can't be moved, which is what he seemed to want to know.' She frowned. 'There's no reason for your diary to coordinate with his. Do you think it's something to do with the Pentecost inheritance?'

'Possibly.' Elliott picked up a couple of pieces of mail from his in tray. 'We'll find out eventually. I suppose you'd better keep him informed, as he's so keen.'

Jenni grinned and tapped something on the computer. 'Done.'

Elliott carried his mail into his own office and walked to the window that overlooked the campus. Two of his postgraduate students were back from research trips – he'd be meeting them to discuss the results next week. A few of the third-year undergraduates were beginning to drift back and dropping into the office, but there were still some weeks to go before the official start of term. The deadlines he had were personal ones for pieces of work.

Absently, he watched a pair of magpies strutting their stuff on the square of grass in front of the building. What scheme was Leyland hatching? A celebration for the acquisition of the Pentecost Collections? The theft of the Necklace had delayed an announcement, but maybe Leyland *had* been given the nod that the University's bid had been successful?

Elliott left the window and strode back to his desk. Whatever it was, Leyland would have to own up eventually.

He sat behind the desk, leaning dangerously against the back of the chair, which as usual tipped and creaked in protest. The Dean's machinations were of far less concern to him than what was going on between him and Maisie Webster. He shut his eyes, conjuring up her face from early that morning and hearing the echo – *This doesn't change anything*. She was far too intelligent not to realise that saying the words meant that it already had. *And for some reason, that alarms her*.

He wanted to know what that reason was, but he wasn't going to push for answers. He could wait. One thing that he did know was that he didn't want to lose her. What they had was tentative, still developing – but it was the most exciting thing that had happened to him in a long time; perhaps ever. And the excitement had nothing to do with stolen necklaces, although that was exciting too. The strange fizzing in his veins was all to do with Maisie and the chemistry between them. Life had developed an edge since he'd met her – even in that first encounter when she'd been playing the bimbo, she'd invaded his consciousness in a way far exceeding anything the circumstances warranted. Simply the sight of her – the thought of her – made his heart thump a little harder. It didn't matter whether the picture he conjured up was of her sitting across from him at a table in a restaurant or curled up next to him, skin to skin, in his bed.

Patience. He had to have patience. As long as he could keep seeing her, it was enough. If she was to end it …

He straightened up, making the chair protest again.

He wasn't going there. It wasn't going to happen.

No way.

Driving was easier once London was left behind, but elation and tension still warred with each other.

Better now though, after a stop at the motorway services for food and coffee.

You did it. You found Maisie Norris.

But now you have to deliver.

Within twenty-four hours, the arrangements would be made. And in the following twenty-four …

The Necklace would be gone. *And so will you.* Five million – money and freedom, a new life …

That man, Elladour, would pay it. Everything was in place to take the money and run. It wasn't perfect. It would be possible to follow the money trail … *but* he *doesn't have the skills to do that. Elladour will have the Necklace so he won't be telling and you'll just be … gone.*

You just have to keep hidden and keep your nerve.

Forty-eight hours.

You can stall that long.

The car nosed into the street of non-descript terraced houses. Back Street, Anytown. Most of the properties were rented out, with a transient population.

No one knows you here now.

He *hasn't found you.*

The shiver was involuntary, cutting deep. It hadn't been a problem until Mumford. Mumford was dead. *Murdered.*

It seemed crazy and yet …

The thought and the fear kept growing. Nerves strung too tight for too long.

You just need to get away.

There was a parking space just ahead, not too far from the front door.

Then back to London. Meet Maisie Norris again. Get Elladour's answer.

After that it will only take a few hours to hand over the Necklace.

Elladour *will* want the Necklace.

Panic rising.

Fight it.

The car slid into the space and stopped.

Nearly there. Go in. Get the Necklace out of the desk. Should have taken it with you – but then the risk of carrying it ...

In and out.

Five minutes, tops.

Then back on the road. Back to London. You can contact Ms Norris tonight. She'll be waiting ...

Leave a message for her, at reception. She'll be waiting.

Take the Necklace and go.

A small silver car was parked across the street. A familiar car. With a familiar figure leaning against it and now walking forward.

Smiling.

Reaching to open the door.

Leaning in.

‘Hello, darling. Good news. It’s all done. The auction is set.’ He was preening – a finger snap and a smug smile. ‘I’ve even got that guy Elladour on board. Am I good or am I good?’

For a split second, everything went dark, as if something had passed over the sun – but the smile was still in place, still smug. *Still triumphant, still preening*. ‘It’s all working, darling, exactly as I planned.’ He held out his hand. ‘Now I need the Necklace.’

Chapter Twenty-Five

Maisie sorted her notes into order. After the weekend and all the excitement of Monday, everything had swiftly deflated. Twenty-four hours, then forty-eight, then seventy-two had gone by with no contact from the mystery visitor in the garage. A package containing a picture of the Necklace on that day's newspaper and another burner phone through which contact would be made, had been left on the counter at the reception desk when both reception staff were occupied with residents. The lobby was crowded and the CCTV showed only the back view of a dark clothed figure in a baseball cap carrying a large satchel with the logo of a national courier firm. Jake had concluded that the man on the crossing had continued to follow Maisie to discover where she lived. The thought that she hadn't spotted a tail was unsettling – although she hadn't really been expecting anything so early in the morning. She wished she could remember even a small detail about him, but there was nothing. The back view of Mr Average. There was still no location or a definite time for the auction. Jake suspected it would not be in the UK.

Carl had now added a review of foyer security to his list.

Maisie sighed. The only thing that was making any progress was her investigation into the missing financier – and not in a good way. She'd talked to his colleagues and close friends and managed to get them to open up to her in a way they hadn't to the police. *But you were asking a different kind of question.* Everything she was uncovering suggested that the guy wasn't the thief but that there was a distinct possibility that he was dead. It was closure of a sort, but not what she'd been hoping for. She still had a few more leads to explore here in London, but she was returning to Bath for the weekend. On Sunday, she'd promised Hal she'd do family lunch. Before that though, she would be seeing Elliott. They'd texted, spoken every evening on the phone, and tomorrow he'd volunteered to cook dinner for her.

Saturday night.

Date night.

She was grinning. She knew it, but she couldn't stop. She'd been trying not to admit that any part of the flat feeling she was experiencing was because she was missing him. *Didn't get very far with that though, did you?* She shrugged off the sarcastic voice. She could do quite well without a man in the picture. Life was just a lot more … *more* … when Elliott was around.

Everything was still okay between them. She'd wondered, after that over-dramatic declaration – true, but over-dramatic. She couldn't, *wouldn't* contemplate taking what they had any further than ... what they had. No meeting the family, no Sunday lunches, no seeing avid excitement in her mother's eyes …

No. Just no. Not going there. No reason to.

Elliott looked around the kitchen. The main course was ready – chicken with lemon and rosemary – keeping warm in the oven on a low heat. The salad was assembled. He'd balked at attempting bread and dessert, buying crispy baguettes and a gooey tarte tartin from the French bakery in the next street. There was a bottle of Chardonnay chilling in the refrigerator, all the windows were open to let in a breeze, and there were fresh sheets on the bed. Elliott took a sip from the half inch of wine left in the glass he'd added to the chicken. It was the first time he'd prepared a meal in this kitchen for a date. With other lovers, he'd kind of got stuck in a round of restaurants and then "coffee" at her place.

Another way that Maisie was different?

He jumped slightly when the intercom buzzed and his stomach did a funny little flip of excitement. *Pe-er-lease ... What are you, sixteen?* He pushed the release for the outer door and went out on the landing to welcome his guest, knowing he really should have waited and checked out the caller from behind his own door, using the fancy new security camera. Hopefully he wouldn't get it in the neck for that, but he was too nervous to wait. *Nervous?* Hell yes, he *was* nervous. And here she was, looking stunning in a slim green dress with her hair piled up on top of her head in a messy knot. He let out a long breath. Later he would dismantle that knot …

Then she was in his arms, turning her face up for his kiss, and everything went hazy and hot.

'Something smells good.'

'Chicken – it's chicken.'

'Nope.' She had her nose buried in his shirt front. 'I think it's you. Cedarwood soap? Something herbal?'

'Possibly.' He really couldn't remember and wasn't sure he cared, but there was one thing. 'There seems to be something rather cold pressing on the small of my back.'

‘Ah.’ She stepped away from him, brandishing a bag with a bottle. ‘Chilled Sancerre.’

‘That would account for it. Would you like to come in and we can find somewhere to put it, or glasses … or something?’

‘Mmm. Something.’ She’d moved in for another kiss and he wasn’t going to argue.

They finally made it over the threshold. ‘I thought we’d eat first, and then you can tell me what’s happening?’

‘Sounds good.’ She was looking up, taking in the plaster mouldings on the ceiling. ‘Original?’

‘I think so. D’you want to look round, while I sort out the food?’

Maisie wandered around the large open-plan space. The furnishings were what she might have expected – modern but not minimalist, constructed on generous lines. Dark wood floors and pale upholstery and a couple of moody seascapes on the walls with a row of photographs of archaeological digs in Egypt – the distant pyramids in the background were the clue. The small display on what was probably an original mantel shelf included a scroll and a rock, a piece of carved masonry and a small sleek statue of a god; black wood and gilt with an animal head – a long snout and pointed ears. The collar around the statue’s neck reminded her of the Necklace.

‘Dinner is served.’ Elliott had laid a small table next to the kitchen alcove. Maisie let out a deep sigh as she walked over to take a seat. She was relaxed, except for that little tingle of awareness that was always there between her and Elliott. With this man she didn’t have to *be* anything. *You can just be.*

Maisie enjoyed the food Elliott had prepared and said so. Now they were settled on the sofa with the remains of the wine as the dishwasher chugged busily in the background. They’d discussed both the approaches about the Necklace and Elliott had updated her on the strange behaviour of Dr Leyland.

‘Hmm.’ Maisie leaned her head on Elliott’s shoulder. ‘You don’t think there’s any way Leyland could be mixed up in this?’

‘I don’t really see how.’

Maisie straightened up, shaking her head to clear away an unwelcome thought about the death of Professor Mumford. *Not going to spoil tonight with that.* She looked round the room, remembering a question she'd been meaning to ask. 'Who's the rather spectacular god on the mantelpiece?'

'He is, isn't he?' Elliott responded smoothly to her change of topic. 'Anubis, god of the underworld – some say god of the dead. He was a present from a colleague in Egypt.'

'He looks quite at home up there.' She turned her head to indicate photographs. 'Those are impressive.'

'First dig I worked on.'

She sensed a restlessness in him. 'And you'd be there now, if it wasn't for your academic commitments and the guest lectures?'

'Well, planning a trip, at least. I haven't given up hope.' He pulled her a little closer to him. 'I'm not really complaining. It's an honour to be asked to deliver those guest lectures and the reception shouldn't be a hardship. The Society has a very good cellar, laid down by a few of the Fellows after the war. You're still okay to come as my plus one?'

'No way I'd miss it. I want to meet the secretive Dr Leyland.'

Elliott laughed. 'The chance to scrutinise him in person.'

Maisie didn't respond to that. She'd asked Michelle to enlarge on the background she'd prepared for her for Torquay, but it hadn't yielded much that was useful. With the man's uncharacteristic behaviour and the warning that Ben had given Elliott over his suspicious speculation about *her,* she was certainly ready to scrutinise him in person. She settled more comfortably into the curve of Elliott's arm, enjoying the warmth of his body close to hers. She'd put her toothbrush and spare underwear in her handbag. *Hope or foresight?* She didn't think she was going to be disappointed.

She tilted her head back, studying the complex moulding around the central ceiling light. 'Are you renting this place or buying it?' she asked idly.

'Neither – couldn't afford it on an academic's salary, even with the extra from the TV. I inherited it, and the Morgan, from my uncle.'

Maisie sipped her wine, digesting the information. 'You were close?'

'I was the only member of the family he spoke to.' Elliott grinned. It did good things to Maisie's stomach. 'He was the black sheep of the family. Made his money *overseas*.' Elliott's emphasis gave the word some slightly sinister quotation marks. 'My parents were convinced he was a drug smuggler – in fact, he was just pretty astute with investments. He'd had three wives but no kids so he left me his two most prized possessions – the flat and the car. I enjoy them both, as he meant me to. I think Mum and Dad would have liked me to refuse to accept them, but the value of the assets won out in the end. Set up for life was the expression that was used.'

'Mmm – so you're quite a catch then?' Maisie stiffened as she registered what she'd said – stupid, thoughtless words drifting out of her mouth over the distraction of physical awareness. Words she could hear echoing in her head, in her mother's voice. Afraid of an ominous pause, she crashed hurriedly into a new topic. 'I meant to ask you, have you ever been anyone's best man?'

Elliott didn't seem to notice the quick change of subject, or the way her mind was still running on weddings.

'Once – for my friend, Ben. Sadly, the marriage didn't last.' He didn't query why she was asking, just raised an eyebrow. *Very Elliott.*

'My brother is marrying his boyfriend,' she explained. 'He's asked me to be his ... best person, I suppose. I'm not really certain what it involves.'

'From what I can recall, the key duties were looking after the ring and making sure Ben didn't get embarrassingly drunk on his stag night – oh, and making a speech at the reception.'

'That's what I thought.' Maisie nodded. 'I can do that, if that's what Hal wants.'

'I have every confidence in you.' Elliott raised his glass in a salute.

Maisie braced herself, waiting for the obvious questions about her family, given that she'd quizzed him about his uncle, but they didn't come. Instead, Elliott topped up their glasses and asked about her plans for returning to London the following week.

By the time he stood up, pulling her up with him and into his arms for a long luxurious kiss, her nerves had settled. His hands, running down her back, were both soothing and arousing. She leaned into him, tilting her head as his mouth followed the curve of her neck to the deep vee of her dress. His hands skimmed her body, tantalising barely-there touches that stoked the heat deep within her.

Slowly, a few paces at a time, they made it into the bedroom. Maisie was aware of dark grey walls and the windows open to the gathering dusk and the sounds of the city before they collapsed onto the king-size bed. Then her focus was only on Elliott and the sensation building between them.

Somewhere close a clock was chiming. Elliott moved his arm to settle Maisie's sleeping form more comfortably against his side. *Three a.m. and all's well.* And all *was* well. Making love the previous night had been every bit as amazing as it was the first time.

He blew softly to dislodge a curl tickling his chin. Taking the pins out of Maisie's hair had been as sensuously arousing as he had hoped. Everything about Maisie Webster was arousing and somehow completely *right.* He was glad that he was awake now, to enjoy lying quietly beside her. She'd be gone in the morning. *Family obligations*. He'd understood instinctively not to ask questions, but there had been a few tell-tale signs that he thought he could read – shifts in Maisie's body language when they'd accidentally strayed into guarded terrain. *Something with her parents – a matchmaking mother?* He wasn't worried. It was the woman in his arms he wanted, not her family. He wanted her to be happy and to trust him – that was a bone-deep certainty. He'd do whatever he needed – whatever *she* needed – to make it happen.

Chapter Twenty-Six

Maisie parked her car outside her parents' house and sat for a moment, collecting her thoughts. She'd much rather have spent the day with Elliott, but she'd promised Hal and she wasn't going to renege on that promise. Besides which, she was curious to meet Stephen. *Checking that he's good enough for your brother?* Smothering a grin with a sigh, she got out of the car, frowning a little. Was that Fran's yummy mummy SUV? She was sure it was. *Looks like the gang's all here.*

Lunch was … predictable. Mum was coy and fluttering, Dad the quiet observer, Hal nervous, proud and in love. Stephen was tall, dark and a little wary, also in love. Maisie realised this quickly, with a relief that surprised her. *Your brother will be okay with this guy.* As they ate, she'd done her part to keep the conversation flowing. It had gone much better than she'd feared except that her sister was obviously jumpy. At moments when she wasn't part of the conversation and her features were at rest, she didn't look at all well.

The twins had gone with their father to visit Paul's parents, which was a bit odd. Maisie could see that her mother was puzzled and disappointed at the absence of her granddaughters, but maybe Fran had the right idea, not inflicting Stephen with too much family all in one go. She loved her nieces, but they *were* exhausting. She studied her sister again; Fran was running a hand up and down the stem of her wine glass with a nervous gesture that seemed to be unconscious. Maisie caught her eye and shook her head. Fran started, looking down at her hand and pulling it hurriedly into her lap, flashing her a wan smile. *Definitely something wrong.*

Once the meal was over, the men departed to her father's man-cave to watch whatever sport was taking place on a Sunday afternoon. She resisted the temptation to go with them. She needed to make space for Fran to talk, if she wanted. Mum disappeared into the kitchen, waving away offers of help once the plates had been carried through. Maisie would have taken a bet that she would be emerging soon with wedding brochures. Which just left her and her sister.

'Come for a walk?' Fran suggested. 'The park?'

'Why not?' Maisie stood up. Maybe now she would find out what was going on.

After they'd walked for about ten minutes in silence, she began to doubt it. They'd almost reached the park where they'd all played as children – but not together. The age gap was too wide. She tried to think what might be bothering Fran. Redundancy? Illness? If it was the latter, surely her sister would have shared that with their mother?

They'd reach the park gates. Fran gestured to an empty bench in the shade of a tree. 'Shall we sit down?'

They sat. Maisie stretched out her legs and looked at her feet. 'Whatever it is you want to talk about, Fran, I'm listening.'

Fran gave one of those jerky starts again, put a hand up to rub her eyes, then let it drop. 'Thanks … It's just … I can't tell Mum or Dad or anyone … but if I don't talk to someone…' Maisie heard her swallow. 'I can't believe I'd ever be saying this – but … I almost had an affair.'

Maisie wasn't sure she would have believed it either, except that she'd seen Fran with the stranger in the coffee house. She wasn't going to reveal that though. 'Almost?' She latched onto the part that didn't quite add up.

'Almost,' Fran confirmed. Her voice sounded stronger. 'It was *stupid.* I really don't know what I was thinking. I never slept with him. It was just a few kisses. Paul knows. He understands, or he's trying to. It's going to be all right.' Maisie watched her sister's hands clench in the folds of her expensive linen skirt. 'We'll get through it, I know we can. It's *over,*' she emphasised. 'I ended it, told him I wouldn't see him again, that my husband knew …' Her sister's voice broke a little. 'But now … now he won't stop. He says he's not ready to give me up.'

Maisie sat up straighter on the bench. That *did* sound strange. *And disquieting?* 'I think you'd better tell me all of it.'

It wasn't really a very remarkable story – a marriage grown fragile under the weight of time, two demanding careers and the responsibilities of parenthood. It was just one that Maisie had never expected to hear from her sister.

'And then I met Julian Holt.' Fran's voice trembled a bit, but she ploughed on. 'I was on a training course for work. He was on another one at the same centre. At first it was just drinks in a group, then one evening there was a mix-up. All the others had gone out for pizza or something, but somehow the message hadn't got passed on and it was just him and me, so we had dinner together.' Fran looked up, meeting Maisie's eyes. 'I enjoyed it. Julian is very charming, very good-looking. It wasn't hard to be with him and it was good to have a man's attention, just for *me*.' She shrugged. 'When the course ended, it didn't stop. He doesn't live in Bath, so we didn't meet up that often, but we *did* meet. For coffee ... and dinner.' Maisie could see her sister was blushing a little. *That's when the kissing started.*

She waited for Fran to continue. 'Then ... then he asked me to go away for a weekend. And I said yes.' There was another pause. Maisie didn't fill it. 'He booked a hotel, outside Stratford-upon-Avon. I drove all the way there, but then, when I was about to get out of the car, I realised what I was doing – throwing away everything Paul and I had for a man I hardly knew. I left a message at reception and drove straight back and told Paul everything. It wasn't actually that much.' She gave a stilted laugh. 'Not exactly a big affair. Paul … Paul was great. He'd realised that there was something, knew that we had to fix things. I think there might have been someone too, in his office. But we're good now. We're working on it.'

'But you still have a problem with this guy, Julian.'

Fran hooked her blonde hair back behind her ears in an abrupt, frustrated gesture. 'He just won't go *away*. I met him once, after I told Paul, in a café in town. I told him to his face that it was over.' *And that's when I saw you.* Maisie nodded but didn't speak. 'I *told* him, but he's still *there*.' Her sister's voice rose a fraction. 'When I meet the girls from school, outside my yoga class – "likes" on social media …'

'He's a stalker,' Maisie suggested quietly. Something disturbing was niggling in the back of her mind.

'That's *exactly* what he is. Paul said it too. That's why he's gone to his parents today – to ask if we can go to their place in Sardinia and if they'll have the twins to stay, so they don't miss the beginning of term. If we can get away, Julian will *have* to stop.'

Maisie wasn't too sure about that, not without a little outside intervention, but that wasn't what Fran needed to hear.

'I think that's a good idea. How soon could you go?'

'Tuesday morning, I hope.' Fran turned to meet Maisie's eyes. Her face looked less strained and her movement less jerky. 'I needed to talk to someone. Tell someone. And who can I trust better than my sister?'

Maisie didn't quite know what to do with that, so she just nodded. 'I think it's a good idea for you to get away,' she repeated.

They sat silently together for a few moments, watching a couple of small boys and an exuberant Cockerpoo chasing a ball and each other.

Fran broke the silence. 'When we're in Sardinia, we're going to try again for another baby.'

'Again?' Surprise made Maisie blurt out the word.

'Yeah.' Fran's mouth twisted. 'We …' She didn't finish the sentence. 'Third time lucky – maybe. The girls would love a little brother.' She looked down at her watch. 'I think it's time we went back and rescued Hal and Stephen.' She looked up, her face much more relaxed now. 'Thanks, Maisie – it was good to talk to you.'

They got back to the house to find their mother in full flow, with brochures and wedding magazines heaped on the coffee table. Hal and Stephen were sitting together on the sofa, holding hands and looking shell-shocked. Exchanging grins, Maisie and Fran waded in to direct their mother away from themes involving horse-drawn carriages, rose bowers, kilts and tartan.

Grandmother's name was not mentioned.

When it came time to leave, both Hal and Fran hugged Maisie hard. It felt strange. *But good.*

On Monday she got to the office early so that she could make a call while it was still quiet.

'Maisie Webster for Detective Sergeant Casey, please.' She waited to be connected. 'Gary? Yeah, fine, you too. Look, you're the one handling the bank jobs – the ones in Gloucester and Cheltenham? Yeah – I heard a rumour that there was inside help, but that you weren't getting anywhere?' She held the phone away from her ear, avoiding the discontented cursing on the other end. 'No, I haven't rung to gloat. I had an idea – just listen, will you?'

She replaced the receiver ten minutes later, satisfied with what she had put in motion. Maybe she was wrong, but she had a gut feeling …

She picked up a pen from the desk and started to play with the cap. She'd got a whole new view of her family this weekend. Well, not Mum and Dad, nothing would really change there – her mother would still steamroller along and her father would simply watch – but Hal and Françoise? Her brother was in love and ready to make a statement about it in a way that far too many people would still find unacceptable. And her sister's perfect marriage … well, it wasn't perfect, after all. And they'd both reached out to her.

So maybe it's time to think about that?

Chapter Twenty-Seven

'Ah, Elwood – the President thought I might find you up here.'

Elliott turned to greet the Secretary of the Academic Society, who'd followed him into the gallery at the top of the Society's London headquarters. In his early sixties, retired from a successful career in business, Grant Carmichael was one of the youngest of the Society's Fellows, appointed as much for his commercial background as his keen interest and expertise in Egyptology. That business acumen was raising the Society's profile with lectures, sponsorship and the upcoming gala reception.

Now he had clearly been sent to scoop up the guest speaker and shepherd him back to his responsibilities. Elliott couldn't argue with that. He'd only intended to spend a few moments here in the gallery that housed a selection of the Society's rare books and some of the smaller items from its extensive holdings. He'd done what he'd came for, checking the original publication date of one of the oldest books, but his eye had been caught by a small display case that had made him linger. He walked to join Carmichael at the door. He'd enjoyed an excellent lunch and now it was time to sing for his supper … er … lunch.

'I was distracted by the jewellery,' he said. 'Some of the pieces have been moved?'

'Oh. Yes.' Carmichael looked over at the gaps in the display. 'Downstairs – part of the exhibition for the gala,' he explained. He was holding the door open ready to usher Elliott through. 'The Members and Fellows in attendance are greatly looking forward to your presentation and, of course, the public lecture afterwards.' They approached the staircase. Elliott stood back to let the older man precede him. 'The committee has been immensely gratified over the response to that. Fifty people here in person and several hundred registered for the webinar – an international audience. The recording will be kept available afterwards for subscribers …'

Elliott was only half listening. He was happy to help promote the Society and swell the coffers that maintained the building and funded digs and bursaries, but his mind was wandering back to the exquisite pectoral in the display case – a depiction of the vulture goddess Nekhbet in gold, inlaid with slivers of glass and semiprecious stones.

Once on the ground floor, Carmichael pulled open the double doors into the Society's lecture room. A swell of noise came to meet them – conversation, the scraping of chair legs on parquet, clearing of throats. Elliott moved past the Secretary, murmuring thanks as he walked towards the dais where the President was waiting to introduce him to the audience.

In the borrowed Chelsea flat, Maisie slithered the blue lace dress up over her hips and reached around to zip herself in. She was meeting Elliott in the bar of a hotel close to the Strand for an early dinner before walking down to the Society's building. The reputation of the hotel and a little homework on the sponsors of the gala had prompted her to raid her official work wardrobe for the slim-fitting cocktail dress from a designer patronised by some of the younger royals. Cassie had lent her a gold and diamond tennis bracelet and she'd added her own plain gold studs, navy pumps and a vintage beaded evening bag. The dress was one of her favourites for a certain kind of undercover work – chic but understated, except to those who knew about these things. *Not the sort of dress you were wearing when you first met Dr Elwood!*

She grinned at herself in the mirror. She'd pinned her hair into a smooth chignon and, in deference to the occasion, had added a Cleopatra-style flick to her dark blue eyeliner; she was pleased with the results. She was ready. She picked up the house phone. If she dialled down now the concierge would have a cab waiting by the time the lift reached the lobby.

Elliott's reaction when she walked into the bar of the hotel was everything she might have hoped. The dress and Cassie's diamonds were earning their keep.

'Wow!' He stepped forward to greet her with a kiss. 'I've changed my mind – let's skip the gala and just get a room.'

'No way!' She took a step back, laughing. 'I'm expecting to be fed and to meet a lot of antiquarian Egyptologists – not to mention your mysterious Dr Leyland.'

'Oh well, if we must.' He handed her the white wine spritzer that was waiting on the bar and picked up his own glass. 'Our table is ready, if you want to go through to the restaurant.'

Over a delectable seafood salad, Maisie outlined a little of the work she'd been doing on the missing financier – she'd found a lead that made her more hopeful of a positive result. Elliott brought Maisie up to speed on the two lectures he had given the day before. 'I also had a look at one of the jewellery exhibits in the Society's gallery.'

'Yes?' At the tone of his voice, Maisie's interest sparked.

'It's a pectoral – something like a necklace – and the workmanship is exquisite. The Cleopatra Necklace is beautiful, but a very much simpler design. It just made me wonder if the Necklace really *is* authentic.' He shrugged. 'I've only seen both of them briefly behind glass. It would be good to be able to compare them.

'That would tell you if the Cleopatra Necklace was a fake?'

He chewed his lip, considering. 'I think that would be pushing it too far, but it would be good to examine it with other pieces in the Society's collection. Whatever the result, in broad terms it's not a fake – it *is* the Cleopatra Necklace and it has all those legends attached to it. A collector would be buying all that. But is it actually Egyptian?' He gave her a rueful grin. 'I'm being pedantic. It doesn't really matter – a case of buyer beware. As long as Jake doesn't end up buying it.'

'Well, he did say he needed an anniversary present for Cassie.'

As they both laughed, the waiter materialised beside the table offering dessert menus. Maisie shook off a tiny someone-walked-over-my-grave shudder and bent her head to make her choice. The doubts Elliott voiced had resuscitated all the ones she had buried. If there was any question about the Necklace – if someone *did* want it authenticated – that put Elliott right back in the frame. She inhaled and handed the menu back with her order. All that was conjecture – it might never happen. *And it certainly isn't happening tonight.* She pushed the doubts resolutely out of her mind – tonight was about enjoyment and seeing Elliott in his professional world. She was looking forward to that.

They walked slowly through the crowds passing along the Strand on a warm late summer evening. Ahead of them a few other people peeled off to enter the shadowy passageway that led to the Society's headquarters. They followed, emerging into a small enclosed courtyard.

'Good grief!' Elliott had come to a standstill, staring up. Tonight, the Society was clearly *en fête.* Every window in the tall Georgian building blazed with light. Flower displays and potted trees flanked the shallow steps and a red carpet ran from the cobbles of the courtyard in through the open doors. A banner along the metal railings announced the exhibition with a discreet roll of crests and coronets indicating the august patronage enjoyed by the gala's sponsors. Faint strains of music and a gust of exotic scent drifted out. A press of people was visible behind the windows, holding glasses, talking and laughing.

Maisie looked up at Elliott's stunned expression and tried not to laugh herself. She didn't quite manage it.

'I didn't expect all *this*,' he defended himself indignantly. 'I knew there was a jewellery firm involved—'

'Not just *any* jewellery firm.' Maisie pointed to the "by appointment" insignia on the banner, then edged out of the way of a couple who were walking towards the red carpet. She took his hand. 'Come on, let's go and join the fun.'

Once they'd mounted the steps to the open doorway, Maisie really didn't know whether to look at her surroundings or to watch Elliott's face, which was a picture of disbelief.

'I'm guessing it doesn't normally look like this,' she suggested, still unable to keep the trace of laughter out of her voice.

'It certainly does *not*.' The touch of chagrin was priceless. They'd reached the meeter and greeter stationed just inside the door. The man's bulk and the width of his shoulders suggested a dual role as door security. People ahead of them had produced invitation cards. Elliott was patting his pockets in a distracted way, but when the greeter saw him, he simply smiled. 'Dr Elwood and guest. Please go through.' The man waved expansively at the hallway behind him. Doing as they were invited, Maisie took time to look round. The building would have been impressive in any circumstances, with a marble floor, delicate plasterwork and a graceful sweeping staircase. Tonight, the space had been carefully dressed for the occasion in the same way as the guests. There was more sharp Italian and classic Savile Row tailoring on the men than you could shake a stick at. *If you had a stick and wanted to shake it.* The array of designer dresses on the women made her very glad once again that she'd raided her work wardrobe. *You read this one right, my girl.*

There was, predictably, a lot of notable jewellery but Cassie's bracelet did its job nicely – satisfyingly glittery but understated. There were more flower arrangements and carefully positioned diffusers wafting a complex designer fragrance into the crowd. It made the space smell *very* expensive. Small placards at strategic points indicated that the perfume had been specially created by a leading cosmetic house – a *very* famous name – to complement the jewellery collection. Samples would be included in the gift bags for the guests to take away when they left. Maisie smiled. She did love an upmarket goody bag.

Elliott, who seemed to have recovered a little from his surprise, had liberated two glasses of champagne from a passing server and handed her one. She sipped and appreciated. Elliott hadn't been wrong about the quality of the Society's cellar – or maybe this too came from the sponsors.

She took another sip. 'Should you be making your number with anyone?'

'Not really. It wouldn't be easy to find anyone in this crush anyway.' He looked round, clearly not spotting anyone he knew. 'It isn't what I expected,' he repeated, frowning.

'No,' she agreed. She nodded to a sign indicating the way to the main hall. 'Shall we go and look at the display?'

A much larger notice at the entrance to the hall indicated that the exhibition would be officially opened at 8.30 p.m., with a special guest appearance by Nevada Shaw, who was to be the "face" of both the jewellery and perfume ranges.

'Nevada Shaw.' Elliott was studying the name. 'Isn't she …?'

'Hollywood A-lister – nominated for an Oscar last year.'

Elliott was looking more and more confused. It really was adorable. *Who would have thought stuffy Dr Elwood would ever look adorable?* Maisie hid a smile in her champagne glass. Elliott's frown had got more pronounced.

'That can't be right. Someone must've made a mistake,' he said emphatically. 'I doubt if any of the Fellows would have any idea who she is, let alone invite her.'

'I expect the sponsors invited her.'

'I suppose so.' He didn't look convinced. Maisie suspected he might be underestimating the Fellows. Nevada Shaw was devastatingly gorgeous, as well as being a very fine actress, so Elliott's bewilderment really was totally endearing. He'd warned her, over dinner, to expect a sedate evening of scholarly debate in the company of a significant number of octogenarians, and was clearly still having difficulty squaring expectation and reality. She tapped his arm. 'Come on, let's go look at the exhibits.'

They moved into the long room. It was less crowded here than in the hall and the reception rooms on either side of the front door. Statues and sarcophagi from the Society's collection lined the walls, accessorising the display and reminiscent of the ones in the Egyptian Room in Pentecost Place. *Hope none of these have a secret panel attached.* She could see from Elliott's quick grin when he caught her eye that he was thinking the same thing.

Out of habit she noted the low profile but substantial security presence, situated at key points in the room or mingling with the guests. Their dark suits and their stature identified them to her experienced eye. They were of the same mould as Jake's security and close protection squad.

'Are you ogling the security staff?' Elliott, who had been making the acquaintance of a large statue with a complicated headdress, came up behind her to whisper in her ear.

'Professional assessment only,' she responded with dignity. 'Good to see it being taken seriously.'

Elliott slid his arm around her and they moved over to the main display, where the need for security became obvious. The modern jewellery was stunning, each piece arrayed with the original artefact that had inspired it. The Society had allowed the contemporary designers full access to its collection for the purpose. Those original pieces were also stunning, but in a different way. Everything in the room that was offered for sale was stratospherically out of her price range, with diamonds and precious stones replacing glass and crystals. Remembering that anniversary present though, she slipped one of the fancy publicity postcards into her bag to pass on to Jake.

'It's all beautiful,' Elliott said softly as they pored over the last case.

'But you prefer the originals.'

He shrugged, a little helplessly. 'I can see the merit of what's been done, but it doesn't …'

'It doesn't speak to you?'

'No.' His eyes lighted at her understanding. 'There's just something about the ancient pieces.'

'They're your job. And your passion,' she added softly. The realisation of a man so at home in his skin touched a chord deep in her chest. Competence and professionalism were sexy as hell, but this was something more. *A glimpse into a soul?*

Momentarily distracted by her thoughts, Maisie started a little at a movement behind them. People had begun to come in from the front of the building and dignitaries were taking their places on a platform at the end of the room. 'Looks like things are happening. It must be eight-thirty.'

The Society's President, clearly one of the octogenarians, gave a simple but clearly delighted speech of welcome. The CEO of the jewellery company responded, then graciously introduced the celebrity guest. Nevada Shaw, as breathtaking as the jewellery from the collection that she was wearing, stepped forward. The atmosphere was electric as she spoke about the honour of being chosen to represent both jewels and perfume, but also about the historical role of the Society and the good work which would arise from this sponsorship by way of grants and bursaries, proving that she had done her research as well as vibrating glamour. As she was ushered off the stage to pose for photographs, an enthusiastic line of elderly Egyptologists was already forming to beg the honour of selfies. Maisie heard Elliott take a deep breath that was rueful and still a little disbelieving.

'Well … that *was* Nevada Shaw.'

'Yes,' she agreed solemnly, earning herself a poke in the ribs.

'Stop laughing at me. I was wrong. I admit it.'

'Oi!' She objected to the dig in the ribs. 'Do you see me laughing?' She showed him a serious face, but knew that he wouldn't miss the amusement bubbling up in her eyes.

'Hmm – I really never imagined all this.' He was looking narrowly at the suave grey-haired man who was deep in conversation with the jewellery CEO. 'The new Secretary obviously has hidden depths.'

'And good contacts,' Maisie responded, nudging him in return. 'Are you going to join the line for a picture then?'

'I don't think so, but I suppose it would be good to circulate a bit.'

'Then that's what we'll do.'

They sipped more champagne and mingled. Elliott introduced her to colleagues that he spotted amongst the crowd and she was happy to people-watch if he got drawn into academic discussions. It was particularly endearing to watch elderly members of the Society as excited and blushing as schoolboys at having a real-life film icon in their midst. Mr Suave, the Secretary, noticing Elliott in the crush, had brought the star over to meet them. And Nevada Shaw *was* a complete star. The glorious smile was genuine – all the way to the eyes. As the Secretary navigated her on to meet other guests, someone hailed Elliott from behind them.

'Elwood! Almost missed you in the melee.' A tall man with hawkish features and suspiciously dark hair was bearing down on them.

'Dr Leyland – I wondered if you were here.'

'Of course – couldn't fail to turn up for such an important event.' Maisie decided the man's smile looked decidedly smug. *Now why is that?*

Having greeted Elliott, Leyland was looking at her with curiosity. Despite Ben's warning, Elliott took the hint and introduced them. Maisie found herself being charmed to a professional level – polished and urbane. Maisie guessed urbane charm was Leyland's default mode in social settings, and he was good at it.

But who are you really, *Dr Leyland? And why are you here?*

That was the actual puzzle.

Underlying the smooth surface, there was an air of suppressed excitement about him that put her senses on alert.

He's waiting for something to happen. What?

She didn't get a chance to probe as Leyland was drawn away by the Secretary. Maisie watched them go – *another smoothie in the same mould.* Her observation was interrupted by a woman in a spectacular vintage frock who stopped to admire Maisie's evening bag.

When she turned back from an exchange of pleasantries over the delights of vintage clothes, Elliott had become absorbed in a discussion with a group of elderly Fellows in equally elderly suits that were probably classic tailoring forty years ago. *At least the old boys can still fit into them.* They were a leathery, healthy-looking group. From small colourful badges on baggy lapels, Maisie deduced that these were members of the Society's committee, keen to discuss contentious points in Elliott's lectures. She stood quietly watching. Seeing Elliott in intense professional mode gave her a distinct buzz. She'd enjoyed herself tonight, but now maybe it was time to leave …

Diverted by what they might do *after* they left, she reacted with surprise when a man stopped beside her.

'Sorry. Didn't mean to startle you. Can I offer you a refill?'

She turned to study him. Not as tall as Elliott, brown hair and a pleasant if unremarkable face. He was holding two glasses of champagne. She'd been nursing an empty glass for a few moments. *And whoever he is, he noticed.* She put the glass down and accepted one of the full ones he was proffering, eyes slightly narrowed. *Is this a pick-up?*

When he had a hand free, he held it out. 'Ben. Ben Bartram. And I'm guessing you're Maisie. I work with El,' he explained.

'Oh!' She considered the newcomer with interest. 'He's mentioned you. You're old friends.' She did a quick mental review of what she knew – a mate from undergraduate days, divorced, working alongside Elliott at the university … or maybe not quite alongside. Wasn't he some sort of assistant to Leyland? She wondered if he knew the reason for the man's excitement, but she wasn't about to ask.

'Too bad of El, neglecting you for a bunch of old codgers.' Ben raised his glass to indicate the group clustered around Elliott. 'His loss is my gain.' He grinned engagingly, putting on the charm. *Another one!* Maisie smiled to acknowledge the heavy-handed compliment and sipped her drink. *Come on, this is Elliott's best friend. Be nice.*

'Elliott didn't mention that you'd be here. You're not an Egyptologist though, are you?'

'Hell no! I'm an English lecturer. Dr Leyland brought me along because he needed someone to fetch and carry for him.' The touch of bitterness was unmistakable, then Ben laughed. He had an attractive laugh. 'Oops – shouldn't be talking about our esteemed Dean in that way, but he can be … demanding?' The brown eyes invited Maisie to laugh with him and she found she was. There *was* charm there. She relaxed her shoulders, only just aware that she'd tensed them. *When she'd been speaking to Leyland and she'd picked up on that excitement?* Ben was still speaking, 'I wasn't going to miss an all-expenses-paid trip to the big city and the chance to witness a pal's triumph.' His glance shifted over to where Elliott was standing, with an expression Maisie couldn't quite decipher.

'Triumph?' she queried instead.

'Oh.' Ben looked back at her, clearly disconcerted. 'Damn, I forgot—' he broke off, relief flooding his face as he glanced over her shoulder. He gestured with his glass. 'Looks like it's happening now.'

As she turned, the lights dimmed for a second. On the other side of the room the Society President was calling for quiet. As the babble of conversation faded, Maisie was aware that the committee members surrounding Elliott had stepped back a pace, leaving him alone in a small island of parquet floor. Suddenly on the alert, she straightened up, her eyes on the crowd. There was a distinct sense of anticipation in the air now. The crush had thinned. The guests who'd come to see and be seen had moved on to whatever event was next on their social programme for the evening. The ones in the room now looked much more like they belonged here.

The President had been joined on the platform by the jewellery CEO and another man. Maisie recognised Leyland, wearing a distinctly cat-got-the-cream expression.

What's going on?

Chapter Twenty-Eight

Maisie caught Elliott's eye as he turned towards her, looking equally baffled. She hauled her attention away from him to rake the crowd, again assessing for threats – although what the hell they might be, she couldn't think. She intercepted a few glances cast in Elliott's direction but nothing here felt hostile – there was only that muffled sense of anticipation. Ben seemed to have melted back into a group of bystanders.

The President stepped closer to the edge of the platform, looking out over the room, to address the spectators with another round of thank-yous and gracious compliments.

Smiling benignly, he seemed to be looking their way.

'And now, my friends, I have a very welcome duty to perform.' He glanced round, gathering his audience. 'The committee of the Academic Society held an extra special meeting this morning to approve the awarding of a Fellowship to an outstanding colleague who is making a name for himself within the profession and on the public stage. It is my great pleasure to make the announcement now. Members and distinguished guests, I ask you to welcome our newest Fellow – Dr Elliott Elwood.'

The committee members circling Elliott broke into applause, quickly taken up by other people in the room. The President was beckoning him onto the stage. Seeing that Elliott was totally stunned by the announcement, Maisie stepped forward to take his glass from a limp hand – luckily it was empty – before giving him a little push and a grin. 'Go on.'

Guided by the committee members, the crowd parted to let Elliott through. Once he reached the stage, there was a round of vigorous handshaking but Maisie could see that he still looked dazed.

Then the CEO stepped forward to the microphone. 'Before Dr Elwood has chance to speak—' He turned to acknowledge Elliott, who was standing in front of Leyland. The Dean had a proprietary hand on Elliott's shoulder and an exceedingly self-satisfied expression. 'This evening marks only the beginning of what we all hope will be a memorable partnership with this august Society. I'm pleased to take the opportunity to announce tonight that my company will be hosting a major exhibition of Egyptian treasures in cooperation with the Society and the University of Aquae Sulis.' He paused to acknowledge the President and Leyland, and to allow another burst of applause. Maisie clapped along with the rest. That explained the excitement. *But how is Elliott mixed up in this?* She could see, from his expression, that he was wondering the same thing.

The CEO, clearly happy with the reaction, gestured for silence again. 'As part of this exciting joint initiative, the company intends to establish an annual programme of public lectures. It is my great pleasure to invite Dr Elliott Elwood, the Society's newest Fellow, to deliver the inaugural lecture as our guest at the company's international headquarters in the Principality of Monaco.'

'Now we know what that devious sod Leyland was plotting – and why he was so keen to make sure I would be at the reception and that my diary was free.' Maisie looked up from where she was making tea in the kitchen recess of the Chelsea flat, startled by Elliott's uncharacteristic language and vehemence. It was gone midnight. Once the bombshell had been dropped, there was no way that they were going to be able to sneak away. People had been lining up to congratulate him on the Fellowship and the trip to Monaco. Reporters from a trade periodical and a glossy women's magazine had turned up to do interviews. Elliott had been photographed with Nevada Shaw in front of a display of the new perfume. It had all been rather hectic.

'Ben knew about it too,' Elliott continued. 'And he didn't tell me.'

'Yes, but he couldn't really go against Leyland's orders,' she pointed out, the voice of reason. 'There must have been people at the Society who knew, and no one gave you a hint.'

'Mmm.' Elliott grunted a response then sat up with a jerk. 'That girl, at the photoshoot at the Museum – Sophie. She was wittering on about a special occasion, and she mentioned Leyland. I thought I'd misheard. She must have known too. It seems like everyone knew about it except me!' Maisie carried two mugs of tea over to where Elliott had flopped back on the sofa, resting his head against the cushions, glaring at the ceiling. He'd taken off his tie and opened the top button of his shirt. The column of his throat looked … enticing.

'Move over.' She gave him a nudge with her foot as she bent to put the mugs down on the table.

'Oh, yes. Sorry.' He shifted to let her sit down and reached for the tea. 'Thanks.'

Maisie blew on hers, so that she could drink it, and studied his profile. She could understand – Elliott had been manipulated and he didn't like it. She didn't blame him for that, but even so …

'Is becoming the youngest ever Fellow of the Academic Society and scoring an all-expenses-paid weekend to Monte Carlo in the company of one of the most glamorous women in the world really so bad?'

The lectures would form part of a festival that included the Egyptian jewellery exhibit, relocated from the Society's HQ to Monaco. As the jewellery and the fragrance lines would have their international launch there, Nevada Shaw would also be making the trip.

'I suppose not,' he grumbled, clearly not convinced. 'If I was going to be away from the University, I'd rather it was for an expedition to Cairo with my postgrads. And if I was going to Monte Carlo, I'd rather it was with you,' he added gruffly.

The bubble of happiness that rose in her chest made her smile.

The Monaco exhibition would focus initially on an augmented version of that evening's display as part of the closing weekend of a month-long arts and culture festival currently being held in the Principality. Elliott would deliver two public lectures on Saturday morning, the weekend after next. Once the festival was over, the Egyptian element of the exhibition would be enlarged again and continue for six months.

'The extra items are coming from Aquae Sulis – which can only be the Pentecost Collections. Leyland *must* know that the University is going to get them.'

Maisie was finding the combative glint in Elliott's eye quite fascinating. *Remember – don't piss off Dr Elwood – oh – actually, been there, done that. Fell out of the dress.*

She put down her tea and leaned over, tilting Elliott's chin so he was facing towards her. She leaned in. After a second of resistance, the hard line of his mouth softened under hers. She teased gently with her tongue until he responded in kind. When his hand came up to unpin her hair, she knew that she'd succeeded in diverting him.

She straightened up and away, gratified when he gave a growl in protest. 'Come on.' She reached for his hand. 'Let's go to bed.'

When Maisie got back to the Bath office, late the following morning, the phone on her desk was ringing.

‘I owe you a drink.’ The laconic greeting didn’t disguise the satisfaction in Sergeant Casey’s voice.

‘It *was* blackmail.’ Maisie knew her face had lit up with a grin.

Her previous telephone call to Sergeant Casey had suggested a new line of enquiry on the bank robberies he was investigating – that Julian Holt, the man who had been trying to lure her sister into an affair, was part of a gang of thieves who were using blackmail to coerce bank employees to supply inside information. She’d outlined her “theory”, without naming Fran or giving details. Casey was too good a copper not to realise that there was more to the story, but had agreed to follow it up.

Holt’s stalkerish attempts to continue the affair with Fran had immediately rung alarm bells with Maisie. Knowing about the unsolved robberies, she’d quickly put two and two together. As assistant manager of a large local bank, she’d suspected that her sister was being lined up as Holt’s next victim for a honey trap – the collection of compromising material with which to apply pressure; pressure that would be exerted to make Fran disclose vital details about the bank’s security system, with the threat to publish graphic photographs. Holt had clearly been reluctant to see his weeks of work go to waste when she ended the relationship.

‘Yeah,’ Casey confirmed. ‘The assistant manager of the bank that was robbed in Cheltenham admitted to an affair. Holt threatened to break up her marriage with the whole mess *that* involves – kids, property, whatever – the price of silence being inside info on the bank. We picked Holt up yesterday. I think he’ll roll over. We got nothing on the Gloucester job though – all the upper management there is male, so they may have used a woman for that. We’ll find out.’

Maisie assured him of her confidence that he would, and arranged a meeting in the pub for the promised drink. She replaced the receiver and sat back with a sigh of relief. With luck, by the time her sister got back from Sardinia, Holt would be completely enmeshed in the legal system and out of her life for good. Fran’s secret was safe. *And she’ll never know what you did.* Maisie was still figuring out why that was important when Michelle put her head round the door.

‘Jake’s office – now.’

Maisie was on her feet and following her colleague in a heartbeat. ‘Contact?’ She asked quietly as she caught Michelle up in the corridor.

‘Must be.’

When they reached Jake’s office, the burner phone was sitting in the middle of his desk. ‘The thing went off fifteen minutes ago,’ he said.

'Scared the crap out of me. The auction is on, but the bastard is still being cagey. No details – just that it's set for the weekend after next, in Monaco.'

'Monaco!' Maisie heard the rising intonation in her voice. Her skin had gone as cold as if someone had dumped a bucket of ice water over her.

'What?' Michelle's hand gripped her arm hard, bringing her back to focus.

'Elliott … Dr Elwood. The Dean of Humanities has arranged for him to give two lectures the weekend after next … in Monaco.'

Chapter Twenty-Nine

'It *could* be a coincidence,' Michelle didn't sound as if she believed it, even as she said it.

'Not impossible,' Jake agreed. 'Monaco is full of very rich people – Mickey has already identified two possible collectors. One of them is in his eighties and unwell. It would make sense to take the sale to him, rather than the other way round. But it still puts Dr Elwood in the wrong place at the wrong time,' he observed. They were sitting at the table in Jake's office. On his instructions, they'd cleared their diaries for the rest of the day. Elliott had been invited to join them and was due any minute. Cassie would also join the council of war when he arrived.

'It potentially increases our chances of identifying the seller.' Michelle's eyes gleamed as she thought it through.

'*If* the seller is intending to have Dr Elwood authenticate the piece,' Maisie objected. 'We can't be sure of that.' She definitely wasn't happy about where this was going.

'Michelle is right though – it could be something we can use,' Jake suggested. Maisie tried not to glower at her boss. Sometimes Jake could be so damn reasonable she wanted to throw things. 'I don't like the involvement of this Humanities guy – Leyland,' he added. 'You said he was the one driving this exhibition thing.' Jake nodded to Maisie. 'That links us back to the University … and the death of Professor Mumford.'

Maisie swallowed. Her impression of Leyland was that he was a smug prick – but a murderer? She couldn't see it. *Yeah, but how many friends and neighbours of murderers and terrorists say what nice people they seemed? And Leyland doesn't even seem* that *nice.*

'You think Leyland orchestrated this to get Elliott to Monaco?' she asked flatly.

'It's difficult not to see the possibility,' Michelle observed. 'Okay – he couldn't have controlled the jewellery exhibition or the Fellowship, but he must have offered the artefacts and he might have had some influence over the lectures. He could certainly choose the site of the auction. Locating it in Monaco gives it cachet – money and glamour. And getting most of the bidders off their home turf might be an advantage to an amateur outfit with no backup behind it,' she suggested, running with the idea. 'The whole thing *could* have been done electronically – no one had to leave their office. It could have been over in ten minutes.'

'But not as much fun for the collectors if the bidding war is part of the attraction,' Jake responded. 'The fact that they seem to have assembled an auction supports that.'

'This insistence on the bidders travelling is also a power game.' Michelle was still thinking aloud. 'He/she/they hold the cards – but it gives us something to work with. We have to be grateful for that.'

Maisie wasn't feeling at all grateful, but she could see Michelle's point. Didn't mean she had to like it.

Jake was also looking thoughtful. 'It's theatrical, flashy, "Look at me, I have something you want and you'll jump through my hoops to get it." Does that sound like Leyland?' he asked Maisie.

'I don't know him that well, but he has a reputation for arrogance and for being a schemer, so it might. I'd guess he enjoys power plays. Elliott can tell you more when he gets here.'

'Being able to produce your own expert to validate the piece *is* pretty cool,' Michelle mused.

'I suppose so,' Maisie conceded. 'We're loading a lot onto the idea that Leyland is the mind behind this.'

'True,' Jake agreed. 'But, whether or not his presence was manipulated, Dr Elwood will be in Monaco at the same time as the auction. He has to be protected. If he *is* to be involved, he will have to be shown the Necklace at some stage. It could be a vulnerable point for them. And we have one advantage – they don't know that *we* know.'

Maisie slumped in her seat. She would prefer that Elliott was a million miles away from it all, but Jake's mention of protection had slightly cooled her impulse to stamp about and wave her arms. Elliott would have protection. *Me. That has to be me.*

Jake looked up as the phone on his desk rang. 'I think Dr Elwood has arrived.'

He doesn't suspect. He doesn't suspect. He doesn't suspect.

After days of walking on egg shells, the wave of realisation and relief was almost overwhelming. Nothing had changed. He'd accepted the attempt to disappear. *I didn't know* he *knew about that house – a place from the past.* He had known, and he'd remembered. But he'd acknowledged, even applauded using it to slip quietly off the map, never realising that it was meant to be *his* map. *Too puffed up with how clever he's been to think about it.*

Now arrangements for the auction were made. Yesterday, the last piece had fallen into place. Elliott Elwood would be in Monaco. It was all going ahead.

He doesn't suspect.

It was all going to be fine.

Yeah, but now he *has the Necklace.*

I don't trust him. *I don't feel safe. I'll never feel safe now, with* him.

Deep breath. No need to panic. For now, they were still "partners". There still might be a chance.

A pulse of adrenaline surged. Maisie Norris's boss was one of the four invited to the auction. And Elladour hadn't let on about the second offer.

Probably thinks it was a hoax or a con.

But it wasn't, *Mr Elladour.*

And maybe we'll both still get the chance ...

The Necklace wasn't sold yet. *He* was *so* pleased with himself. Full of pride that Elwood would be in place to authenticate it. But to authenticate it, Elwood would have to *see* it.

Would that be where the chance came?

Elliott waited at the back door of the honey-coloured Georgian building that housed the Kings Detective Agency. Jake McQuire had explained the situation succinctly over the phone and given him instructions of how to approach the offices by the staff entrance to avoid the risk of being seen. He looked around with interest. The access through a narrow alley led to a small enclosed courtyard. High walls clothed with prickly looking shrubs helped to shield the approach. He was looking forward to seeing where Maisie worked, although he had a suspicion that she might not be quite so pleased to see *him* there. He turned when the black panelled door swung open. He'd passed muster with whoever was monitoring the small security camera mounted on the frame.

When the secretary who collected him escorted him to McQuire's office on the top floor, he found McQuire himself, his wife Cassie, whom Elliott knew from various charity activities, an attractive young woman introduced as Michelle, and Maisie. From the stiffness of her mouth, he deduced that his suspicion was correct. She was not happy to have him involved. He had a good idea why. He took a breath. *May as well get the thing out in the open straight away.* 'You're making plans to try to recover the Necklace and apprehend the thieves – and you want me to act as bait.'

Maisie had to swallow down the hard lump in her throat at the even tone of Elliott's voice. Now *he* was being reasonable. *What is the matter with these people!*

She must have moved or something, because he looked over at her as he took a seat at the table. She arranged her face into a disapproving frown, but he was smiling. *Smiling*! And Jake was laughing. 'That's a bit blunter than I would have put it, but it seems possible that you've been deliberately inserted into the equation. We have to grab whatever advantage we can find.'

'And if someone wants me to examine the Necklace, I count as an advantage. I get that. Unless I refuse to lecture, I'm going to be in Monaco at the critical time whatever happens. I'd rather be part of your plans than not.' He gave Jake a level look. 'If Vaisey Leyland is mixed up in this somehow, I want to know.'

Maisie didn't miss the flash of steel in Elliott's eyes and the combative set of his jaw. *Okay – if you suspected a colleague was setting you up, you'd want to do something about it too.*

'Do you think he is?' Jake addressed the question directly to Elliott.

Elliott shrugged. 'Honest answer? I really don't know. I don't want to believe it, but I think he might be capable of it. I've never really got on with the man, so my judgement might be skewed,' he admitted. 'He enjoys intrigue. He must have manoeuvred to get the University involved in the exhibition and he might have had some influence in the matter of the lectures. I really don't know,' he repeated. 'I suppose he might want money.'

Jake looked automatically at Michelle. She shook her head.

'Nothing in his finances indicated problems. He lives within his means, but we know he's a gambler. He could have unrecorded debts.'

'He could be doing it just because he can – almost an intellectual exercise – or to funnel money into relocating the Pentecost Collections to Pentecost Court,' Elliott said. 'Either of those motives might make sense to him. The connection to the University seems too strong to ignore it.'

'I don't think we can,' Jake said quietly.

Abruptly, the resistance inside Maisie crumbled. *This is happening. You can't avoid it, much as you would like to.*

With an effort, she pushed her objections into submission. Elliott was right; he was in this whether *she* liked it or not. It was better this way. Elliott wouldn't be alone. She had to focus – their plan had to be as good as they could make it, which was going to be a big ask as there were so many unknowns. *You need to be all over this.*

Jake had been doodling on a pad while they waited for Elliott to be shown up to the office. She could see that he'd drawn a Venn diagram, with overlapping circles, but she couldn't read what he'd written in the sectors.

'Given that we can't change what Dr Leyland may have initiated, I suggest we circumvent his arrangements and those of the thieves as far as possible.' Jake turned the sheet of paper around to display his doodle. One circle was marked Augustus Elladour, the other had Elliott's name and the overlapping section in the middle was her. Jake was grinning one of his wolfish grins. 'We've inserted me into the scenario, as the mysterious billionaire Augustus Elladour, but I think I shall continue to be a very secretive billionaire.'

Jake shot a glance over at his wife. Cassie had been quiet, following the various arguments. Now she had her head tipped on one side, which Maisie knew was her thinking position. 'Like maybe you're a squeaky-clean type who plays with the good guys but has a very particular and very illegal hobby that he doesn't want known?' she suggested.

'Exactly,' Jake agreed.

Something twisted in Maisie's chest at the rapport between Jake and his wife. She knew the feeling was envy. They connected on so many levels.

Jake tapped the diagram. 'The link in all this is Maisie. I want her to continue to represent me in the negotiations for the moment. She also has a personal connection to Elliott.' He glanced between the two of them. 'I propose we set you up in a villa in Menton rather than whatever accommodation Leyland has negotiated. It's close to Monaco but it gives us some space to work with. We already have people in the area.' *That's whatever squirrelly thing Mickey is involved in.* 'They can provide an element of backup, should we need it,'

The knowledge made Maisie feel a fraction more relaxed. It was a very small fraction.

Jake was still speaking. 'I can be present to step in when the crunch point is reached, but I don't propose to have a high profile until then. Keep them guessing.'

'Use the yacht,' Cassie suggested. 'You can come and go anywhere on the coast as you please.'

Maisie found herself trying not to smile. *How the other half lives.* The lump in her throat had dissolved a bit. She still wasn't comfortable about Elliott's involvement, but if she was going to be with him in their own villa …

Michelle was leaning back in her chair, playing with a pencil. 'The secret billionaire thing. Are they going to be trying to find out more about Augustus? Find out who you really are?' She looked at Jake.

He grinned. 'And as you were the one to set up the profile for Augustus Elladour, if they do go digging, we know that it's as good as it gets.'

Maisie could see her friend trying to look blasé at the compliment and almost succeeding. 'It was a rush job though,' Michelle complained. She put the pencil back on the table. 'I suppose if anyone did somehow make a connection with the detective agency that squeaky-clean/secret vice thing would work. They wouldn't be sure what your role was.'

'That would be the idea – but I'd much prefer that they don't make the connection, so Maisie acts as principal for as long as possible.' Jake shot Maisie a grin of approval. Despite the tense situation, she couldn't help the flicker of pride – she was trusted to do her job. She *mattered.*

Jake continued. 'Not knowing exactly what we're up against doesn't stop us, but we need to take every precaution.' He shot a warning glance around the group. 'No one goes out on a limb for this. We don't have a client to please, and with the greatest respect to Dr Elwood's professional interest, the Necklace is not worth the possibility of anyone getting hurt.'

Maisie looked over at Elliott. He was nodding, endorsing what Jake had said. Even with Jake's caution, the reminder of risk sent a small shiver through Maisie. The thieves probably weren't a professional gang. Amateurs might be more reckless. *And at least one of them is probably a murderer.*

You can never forget that.

Chapter Thirty

Elliott leaned back in his office chair and clasped his hands behind his head. The plans for the remodelling of Pentecost Court were spread out on the desk in front of him, weighed down at the corners by large pebble, an ancient Oxford dictionary and a stone model of the Sphinx. Everything was looking good. Leyland had confirmed that the University's bid for the Pentecost Collections *had* been approved, but the announcement was under wraps until various formalities were completed. Leyland was masterminding an official statement, with suitable ceremony, for the beginning of term, when he was sure of maximum attention. An announcement in the last weeks of the vacation just wouldn't cut it. He hadn't mentioned the Necklace and Elliott hadn't asked.

Elliott ran his hand over the plans. Currently, his acting ability was peaking at Oscar class, but he was finding it difficult to be around the Dean, suspecting what the man might be. He could feel the muscles of his neck and shoulders tensing now and Leyland wasn't even on the campus. He was in Torquay, wading through inventories and provenance.

And after that, will he be on his way to Monaco?

Maisie was eating lunch in Jake's office. They were having a short update meeting and Cassie always arranged for catering even if, as today, she wouldn't be there herself. Maisie wiped a blob of mayonnaise off her hand. The chicken salad sandwich had been delicious. The things they were discussing less so. Cassie had the right idea though; good food helped.

The arrangements for the auction had finally been disclosed in a further letter left at reception at the Chelsea apartment. Acceptance was confirmed using another untraceable burner phone. No objection had been raised to Maisie acting as Elladour's representative. They'd speculated that other bidders were doing the same.

And as for the auction itself …

'Too clever by half.' Jake indicated the admission ticket for the masquerade ball on the Saturday night that marked the end of the arts festival. Bidders would attend the ball and be contacted there. A brief note also set out the arrangements for electronic transfer of the purchase money.

'It rather is, actually.' Michelle picked up the ornately embossed card in one hand while holding a BLT in the other. 'Dress code. Visards. Costume or dominos,' she read aloud, taking a bite from the sandwich. 'I'm assuming translated that means masks and fancy dress, which lets all the participants remain anonymous. What the hell is a domino?'

'Hooded cloak,' Maisie replied absently. 'I had to look it up,' she admitted when Michelle raised her eyebrows. She'd done it when Elliott had received his own invitation, personally endorsed by the CEO of the jewellery firm. She glanced over at Jake. 'The process for the auction might start at the ball but it doesn't have to end there. Our clever friend might be planning to load everyone into a minibus and drive off to who knows where.'

'It's a possibility,' Jake agreed blandly. Maisie stopped playing mentally with the implications of a mass kidnapping of billionaires with dodgy obsessions and considered her boss with narrowed eyes. He was up to something.

But when isn't he?

He would attend the masquerade, but they'd agreed to decide whether he stepped in as Elladour when they had a better idea of what was going down.

If we ever do.

She would be at the ball.

Jake would be at the ball.

Elliott would be at the ball.

The thieves would be at the ball.

It's going to be a really fun evening.

It was Sunday. Somehow, she was here at her parents' house again for family lunch. On the whole, the day was going okay. *And maybe it will get better later.*

The roast lamb was perfect and her mother had plenty to divert her with the wedding, her granddaughters, who were meeting Stephen for the first time, and the photographs of Fran and Paul's trip to Sardinia. When Fran had hugged Maisie hello, she'd whispered how well the trip had gone. She was certainly glowing and it wasn't just a holiday tan. Maybe the baby plan had also succeeded? Maisie found that she was hoping so.

When the conversation turned to wedding favours, she tuned out, only tuning back again when her father made to top up her wine. She put a hand over the glass with a smile. She didn't want any more; she was driving. Her mother was asking Fran about a new recruit to the bank – something to do with foreign currency. 'I'm sure it must be quite an upheaval for the young man, moving to a new area. You must invite him to lunch, Françoise. He'd be very welcome.'

You bet he would.

When her mother gave a heavy sigh, with a speaking glance in her direction, Maisie frowned at her sister across the table, trying to convey a hard "No" with her eyes. Fran was laughing, tilting a hand in a maybe-I-will, maybe-I-won't gesture. Maisie added the threat of retribution to her disapproving glare. It was clear what her mother had in mind, but she didn't need to be introduced to some random stranger. She had a man in her life.

Yeah, but no one knows about him.

She quickly pulled her thoughts away from *that* and asked a question about the damn wedding favours.

Now she was sitting in her parents' garden, knowing she was about to be cornered by her brother-in-law.

Once the meal was over, she'd escaped here to allow a decent amount of time to elapse before she made her final getaway. Hal and Stephen had retreated with her father to the den and the sports channel, but Paul hadn't joined them. Her mother and Fran had taken the twins to visit a neighbour whose cat had kittens. Thinking that two adults and two excited nine-year-olds would be quite enough for the new mother, Maisie had declined the treat. And now her sister's husband was approaching her refuge in the rose arbour with a very determined expression. Paul was tall, dark and brooding. *Not unlike Elliott.* It seemed that this generation of Webster women went for brooding; a word that could never be applied to their father's sandy hair and boyish features.

'Hi.' She shaded her eyes with a hand to look up at Paul, shifting on the bench so that he had room to sit down. 'The raiding party isn't back yet?'

Paul gave a rather twisted grin. 'No, but I suspect cat ownership will occur in our family's imminent future.' Despite the grimace, he didn't seem too bothered by it. Instead of sitting down, he stopped in front of her. 'I'm glad you didn't go with them. It gives me the chance to say thank you.'

Maisie's heart began to thump. 'What for?' she asked cautiously.

'Julian Holt was arrested while we were in Sardinia. As the result of a tip-off. It was in the local paper,' he responded obliquely, turning to lean against the arbour and look out over the garden.

'Julian Holt?' Two could play at oblique, but her heart was still thumping.

Paul watched a bird bouncing across the lawn before taking flight to a nearby bush. 'You're not just a receptionist at Kings any more, are you, Maisie?' He shifted slightly to look down at her. 'My firm had some background checks done on new employees recently. The HR manager mentioned that the detective who did the checks had the same first name as her newest granddaughter. *Maisie.* She was very impressed with the way everything was handled, by the way. She said the agent was very professional and experienced.'

Maisie considered possible responses and decided on silence.

Paul gave her a lopsided grin, as if he'd expected it. 'I realised a long time ago that you're the changeling in the family. Or you view yourself that way,' he said, after a pause. 'It's your choice – I'm not going to say anything more, except that I've not told Fran about any of it. Maybe you can think about whether you still need to embrace the changeling thing though?' He took a deep, shaky-sounding breath. 'And thank you for protecting my wife and helping to save my marriage.'

'I—'

Maisie wasn't sure what she'd intended to say, but it didn't matter. The kitten-visiting party had arrived back, streaming across the lawn, the two girls in the lead and bubbling with excitement. Paul's face changed when he saw his wife and daughters and Maisie knew what she was seeing. *That's love.* She found she had a lump in her throat.

'You're welcome,' she whispered the words, knowing he wouldn't hear her.

Then Rosie, normally the quieter of the twins, planted herself beside her on the bench to seek an opinion on whether they should choose a black-and-white or ginger kitten, and the moment passed.

Elliott dumped the bag with his kit on the floor by the door and headed for his power shower, which he preferred over using the ones at the gym.

Once showered, dressed and sitting down with a pot of tea, he wondered what Maisie was doing. She'd been evasive over her plans for the day, which he took to mean that there was some sort of family stuff going on. He hadn't pushed.

Of course, it might not be family at all.

Maybe there's an old flame in town for the weekend.

The thought hit him so hard and unexpectedly that he lost breath and winced.

No – that wasn't true. Couldn't be. Maisie wouldn't do that. *Why would she?*

Of course, for the moment they were brought together by the Necklace. *Forced proximity.*

And deception was part of her job …

Elliott huffed hard at his thoughts and took a sustaining mouthful of tea. What he had was Sunday afternoon blues, with nothing to look forward to but an evening of mundane offerings on the television. He wanted company. He wanted Maisie. It didn't matter if that was just both of them dozing in front of the TV with a bottle of wine. He needed to know that she was *here.*

Oh, for heaven's sake! Get a grip.

He finished the tea and stood up. Maybe he'd go for a walk. Perhaps he should get a dog? That would be company.

He stopped in the middle of the room. *Would you look at yourself? Get a dog!*

He was quite capable of spending an evening alone. He was bored. That was all. And who wouldn't be uneasy with the spectre of that damn Necklace looming over them? Perhaps the thing *was* cursed.

They'd agreed that, with the arrangements set for Monaco, he was unlikely to be under threat here in Bath, but even so there was always that niggling doubt in his mind, putting him off balance and planting all sorts of stupid ideas in his head. He wanted a diversion. Maybe he should go to the cinema? There must be something worth seeing either here or in Bristol. He'd watch some mindless action movie and eat popcorn. He rummaged in a pile of papers on the coffee table for the local *What's On* magazine.

Maisie locked her car and made her way to the front door of the block. The day was softening down to evening. *Sunday evening*. She wasn't too keen on Sunday evenings after she'd been to Sunday lunch. *Left over time. Neither one thing nor another*. It stirred up uncomfortable feelings – made her restless. She didn't fit into her family and she'd always known it.

Except that today it had felt different.

Did it feel *different or were* you *different?*

The idea gave her an odd churning feeling in her abdomen.

She let herself in and climbed the stairs to her flat.

Fran had teased her and Paul had thanked her, and Hal and Stephen had both hugged her when they arrived and when they left, and it all felt a bit strange.

As if you're actually part of the family?

She pursed her mouth as she turned the key in the lock and pushed open the door to step inside. The air in the flat was warm and heavy. She crossed to open the window and stayed to look out. The street below was quiet.

What had Paul called her? The changeling? *You never seem to be ... enough.* She was the accident, the afterthought, the red-headed embarrassment who arrived after the perfect family was meant to be complete …

She'd heard that often enough from her grandmother when she wasn't supposed to understand grown-up conversation.

She'd never fitted into her family. She fitted with Elliott, but who knew if that was going to last? Once Monaco was over, there would be nothing to tie them together. Maybe what they had would just drift away slowly into nothingness. Elliott would go back to his life, and she to hers, and they might meet occasionally for a drink

She rubbed absently at her chest; an uncomfortable sensation behind her rib-cage. Everything was fine at the moment, so why was she worrying about the unknown?

She sighed and moved away from the window. *Sunday night blues.* She could do something about that. By Friday, they would be in Monaco with everything that involved, but for tonight – it was still warm outside and would be daylight for a couple of hours yet. She dug her phone out from her bag.

'Hi – yes, just got in. What are you doing? Fancy a walk? Along the canal to look at the boats? Maybe find a pub with a garden?'

Chapter Thirty-One

Jake leaned casually against the deck rail, looking back at Nice harbour and the town beyond, basking in the warm sunshine. 'If Leyland is here, he's lying low.'

'*If* he's here?' Maisie raised her eyebrows at her boss. 'We know he's not in Bath, or Torquay.'

Jake grinned. 'That still leaves lot of other places he could be.'

Maisie shrugged. She'd come straight to the ship from the airport, off the early morning flight. She'd wanted to check in with Jake. Okay – she also wanted to see the yacht. She wrinkled her nose. *Billionaires' toys*. The thing was huge, with facilities comparable to those of a luxury hotel – owner's suite, guest suites, lounge, dining room, staff quarters, multiple decks, swimming pool, the place at the top where the driver sat …

And it floats.

She was trying not to be impressed, but it wasn't working. The damn thing was gorgeous and she had definite pangs of envy. She'd like to scoop Elliott up when he arrived on the afternoon flight and sail off into the sunset, away from that damn Necklace.

Not going to happen.

She sighed and leaned against the rail alongside Jake. 'Leyland is here somewhere,' she said with conviction. 'But he won't know where *we* are.'

Michelle had phoned the festival organiser this morning in the guise of Elliott's PA, to let her know that Dr Elwood and his companion had accepted an invitation to stay at a friend's villa instead of the accommodation that had been reserved. The harried administrator had taken a moment to register Elliott's name. Once Michelle had confirmed that Dr Elwood would make his own way to all the events he was expected to attend, the woman had rung off quickly with a relieved goodbye, obviously moving on to the next pressing thing – which suited them just fine.

Maisie knew that it was malicious to hope that Leyland, and whoever he was working with, had a few uncomfortable hours when they realised Elliott was off their radar, but she didn't feel guilty over it. At best they were thieves, and at worst Leyland was a murderer. 'You have everything in place for Saturday night?' she asked instead.

The gala masquerade ball would mark the culmination of the festival – and the night of the auction. Jake had made certain arrangements, but he hadn't disclosed what they were. She knew he would be at the ball, ready to step in if necessary. There was no way of telling whether the other auction participants would appear in person, or act by proxy through agents. Mickey reported that two notable dealers were in town, which suggested the latter in regards to a couple of the bidders, but wouldn't an avid collector want to handle the Necklace for themselves?

'Everything is done,' Jake confirmed. 'As far as everything can be.'

They were working with so many unknowns. *Too many.* What they were doing was crazy. But whatever they were doing and whether they were here or not, Elliott would still be in the middle of it. *So it's much better that we* are *here.*

She straightened away from the rail. 'Time I was on my way to Menton. I'll keep in touch.'

'This place is awesome.'

'It is – but you haven't seen the yacht.' Maisie stood beside Liam on the highest terrace of the villa in the hills above Menton. The building was a pile of blinding white sugar cubes and plate glass. Palm trees shaded the edge of the terrace. Bougainvillea flared in vivid shades of pink and purple. Below them, on a lower terrace, an infinity pool glittered turquoise in the sun. Beyond that, the sea shimmered blue-grey, dotted with boats of all shapes and sizes.

'You think Jake owns this place?' Liam speculated.

'He said it belongs to a friend.'

'I should have such friends.' Liam let out a long sigh, then reverted to business. 'The security is solid – alarms, high perimeter wall, good locks. The gates to the grounds will discourage vehicular access.' He turned to look at the huge windows behind them. 'If this was a threat on someone's life then I would not be happy with *those*, but our unknown isn't looking to kill Elwood.'

Despite the gloriously warm day, Maisie shivered. She was glad that Jake had arranged for Liam to look over the place and stay on hand in the staff accommodation above the garage. They really didn't know what to expect. Would the thieves attempt to abduct Elliott before the ball? Might the thief who had tried to do the separate deal manage somehow to turn up here, to offer Jake the Necklace? That would kill two birds with one stone with Elliott on hand to evaluate it.

She gave another tiny shudder. *No, not kill. Don't think about killing.* If the second seller turned up, it would mean they'd eliminated one of the thieves. That was good. But if Leyland *was* involved, he could be a murderer. She took a deep breath of jasmine-scented air. Her thoughts were going around in circles. Bottom line – they didn't *know.*

All they could do was wait – and react.

The parameters of the operation pulled in two directions: protecting Elliott, without being seen to do so, but allowing anyone who had a necklace to authenticate to make contact. *No pressure then. No pressure at all.* Her personal choice would be to lock Elliott in a windowless room somewhere, with a guard outside the door, and leave him there until the damn Necklace was sold to somebody, *anybody*. But that wasn't what this was about.

'They want his expert opinion, Maze, they're really not going to kill him,' Liam said softly.

Maisie jibbed a little at the fact that Liam could read her so well before she semi-relaxed. *He's an experienced and trained observer, remember?* 'I know. I keep telling myself that – but this whole thing is so damn … up in the air. We're knitting fog. All we really know is that *something* is going to happen at that damn ball.'

'Control freak,' Liam chided, with a low laugh.

'Yes. All right.' Maisie held up her hands, acknowledging the accusation.

'I don't like it either,' Liam admitted. 'But we do the best with what we have.' He looked at his watch. 'Your guy should be here any minute. I'm going to disappear to the staff quarters. Buzz if you need me.' Maisie was surprised when he pulled her into a swift hug. 'Make the most of this place – and your time.'

He walked briskly away. Maisie followed him more slowly. *Her guy.* She rather liked that. *Maybe more than you should?*

To hell with questions, they had nearly eighteen hours before Elliott delivered his first lecture and reappeared on the thieves' radar. She *was* going to make the most of them.

A taxi was discharging its passenger when she reached the front of the house. Liam must have released the gate. She walked over, ready for a hello kiss as the car pulled away down the drive.

Elliott kissed her with enthusiasm, but she sensed that some of his attention was focused over her shoulder, on the car standing in front of the house. As they broke apart, she gave him a reproving look.

'I know – sorry, sorry, but wow! Just wow! A vintage Sunbeam Alpine,' he said reverently.

'The car Grace Kelly drove in *To Catch a Thief,*' Maisie confirmed. 'Only hers was a current model then, and it was sapphire-blue.' This one dated from the 1960s and was gleaming red. She really couldn't blame Elliott – she'd had the same reaction when the hire car was delivered.

She pulled his hand so they could walk over to inspect it.

'Wow,' he said again. 'You have a very cool employer.'

'He is that,' she agreed. The car was a generous gesture, one which Jake knew she would appreciate. It was also distinctive enough to make them easy to follow. *And isn't that what we're here for – to catch a thief of our own?*

'Elwood never checked into the hotel.'

'He must have – you must have missed him.'

'I did *not* miss him. I sat in that foyer for two hours.' *Ordering expensive coffee and pastries and trying to blend, until the point where it got embarrassing.* 'Was there a delay at the airport?'

'No – the flight came into Nice on time. He was booked on the helicopter transfer – he should have been at the hotel by four-thirty at the latest.'

'Well, he wasn't. I sent in a parcel. It wasn't delivered.'

The lavishly wrapped bottle of champagne was the kind of welcome gift visitors to the hotel might expect to receive from a friend or a business colleague. The package had been delivered within ten minutes of placing the order and had been accepted by the receptionist. It sat on a table beside the concierge's station for an hour before the man ambled over to the desk, pointing at the package, clearly with a question. The receptionist consulted the computer below the desk, grimaced and shrugged. The champagne was carried off into an inner office.

'He's staying somewhere else. Has to be. With the Norris woman.' The voice on the phone was flat and uncompromising. 'We need to find out. We need to be sure of him.'

Chapter Thirty-Two

'This place is—'

'Awesome?' Maisie looked over with a smile that sent a kick of warmth through Elliott's chest.

'I was going to say amazing, but awesome will do just as well.' He sat back in his chair, absently passing his wine glass from one hand to the other and soaking up images – the red-tiled terrace where they'd eaten dinner as the sun sank, the white geraniums that spilled from terracotta pots, the twisting bougainvillea. Tiny fairy lights twinkled high in the spiky leaves of the palm trees that leaned in overhead, casting the edges of the space into mysterious shadows. Light spilled out from the wide windows of the villa behind them, and below them submerged lights in the pool shimmered up through the water. The scent of citronella candles mixed with the heady fragrance of jasmine from somewhere in the garden.

The remnants of their meal of salad Niçoise and a tart glistening with fruit lay on the table between them. Maisie sat across from him, her hair pinned away from her face, in a slim linen dress of the same blue as the pool. Her nose was faintly dusted with freckles and her arms were lightly tanned from the sun. Her eyes were laughing and her mouth was warm and full.

She's never looked more beautiful.

Something squeezed in his chest, hitching his breathing. He put down his glass carefully, aware that his grip might not be quite steady. And there was that kicking in his chest again. He held out his hand across the table and she took it, her fingers closing on his.

'I …' Suddenly, he didn't know what he was going to say. The night was warm and dark and enfolding, wrapping them in a cocoon of shadow splattered with sparkling lights. 'Perfect.' The word rose up from somewhere but he wasn't sure what it meant – the place, the woman … everything?

'It is, isn't it?' Maisie squeezed his hand. 'And tonight, it's all ours.' She stood up suddenly, letting go of his hand, laughing. As she slipped from his grasp, his fingers felt strangely cold.

'Just look at that.' She gestured to the pool, glowing turquoise below them. She turned back to him, her eyes alight with life, with intent. 'We should swim.'

'Yes, we should.' The night and the place were magic. He wanted to absorb all of it, to take it all in. The feeling made him breathless. 'We must.'

Maisie reared up from the water, letting her feet touch the bottom and pushing her damp hair out of her eyes. Swimming like this, in the lighted pool with the stars above them, was a totally new experience. She'd reluctantly relinquished the idea of skinny-dipping when she remembered that Liam had promised to make a couple of patrols of the grounds. *But we will do it. Some day. Soon.* Even decorous in a bikini, the contrast between the water and the faint chill in the night air was sending goosebumps over her skin. *Or maybe that's being here, with Elliott?*

He splashed to a stop beside her, and she turned naturally, without thought, into his arms. The extra contrast of warm skin made her senses ripple like the water. The kiss was long and slow and deep, part of the night. She was wrapped up in the scent of jasmine and Elliott, the rustling of the palm leaves as they caught a tremor of breeze, and the navy darkness of the sky and the sea.

They sat together for a while on the edge of the pool, staring out at the drop into infinity, at the stars and the lights of the boats on the water. Her wet skin was chilling but Elliott's arm around her was warm and secure. She turned her face into his shoulder.

'Ready to go in?' he asked. She nodded, cheek brushing against his warmth, before pushing herself up and away from the pool, reaching for his hand.

The master bedroom was on the ground floor at the back of the house, dominated by a bed that had to be more than king-sized. The long windows that led to a small secluded terrace were covered now with drapes of filmy voile. In the golden light of two tall, slim bedside lamps, the white curtains, walls, carpet and linens merged into a cloud-like enclosing haze. Sodden bikini discarded, Maisie dropped naked onto the welcoming softness of the bed, reaching to pull Elliott down beside her. She put her hand on his chest, holding him still, taking a long moment to absorb him, skin to skin.

She wanted him. That was as it always was now, but tonight there was something different in the mix. *It's this place. Has to be. Wrapping you up in magic.* She felt breathless, her skin sensitised, her breasts needy and aching, but not with urgency. Every moment tonight had to last, be noted, and not lost in a blur. Elliott seemed to understand. He was gently sifting his fingers through her still damp hair, combing it away from her face, his eyes dark, focused on his task.

'What do you want?' he asked softly.

'I want you.' She breathed in. 'Just you.'

They'd made love so often now – but never like this. Each small touch set her nerve endings humming, pleasure blooming under the skin. It wasn't sparks and fire but a long, slow-building crescendo of touch and taste. They were in tune like never before. Elliott knew her body now; the sensitive places where the caress of hand and mouth brought her to the brink of sobbing need. With exquisite control and murmured words, he explored her slowly; mouth, breasts, stomach, thighs, until she hung on the brink of shattering. At last, with his mouth on the most intimate part of her, lapping inside her, she broke, spinning into darkness, eyes pressed tightly shut, hands clawing against the sheets.

After long, dizzying moments when the world was only sensation, her eyes finally flickered open as the room righted itself. She reached to kiss Elliott, knowing the taste she would find on his lips. 'Now you.'

In response to Maisie's insistent pull on his shoulder, Elliott rolled on his back, holding himself still as her mouth roamed over him. He didn't quite know how he was holding on, only that he was. Torment and pleasure and ... no words. He and Maisie had built something here tonight in this vast bed and he didn't want it to end. He held on and slid into pleasure on pleasure, deep into a closeness that he'd never experienced before. When she took him into her mouth, he was sure he was levitating. His hand brushed the top of her head and she gently let him go. 'Now?'

'Now,' he confirmed. His hands were clumsy as he fumbled the condom from its packet, but then he was *there,* sinking into welcoming heat, feeling small muscles adjust. Everything he was had centred on Maisie's enraptured face. On the edges of his vision, there was only darkness. As he rocked into the tight, wet heat, waves of sensation broke at the base of his spine. The sense of completeness was the eye of the silent storm.

'This is *right* … this is *everything*.'

Maisie gave a smothered gasp. Her muscles contracted and he watched, caught and held in the spell, as she came apart in his arms, before he came apart in hers.

Maisie was sleeping, her breath soft on Elliott's shoulder. He was lying awake, staring at the ceiling.

Tonight … Tonight had been like nothing that he'd ever experienced before, in a place he'd never been. He wanted to get up and pace around the room, but he couldn't wake the woman who slept by his side. The woman who …

He still couldn't shape it into words, although his mind was racing.

You know. You know what this is.

He'd never imagined this. Something so huge, so random, so out of his expectations. And it would never have happened if they hadn't been tossed together by a threat and a mystery. Emotion twisted in his chest that had nothing to do with the fact that both those things were still out there. The ache under his ribs was the potential for loss, and that had never happened before either. For a moment, his mind flashed back to that first morning-after; Maisie standing at the door of his Chelsea hotel room, announcing nothing had changed. But of course it had. He'd felt a whisper of it then, but he hadn't been ready – hadn't understood where this was going. Making love tonight had been magical because it *was* magical. *Because you were making love with the* woman *you love.*

He stared at the ceiling and faced the inescapable truth – the one that had been trying to ambush him now for days, maybe weeks.

He was in love with Maisie Webster.

The admission welled up inside him, surprise, shock … joy?

He could wake her now, tell her, make love with her again. He could just turn over, rouse her with a kiss—

Abruptly, his racing thoughts came to a jangling halt. He stared down at Maisie, lying beside him, her hair shadowing her face, a wild tangle of curls silhouetted by the faint light falling through the voile drapes. He had no idea how she felt about him. She liked him, he was sure of that … but could there be more?

The bleakness of the possibility of "no" and "never" floated on the edge of his thoughts, making him close his eyes. *Not going there.* Self-realisation was enough for one night. He blinked up at the ceiling. *I'm in love with Maisie Webster. This is the woman I want to spend the rest of my life with.*

What the hell do I do now?

Chapter Thirty-Three

Maisie walked slowly down through the gardens that led to the Casino. Fountains sparkled in the sun, exotic strelitzia lit up the flower beds, and the round heads of the agapanthus flowers were as blue as the sky. The sky itself was reflected in the modern sculpture in front of the Casino. Anish Kapoor's polished steel disc presented a wavy, upside-down view of buildings and palm trees, in contrast to the intricate Belle Époque splendour of the building standing behind it. It made her think of a wedding cake; all frills and tiers. The contrast with the sleek lines of the mirror seemed to work.

She glanced regretfully at the wide shallow steps and tall door giving on to the interior. She would have liked to go inside and wander around the highly decorated rooms. Just another tourist, like the small gaggles clutching guide-books and taking selfies that she had to keep navigating around. *Later? When this is done?*

This morning, her object was beyond the square: the upmarket hotel where the masquerade ball would be held that evening. She didn't expect to get anywhere near the ballroom itself, but she still wanted an idea of the setup.

She walked on.

Posters and banners for the festival and the ball competed with promotion for the exclusive "Egyptian" jewellery and perfume lines. Nevada Shaw's face smiled out, somehow managing to convey sultry and friendly in a single expression. She really was a good actress. She'd also been in the audience for Elliott's first talk that morning, pleasing the small contingent whose chief objective in being present was to see and be seen, and adding an unexpected thrill for those who had come simply to listen. She'd given the crowd their money's worth by standing up to ask a perceptive question at the end.

Maisie had enjoyed the lecture, even though part of her mind was turning over with other things. Elliott had captured his audience within a few minutes of starting to speak, even the ones who were less invested. Maisie had experienced a surge of unexpectedly possessive pride. She'd slipped out at the end, knowing that Elliott would be safely occupied for another two hours, repeating the lecture for a second audience, and that Liam was close by. She didn't think they were being observed, but she was carefully walking a line between keeping Elliott safe, while acting the part of billionaire's representative and academic's girlfriend. Her mouth twisted in a smile – now *she* was the actress, calling on all the skills she had.

The hotel she was looking for was ahead of her – another Belle Époque wedding cake, with fluttering flags and a red carpet. Flowers were being unloaded and arranged around the entrance, supervised by hotel staff with clipboards.

Maisie avoided the front and slipped down a side turning to see what she could of the back of the building, taking note of basement steps and emergency exits. The rear of the hotel was blocked off with high gates but the cul-de-sac on one side would be a good place to park a vehicle – for transporting bidders or making a getaway. There were two fire exits from the building and two basement stairwells, enclosed with metal railings, with steps up to street level.

Maisie looked suspiciously at a white van bearing the logo of a Nice wine merchant. There was no sign of the driver and what she could see of the interior yielded no clues. Was this the thieves' vehicle, in place already? She took note of the number, just in case. Unable to view any more of the hotel, she retraced her steps, deep in thought.

There had been nothing out of the ordinary so far today. Breakfast on the terrace at the villa had been uneventful. Elliott had been quiet, but she'd assumed he was thinking of the lecture and left him in peace to brood. They hadn't been tailed on the way in. When they got out of the car at their destination, he'd given her a smile that had made her vibrate all the way to the soles of her shoes. She'd seen no one in the audience who had given her cause for concern – except … She frowned. There *had* been a woman, tall and slim in an expensively simple linen dress, with a silk headscarf over blonde hair and oversized sunglasses, who had briefly seemed familiar – but it had only been for a second. As the woman had been walking rapidly away from the lecture hall rather than hanging around inside, it was probably nothing. *Probably familiar because she was channelling vintage Grace Kelly, big time.*

Filing the memory away, Maisie headed back towards the Casino and the Café de Paris for a seat on the terrace, expensive coffee and people watching. Shown to a table, she sat down, found her own sunglasses, not oversized, and settled in to be a tourist. She concentrated on projecting relaxation, but kept alert to her surroundings and to the people around her. She hadn't been followed and no one here looked suspicious – excited tourists and a smattering of local inhabitants distinguished by their designer clothes, stylish jewellery and an indefinable aura of belonging in a glamorous location.

Lectures complete, Elliott said goodbye to a few stragglers who were still asking questions and made his escape to the late morning sunshine. Maisie had texted him that she was waiting at the Café de Paris. He headed in the direction of the Casino, knowing that Liam was walking at a discreet distance behind him. They weren't expecting an attempt to make contact, but they couldn't ignore the possibility.

Elliott walked slowly, welcoming the chance to get his thoughts in order. The realisation that had come to him in the early hours of the morning had been a surprise, and yet not. He'd known from the first moment he saw Maisie, falling out of that tight pink dress on the arm of a man old enough to be her father, that there was a spark – which was probably part of the reason he'd taken refuge in disdain.

And now …

Is this the woman you want to spend the rest of your life with?

He was painfully aware that a whole chorus of voices in the depths of his mind was yelling "The hell, yeah!" But it wasn't that simple. If he made a declaration … if he asked …

He inhaled sharply, feeling a heavy grey weight settle on his chest, despite the warmth of the sun. *What will happen if she says no?* He had a strong suspicion, more than strong, that Maisie's reaction would *not* be what he would be hoping for.

Realising his steps had faltered as his heart rate accelerated, he steadied his pace and his breathing. They could go on as they were. No need to disturb anything. *No need to put your heart on the line.* He'd never thought before about having a heart – not in any other context than a biological one, an efficient pump plodding away in his chest. Now he was finding out.

Now that he knew that Maisie had the power to break it.

Maisie was watching the street. *Nothing to see here.* Just people passing by, enjoying the sun and the sights. She drained the last of her coffee and set the cup down. A man was walking towards her, silhouetted by the sun.

Elliott.

Her breath flattened in a sudden complex wave of sensations. Recollections of last night flickered in her brain. It had been—

With an effort, she shook free of her memory and some emotions she couldn't define. *Today you have work to do.* She looked up to greet him with a smile. About to ask if the rest of the morning had gone well, her voice inexplicably faltered as her mind spun off again into space. The intensity in Elliott's eyes as he looked at her sent a frisson over her skin. Then he pulled the second chair out from the table and everything settled again. He gave her a lopsided grin. 'Are we eating here? I'm starving.'

They ate lunch, sharing an ice cream, and then located yet another hotel where the jewellery exhibition was housed. The display was even more impressive than it had been in London, security was heavy and patrons were clearly impressed. Life-size images of Nevada Shaw photographed at notable locations in the Principality and wearing pieces from the collection adorned the walls.

'I think they have a hit on their hands,' Elliott said, steering her out of the way of a pair of gem-encrusted ladies who were clearly intent on adding to their collections.

They ambled back to the car. Maisie kept a wary eye out – although she didn't quite know what she was looking for. Or who? Michelle had not had much luck yet in finding detailed information on the giggler from Torquay. The woman was half way through a twelve-month contract with one of the museums. Prior to that, she'd been backpacking around Europe for a couple of years, supporting herself with casual work while researching to complete her PhD on the history of alchemy. In theory, the academic connection might have brought her into contact with Leyland, but there was no concrete evidence either way. The giggler was still in the frame.

Maisie scanned her surroundings yet again. The thieves, the buyers, and presumably the Necklace, would all be at the ball tonight, as would Elliott. Why would they need to approach him now? She consoled herself with the voice of reason while acknowledging that she'd be happier if she had some idea where Leyland was. *But, actually, would you really be happier to know that he's visiting his dear old mum in Scarborough? That would make the thieves complete unknowns. Better the devil you know than the one you don't?*

She'd tried to persuade Elliott that there was no need for him to leave the villa tonight. He could stay there with all the security and Liam for protection. He hadn't even advanced any arguments in reply, just given her a *look.* And so he *would* be at the ball.

When they reached the small shady courtyard where the car was parked, she slid into the passenger seat and let Elliott take the wheel. His grin was another toe-curling moment. Pulling herself back to the job in hand, she opened her phone to text Jake.

Anything on Leyland?

The response came back straight away. *Zero.*

She put the phone down to concentrate on observing the traffic around them, unable to decide if that knowledge was good or bad.

Chapter Thirty-Four

'What you think?' Elliott appeared in the doorway of the dressing room off the main bedroom, where Maisie was putting the finishing touches to her make-up; a tricky operation as it had to survive under a mask for at least some of the evening. She looked up and her heart – well, something in her chest – did a long, slow, swooping dive.

They'd avoided the fancy dress option as potentially too restricting. The masks and dominos – hooded cloaks in light silk – could be rolled into a ball and tossed aside in a matter of seconds. She'd tried it to make sure. Now Elliott was standing in the doorway in classic white-tie evening dress with a black domino tossed casually over his shoulders. The sight did strange things to her insides and made it momentarily difficult to swallow.

She wanted – *really* wanted – to entice him onto the bed and slowly dispose of the clothes, starting with that perfect white tie … She wanted …

The things she wanted were too complex to decipher now.

'Very distinguished?' she suggested.

Elliott's knowing look told her that he'd picked up the desire in her eyes and that he shared it.

For a crazy second, she considered, seriously considered, staying at the villa and making her fantasy a reality and to hell with the Necklace, cursed or not.

Biting her lip, she pushed the temptation away.

Later.

When this is done.

She turned back to the mirror for a last check on her handiwork. Tonight, she'd chosen a dark red jumpsuit from a young American designer. There was a subtle sparkle in the fabric, and a complex pattern of embroidery scattered with fake gems glittered over one shoulder. The wide legs made it look like a floor length gown but gave her more ease of movement, should she need it. This time Cassie had supplied a ruby choker to go with the diamond bracelet that was becoming Maisie's signature jewel. She sighed. She was going to miss the bracelet when she had to give it back.

Her mask, an exotic confection of gems, sequins and feathers, was displayed on a stand on the dressing table. Designed to match the jumpsuit, it was a much more elaborate affair than Elliott's plain strip of black silk. It limited her side vision, but she'd decided that to project the right image she'd have to take a chance. Ostensibly, tonight she was a buyer, not a bodyguard.

Elliott came to stand behind her, putting his hands on her shoulders. His palms were warm through the fabric of the suit.

'You look wonderful.' His voice was low and husky, with a note in it that puzzled her. He bent his head to press a kiss to the nape of her neck, sending tremors through her. She put up her own hand to cover one of his as he straightened, meeting his eyes in the mirror. The emotion she saw, or thought she saw, in the dark depths shook her as much as the kiss. *No time now.*

She hauled in a deep breath, picking up her evening bag to drop in her lipstick.

Only a few more hours and this would be over.

And then ...?

She lifted the mask from the stand and tucked her bag under her arm.

'I think it's time to go.'

Maisie had been to a couple of proms and grad balls, and once to a May Ball when she'd briefly dated a lecturer from a Cambridge college. She hadn't realised she had form for fancying academics. The whimsical thought grounded her and eased a little of the tension she was trying not to show. This event was on a whole different scale to anything she'd been at before.

Money. It almost glittered in the air. Maisie surveyed the room. The sumptuous setting of the hotel – gilt, crystal and elegant artwork, augmented with plants and flowers and small potted trees – all still faded in comparison with the guests. There was a sprinkling of fancy dress – mostly historical or fairy-tale figures. A number of women had taken up the Egyptian theme, with variations on Cleopatra or Nefertiti. Maisie's heart stopped briefly for a second when she glimpsed a Tutankhamun mask, before realising that this one was moulded, gilded and jewelled rather than cheap, flat cardboard. The majority of guests had opted for evening dress with dominos and masks – the men in formal white-tie, the women in designer gowns and fabulous jewels. She recalled reading somewhere that a white-tie event implied that royalty might be present. She could easily believe that was possible. There was a traditional big band, a jazz quartet and a celebrity DJ, who would provide the music for the dancing at various points in the evening. A lavish buffet in a side room sparkled with ice sculptures and the shining cubes mounded around platters of charcuterie, seafood and salads, flanked by a table with stands of delicate desserts. Proceeds from the extravagant event were going to a selection of arts-based charities on the Côte d'Azur.

The atmosphere was heady, with an edge that she guessed came from the intrigue supplied by the masks.

Or maybe it's just your nerves?

She was aware of tension ratcheting up inside her and fought it, dancing with Elliott, with Jake, with the CEO of the jewellery company and with several strangers, while waiting all the time for a tap on the shoulder. Was Leyland here somewhere?

'When do you think they'll make contact?' Two hours had passed and she was waltzing with Jake. It was strange – dressed for the ball, he was almost a mirror image of Elliott. Well, not quite – Elliott's evening dress fitted well but Jake's subtly whispered bespoke tailoring. His cufflinks and studs sported diamonds – the design looked old, but not vintage, and more flamboyant than her boss's usual laidback style. Maisie guessed they were inherited and worn to advertise wealth and perhaps a certain lack of taste in a collector of dubious artefacts. The black silk of the mask made the blue of his eyes even more pronounced. As a discerning female, she could fully appreciate the whole presentation, but Jake was just Jake. Her skin didn't heat to his touch or her heart speed up when they danced the way it did when Elliott took her in his arms. *Just as well. Cassie would murder you.*

She realised with a jolt that her thoughts had drifted. Jake was covertly scanning the ballroom, over her shoulder.

'A little before midnight, I'd guess,' he answered the question she'd almost forgotten she'd asked. 'Just before the witching hour and the traditional time for unmasking.' His eyes flickered towards the ornate gold clock over the band's dais. It was ten past eleven. 'We need to keep an eye on our targets.'

Although the room was crowded, within an hour of arriving they had picked out candidates for the other bidders. A heavily built blond man in a half face mask and what was clearly a rented suit leaned against one wall, nursing an empty glass. He was making no attempt to participate in the ball, but looking impatiently at his watch from time to time. They judged him to be an agent for a bidder who wanted to remain anonymous. In an alcove, a hunched figure wrapped in a red cloak sat quietly in a wheelchair, flanked by a burly attendant in impeccable evening dress. Both men gave every appearance of enjoying the event. From time to time, various people stopped by the chair to chat for a few moments. They'd identified him as Emile Le Clerc, the collector who actually lived in the Principality. Liam and Mickey, who had been attached to the hotel security detail for the evening to act as backup, had confirmed that a known dealer from Marseille was in a side room that had been commandeered by a group of guests who preferred to play cards rather than dance. He was winning modestly and also watching the clock. 'Looks like the gang is all here – still.' With a professional twirl, Jake stopped beside their table where Elliott was sitting, before disappearing back into the crowd.

'Shall we get something to eat?' Elliott suggested. When Maisie hesitated, he took her hand. 'They will find us, wherever we are.'

Reluctantly, she nodded, accepting. 'Have you seen anyone who might be Leyland?' she asked as they made their way to the refreshment room.

'Not really. Surprising how good a disguise a hooded cloak and a simple mask are. It was a clever idea.'

'I suppose it was,' she agreed with a stifled sigh. The whole thing was such a mixture; complicated and simple, clever and slapdash. *Devised by someone just a little too clever for their own good – or who thinks they are?* Did that fit Leyland? Somehow, from what Elliott had told her, it didn't feel right, but she didn't really know the man.

They drifted around the buffet making a plate to share before finding a place to sit. They ate in a near silence that Maisie knew was too tense – she was surprised she could get her jaw to function, but the food was delicious. Some of the nervous energy dissipated when Elliott stretched across the table to touch her hand. At twenty to twelve, they were back in the ballroom. Jake was lounging at their table. It took Maisie a second to realise that the man standing in the shadow of a potted tree behind him was Mickey in the uniform of hotel security.

'Le Clerc has gone,' Jake said softly as they sat down. Maisie looked over. The alcove where the wheelchair had stood was empty. 'A woman in fancy dress collected him and his escort a few moments ago.'

'Maybe they needed time to deal with the complication of the chair?' Mickey suggested from the shadows. 'Ah! She's back. And aiming for our friend in the ill-fitting suit.'

Maisie turned as casually as she could to scan the room. She froze as she caught the back view of the figure threading her way through the clumps of people gathered on the edge of the ballroom watching the dancers – a glimpse of pale blonde hair under a hat and the distinctive pastel checks of a flounced and stiffened skirt.

'What is it?' Elliott leaned towards her, unable to see from where he was sitting.

'The fancy dress the woman is wearing.' She breathed out, deliberately turning her head to answer him, although she wanted to keep watching. 'It's the Columbine costume from the Pentecost Collections, or a copy. That's Dorothea.'

Chapter Thirty-Five

Maisie could almost feel images clicking into place in her head, like lines in the slot machines in the Casino. The Grace Kelly imitator from that morning watching the lecture, and before that—

'She was the insider.' Elliott took the words out of her thoughts. 'The one in the Tutankhamun mask.'

Maisie nodded, surprised at the small spike of relief. She had *known* that they hadn't imagined or mistaken that face in the dark, or where it had come from – inside the house. 'I think it was her in the garage in Chelsea. I had the feeling it was a woman.'

'In that case, *was* she attempting to double cross her partner?' Jake asked quietly. 'If she was, they're working together again now.'

Maisie shifted in her seat. She wasn't sure what that might mean, but she also wasn't sure that it was good. The whole thing was so damn precarious. Aware of her muscles tightening for flight or fight, she met Elliott's eyes – the calm confidence there settled the churning in her stomach. *All we have to do is walk through this and keep walking – if all else fails, Jake will buy the damn Necklace.*

She looked over at Jake, who was still watching Dorothea. She waited until his attention came back to the table. Mickey had already melted away.

'They left through one of the fire doors,' Jake reported. 'From the body language, the guy was suspicious … She showed him something that convinced him.'

Elliott looked over at Jake. 'When the mysterious chaperone comes for us, do we recognise her?'

'Hmm. Think we have to play that by ear – react to whatever she does. She's cutting it fine.'

Instinctively, they all looked at the clock. There were less than ten minutes to go. Already the bandleader was making jokes about the countdown to the midnight unmasking. Waiters were circulating with champagne cocktails to toast the successful end of the festival.

They waited. At three minutes to midnight the atmosphere in the room crackled with energy, a lot of it hovering around their table. The bandleader put a finger to his lips, exaggeratedly calling for silence. Jake had risen, moving a few steps away.

'Ah!' Elliott let out a long low exhale. 'The psychopomp approaches.'

'Psycho what?' Despite herself, Maisie found she was laughing, the tension lifting. *Only you, Elwood.*

'Psychopomp. Guide who takes you to the underworld,' Elliott explained smoothly. He gave a tiny nod.

Getting the message, Maisie swung round slowly. Dorothea had almost reached them. Maisie looked at the costume – not a copy she was sure, but the genuine article, topped by a black mask and a perky tricorn hat. And this was the genuine article too. The real Dorothea; not the droopy, colourless hostess from the weekend in Torquay. *And strung as tight as a tripwire*, Maisie recognised. *Takes one to know one.*

An excited, expectant hush was spreading around the room as the clock ticked down. Two minutes to midnight.

'Ms Norris.' Dorothea kept her voice low. 'So nice to meet you again.'

Maisie let out her pent-up breath. 'And you, Dorothea – quite a surprise.'

Dorothea made a dismissive gesture, already turning towards Elliott. 'A pleasure to see you too, Dr Elwood. I trust you will be making one of our party?' She tilted her head in a question.

Elliott gave a brief nod in answer.

'Excellent. A welcome addition to our evening's proceedings.'

Dorothea's eyes glittered, outlined by the mask. Her focus had moved over Maisie's head. 'And this is?'

'My employer,' Maisie said. Jake took a pace forward.

Remaining conversation and chatter in the room was rapidly fading as people prepared to clap down the seconds.

Dorothea gave Jake a rapid inspection, clearly assessing the tailoring and the diamonds. 'Oh.' She smiled. 'Mr Elladour. I'm *very* pleased to meet you,' she purred.

She really was. Maisie could feel it, but the tension in the woman had slid up yet another notch. *This is not good.* Jake gave a small bow, muttering something in response.

Dorothea smiled widely. 'If you would all come with me.' She indicated the closest fire exit, slipping past the table to lead the way. As they stepped through the open door, the countdown to midnight began.

'Ten, nine, eight …'

Chapter Thirty-Six

The corridor beyond the fire door was lit only by emergency lighting. The white paint on the walls was scuffed and had yellowed in patches. Dorothea led the way. Elliott walked behind Maisie, with Jake at the rear. A tangle of service pipes ran alongside them, just overhead. At the beginning Elliott tried to count their paces, sure that the others would be doing the same, but once past four hundred, he gave up.

Wherever they were going, it was well away from the main part of the hotel. *Had Dorothea escorted each bidder by a different route?* He suspected that might be so, given the varying times it had taken her to return to the ballroom. It appeared that theirs might be the longest – and psychopomp was right. Dorothea was leading them down into the bowels of the building; a deserted liminal space. *She didn't show any hesitation in inviting me along – or any surprise. They were watching. You were always going to be part of this, willingly or unwillingly.*

They passed through two more doors, crossed two intersections and descended two short flights of steps. Any sounds from the ballroom had long since faded. The corridors seemed indistinguishable from each other, but Dorothea moved confidently, sure of where she was leading them. *How well does she know this place?* Once this – whatever this was – was concluded, Elliott wasn't sure about finding their way out again – but that was a worry for later.

They clattered down yet another set of steps, through another door, and then it seemed that they had reached their destination. It was a basement storage space, low ceilinged and sparingly lit. Boxes of what appeared to be catering supplies loomed over them. The place smelled of cardboard and a faint sweet odour that Elliott thought was vaguely familiar. Ahead, a bright light was visible over the boxes. Dorothea ushered them sideways into a narrow passage that had been fashioned in the stacks, illuminated by a string of small bulbs. The passage opened into a hollow area where the containers had been shoved aside. The bright light was much closer now.

As they emerged cautiously into the space, Dorothea abruptly twisted sideways and, flattening her skirt with her hands, squirmed through another narrow opening and disappeared. Confused, Elliott turned towards the light. Then he understood the setup. A ring of what looked like stage spotlights illuminated a clear central area. Around the edge were three more hollows like the one they were standing in, rather like boxes in the theatre. In contrast to the spot-lit centre, these gaps were largely in shadow, giving the people in them a degree of anonymity if they stood well back, although Elliott made out a metallic gleam that he thought was the sides of the wheelchair in the opposite "box". A small torch rested beside a computer tablet on an upended packing case. Jake picked up the tablet.

'How the bids will be made,' he said softly. Michelle had done what was needed and set up the electronic account enabling funds to be transferred. A post-it note with a letter *D* printed on it was attached to the tablet to identify the bidder.

'For fuck's sake, can we just get on with this?' The loud and irritated demand came from the adjacent space. Elliott guessed it was the big guy who had argued with Dorothea. Elliott felt rather than saw Maisie stiffen in the darkness. He put out a hand and found hers. She squeezed his fingers, then let go. The contact was reassuring. Quickly analysing his feeling, Elliott decided that he wasn't exactly afraid, but apprehension and stretched nerves were definitely in the mix.

'All in good time.' Elliott took a surprised breath that he heard echoed around the circle. The response to the angry demand had come from somewhere behind the spotlights. The voice was mechanical, distorted. Male, he was sure, but that was all he could distinguish. *Is it Leyland? All these electrical gadgets? Is the man* that *tech savvy?*

The questions fled as another surprise jerked through him. A grotesque figure stepped out into the circle of light; an enfolding black cloak, an exaggerated stove pipe hat that stood up maybe a foot, confusing any impression of the man's height, and below that the long-nosed mask of the most sinister character to be associated with the *Commedia dell'Arte* – the Plague Doctor.

'Gentlemen – and lady.' The figure nodded its head to where Maisie stood. *How much can you see?* Elliott guessed not much, but of course *he* knew where Maisie was. 'Thank you for attending tonight,' the distorted voice went on. 'I apologise for the somewhat … theatrical … nature of the proceedings, but I'm sure you appreciate the opportunity being afforded to you.'

You're not sorry. The conviction came strongly, almost like a voice in Elliott's head. *You're enjoying this.* He was aware of movement behind him in the darkness. Maisie and Jake had both discarded the masks and silk dominos. He unfastened his own, rolling them up and shoving them into a small indentation between the boxes.

Maisie stepped close. 'Is it Leyland?' she breathed in his ear. He inhaled her scent, wishing he could give her a positive answer.

'I'm sorry, but I really don't know. I can't say that it's not.' It was the best he could offer. He sensed her nod rather than saw it; understanding, not reproach. Which made him wish even more that he could give her a definite yes or no. If he concentrated? There was something ... or was there? *Just wishful thinking?*

The Plague Doctor was running through the arrangements. Bids would be made using the computer tablets until there was one final bid.

'After a short delay, while the transfer of funds is verified, you will be escorted back to the ballroom.' The man reached down to roll out a tall trolley, on top of which rested a laptop computer. 'The successful bidder will, of course, remain behind to take charge of the Cleopatra Necklace. My commiserations in advance to the losers.' The voice broke up a little as the man laughed. 'I look forward to your bids, gentlemen – but first—' with gesture like a conjuror, which Elliott had begun to recognise fitted the man's personality, he held up an object that shone and glittered in the lights as he displayed it aloft between both hands '— I give you the Cleopatra Necklace – an item, I am sure you will agree, that is worth a king's ransom … or maybe a queen's ransom?' he suggested silkily. Even with the mechanical interference, the sly goading in the words came through. *Definitely enjoying this.*

Elliott squinted at the Necklace, his mind flipping over what the speech might have revealed. Was it Leyland? He just couldn't be sure – and the Plague Doctor had spoken only of himself. *Where does Dorothea fit in this?* Simply an escort? Would they really be guided out when this was done; three sets of disappointed and potentially hostile bidders?

As if on cue, an angry voice spoke again out of the dark in the next box. 'And how the fuck do we know that it's the real thing? It could just be paste. You can forget all this cheap conjuring. I expect to examine the goods before we get to any bidding.' There was a murmur of agreement from around the circle.

'I'm afraid that will not be possible … sir.' The honorific was mocking. 'But arrangements have been made, which I trust will satisfy you. The Necklace will be authenticated by a recognised expert, for the benefit of all of you.' The figure swivelled his head to take in all the observers, then made an expansive theatrical gesture of invitation.

'Dr Elwood, would you please join me?'

Chapter Thirty-Seven

No! No! No!

Maisie wasn't sure if she moaned the words aloud as Elliott hesitated, then stepped forward into the light. She bit her lip, calling on every iota of willpower not to follow him. Jake's brief touch on her shoulder reassured her that whatever the cost, it was the right thing to do. It still twisted her stomach into knots.

The Plague Doctor had produced an old plastic chair and was offering Elliott the Necklace.

Elliott received it carefully, then paused to turn before sitting down. 'My name is Elliott Elwood,' he addressed the box-like niches. 'Some of you may know it. I have some expertise with Egyptian artefacts.'

Maisie felt a surge of pride cut through the churning in her abdomen. Elliott's quiet dignity made the Plague Doctor's cheap theatricals look even more tawdry. Elliott was still speaking, 'Whether I can verify *this* artefact, in the circumstances—'

'I have every confidence in you, Dr Elwood,' the Doctor intervened smoothly. Maisie's stomach gave another twist. Even through the voice distorter, there was certainty there. *This man* knows *Elliott. It's Leyland. It has to be.*

There was a rustle of movement around the edge of the circle. 'I'm willing to take Dr Elwood's opinion.' The voice came from the space opposite – the man in the chair.

'I also,' Jake chimed in from behind her.

'Thank you, gentlemen.' The Doctor gave an exaggerated bow. 'If the two other bidders wish to withdraw …' He let the sentence hang. There was a short pause. No one moved or spoke. 'In that case, Dr Elwood, if you would be so good.'

Elliott sat down, weighing the Necklace in his hands. There was a pain now in Maisie's chest. Okay, so Elliott was an expert, his opinion counted, but authentication needed other things too – provenance, paperwork. Inside, she was cursing the damn Doctor, hanging all this on Elliott. And Dorothea too, wherever *she* was.

As if picking up on Maisie's thoughts, there was a movement behind the lamps and another figure stepped into the light; a figure in the glittering, pastel-checked costume of Columbine.

Dorothea.

Dorothea, holding a gun.

She gestured tightly with the weapon, holding out her free hand. 'Thank you, Dr Elwood. I'll take the Necklace now.'

'What the hell do you think you're doing?' The Plague Doctor stepped forward. Dark cloaked shoulders bristled with shock and anger.

'Taking what's mine.' Dorothea's voice sounded very calm. The gun was very steady.

'You *can't*.' The Doctor waved his hand at the computer. 'This is stupid. Everything is set up.' He gestured around the space. 'Darling, in a few more moments we'll be *rich*.'

'Set up,' Dorothea echoed the words. Under the harsh lights, Maisie could see her lip twist with contempt. 'Did you really believe all that James Bond stuff – interactive computers, instantaneous transfer of funds?' She gave a harsh laugh.

'But… you put it all together … you *said* you'd done it.' Even through the voice distorter, the incredulity was clear.

'I lied,' Dorothea said coolly. 'I'm taking the Necklace now. I don't need all this.' She gestured with the gun. 'I have a buyer.'

Maisie's stomach dropped when she realised the implications of that statement. A muffled exclamation from the darkness where Jake was standing confirmed that he had reached the same conclusion.

Dorothea held out her hand, cupped imperiously. 'The Necklace please, Dr Elwood.' Elliott had risen when Dorothea moved into the light. Now, after a brief hesitation, he stretched out and tipped it into her palm. Possessive fingers closed on it, holding it tight. 'Thank you.' Dorothea took a small step back. 'I'm leaving now. If anyone tries to interfere, I *will* shoot them.'

'Darling, please.' The Doctor moved forward.

Dorothea levelled the gun.

The sound of the shot split the air, loud even with the dampening effects of the cardboard boxes. Maisie's breath tore out of her lungs like shattering glass as she gasped. For a long second, as the reverberation died away, nobody moved – shock held everyone still.

The three central figures under the harsh lights formed a tableau, illuminated and motionless, like players on a stage set. Then Maisie saw a shudder run through Dorothea. The woman was looking down, her hands clutched to her chest. Under her fingers a dark stain was spreading over the delicate squares of the Columbine costume. With a snatched, choking gasp, Dorothea sank to her knees, then toppled to the floor. The gun and the Necklace clattered away as she fell.

As if her collapse unlocked a spell, the circle of bidders came alive in a ripple of protest, alarm and disbelief. Elliott was moving towards Dorothea as the man attending Monsieur Le Clerc rushed forward to join him. Focused on the two men bending over Dorothea's crumpled body, Maisie was dimly aware of other noises, coming from outside – doors crashing open, voices, a loudhailer – 'Attention in the building. Attention in the building. This is the police.'

The Necklace and Dorothea's gun had landed inches from the Plague Doctor's feet. He bent to scoop them up, tugging at something as he straightened.

Maisie had a brief glimpse of the metallic glint of his own gun before the basement plunged into total darkness.

Chapter Thirty-Eight

The last half-hour had been … crowded.

Maisie put her hand to her head. There was a sharp pain building behind her eyes, making it difficult to process everything that had happened – seething movement in the darkness, shouts, piercing beams of torches, confusion. Then eye-blinking brightness as the lights were restored.

Now she was sitting on a box beside Monsieur Le Clerc's chair. His attendant was standing behind them and Elliott was beside her. They were all in one piece, if shaken. Le Clerc was hunched in his chair, pale but composed. Instinctively, Maisie raised a hand to cover Elliott's, where it rested on her shoulder.

'He *shot* her.' Maisie could still barely believe it, except that Dorothea's body remained where it had fallen. She kept her eyes away from it. Le Clerc's manservant had wanted to cover her face with his coat, but the police had vetoed it. A CSI team had just arrived. Jake was somewhere with the leader of the police squad. She straightened her shoulders when she saw him coming back to them, carefully skirting the central space.

'It's okay for us all to leave now.' Jake looked from Maisie and Elliott to Le Clerc and his attendant. 'They'll want to take statements in the morning.' Monsieur Le Clerc inclined his head, with a murmur of thanks.

In the inky darkness after the Plague Doctor had yanked the cables, cutting the lights, the dealer from Marseille had run headlong into the arms of a policeman when attempting to get away. The angry bidder had disappeared completely. So too had the Plague Doctor, the Necklace and Dorothea's gun.

A young police officer came forward to navigate the wheelchair out of the basement, via the cargo lift. Jake indicated a narrow passage that had been made by moving some of the boxes. 'We can go that way.'

Maisie got to her feet, glad to find her knees were not as wobbly as she had feared. Elliott moved alongside her, slipping his arm around her waist. She leaned in to him, grateful for the warmth and the familiar scent of his aftershave. He dropped a quick kiss on the top of her head where it rested on his shoulder.

A small flame of anger was still flickering inside her. 'He *shot* her, just to get that cursed Necklace. He could have shot *you*.' She could hear the brittle edge of remembered fear in her voice.

'But he didn't.' Elliott kissed her again and then let her go, so they could squeeze through the passageway after Jake. 'And Dorothea did try to double cross him. I know that's not justification—'

'But it would have been to him,' she said bitterly. 'And he got away.' The man had simply melted into the darkness, evading the police swarming the basement. 'I hope that damn collar morphs into a snake and strangles him.'

'An alluring if impossible idea,' Elliott agreed. They were almost at the end of the passageway through the piled-up boxes, which ended in a small clearing in front of an emergency exit. They caught up with Jake as he tried to push the door open.

'It's not locked.' Maisie frowned. She could see light from the street around the edges of the door, which must have been one of the ones leading to a stairwell that she'd noted the previous morning. It seemed a long time ago.

'No, something's blocking it.' Jake gave it a shove with his shoulder and the obstruction shifted, allowing the door to open and revealing what had been holding it shut.

For a moment, Maisie couldn't make sense of the shape – a dark rolled bundle, with something sticking out at the end. After a second, she realised what she was looking at. It was a pair of feet. A pair of feet and a black cloak.

A body, huddled at the bottom of a set of steps.

Jake pushed the door wide. It fell back against the outer wall and caught automatically, fastened open. Now they could see the whole of the body and the grotesque effigy of the Plague Doctor's mask. Light from a column in the street fell gently into the stairwell, showing where the mask had slid sideways to reveal the face beneath.

Maisie heard Elliott's indrawn breath at the moment she recognised the dark fall of hair and hawk-like features.

The man at the bottom of the steps was Vaisey Leyland.

Chapter Thirty-Nine

Sunshine glittered, almost blindingly, on the water. Elliott adjusted his sunglasses. He was discovering that a long night involving sudden death and police investigations felt very like a hangover. They had spent what remained of the night, after the discovery of Leyland's body, on Jake's yacht. Now he was having a very late breakfast with Maisie on deck while the crew made ready to move the boat to its regular mooring in Nice. Across the table, Maisie was also wearing dark glasses. Her shoulders sagged in an uncharacteristic slump. Elliott identified an emotional crash landing after the events of yesterday.

Jake was off somewhere with the police – an officer had arrived earlier to take statements and escort him to some sort of meeting. He had been the one who'd arranged the police presence surrounding the back of the hotel. An overheard snippet of conversation suggested that the police had used some sort of thermal tracking device to determine where the bidders were gathered. Maisie had suspected Jake might also have been wearing a wire, possibly even a body camera, but he was tight-lipped on the subject and she knew not to ask questions. The authorities were taking the basement apart, inch by inch.

Dorothea had died of that single bullet wound to the chest, Leyland, from the evidence of his position and bruises on his body, from a fall on the stairs while making his hurried getaway. Frustratingly, he had not been carrying either the Necklace or the guns. He was assumed to have hidden them somewhere before making his escape, hence the painstaking search. Amazingly, the police activity at the back of the hotel had been kept totally discreet. None of the revellers attending the ball had any idea what had been happening while they celebrated and drank champagne.

Elliott cut up a peach and put a piece on Maisie's plate. He watched as she picked it up and ate it absently.

'Trying to figure out where Leyland stashed the loot isn't really going to do any good,' he suggested. 'It has to be in the basement somewhere. The searchers will find it.'

'I suppose so.' She sighed. 'I don't really understand why he would have hidden it.'

Elliott shrugged. 'So he wouldn't be found with it if the police caught him?'

She shrugged in response. He could see she wasn't convinced. She'd taken off her glasses. Her eyes were beautiful, and tired. A swell of protective love made it hard to breathe for a moment. He sipped coffee and looked at the sea.

'I suppose it *was* Leyland – the Plague Doctor, I mean?' she asked after a moment. 'Was there *anything* familiar about him? You knew him best, and you got closest to him.'

'I really can't say.' Elliott put down his cup. That was another frustration. He thought that there *had* been something familiar about the grotesque figure, but he couldn't confirm categorically that it was Leyland. With the tension, the lights and the theatrical getup, he couldn't be *sure*. 'He was wearing the costume. It *has* to have been him.' He'd rationalised this since they'd found the body. 'He was running up the steps to the street, trying to get away and he slipped and fell. It all makes sense.'

Except that the Necklace is still missing. The damn thing really is *cursed.*

He looked over at Maisie again. She was yawning. 'Why don't you go down and have a nap?'

'I don't think I can sleep, but I do want to shower.'

She got up, moving stiffly. Elliott caught her hand as she passed, bringing her fingers to his lips. "I love you," hovered on his tongue. He bit down on the words.

Not now. Maybe not ever?

He pushed that thought aside. They were together, they were unharmed, the people behind the plots were both dead – even knowing what they were, he could regret that – but the sun was shining and this was the Riviera.

All in all, he didn't give much of a damn if the Necklace was never found. The thing was nothing but trouble, and he wasn't even sure—

He discarded that thought too in favour of watching Maisie as she walked away down the deck. *Walked away.* The cold twist in his chest at the implication of the words was no surprise. Would she soon be walking out of his life for good, now that there was no mystery to hold them together?

He rose, pacing over to the rail, watching the activity on the dock. Sunday morning in Monaco. Nothing to see here except normal life. *Normal life as lived by millionaires and billionaires.*

He was borrowing trouble. There was no reason to doubt that he and Maisie would still be together in six months, in a year … but forever? He wanted forever. The knowledge was a deep, hollow ache inside him. He was only guessing that Maisie wasn't ready to commit. Maybe, given time—

'Hey! Elliott! Hello!' Elliott shifted slightly to find out who was hailing him by name from the dock. He squinted into the sunshine, making out a familiar figure walking towards the yacht.

'Ben!' He turned and hurried down to the head of the gangplank, still in place for Jake to come aboard before the boat sailed. Ben had reached the bottom and was hesitating. Elliott nodded to the member of the crew nearby, indicating that Ben was a friend, and waved him up. 'What are you doing here?'

Ben reached the top of the access in a few hurried steps. His face twisted. 'You may well ask. I have absolutely no idea. Leyland rang me yesterday and insisted I had to fly out. I didn't even know he was here. He said he couldn't explain over the phone.' He put his hand to his head. 'I just arrived, a couple of hours ago … and now the police say that he's dead? What's going on? Do you know anything?'

Elliott saw the distress and confusion in Ben's face. He gestured to guide his friend to the upper deck. 'It's complicated. I think we need coffee.'

'That,' Ben agreed, exhaling with obvious relief, 'would be brilliant.'

As he ushered Ben up the companionway, Elliott's mind was ticking over. He wasn't sure how much he should divulge, how much he was *allowed* to divulge. When they reached the table on the upper deck, one of the catering staff was clearing used plates and cups. Elliott, rather self-consciously, and aware of Ben's eyes on him, requested another pot of coffee and clean crockery. The steward acknowledged the request with a smile. 'Coming right up, Dr Elwood. We'll be sailing in about ten minutes – as soon as the boss gets back. He's on his way.' He gave Ben an enquiring look before leaving with the plates.

Ben's eyes had widened a little. 'Sailing?'

'Just as far as Nice,' Elliott explained. 'It won't be a problem to get back to Monaco from there, if you need to – or we can go ashore now – find a café?'

'No, that's fine – if it's okay for me to hitch a ride? I left my bag at the airport. I can get a hotel room in Nice. I suppose someone will have to arrange for Leyland's body to be taken back.' He frowned. 'What happened? Was it a heart attack?'

Elliott had decided he needed say as little as possible. 'I gather it was the result of a fall. The police are investigating.'

'Oh!' Ben still looked confused but Elliott saw a glint in his eyes. *Just realising that there might be something in it for him – promotion?*

They sat down at the table. The coffee arrived with a fresh basket of croissants. Helping himself, Ben looked around. 'How the other half lives, eh?' There was a shade of envy in his expression. 'Fancy friends you have these days, El.'

'Maisie's boss,' Elliott corrected. 'He treats his employees well.'

'I'll say.' Ben was attacking a croissant, lavishly spreading butter. Elliott felt momentarily uncomfortable, wrongfooted somehow by Ben's tone.

Elliott poured himself another coffee, not sure if it was wise to have any more caffeine. He should have asked for orange juice. He was on edge, strangely jumpy, and he didn't really know why. *Probably lack of sleep.* He was sitting in the sun on the deck of a luxury yacht chatting to his best friend. What could be wrong?

He stirred a little as the boat's engines revved and they began to glide gently away from the mooring. Jake must be back on board. He was aware of a certain apprehension. If McQuire joined them, he hoped Ben wouldn't pass some crass remark. His friend was sitting back now, relaxed and munching on the croissant. 'I needed this.' He gestured to the table. 'Thank you.'

'No problem.' Elliott looked back at the harbour as they moved slowly away from the mooring and out to open water. He knew that they would follow the coastline on the way to Nice. Maisie would probably be here in a few moments to watch as the Côte d'Azur unravelled beside them. He took a deep breath, feeling more at ease now that they were moving. All the tension and tumult they had experienced in Monaco was behind them.

'Ms Norris not around?' Ben had finished eating and drawn a small gadget out of his pocket. Elliott recognised a brightly coloured vape.

'I hope she's catching up on some sleep.' He watched Ben take a pull on the device, feeling slightly irritated. He'd been enjoying the freshness of the sea air.

Ben must have picked up on his silent disapproval. He waved the vape. 'You don't mind?'

‘Er, no.’ Elliott smothered his initial dislike. They were on deck after all. The fumes would dissipate. ‘I didn’t know you used one of those things.’

‘Secret vice.’ Ben put the vape to his lips again with a smile. ‘You must be a bit knackered too, old chap – dancing until the small hours.’ He grinned, eyes glittering. ‘Good night, was it?’

‘Yes,’ Elliott agreed, slightly stiffly. It would have been very good without the machinations of a control freak thief – and murder. Despite that, some parts of it *had* been very good indeed – the bits where he’d held Maisie in his arms.

He looked over at Ben, suddenly puzzled over the way his old friend was regarding him, eyes so strangely bright. His tired mind turned over sluggishly. ‘How did you know—?’

He got no further. The sweet, flowery vapour emitted from the device in Ben’s hand wafted over to him. A familiar fragrance. In a series of slow clicks, things came together in his head. The scent in the gallery at Pentecost Place when the hidden passage opened, faint sweet traces in Ben’s office on campus that he’d only half registered, the fugitive scent lingering last night in the cardboard alleys of the basement …

Ben was still watching him with those over bright, knowing eyes.

‘You know … about the ball. You know everything.’ Elliott’s breathing had gone thick. ‘It was *you*, not Leyland at all. You stole the Necklace—’ Horror splashed a bone-deep chill over him. ‘*You* murdered Dorothea.’

Chapter Forty

Maisie had given in and napped for ten minutes. Now, after a shower, she felt more alive and alert. When she was in the bathroom, the yacht had cast off. Now there was a view of the coast from the windows – they were actual windows, not portholes. She stood for a few moments watching the scenery – small coves, a straggle of pastel-coloured houses clustered around a pocket harbour, tree-clad cliffs dotted with villas; some close to the water with their own landing stages. Although she was watching the panorama unfolding, her mind was still turning over last night. Had the police search turned up anything? Had the Necklace been found? Jake would probably have the latest update. She pulled on a pair of shorts and a slouchy T-shirt and set out to find him.

'Leyland!' Ben's voice dripped scorn and venom. 'You really think *he* could be behind something like this?'

Well, no – because he was an honest man. Elliott realised, with a jab of remorse, that he really *should* have known. Leyland was contrary and arrogant but essentially honest. Maybe that was the reason for the whisper of disbelief, even when everything pointed to him. *You should have known it was a setup.*

A setup engineered by the man sitting across from him. The friend he no longer recognised. Brief vignettes from the past flashed through his brain – all the good times, yes, but also the instances of small items that went missing, jobs poorly completed, ambitious plans that somehow never worked out – always the fault of someone else. Not a case of Ben *taking* the blame, as he'd always accepted – without enough thought, he realised abruptly – but of him *shifting* the blame. And then there were the complaints of slights, of opportunities missed and promotions passed over. He'd taken Ben's side because they were friends, and because of those good times. Where and when had things changed? He looked at Ben now, his face alive with a malicious self-satisfaction that was almost feral. *Did I ever really know you?* And two – no, possibly three people were dead. 'Did you kill Professor Mumford?' he asked abruptly.

Ben shrugged. 'He'd had his three score years and ten. More like twenty. It was time he moved on but he wasn't prepared to go.' There was no remorse in those eyes, only triumph and contempt. 'Maybe if he and Leyland had realised that I was worth much more than simply being their errand boy – well …' He shrugged again, with a half laugh. 'I rectified *that.*' He took a final pull on the vape and put it down carefully on the table. 'Not that it wasn't useful, having the inside track on all Leyland's little plots and intrigues. Very useful.' He gave a soft laugh.

'You were working with Dorothea?' Elliott asked cautiously.

'She was in love with me.' The way Ben preened over the words made Elliott feel sick before the man's face fell into the discontented lines of a thwarted child. 'She was *meant* to be,' he muttered. 'But she didn't want to give me the Necklace. I couldn't trust her. She had to go.' He pouted disconsolately. 'She told me she could work the computers to transfer the money. Said it would be untraceable. That was a lie. She let me down all round. We really could have gone places together, but she didn't appreciate me and the things I can do.'

Elliott's nausea increased. Even if everything had gone exactly as planned, he wondered how long Dorothea would have survived. How soon before the monstrous ego sitting across from him found something new to displease him? *No wonder she was trying to take the money and run.* He could see that Ben had settled in to tell his tale as he had done so many times before, sure of his friend's unquestioning support. *What a dupe you were.*

'Always a mistake to trust a woman,' Ben continued. 'Take Sara …' Ben's face twisted at his ex-wife's name. 'It was you she wanted, you know?' he said conversationally. 'I was second best – the also-ran. I *loved* her. She was everything ...' His voice broke and the twist in his expression flashed briefly into pain, quickly gone. 'She married me to stay close to you – I think she still had hopes. But you were never interested, were you? Wouldn't have taken my leavings. And *she* wanted more – always – prestige, an expensive house, a fancy car, a husband who was *going* somewhere. I did what I could, but it was never enough. I wasn't *you.* That's when it started to go wrong. I needed more *money* ...' His voice faded briefly, then revived. 'And that was when I realised – life isn't fair. Some people get all the luck. But you can make your own luck. You just have to have the guts to help yourself. And you know what?' The self-satisfied grin resurfaced. 'I found I did. And I found I didn't need *her*. I was finally using my brains, getting what *I* wanted. When she ran off with that film producer, I was glad to see her go. I had so much good stuff going on. And no one knew. No one. Not even you, El.'

Swallowing hard, Elliott fought nausea. He could see it all now – the small character flaws that would have stayed small, if it wasn't for a lover's betrayal. Or would they? Was he falling for Ben's version of events yet again? Had this monster always been there, hidden under the engaging smile and the self-deprecating charm? And Ben *had* had charm, and humour. Had all that really been wiped out by the loss of the woman he loved? Or was blaming his ex-wife just another of Ben's self-justifications? Would another wrong turn in his life, a different one, have had the same result? Elliott recognised that he would never know. The man sitting across from him wasn't the friend he'd always thought he was, but where that friend had gone—

A small breeze lifted the edge of a discarded napkin on the table. It fluttered for a moment, drawing Elliott back to the present. Digging into the past and mourning a friendship, and his own lack of awareness, wasn't going to help now. He had to concentrate. If he could keep Ben talking until someone else came ... *But please don't let that be Maisie.* He had to look interested, encouraging, sympathetic. If someone came, surely together they could overpower Ben? Elliott pushed the spectre of the two missing guns out of his mind. *All you can do is keep him talking. So keep listening – the way you have so often in the past.*

'What ... what made you decide to go for the Cleopatra Necklace?' It was the only question he could think of. Ben would want to boast about his cleverness. *Feed that ego.*

'Finding Dorothea, of course,' Ben said patronisingly, the expert disclosing his cleverness to the slow pupil. 'I met her at a poetry slam in Cheltenham – showcase for a couple of my students. All crap, of course, except for Dorothea. She was seriously good – the star of the show. Then I discovered she was one of the Pentecost heirs. She thought she was going to inherit from her aunt, the one she was caring for, but the old bitch had mortgaged her house behind her back to pay for some operation or other. All Dorothea had was the income from renting out her own house, just a little terraced place in Gloucester, and the bank was getting most of the money from that. And that idiot Barnabas had committed to using the Pentecost fortune for charity.' Ben almost spat the word. 'Getting Dorothea on side was easy. Disappointment is a powerful thing. She had plans; she was going to travel, meet someone, get married even. Didn't take much to convince her that she'd found what she wanted with me.'

You preyed on a lonely and desperate woman.

'I had the contacts, you see,' Ben elaborated. 'Been selling stuff for years – books mostly.' *All those missing items from the University Library*, Elliott realised with a sudden shock. That had been Ben. 'The Cleopatra Necklace though, that was something else. Dorothea knew how to work it. There was a mechanism in the case and the secret passage. Old Erasmus liked all that stuff. Dorothea had stayed in the house as a child. No one else knew about it. Her uncle, Ignatius, showed her and she had the chance to make sure it still worked when she was getting ready for the house party. You and Ms Norris turning up that night was a bit of a shock, but in the end it came out all right. Better even, with all the confusion.' He acknowledged Elliott with a small salute. 'Police don't know their arses from their elbows.'

Ben had made himself comfortable in the chair now, reminiscing and exulting over his cleverness. 'She was a good little actress – Dorothea – performance poet, you know? She fooled you that weekend.' The statement was a challenge. Elliott nodded to admit that she had. 'The woman you saw that weekend, that wasn't Dorothea,' Ben asserted. 'She was playing a part. Did it well.'

A spark of memory surfaced in Elliott's mind. 'It was her you came to meet when I ran into you in the street in Torquay, not me at all, or your aunt in Brixham. She was the woman in the trench coat.'

Not at all like the Dorothea of Pentecost Place.

'She was.' Ben looked pleased that Elliott had remembered and noticed. 'I had to come down. We thought that we were sunk with that stupid girl trying to steal stuff from the Clown Room. It was all right in the end though,' he repeated thoughtfully. 'Dorothea was different after Mumford. I didn't tell her it was me, but she knew.'

She must have been terrified.

'Why did you kill him?' Sickeningly, Elliott thought he knew the answer, but he had to ask.

Ben's smile was suddenly wide and sunny. 'To get you on board, El. Didn't you realise that?' Ben shook his head sorrowfully at Elliott's lack of perception.

'Leyland could have decided to go himself, or sent a team, like the museums did,' Elliott countered.

'Nah. He had a big poker tournament that weekend. Why miss *that* when he had a resident expert on tap? Mumford would have gone alone, so I convinced him that it would take too long to assemble a team – all that inter-departmental squabbling for glory? He knew from the Prof what the Collections contained, and what to bid. You were a bit of icing on the cake – renowned Egyptologist, Dr Elliott Elwood. And he knew then the Academic Society was considering the Fellowship – that smarmy Secretary contacted him for a background check. And *I* wanted you there for the Necklace. Knew your name would sell the thing. Now, speaking of that, we need to get on with it,' he said briskly.

'Get on with what? Why did you come here? What do you want?' Elliott already had a stomach-churning inkling of what it might be. He knew he was right when Ben produced the Necklace from the pocket of the loose jacket he was wearing. Elliott swallowed again, controlling the wave of nausea. He had to stay focused. He concentrated on the irony. Jake McQuire had been afraid that professional thieves were a threat, forcing him to authenticate the Necklace. The threat had been real, but instead it had come from a man Elliott had counted as a friend.

'We're going to do what we were supposed to do last night, old boy. You're going to verify the Cleopatra Necklace, while I film it.' He placed the Necklace on the table in front of Elliott to bring out his mobile phone. 'Then, when the boat reaches Nice, I walk off and disappear. No one gets hurt.'

Elliott was about to ask why he would do that. *Is he really expecting friendship to go that far?* Then he saw what else Ben had withdrawn from his pocket. A small, wicked-looking gun. 'I'm not too good with this sort of thing.' Ben displayed the weapon, holding it awkwardly. 'Brains, not an action man. But a gun is a gun.'

'You managed to kill Dorothea with it,' Elliott pointed out. *Really, do you want to remind him of that? Do* you *want to remember it?* Under the words, his mind was working frantically. Jake was somewhere on the boat, as well as four or five crew… and Maisie. God, he hoped that she was flaked out asleep in the stateroom, away from this madness. If he could continue to keep Ben talking …

Ben's mouth twisted again in discontent. 'Dorothea was an accident.' Abruptly, he changed his story, offering the justifications that had become second nature. 'I didn't intend to *kill* her – not that the traitorous bitch didn't deserve it. She moved at the wrong time. Must have.'

'And Leyland?' Elliott wasn't sure that he should ask that either, but knew that he needed to.

Ben's eyes lit with dark satisfaction. 'I decided he could be useful for a change. When I phoned him with an invitation to the festival, the silly old fool couldn't get on a plane fast enough. I told him he'd been especially asked for and the self-important idiot lapped it up. But then when he arrived, he started to ask too many questions about what I was doing here and what was going on. I had to hit him to keep him quiet. Can't say I didn't enjoy it though,' he affirmed with satisfaction. 'He must have had a thin skull or something. I only meant for him to be a diversion while we got away, something to keep the police occupied, not for him to actually die.'

Elliott seriously doubted that. He'd seen Ben shoot Dorothea point blank in cold blood. Leyland's body had been dressed and arranged at the foot of those steps. There was planning and premeditation in that. It had to have been done before the scene in the basement was staged. If Leyland had only been knocked out, he might have come round and raised the alarm. Much better to be sure that wasn't going to happen ...

If you've already killed once ...

And there it was again. *"It wasn't me. It wasn't my fault."* A refrain Elliott had been hearing for years and never really noticed or questioned. *Was I a poor sort of friend? Would it have made a difference?*

'You know all this could have all been avoided if you'd done what I wanted, back in Torquay. You could have given me a written authentication then. I did ask you, when we met that Saturday morning after the clown fiasco,' Ben pointed out plaintively. 'Instead of which, we have this.' The gun barrel caught the sun as he waved it. Elliott felt his throat getting dry. *You could reach for the drink and throw the contents of the cup in Ben's face, like in all the best action movies?*

Yes – but you're not close enough to grab the gun. Ben could still fire.

Realising with a jerk of alarm that his distraction might have given his thoughts away, Elliott focused again on the man who had once been his friend, only to realise that, inexplicably, Ben was giggling. 'I have to say, this thing had its moments,' he spluttered through the giggles. 'Sorry that we interrupted your bit of nookie with Ms Norris amongst the sarcophagi by the way … That was *so* funny. Didn't think you still had it in you, El. Sort of thing we would have got up to when we were students.' Elliott realised, incredulously, that the expression on Ben's face now was one of indulgent nostalgia.

Then the look faded to be replaced by a pout of discontent. 'It should have been so simple – in and out through the tunnel and the rope on the roof to leave the dim-witted plods scratching their heads.' The mobile mouth flattened into a surly line. 'But Dorothea wouldn't give me the keys to the fucking cabinet. She had to *be* there – and use that stupid conjuror's box. She didn't want me to have the Necklace. I organised a safe deposit box, but she wouldn't hand it over. Claimed that she was superstitious – afraid of activating the curse. Acted as if she didn't *trust* me ... She had to give it to me in the end.' Ben's small smile was chilling. Elliott felt as if something unclean was crawling up his backbone. Ben's eyes had lighted again into laughter. 'Stealing it that night – right under your nose – that *was* funny. All that dodging about in the dark.' His look invited Elliott to agree. With a dry swallow, Elliott nodded his head.

'And then that day in my office,' Ben continued. 'When you cold shouldered me over whether Ms Norris was involved in pinching it – couldn't resist that, mate. Pulling your leg. Got it bad for her, haven't you? Can't say I blame you. Lovely girl – and I reckon I can take credit for bringing you together.' He nodded happily, but then in a second seemed to realise the presence of the gun in his hand. His face went cold. There was a matching coldness in Elliott's chest as he met Ben's eyes. Now he could see it – obsession – just as much as any collector – but for the money that the Necklace would bring and his cleverness in taking it.

'Right then.' Suddenly, Ben was all business, breaking into Elliott's thoughts again. 'You authenticate the Necklace, or I shoot you. The knee. The elbow ...' He waved the gun in a sloppy arc. 'At this range I couldn't fail to hit you, but that won't be necessary – all you have to do is validate the Necklace for a future buyer.' He looked around, assessing their surroundings. 'Unless Ms Norris's boss would like to make an exclusive bid? I could be open to offers.'

Surging adrenaline had wiped out Elliott's tiredness. He tried to keep still, to look relaxed – as relaxed as you could be with a gun in your face, but his mind was racing now. Ben knew that the yacht belonged to Maisie's employer and that he had been with them last night, prepared to bid. *But he doesn't know who McQuire really is*. Could that be useful somehow?

Whether it could or not, Ben couldn't know the truth. Elliott wondered where on the boat Jake was and whether he might come on deck. They could send a crew member to find him. He was sharp enough to assess the situation and play the cards as they lay. *Could we use Ben's greed?*

Stalling for time, Elliott reached out to take the Necklace. For some strange reason, he'd expected the metal to be cold but, of course, it was warm from the sun shining on the table and from Ben's pocket. Somehow, that warmth felt more sickening than having a gun pointed at him.

'That's right,' Ben encouraged. 'Have a good look, then tell me what I want to know. I know you can.'

Maisie found Jake in the forward cabin, talking to one of the crew. He was still in his evening clothes from the night before. The well-cut suit was looking a little tired, as was its wearer. 'Hi.' He greeted her with a wave of his hand as the crew member left. 'How you doing?'

'Fine,' she responded automatically. 'Any news?'

Jake shook his head. 'No sign of the Necklace. They found one of the guns – probably the one Dorothea dropped, not the one that was used to kill her. There's nothing official yet, but the word is that not all of Leyland's injuries were consistent with a fall.' He ran his hand wearily through his hair. 'It's all in the hands of the authorities now. I was lucky to get that much.'

Maisie doubted that it was all luck. She knew Jake was involved in some sort of operation on the Riviera and in Paris, the details of which were highly confidential, but that wasn't the issue now. She latched onto the core of what Jake had said. 'If Leyland wasn't killed falling down the steps—'

'Then someone else killed him,' Jake finished.

'Oh God.' Maisie's stomach heaved a little as she understood the significance. 'There was a third person involved? Or the Plague Doctor we saw *wasn't* Leyland?' Her thoughts unravelled, making her stomach lurch some more. 'Maybe he was never part of it, except as a bystander and a victim?' She stood still, controlling the nausea, sifting through implications. The ten-minute nap had indeed sharpened her brain. 'Someone else connected to the University?'

'Oh – Mr McQuire.' The member of staff that Jake had been talking to came back into the salon. 'Sorry – I forgot to tell you. Dr Elwood has a guest on board. They're both on deck.' The man smiled and withdrew.

'A guest?' Jake raised his eyebrows. 'Someone from the University?' he repeated the suspicion Maisie had just voiced.

'I'm going up to find out,' she decided. 'Will you come up after a few minutes but stay out of the way until we work out what's going on.'

Really it wasn't a question. She could see from Jake's face that he wasn't happy about it, but she wasn't leaving Elliott alone up there with whoever it was. 'You could change,' she suggested.

Jake looked down ruefully at his suit. 'Probably a good idea. Give me five minutes. I'm going to alert the crew as well.'

Maisie walked briskly to the companionway that gave onto the deck where they'd had breakfast, thinking about Jake's last remark. If you worked for someone like Jake, you had to be ready for … well, anything, even as the crew of his yacht.

The thought of the "anything" that might be waiting above quickened her heartbeat.

She'd reached the stairs.

In the sunlight on deck Elliott dropped the Necklace on the table, regarding it as he might a snake. He knew it was an illusion that the thing looked like a pool of darkness, even as it glittered in the Mediterranean sun.

'Go on,' Ben prompted, raising the camera. 'Authenticate the Necklace. The Elwood Magic Touch – make it good,' he encouraged.

'Ben …' Elliott's chest contracted in what he recognised was incipient panic. He fought it down. 'I really can't do that – proper authentication is more than just looking at the thing—'

'No!' Ben interrupted. 'All *you* have to do is handle it. The Elwood Magic Touch,' he repeated.

'Ben – please.' Elliott shook his head. 'There's no such thing. It was a *joke*.'

A joke going back to his student days when his discovery of some broken fragments of a statue had led to the opening of a previously undiscovered minor tomb; small but with more statues, that were still intact. There had been ribaldry in the camp, some of it he knew tinged with envy, when the director of the excavation had singled him out for a special mention over a celebratory dinner – "*Elwood's Magic Touch … all he has to do is pick something up.*"

'No!' Ben repeated the denial louder, waving the gun. 'Dorothea told me. She was watching from the hall when you went into the Egyptian Room at Pentecost Place. When you saw the Necklace, you *knew* it was real, even without touching it.'

'Ben … I …' Elliott's response tailed off.

How can I explain that what Dorothea saw was my imagination – envisaging the Necklace around Maisie's neck?

It wasn't going to work. He could see that. Reluctantly, he fingered the Necklace. 'What do you want me to say?'

'Authenticate it.' The impatience in Ben's voice was clear. 'Say the things to let buyers know it's the real deal. Like you do on the TV.' The slight sneer in the words spoke volumes.

Elliott picked up the gleaming collar, swallowing his distaste. *It's just a piece of jewellery.*

Ben raised the camera, standing and stepping back to get Elliott's face and hands, with the Necklace, into the shot. The gun was still in evidence but held loosely now, pointing towards the sky.

Elliott scanned the table. If he threw something, even pushed the table over—

As if he'd heard his thoughts, Ben gripped the phone awkwardly in his left hand and levelled the gun again, frowning and making a get-on-with-it gesture with the weapon, which flashed in the sunlight.

Elliott seized a second to ground himself. He couldn't afford more. The camera was running. He took a deep breath. 'Um … well … I'm Dr Elliott Elwood, Senior Lecturer in Egyptology at the University of Aquae Sulis. What I have here—' he held up the Necklace to display it '—is an Egyptian-style collar of gold, inset with crystals and lapis. The workmanship …' He faltered, drawing in another deep breath. He was winging this, trying not to say too much about the actual provenance of the Necklace, which lay like a piece of dead metal in his hands. If he really believed in that Magic Touch, he'd have said that the collar was screaming *fake* at him, but he knew that was all in his mind. He ran his finger over the gold. It felt smooth. He tried to concentrate. Would a genuine artefact feel—?

'Ben! What on earth are you doing here?'

Ben cursed and fumbled the phone and Elliott dropped the Necklace back onto the table as Maisie strolled down the deck towards them.

Chapter Forty-One

You should have known it was Ben.

Ben – with a gun, pointed at Elliott.

Uncertainty gone, her thoughts in ice-cold overdrive, Maisie held down the impulse to charge at Ben, wrench the thing out of his hand and throw it overboard. *Too risky. You're going to have to finesse your way out of this one.*

She forced herself to walk normally, to keep her face in an expression of confused but welcoming enquiry. 'Oh!' She faked spotting the gun for the first time. 'Ben! What's going on?'

Her mind was sorting through the new situation, even as she got nearer to the table. It should have been obvious, really. If it wasn't Leyland, who else could it be? *But he's Elliott's friend.*

Was Elliott's friend, by the look of anguish on Elliott's face and the flicker of repulsion she could discern in his eyes. She hoped Ben wasn't as good at reading Elliott's emotions as she was.

Why is he here?

Her stomach heaved a little when she spotted the mobile phone and the penny dropped.

Authentication.

'Er … Ben … Ben had the Necklace.' Elliott made a reluctant gesture towards the collar, which was now a seductive pool of gold and sparkles, gleaming warmly on the table.

'You found it?' Maisie stepped closer, peering at the prize. 'After Leyland dropped it?' She forced her facial muscles to show admiring astonishment. What she was saying didn't really make sense, but accusations weren't going to get Elliott out of the range of a bullet. Instinct told her that Ben wouldn't expect clear reasoning from a female. She needed to give him some space – a lifeline.

'Yes.' Ben nodded, eagerly grabbing the line she'd thrown. 'Leyland called me, last night … He said he needed me ... When I got here… There were police at the hotel … I … I just picked these up in the street,' he finished with a rush. He gestured to the Necklace and the gun, now held loosely in his palm. His mobile phone had disappeared back into a pocket. 'I didn't know what to do. I panicked.' The smile was self-deprecating, disarming, if you didn't look at the calculation in his eyes.

‘I couldn’t think … I was afraid the police would assume I had something to do with it. I came to Elliott.’

He threw a glance at Elliott that she knew was a warning as he turned more fully to face her. Elliott stayed silent, letting her lead. ‘Your boss. He’s here, isn’t he?’ There was excitement now in Ben’s voice. ‘This is his boat. He wants the Necklace. Perhaps we could do a deal? Elliott and I—’ He gestured between them with another hard glance at Elliott that she wasn’t supposed to notice ‘—we can make sure that the money goes to the University – an anonymous donation without any middle men involved. A private transaction, just between us.’ That boyish grin again.

‘That sounds …’ *As if it has more holes in it than a fishing net, but just go with what works.* Maisie had caught a small movement at the other end of the deck that suggested that Jake was closer than Ben might be expecting. She was also conscious that the yacht was slowing down. ‘It sounds like something Mr ... Mr Elladour might be interested to discuss.’ She remembered just in time to use Jake’s fake name. Ben might know that wasn’t the name of the owner of the yacht, but the secrecy wouldn’t be a surprise. There would have been very little time for him to research Jake McQuire’s real identity. She could only count on that – and the anticipation and greed she saw in the man’s eyes.

‘Maisie, Elliott? Jake lounged out of the shadows at the end of the deck. ‘I’m intrigued. What would I like to discuss?’ He smiled and held out a hand to Ben. ‘Hello! I’m Elladour – welcome aboard. Any friends of Elliott’s, and all that …’ He looked enquiringly over at Elliott, inviting an introduction.

‘Oh …’ Elliott visibly gathered himself together. ‘This is Ben Bartram, a colleague from the University.’ *Colleague – Elliott won’t be calling this man a friend ever again.*

Ben had turned, holding out his left hand. If the situation hadn’t been so macabre, Maisie would have laughed at his preening self-satisfaction at finding himself actually shaking hands with the mystery billionaire. She had relaxed a little once Jake appeared, but Elliott was stiff with tension, although he was doing his best to cover it. The gun was held now at Ben’s side, pointing down at the deck. Out of sight. *But it’s still there.* And the damn Necklace was sitting on the table, glittering placidly in the sunshine. The evil thing *was* cursed.

‘I … I thought that you might like to purchase the Cleopatra Necklace.’ Ben was back on his mission. She could see him bracing himself as he stepped back, away from Jake, scooping up the collar from the table. She saw the shiver of determination run through him as he straightened and lifted the gun, pointing it at Elliott.

No!

'Dr Elliott was about to authenticate it. It's yours for ten million.' All pretence had dropped away completely. Ben was revealed – a thief and a murderer, doing business. 'When we reach Nice, Dr Elwood and Ms Norris will stay with me here. You get the money for me in exchange for the Necklace. I leave and that's the end of it.'

Maisie made a muffled exclamation, pretending shock and confusion. *The feeble little woman.* Ben ignored her.

Jake was standing very still. His eyes were on the gun. Maisie knew he would be figuring out a way to neutralise the threat, but now he simply looked unimpressed. 'I'll certainly take the Necklace. There's no need for you to wave that thing around.' He'd stepped a little closer to the table without Maisie really registering. *Ben could shoot any one of us.*

Elliott got to his feet, pulling Ben's attention towards him. *Dividing his concentration. He can shoot any of us – but he can't shoot* all *of us.* 'I can't verify that this Necklace is a genuine Egyptian artefact,' he said levelly.

Jake gestured the caution away. 'I'm willing to take the chance.' Maisie inhaled sharply. Her boss was good. She could see avarice and the desire of the obsessive collector clear in his face. 'Ten million. No problem, but it will take a few hours to get hold of it.'

Ben was grinning now, his eyes alight with satisfaction. *Everything he's dreamed of, right here.* He inclined his head to Jake, almost like pharaoh might have, acknowledging a bargain. *Or an offering.* 'Dr Elwood and Ms Norris and myself simply remain as your guests until the money is available.'

'How do you want the payment made?' Jake asked, as if he was buying bread in the supermarket, instead of offering millions to a gun-wielding thief for a cursed Necklace. Ben was concentrating on Jake, his body language still taut although edged with triumph. She and Elliott were secondary figures; useful pawns, but not important.

But still in the line of fire.

She shuffled a tiny pace closer to Elliott. Something was about to happen. Ben hadn't noticed; too intent on rehearsing the details of a money transfer with Jake, but the yacht had virtually stopped. There were subtle movements too on the other end of the deck.

She edged forward again, ready to pull Elliott away from the table if she had to. Her heart was beating very fast but her mind was clear. She saw the second when Ben took in the change in his surroundings, saw his eyes widen as a uniformed figure appeared from where Jake had been standing moments before, saw him make the decision to fire.

The bullet, aimed at the police officer, went wide. Her hands were on Elliott's arm, pulling him towards her as Jake dived in the opposite direction, splitting Ben's potential targets. Ben was pivoting wildly, waving the gun as more uniformed figures moved in behind the first. 'Stop! I'll shoot!' The threat was a panicked yell.

For a gut-wrenching moment, the gun was pointed at Elliott. Ben's finger squeezed the trigger. A scream built in her throat as she yanked Elliott down to the deck, bracing herself for the report.

It didn't come.

There was just a hollow click. Ben, his face a mask of disbelief, stared down at the gun, shaking it and pulling the trigger over and over. With a howl of frustration, he pitched the weapon in the direction of the advancing police and sprinted to the rail of the boat. Before she could fully comprehend what he meant to do, he had scrambled up and over.

The last thing she saw as he plummeted towards the water was the flash of the Necklace, still clutched in his hand.

Chapter Forty-Two

Feet clattered on the deck as they all rushed to the side – Maisie, Elliott, Jake, three uniformed policemen and two of the crew.

'He'll never make it,' one of the crew men exclaimed in dismay.

'He is though,' Jake pointed out. Ben was already some distance from the boat, moving fast and steadily towards the shore, where one of the private landing stages jutted out into the water.

'He's a strong swimmer.' Elliott was leaning almost over the rail, following Ben's progress as his light brown hair turned slick and dark against the blue water. 'When we were at university he used to swim competitively.' Behind them, one of the police officers was barking orders into a phone, setting up an intercept. The rest of them just leaned on the rail, watching that dark head rising and falling in regular rhythm, getting closer to the landing stage by the minute.

But something was happening on the landing stage. A group of people in swimming gear were gathered at the very end of the jetty, laughing, jostling and joking.

'Speedboats. They've got a couple of speedboats,' Jake called out.

Even as they watched, the group divided and tumbled into the boats, roaring away from the jetty, the occupants in an impromptu race, laughing and calling across to each other. They were heading straight for the yacht, probably intent on circling it, showing off to the intruder.

Straight for the yacht and the unseen swimmer in the water, too absorbed in the fun of their contest to heed or understand the warning waves and shouts.

Maisie turned away, nausea rising in her throat when the inevitable happened, burying her face in Elliott's chest as he held her in his arms.

Elliott felt as if he had been chewed up by a large beast and spat back out again. Lack of sleep, the tension of the aborted auction, witnessing murder, the realisation that his oldest friend was a manipulative thief and a killer …

Watching that friend die …

Ben's body had been retrieved quite quickly, along with that of a female passenger from one of the speedboats, who had been thrown into the water on impact.

Four deaths. Ben was responsible for four deaths. And his own.

Elliott knew what some people would say – it was the curse of the Necklace. Maybe it was, if curse equated with obsession. Whatever it was, the thing was gone now. Ben's body had been recovered but there was no trace of the collar. It was assumed that he'd still had it in his hand when he went down.

Now it will be exerting its curse somewhere on the seabed between Monaco and Nice. Will it create its own Bermuda Triangle of lost boats and mysterious accidents?

With a shudder, Elliott realised how badly his mind was wandering. He'd held things together during what felt like days of polite questioning from various authorities, in and out of uniform, but which had, in reality, only been a few hours. Now he and Maisie were back at the villa in Menton. Jake had suggested they stay on there for a few days. He was remaining on the yacht, where Cassie would join him. Elliott had grabbed the offer of the villa like a gift from the gods. His breath wobbled a little – he wasn't sure how Maisie felt about it. The case was over now …

But she is *still here.* For the moment that was enough for his tired mind to process.

He was standing beside the pool with a bottle of water held loosely in his hands, just staring out at the view. Maisie was inside somewhere, on the phone to Michelle, filling her in about events. Would he do that when he returned to the University? Explain to colleagues what had happened … Leyland and Ben – both gone. There would be plenty of chaos in the Faculty of Humanities when he got back. At present, he wasn't even sure he would admit to being involved. It was all …

His thoughts drifted. His mind was closing down. He probably needed to sleep, but somehow he couldn't anticipate lying down and closing his eyes. Too many pictures to flash behind his eyelids. Ben on deck, Ben holding a gun, Ben in the water, the speedboat …

After the clear-up at the hotel basement was completed, the police had found out about Ben's presence in Monaco and his connection to Leyland. They had missed the chance to interview him when he boarded the yacht, which sailed almost immediately. When a member of the crew alerted the authorities to what was happening on board, a unit had been sent by boat to intercept. No one had envisaged what would happen.

Not even Ben. He thought he was invincible.

Elliott had known true fear, maybe for the first time in his life, when Maisie had walked into range of the gun. He'd been ready to throw himself into the path of a bullet – and she'd reacted the same way, pulling him to the deck. That meant she cared for him, surely? Or was he still, at base, just a job?

'You okay?' The sound of her voice made him turn around. She was walking towards him, outlined by sunlight. Something shifted in his chest. Something monumental. She was everything he'd ever wanted and hadn't realised he wanted. The fixed point in a world of chaos. Emotions – love, desire, need – bubbled up in his chest. Bubbled into speech. Speech he couldn't control. 'Maisie, I love you. I want … Maisie, will you marry me?'

Chapter Forty-Three

Shock riveted Maisie's feet to the flagstones of the terrace. She'd just received a declaration of love and a proposal of marriage. Like a lightning bolt out of nowhere.

How ...?

She'd finished a phone call, debriefing Michelle, then walked out into the sunshine and this life-changing moment.

A declaration from a man … the man she wanted … the man she ...

She couldn't even force it into words. It was just too much.

Of their own volition, her hands rose in a gesture of repudiation. She was shaking her head. 'I can't… not now … no!'

She spun on her heel, intent only on escape, escape from the stricken look on Elliott's face.

She fled to the front of the house where the car was standing.

So – that went well. Elliott found that he'd let go of the water bottle. It was rolling around at his feet, making a clanking noise. He picked it up, carefully and precisely setting it on a side table. Not exactly the reaction a man hoped for when making his first proposal of marriage. *What the hell were you thinking?* That was it. He hadn't been thinking. The words had risen out of a devastating swell of emotion that he hadn't been able to control.

But they were spoken from your heart.

All his resolve to keep quiet, to be restrained, to wait, had flown away in an overwhelming rush. *You'd guessed how she might react, but you did it anyway. Needy, needy, needy.* The word ricocheted around his head in a mocking chorus. And the result? A resounding "no" and the sound of the car retreating into the distance.

Elliott walked slowly towards the house. It would probably be best now if he packed his things. It wouldn't take long. Maybe he could even be gone by the time Maisie came back.

If she came back.

Her hands were white at the knuckles, gripping the steering wheel. With an effort, Maisie relaxed them, slowing the car and drawing it into a tiny lay-by – a lookout point with a view over red and orange rooftops.

Shakily, she got out of the car and leaned against it, staring down unseeingly at the roofs and the glittering sea beyond.

Elliott had asked her to *marry* him.

She took in a huge breath that was as shaky as her limbs. He *loved* her.

She put her clasped hands up to press hard against her chest, trying to hold down her racing heart. Elliott had asked her to spend the rest of her life with him and she … she …

She took another deep, ragged breath. *What did you just do?*

This was a mess, a total and utter *mess*.

And you *made it.*

The sun was warm on her face. She tilted her head back to feel it, absorb it into her skin.

Mess.

Her mind couldn't seem to let go of the word. And under the mess was the complete, certain conviction that yes, she was in love with Elliott Elwood. Irrevocably in love. *How the hell did you miss that?*

The realisation made her heart pound even harder. Why had she not realised it?

Panic. Ingrained panic.

She'd met the man she wanted to spend her life with. Marriage … she couldn't face up to the idea of marriage – but to lose him? No – she couldn't. *Unless you already have.*

What the hell have you done?

Slow realisation crawled up from her stomach to lodge in her throat. For as long as she could remember, the shadow of her grandmother had hung over her family, dictating their lives, even from beyond the grave – making *her* an outcast and a failure simply because her existence offended an old woman's warped sense of propriety.

And you played up to it. Or maybe down?

But you're more than that. You've proved it. Over and over.

And Elliott loves you.

Are you really going to let an arrogant and rigid old woman, who's been dead for over a decade, spoil the best thing that ever happened to you?

She scrambled back into the car, executing a dangerously sloppy three-point turn on a mercifully empty road, to head back the way she had come.

When she reached the gates of the villa, they were standing open. She nosed the car inside and up the short drive. The few miles of the return journey had brought her back in control of herself. She was a fully functioning adult. She had to act like one – to use the analytical skills she brought to her work to unpick the panic and conquer it.

She had a reason, a prize.

Elliott.

There was a vehicle standing outside the house. A taxi. Even as she juddered the sports car to a stop, a tall figure emerged from the villa, carrying a suitcase. She flung open the car door, tumbled out and almost threw herself across the drive, skittering to a stop in front of him. His eyes were dark and shadowed, his face drawn with tiredness and pain that wasn't physical. She stared up at him, her heart racing frantically again.

'Don't go. You can't go.' *Breathe.* 'I love you.' The words came out in a rush, but so easily that she wanted to cry. 'I love you,' she said it again, so that he would know. 'But I need ... I need to explain … I *need* you to understand.'

Chapter Forty-Four

They'd paid off the puzzled taxi driver and now they were sitting across from each other at the table on the terrace. Vividly pink bougainvillea shifted in a tiny breeze and the scent of jasmine enfolded them.

The scent of jasmine. Now it's always going to remind you ...

Maisie studied Elliott's face. His eyes were wary, but hopeful. She was sure they *were* hopeful, but his suitcase remained at the front door, tucked in the corner of the shallow porch. He hadn't carried it back in. *But you did manage to tell him that you loved him. That has to count for something?*

She gripped the edge of the table with both hands, grounding herself. 'I'm sorry I ran out on you like that.' She swallowed hard. 'I panicked,' she admitted. 'It was illogical. And very stupid.'

'Not if there was a reason for it.' There was warmth now in Elliott's eyes. He put out his hand, letting it lie where she could reach it. Tentatively, Maisie released her death grip on the table edge and stretched out to clasp his fingers. The touch of his hand felt so good.

There is no way that you're going to give this up.

She *did* love Elliott – great confusing swathes of love, like she'd never experienced in her life before. *And this man knows you.*

The shock of that realisation caught her under the ribs. Elliott knew *her.* The person she was, not the mask she'd become so used to wearing to hide her inadequacies. The disguise for all the ways she didn't match up.

She lifted her head on a new tide of emotion. Hell – she was good at her job, her colleagues valued her, and if a man like Elliott Elwood wanted to spend time with her ... *Not just time, you idiot. He* proposed *to you.* She let out a soft sigh. If Elliott Elwood loved her, then maybe she wasn't just a misfit and an impostor?

He was watching her now, waiting patiently. The hope was still there in his eyes. She owed it to him, and herself, to drag that stifling illogical panic and the baggage that went with it into the light and the jasmine-scented air. She clasped her fingers tighter on Elliott's hand. He returned the pressure. 'This is about your family, isn't it?' He prompted gently, encouragingly.

‘Yes.’ She could feel an unexpected blush starting up from the base of her neck. ‘I …’ She swallowed again. ‘I’ve never fitted in. I was a mistake. An accident.’ She knew her mouth had twisted. ‘I’m not saying that my parents didn’t love me after their fashion, but well … my sister was twelve when I was born, my brother ten. I was … surplus to requirements. They already *had* the perfect family. Everyone said so, especially my grandmother, my mother’s mother. I was an embarrassment. She thought my mother had made herself a laughing stock by getting pregnant again at her age.’ Maisie made a confused gesture. ‘Mum was only thirty-nine! And, of course, if my mother was a laughing stock, she’d made my grandmother one too.’

Elliott tightened his grip on Maisie’s hand, wondering if she was aware of the tiny tensions and relaxations that told a story underneath her words, of a bewildered misfit child. A child who had gone on to make herself into a vibrant, competent woman. A woman he knew he couldn’t live without. She paused, but he waited rather than prompting her.

‘My grandmother was a force to be reckoned with in the family. She lived to be nearly a hundred and she was a real old-fashioned matriarch – like something left over from Victorian times. She scared me to death when I was a kid. I avoided her as much as I could.’ Maisie grimaced at the memory. ‘She had *very* traditional views about what was “proper”. Sex wasn’t at all proper, even if you were married. I wonder sometimes what sort of a life she lived with my grandfather. She’d expected Mum and Dad to stop “all that” once they’d completed their family. So I was a *real* mistake. A very visible one.’ Elliott saw the pain and regret flit across Maisie’s face, gone in an instant. ‘With such a strong personality, it’s not really a surprise that some of her influences still linger.’ Maisie looked down at their joined hands, then back up to meet his eyes. ‘My mother is very much about appearances. She worries constantly about what friends and neighbours will think. Her ideal is that her family should be “settled” – that everything should be perfect and that any possibility of gossip or embarrassment should be averted at all costs.’ Maisie sighed. ‘She can’t help it, it’s ingrained. She has a model of the ideal family in her head, and for the most part my sister and brother fit the mould – straight As in school, Oxbridge, flourishing careers, suitable marriages – although things went off the rails a bit with Hal.’ She gave a lopsided grin that tugged at Elliott’s heart. ‘She has *finally* given up putting “nice girls” in his way, hoping that somehow he will suddenly change. To be fair, what she wants isn't unreasonable – for her children to be successful and in stable relationships.'

'But to you it feels like straitjacket?' Elliott leaned forward a little, watching the surprise coming to her eyes.

'Yes, it does.' She sounded as well as looked surprised. 'Mum doesn't get that … and Dad – he just laughs at it all.' She shook her head, still clearly considering what he had said. 'I'm not like Fran and Hal – I was never more than average in school. I enjoyed art and history, but I was never top of the class. I liked sports. Won a few team medals for hockey and netball. But, of course, sports weren't proper either.' Her face clouded with memory again. Elliott imagined those achievements, and they were achievements, being brushed aside in favour of the academic talents of her siblings. He was holding onto his temper with a certain amount of effort. The narrow-minded tartar of a grandmother had clearly cast an enormous shadow, but the past could not be changed. The woman Maisie was now … well, if her family couldn't see her value, it was their loss.

'I know that Mum wants what she thinks is the best for me, but I can never match up to her ideal,' she said softly. 'My choices are never right, my abilities never enough. I've dealt with it by absenting myself. They don't even know what I do; they think I'm still a receptionist at the agency – my old student job.' She gave a rueful laugh. 'Maybe that's actually a good thing – they don't worry about people pointing guns at me.'

'Hopefully that doesn't happen often,' Elliott responded. 'I'll certainly worry.'

'It's never happened before,' she assured him seriously. Elliott knew that he had to accept that and trust. *He* wasn't going to change who Maisie was. *And it was* your *friend – well, ex-friend – who was pointing the gun.*

After a moment, Maisie went on, her eyes now focused on the view out to sea rather than on him. 'I've got by through ducking and diving, staying out of the way. Avoidance. I didn't realise how bad it had got.' Her gaze came back to him, her face slightly flushed. 'When you asked me to marry you … everything just seemed to fall in – I panicked. There's no getting away from that.' She moved restlessly, her face creased in remembrance. 'It was like ... like being smothered. An overwhelming ambush of everything I'd ever tried to get away from – Mum finally getting her way, the organising and fussing, the triumph because I'd finally conformed.' She gave him a long, clear, slightly irritated look. 'She'd just *love* you!'

Elliott wasn't sure he was too keen on that. He'd much rather be loved by Mrs Webster's errant daughter, who was regarding him now with a baffled expression. 'I am deeply sorry about the panic,' she clarified. 'It was stupid and I shouldn't have done that to you.'

'Not stupid! Human. You explained. I can see the reasons. We can put it behind us.' He raised her hand to his lips. 'I love you. I don't want to lose you.'

'I love you,' she repeated. 'I don't want to lose *you*. And I would like to marry you but …' He saw the tiny flicker, the vestige of hurt and alarm, in her eyes.

'We can work something out. Don't worry about it.' He looked around the terrace. Twilight was creeping in, lengthening the shadows. He looked at his watch. It was nearly nine. 'Are you hungry?'

Maisie tilted her head, considering. 'Starving,' she said with surprise. 'Shall we go and see what there is in the kitchen?'

Elliott strolled out onto the terrace, his laptop under his arm, pausing to look out over the view. *A man could get used to this.* He'd spent three days now at the villa with Maisie, mainly in and around the pool and in bed, some of it catching up on sleep. This morning, he'd made the reluctant decision to reconnect with the outside world and check his e-mails. Maisie was off somewhere on the small estate with the gardener, extending her knowledge of greenhouses and flowerbeds. Her meltdown when he'd proposed had not been mentioned since their discussion here under the bougainvillea. He wondered now if she was cautiously exploring the idea of a life that, at some stage, might involve a house and a garden. He grinned. It was good if she was, but he certainly wasn't going to ask.

He set up the laptop on the table, then hesitated about opening it, not sure what he would find. Jake had been keeping them up-to-date with snippets of information by phone and text. The authorities were apparently concluding investigations, piecing things together with a view to closing the case, now that the thieves were dead and the Necklace lost. Ben's room at a small hotel in Villefranche-sur-Mer had been located, but if a search had revealed anything, it had not been made public. He had been there alone, and investigations had not yet uncovered where Dorothea had been staying. How Ben had explained his presence on the Riviera to Vaisey Leyland, and how the man had been enticed to make the trip himself and then positioned to literally take the fall, remained murky. The gun on the yacht had failed to fire because it was out of bullets, which Jake claimed was characteristic of Ben's planning. No action seemed to be proposed in relation to the auction bidders. No stolen goods had changed hands, and Dorothea did have some legitimate claim to ownership of the Necklace and, theoretically, the right to offer it for sale. Elliott wondered how Barnabas and Armand had received the news of their cousin's death. Presumably, the Pentecost fortune would now be split between them. The press had reported briefly on the tragic deaths of three tourists – in a fall, as a result of a domestic dispute and in a boating accident, in which a local resident had also died – but had not made any connection between them. Emile Le Clerc, the collector with the wheelchair, was rumoured to be recruiting underwater salvage experts. *Well, good luck with that.*

Elliott took a deep breath and opened his computer.

It wasn't quite as bad as he'd expected. Congratulations on the Fellowship and the London lectures – it was as if they'd taken place light years ago – enquiries from students, returned work. A couple of dinner invitations from friends. He'd ask Maisie if she would like to accompany him. The hope that she'd say yes gave a little lift to his spirits.

There were predictable shock waves from Leyland's death, but with its usual behind-the-scenes efficiency in a crisis, the University had matters in hand. One of the other Faculty heads was stepping in temporarily, until recruitment and/or promotions could take place. There was a message from the new man, asking Elliott to take over some teaching and supervisions to fill short-term gaps, along with a request to become responsible for the ongoing work on the Pentecost Collections. He grimaced when he read the proposal for a combined memorial service for three lost colleagues. He'd do what he could to see that Ben's name was quietly dropped from a commemoration of the two men that he'd murdered. Jenni had sent a discreetly worded note, indicating that she expected to hear the *full* story in due course. That made him smile.

He'd almost reached the end of the list, reading, replying and deleting, when the name of a sender and subject line sprang off the screen – *Turn up in the books!*, Elliott read. It had been sent by Vaisey Leyland a week ago. It was only a few lines.

Found this amongst the Pentecost papers – folded in with some invoices for the purchase of three alchemical texts for Lucinda Pentecost's library. Raises some interesting questions, don't you think? Must discuss on your return.

There was an attachment. Elliott clicked to open it and found himself looking at a scanned page – an invoice from a well-known Bond Street jeweller.

Maisie wandered out onto the terrace, having failed to find Elliott anywhere in the house. Her hour with the gardener had been interesting – maybe Elliott would like to go and visit some of the showplace gardens further along the coast that the man had recommended?

Elliott was sitting at the table, staring at his laptop with a blank expression on his face.

'What's the matter?' She hurried over. He jerked visibly at her voice, before turning the machine so that she could see the screen. 'This. It's from Leyland. Sent just before he died. He found it among the Pentecost paperwork.'

Maisie squinted down at the display. She recognised the name of the firm on the headed notepaper, but it was the typed description below that made her blink.

Fabrication of one jewelled collar, in the Egyptian style, to the client's own design and specification. Gold, lapis and crystal – in the sum of seven hundred guineas. The invoice was stamped as paid over a scrawled signature. The day and the month of the stamp were smudged, but the year was clear – *1923*. She looked up at the heading of the invoice. It was dated for the twelfth of December of that same year. The client was Aristotle Pentecost.

'Hell! It has to be the Cleopatra Necklace. It *was* a fake.' She turned to Elliott. He was shaking his head.

'Not necessarily. The Tutankhamun tomb was discovered in 1922 – all things Egyptian were very fashionable. Aristotle was a widower by then. He could have had it made as a Christmas gift for a lady.'

Maisie inelegantly whistled her disbelief. 'Yeah. Or he wanted to own a piece of fancy Egyptian jewellery, and when he didn't manage to dig one up, he had one made.'

'Or that,' Elliott agreed.

‘Come on.’ She nudged his shoulder. ‘Seven hundred guineas would have been one hell of a Christmas gift.’ She pointed to the screen. ‘*That* is the Cleopatra Necklace. It was a fake all along.’

‘It does look that way,’ he accepted, though she could see reluctance warring with probability in his face. ‘There might be more information amongst the rest of the paperwork, but as the thing is at the bottom of the Mediterranean, it’s academic.’

‘Unless Le Clerc recovers it.’

‘Don’t!’ Elliott put his hand up over his eyes. ‘With a gigantic spanner like this in the works, the bottom of the sea is the best place for it.’

‘Maybe we’ll never know.’ Maisie looked thoughtfully at the incriminating invoice. ‘Do you think Leyland might have told Ben what he found? And that was why he was so keen for you to authenticate it?’

‘And it gave him even more motive to kill Leyland?’ Elliott dropped his hand and let out a long breath. ‘It’s all speculation.’ He shook his head. ‘It really doesn’t matter now.’

It did though. Maisie could see it in the set of Elliott’s shoulders. Would Ben have expected Elliott to lie? Tried to force him to do it?

Deceit, thieves trying to outsmart each other, obsessive collectors trying to outbid each other, loss of life. She *really* hoped the thing was never found.

She slid her fingers down Elliott’s arm to take his hand and pull him up from the table, closing the laptop as she did so. ‘Come on – we’ll go and find a good place for lunch and then visit some gardens. I have a list.’ She jangled the car keys in front of him enticingly. ‘You can drive.’

Chapter Forty-Five

Elliott lay on his back, staring up at the ceiling of the bedroom. Beside him, Maisie gave an adorable little snuffle and nestled closer. He glanced down, wondering if she was waking up, but after a second decided that she wasn't. He went back to his examination of the ceiling.

Why was it that sex was so much more … *more* when it was with someone you loved? *Because it's not just sex – it really* is *making love.* He exhaled in deep contentment. His body was relaxed, even if his mind was awake and working. Maisie had done an excellent job of distracting him away from that disturbing e-mail from a dead man, with food, exquisite gardens and, well … herself.

The shock had receded, leaving only questions.

Small memories from the weekend in Torquay kept surfacing, leading him to wonder. Did Barnabas have his own doubts over the authenticity of the Necklace? There was nothing Elliott could put his finger on, just ... questions; the short time that the jewel had been withdrawn from the bank for the Torquay weekend and the security alarms said to limit the time that it might be removed from the cabinet. Was Barnabas keeping the Necklace out of the hands of someone who might identify its origin? Or was it simply that, like his cousin, he feared disturbing the curse by too much handling? *Or was that superstition an invention of Dorothea's because she had begun to distrust Ben?* Elliott remembered the strange look on Barnabas's face when the man had noted his own reaction to the relic. Had it been relief that the "expert" was apparently impressed?

None of it added up to anything much.

Or did it?

Elliott was sure Dorothea had thought the Necklace was genuine. Barnabas – maybe not so much.

Elliott shifted sideways as Maisie stirred in her sleep.

The requirements for hallmarking gold might not have been quite as stringent in 1923 as they were now, but he was confident that the jewellers named on the invoice would have expected to mark their work. Could a client request the process be omitted? Or did the "Cleopatra Necklace" bear the small tell-tale insignia of its manufacturer stamped somewhere on the gold?

It would have been all too easy to destroy the receipt that might be evidence, but Leyland's description of finding it with other unrelated papers suggested it had been overlooked and unknown. Or perhaps just irrelevant – recognised in the family as the bill for an expensive trifle purchased by Aristotle to further his pursuit of a lady?

You could always ask Barnabas?

No – no more. The thing was gone. He wouldn't speculate any more about it. Or even think about it. The whole episode was closed. *And that's for the best.* Their reason for coming to the Riviera was done. The dangerous episode was over. *But you and Maisie being together, that isn't over.* The thought sent a complex glow of warmth deep into his being.

The real world was circling though, outside the haven of the villa. They had one more day here before they returned to Bath, to a new term, to Maisie's cases …

But they were *together* now, which was a big thing, a *huge* thing.

And he had an idea …

Daylight was filtering softly into the cool white room. Maisie opened her eyes slowly, letting awareness drift over her, also slowly. *Their last day.*

A movement beside her made her turn her head. Elliott was propped up on one elbow, watching her. His hair was a mess, standing on end, and his grin was sleepy and satisfied and disgustingly possessively male, but somehow she couldn't raise an appropriate degree of annoyance. Maybe it was the crazy hair – or too much love. Who would have thought that she would ever have that kind of feeling about cold and snooty Dr Elliott Elwood? A slow smile bubbled up.

'What?' Of course, he'd noticed the smile. When she just shook her head and didn't answer, he put out his free hand to trace the outline of her mouth. 'Good morning, Ms Webster. I love you.'

'Me too. You, I mean. I love *you*.' Declaration received and responded to, she shut her eyes.

'Are you going back to sleep?'

She opened her eyes again. 'Probably not,' she conceded. It didn't take much to guess that he had something on his mind. Now he looked edgy. 'What is it?'

'Well, I've been thinking. Going back to the UK – normal life, work, deadlines, the weather ... all that stuff.'

'Don't remind me.' She gave a theatrical shudder.

'We could plan a holiday?'

'I'd like that.' She nodded approval, beginning to be intrigued. There was something going on here. 'What did you have in mind?'

'I was wondering … have you ever been to Las Vegas?'

'No.' She sat up. That was the last place she'd have expected him to suggest. 'Are you a secret gambler then, Dr Elwood?

'Maybe.' There was *definitely* something going on. 'I just thought it would be interesting. And Las Vegas isn't only about gambling.'

'No?' she said cautiously. He was building up to something, very carefully. She was puzzled for a moment – and then she got it.

He was still explaining, 'I thought we could go, just call it a holiday – at Christmas or maybe New Year. Then, if you wanted …' His voice tailed off.

Her thoughts were swooping about like demented butterflies. She really *had* got it. It was making her breathless.

'Quickie weddings, tacky little white chapels, Elvis impersonators …' she recited, watching his face to confirm that was what he meant and seeing that it was. And also seeing the anxiety. 'I *want*,' she decided quickly and emphatically. 'Let's do it, all of it.' She reached over to kiss him. 'Let's run off and get married in Las Vegas, at New Year. It's perfect.'

His smile told her how right that answer was. His grip on her tightened as they kissed again to seal the deal. It *all* felt so right that she wanted to cry, or sing, or both. Maybe not a good idea to actually do it, but there was something else she *could* do.

When they broke apart for air, she gathered her courage. *You* can *do this.* 'I will come to Las Vegas with you, and Elvis can marry us in the tackiest chapel we can find, but … um … before that … would you like to come to Sunday lunch with my family?'

* The End *

Thank You

Hello,
I hope that you have enjoyed *Masquerade on the Riviera*, the fourth in the 'Riviera' series of romantic suspense. Thank you for buying it, or perhaps borrowing it from the library. I'm grateful to every one of my readers. I couldn't do it without you.

As you know, if you have also read other books I have written (if you haven't, I hope that you will soon) I like to write escapism – books that inspire a holiday feeling wherever and whenever they are read. This one was a little different, as quite a large part of it was set here in the UK – although we did make it to Monaco for what I hope was an exciting finale. Writers are often asked where they get their ideas, and quite often we don't really know. In the case of this book, I have wanted for a while to set one of the series on the *English* Riviera. Torquay led inevitably to one of its most famous residents – Agatha Christie – whose books always contain intriguing plots. Once there, I couldn't resist incorporating my own versions of some of Dame Agatha's trademarks – a house party, archaeological treasures, Egyptology, and, of course, if you are venturing into the exotic realm of Egyptian artefacts, there has to be a curse! Combine that with inspiration from what must be one of the cinema's most glamorous romantic suspense films, *To Catch a Thief* – jewel robberies, love and a gorgeous Riviera setting – and you have the ingredients that started me out on writing this story.

Now for a request. If you have enjoyed *Masquerade on the Riviera*, it would be lovely if you could leave a review on any or all of your favourite book sites or mention the book on Twitter or Facebook. You can follow me on both – details appear on the author page which follows. Information on how to find my weekly blog is there too. I really appreciate it when readers take the time to write reviews. Selfies of readers engrossed in the book while on holiday are also always welcome!

Many thanks

Evonne x

About the Author

Evonne Wareham was born in South Wales and spent her childhood there. After university she migrated to London, where she worked in local government, scribbled novels in her spare time and went to the theatre a lot. Now she's back in Wales, living by the sea, and has just completed a PhD in history. She still loves the theatre, likes staying in hotels and enjoys the company of other authors through her membership of both the Romantic Novelists' Association and the Crime Writers' Association.

Evonne's debut novel, *Never Coming Home* won the 2012 Joan Hessayon New Writers' Award, the 2013 Colorado Romance Writers' Award for Romantic Suspense, the Oklahoma National Readers' Choice Award for Romantic Suspense plus was a nominee for a Reviewers' Choice Award from RT Book Reviews. Her second romantic suspense novel *Out of Sight Out of Mind*, was a finalist for the Maggie Award for Excellence, presented by the Georgia Romance Writers' chapter of the Romance Writers of America. Her novel, *A Villa in Portofino*, was also nominated for the Jackie Collins Award for Romantic Thrillers.

For more information visit:
Twitter: www.twitter.com/evonnewareham
Facebook: www.facebook.com/evonnewarehamauthor
Blog: www.evonneonwednesday.blogspot.com

More Choc Lit
from
Evonne Wareham

Summer in San Remo
Riviera Series – Book 1

Anything could happen when you spend summer in San Remo …
Running her busy concierge service usually keeps Cassie Travers fully occupied. But when a new client offers her the strangest commission she's ever handled she suddenly finds herself on the cusp of an Italian adventure, with a man she thought she would never see again.

Jake McQuire has returned from the States to his family-run detective agency. When old flame Cassie appears in need of help with her mysterious client, who better than Jake to step in?

Events take the pair across Europe to a luxurious villa on the Italian Riviera. There, Cassie finds that the mystery she pursues pales into insignificance, when compared to another discovery made along the way …

Visit www.choc-lit.com for more details.

A Wedding on the Riviera

Riviera Series – Book 2

A return to the Riviera on the trail of a runaway groom ...

When out-of-work actor Ryan Calder attends a wedding as the plus-one of successful businesswoman, Nadine Wells, he doesn't expect to get in a scuffle with the groom.

But Ryan has a good reason. He recognises the groom from another wedding where the same man made a quick getaway, taking the wedding money and leaving a heartbroken bride in his wake. It seems he's struck again, and Nadine's poor friend is the target.

Ryan and Nadine decide they can't let it happen to another woman, so with a group of friends they hatch a plan that will take them to the French Riviera, hot on the heels of the crooked groom. But could their scheme to bring him to justice also succeed in bringing them closer together?

Visit www.choc-lit.com for more details.

A Villa in Portofino
Riviera Series – Book 3

From chambermaid to "got it made" ...
When hotel cleaning temp and poetry academic Megan Morrison finds out she's inherited an Italian villa and small fortune from her estranged great-great aunt Olwen, she doesn't quite know how to react. That is, until she travels to Portofino to see Il Giardino delle Rose for herself. Then she knows exactly what she has to do: live there!

Enchanted by the beauty of the house and gardens, fascinated by the history, and more than a little intrigued by handsome hired landscape gardener Gideon West, Megan can immediately see the villa's potential as a dream home.

But having long-lost relatives sometimes means long-lost secrets – and it seems that Olwen had plenty of those. Could these secrets and a jealous obsession be powerful enough to drive Megan out of the house that she's already fallen in love with?

Visit www.choc-lit.com for more details.

Never Coming Home

Winner of the 2012 New Writers' Joan Hessayon Award

All she has left is hope

When Kaz Elmore is told her five-year-old daughter Jamie has died in a car crash, she struggles to accept that she'll never see her little girl again. Then a stranger comes into her life offering the most dangerous substance in the world: hope.

Devlin, security consultant and witness to the terrible accident scene, inadvertently reveals that Kaz's daughter might not have been the girl in the car after all.

What if Jamie is still alive? With no evidence, the police aren't interested, so Devlin and Kaz have little choice but to investigate themselves. Devlin never gets involved with a client. Never. But the more time he spends with Kaz, the more he desires her – and the more his carefully constructed ice-man persona starts to unravel.

The desperate search for Jamie leads down dangerous paths – to a murderous acquaintance from Devlin's dark past, and all across Europe, to Italy, where deadly secrets await. But as long as Kaz has hope, she can't stop looking …

Visit www.choc-lit.com for more details.

Out of Sight Out of Mind

Finalist for the Maggie Award of Excellence

Everyone has secrets. Some are stranger than others.

Madison Albi is a scientist with a very special talent – for reading minds. When she stumbles across a homeless man with whom she feels an inexplicable connection, she can't resist the dangerous impulse to use her skills to help him.

J is a non-person – a vagrant who can't even remember his own name. He's got no hope, until he meets Madison. Is she the one woman who can restore his past?

Madison agrees to help J recover his memory, but as she delves deeper into his mind, it soon becomes clear that some secrets are better off staying hidden.

Is J really the man Madison believes him to be?

Visit www.choc-lit.com for more details.

What Happens at Christmas

A Christmas to remember

Lori France and her four-year-old niece Misty are settling in to spend the holidays in Wales after unexpected events leave them without a place to stay.

Best-selling author Andrew Vitruvius knows that any publicity is good publicity. His agent tells him that often, so it must be true. In the run-up to Christmas, she excels herself - talking him into the craziest scheme yet: getting himself kidnapped, live on TV.

Little do they know they're about to make a discovery and experience a Christmas they're not likely to forget …

Visit www.choc-lit.com for more details.

Printed in Great Britain
by Amazon

37801765R00148